"At last…a well written, captivating novel on the end times. The story probes the subject of spiritual warfare in a vivid way not seen since *This Present Darkness*."
—DR. TED BAEHR, *MOVIEGUIDE* MAGAZINE

"Masterful, Powerful, Frightening. *The Age of the Antichrist* is likely to fly off the book shelves."
—*THE DAILY ADVANCE*, NORTH CAROLINA NEWSPAPER

"Stirring, captivating, intriguing. If you are looking for a book to suggest to *Left Behind* series readers, this is the one. The warfare between the angels and demons will keep you turning page after page."
—CHRIS MCCORMICK, MANAGER, LIFEWAY CHRISTIAN STORE

"We've had dozens of customers come back to buy extras for friends. I've read it, and not only is it a page turner, but also a great read for those addicted to the *Left Behind* series."
—ANITA WOOD, MANAGER, WALDENBOOK STORE

"It left me breathless. I missed a fair amount of sleep reading this book."
—ANDREW LEWIS, TELEVISION DIRECTOR

"This book stirred my imagination. The writing is excellent and intellectual. It has a fascinating plot that brings Revelation to life."
—BRIDGET SHAFFER, EDUCATOR AND READING SPECIALIST

"*The Age of the Antichrist* is an engaging, plausible, thought-provoking story of the end times."
—MIDWEST BOOK REVIEW

"This story is intense!"
—*MESSIANIC JEWISH LIFE* MAGAZINE

the age of the
ANTICHRIST

Dedication

This book is dedicated to my loving wife, Tina. I thank you for
giving me the support that I needed to undertake the greatest hurdle
that I've ever had to cross…writing a book of this depth and
magnitude. I want to encourage anyone who has ever had a dream
to get off the bench and onto the playing field! Surround yourself
with people who say yes…rather than no! I also want to thank God
for giving us His Word, the Bible. Without this, I would be like
a ship without a rudder, or a car without a road.

Acknowledgments

Many special thanks to our faithful Lord. Other thanks to our parents,
Bob and Terry Cash, Gloria Tuccille, and the late Bob Tuccille;
Grandma Geneva Price; Aunt Lillie Belle Woodhouse; the church family
and staff of Atlantic Shores; and all our friends and family who have
helped us through this difficult yet exciting endeavor.

Special thanks to Gini Ward for her editorial assistance,
to her husband Craig for his patience and prayers, and to Suzie Hardy
and Bridget Shaffer who helped us immensely.

Our thanks to Craig Minton for the photograph of Jon.

the age of the
ANTICHRIST

Jonathan R. Cash

Whitaker House

THE AGE OF THE ANTICHRIST

For interviews and speaking engagements, contact Jonathan Cash at:
In the Sky Ministries
P. O. Box 15770
Chesapeake, Virginia 23328-5770
Phone: 757.546.3313
E-mail: intheskyministries@juno.com
Web site: www.theageoftheantichrist.com

ISBN: 0-88368-629-5
Printed in the United States of America
Copyright © 2000 by Whitaker House

Whitaker House
30 Hunt Valley Circle
New Kensington, PA 15068

Library of Congress Cataloging-in-Publication Data

Cash, Jonathan R., 1965–
    The age of the Antichrist / by Jonathan R. Cash.
        p. cm.
    ISBN 0-88368-629-5 (alk. paper)
    1. Spiritual warfare—Fiction. 2. End of the world—Fiction. 3. Good
    and evil—Fiction. 4. Antichrist—Fiction. I. Title.
PS3553.A79373 A73 2000
813'.54—dc21
                                        00-009793

2 3 4 5 6 7 8 9 10 11 12 / 08 07 06 05 04 03 02 01 00

Contents

One

Mystery of the Ages

Icy mountain peaks reached to the sky above the small Swiss town. As the sun moved over the horizon, the snow radiated its own crystal-like light—blinding, but beautiful. Street lights signed off for the night as dawn made its grand entrance. Children began their journey to school, cars littered the streets, and the town bell sounded rhythmically, patiently, as if another ordinary day had begun.

High above the town, on a narrow, winding road, a gleaming white limousine descended cautiously through the curvy terrain. As it entered town, children on their way to school stopped dead in their tracks and stood in awe, as if a foreboding monster approached them. When it passed, they saw one word in large letters on the license plate: "PEACE."

Inside the limousine, the penetrating eyes of the sole passenger stared outside at the rising sun. Then they shifted to the mirror, as the man slowly adjusted the angle of his tie.

"Television, Channel 6," he commanded.

Responding to his voice, the digital image revealed a news reporter somberly recounting the week-old, but still terrifying news.

"No one seems to have any firm answers. With several nuclear blasts behind us, most experts believe that there are more on the way. Some have suggested," she stammered, "that it would take a god to get us out of this predicament."

A satisfied smirk crept upon his face.

"Television, die," he ordered.

He knew that the people of the world longed for a war-free planet. The recent limited nuclear exchanges between some of the Asian nations had sent horrifying images across the world's television screens. These scenes of devastation had numbed their souls. No one felt safe any longer on the fragile planet. The psychological torture of dread and panic had infected the entire world.

9

The limousine pulled into the carport of a colossal, Victorian-style hotel, which towered above the town. A pair of lofty lions stood defiantly on each side of the entranceway.

Four bellboys trotted to the vehicle and stood at attention. One opened the door, and the man quickly exited. Immanuel Bernstate was tall and strikingly handsome. His hair was black and immaculately groomed. Thick eyebrows framed his aqua-blue eyes. He was wearing a black tailored suit, white handkerchief, and bloodred silk tie.

Immanuel strode through the carved mahogany doors and was greeted apprehensively by Theodore Gentile, an obese gentleman with little hair and nondescript features. Theodore, who had grown up in the wine hills of France, had plenty of money, and usually did not hesitate to let one know it. He owned penthouses in Paris, London, New York, and Rome.

"Glad to see you again, Immanuel," exclaimed Theodore, obviously lying.

"Thank you, Theodore," Immanuel responded smoothly.

The anxiety on Gentile's face was obvious. Immanuel stared directly into his eyes and sent the message that he was in charge. He would need to control Gentile if his plan was to succeed, and so far, his strategy was working.

Theodore Gentile was a powerful international banker, but he turned to Jell-O around Immanuel. His only other encounter with Immanuel had been at a United Nations meeting, and it was one he would gladly forget.

"The group is ready," muttered Theodore, feeling the collar tighten around his plump neck.

"Excellent."

Theodore quickly ended the confrontation and graciously motioned for Immanuel to accompany him to the meeting chamber. They strolled through the lobby and into a corridor filled with several elevators. The awkward silence continued until they stepped into an empty elevator, and the doors closed behind them. Immanuel glared at Theodore.

"If you're not with us, you're against us," threatened Immanuel. "People are expendable. Banks are expendable. Nations are expendable."

"Please don't misunderstand me. Your will is my will, Immanuel," purred Theodore. "I trust you, and I believe the plan can work. I just don't understand how. It would take a miracle!" sighed Theodore.

Immanuel smiled.

The elevator doors opened on the sixth floor, and Immanuel signaled Theodore to proceed first. He sheepishly led the way to room 696. Once inside, the men walked to a large closet in the master bedroom.

Above the closet, and unseen to the human eye, was the fallen angel Blasphemy. The demon was a hideous, boisterous, obnoxious creature. A five-star general in Satan's army of defiant spirits, he was the supreme commander over millions of demons. Their mission on Earth was to promote their master's plan of world domination and to spread evil throughout the universe. Blasphemy answered to no one except Satan himself, but he didn't always agree with Lucifer's decisions. In fact, he dreamed of overthrowing Satan and seizing his powers.

"It's time. Proceed with the plan, Immanuel," instructed Blasphemy.

Blasphemy's telepathic directive ended, and a smug grin emerged on Immanuel's face as he dreamed of a world under the control of one superhuman—himself!

The closet wall suddenly opened to reveal a large computer. Theodore placed his left hand on the scanner in the middle of the unit.

"Agent 00169."

A green light appeared. Immanuel impatiently waited his turn.

"Agent 00666."

Again, the green light came on, and the men heard a soft click as a large door opened, exposing a vault. There agent Babel blocked the entrance to an ancient tunnel made of cobblestone. It was remarkably tidy but dimly lit with dozens of candles. Immanuel and Theodore followed Babel into the cool, murky tunnel. They silently journeyed for about fifty yards before the agent broke the ice.

"When we reach the end, I will enter the crystal room first. You will remain outside until I have finished. Agent 00169 will then enter the room alone and complete the requirements for entrance into the chamber. Agent 00666 will follow. Any questions?"

Theodore shook his head, but Immanuel was obviously annoyed with the security measures.

"Just get on with it," commanded Immanuel.

Agent Babel entered first and came back out moments later. Theodore followed, trying to finalize the speech in his head. In just minutes, he would be giving the most important address of his banking career.

The room was in the shape of a triangle. Miniature purple lights were embedded in the ceiling. Theodore moved toward a massive crystal, which occupied the center of the room. An electromagnetic field of energy seemed to violate his body as he placed his hand on the electrode. It felt as if an alien were possessing him, checking his credentials right down to his DNA strands. Unknown to him, Blasphemy was using the security device to realign and reprogram his mind. He struggled to remember his personal security code, which he needed for clearance into the chamber. The light and energy from the rock intensified its spiritual grip and enveloped his spirit. It fed inaudible signals to his brain that chanted, "Obey your master. Obey your master. Obey your master, Immanuel."

Perched just above Theodore, laughing uncontrollably, was Blasphemy.

Theodore methodically nodded his head in agreement as he slowly entered his security code. He roamed through the room and then wormed his hypnotized body out the door. His eyes were glassy, and his demeanor was humbled.

"Enjoy the trip?" asked Immanuel. Theodore opened his mouth but could only whisper an obscenity. He was now harmless to Immanuel's plan.

"Please proceed next, Mr. Bernstate," said agent Babel.

Immanuel confidently walked into the room and approached the crystal. As he touched the rock, the lights grew brighter, and the room became energized with some kind of supernatural force. He seemed to be feeding on the power of the crystal, gathering strength, confidence, and wisdom.

"You will attain your goals and your wildest dreams, but you must be patient. These privileged few have been conditioned to accept our proposal but must be persuaded. Do not despair. Your master will soon join you. He will help you to fulfill the aspirations of the Order by revealing the mystery of the ages," intoned Blasphemy.

The light of the crystal transmitter faded. Blasphemy's orders were clear. The final race was beginning, and the clock was ticking. Hundreds of the greatest leaders of all time had gone to their graves defeated and denied this one prize.

Suddenly, a voice jolted him out of his unspeakable bliss.

"Mr. Bernstate, is everything in order? The group is anxiously awaiting your arrival," interrupted agent Babel.

"Everything is in order. You may proceed," directed Immanuel.

"Sequence activation, Armageddon," commanded Babel.

The stone wall split into two pieces, revealing an elevator. The men boarded without further conversation. Babel opened a panel and slid in a security card. The elevator plunged downward at an incredible speed. Theodore turned pale as his insides were shoved upward. Immanuel was in one of his self-induced trances.

The doors opened to a grandiose medieval chamber. Coats of armor from the Byzantine kingdom stood at guard. Works of art from the early years of the Catholic Church added a flavor of religion to the extravagant atmosphere. In the middle of this exhibition of affluence were a gold and platinum meeting table and twelve chairs.

Immanuel and Theodore were cordially greeted by Lord Birmingham, the hierarch of the European banking committee and mastermind of the "Order." A tall and distinguished-looking man, his smile was cunning yet contagious. Lord Birmingham was a member of one of the wealthiest royal families of Europe. He had the power to destroy banks, national currencies, and even small countries.

"Theodore, how are you?" asked Lord Birmingham, not caring to hear his response. "Are you ready?"

Theodore wore a blank stare on his flushed face. He responded with the few remaining brain cells that the crystal had not mutated.

"I have a speech today?" murmured Theodore in an unusually genuine tone.

All thirteen men at the meeting laughed loudly, causing them to yank their Cuban cigars from their mouths to keep from choking.

Lord Birmingham turned his attention to Immanuel. "Mr. Bernstate, I have heard many good things about you and your work. Some of your unique views on banking and politics in the twenty-first century deserve our attention."

Immanuel smiled graciously.

"I have admired your work and accomplishments, and welcome the opportunity to help the Order achieve its objectives," responded Immanuel.

Lord Birmingham scrutinized Immanuel and said, "I'm sure you understand that, as a new constituent of the Order, your role will be somewhat limited until your credentials are fully investigated." Lord Birmingham's tone changed to that of a teacher lecturing a student. "I am curious about your nationality, your family, and your childhood. Our operatives have documented background intelligence on you for only the previous ten years. You seemingly popped up on planet Earth at age thirty. Did a little spaceship drop you off on the way to the sun so that you could save our sick planet?"

The scattered conversations in the chamber abruptly ended.

"I would think that a solution would be a welcome relief no matter where it came from," offered Immanuel. "Forgive me. You want some answers for this strange lack of documentation. Very well. I was born in Switzerland and grew up in a tiny village near Geneva. I lived there until my twenty-second birthday. It was then that the town was destroyed, along with all its records. My family moved to Israel. We were peasants, and were not issued a visa or any kind of paperwork establishing our identity. Then, I moved to Germany—"

Lord Birmingham interrupted Immanuel with a mere hand gesture.

"I know your history while in Germany and your brilliant accomplishments in banking and politics."

Immanuel interrupted him with a smile. "Of course. What you really want to know is, am I Jewish, right?"

Lord Birmingham looked him straight in the eye and nodded.

"Well, let's see. My father was German, and my mother was Arabian," Immanuel offered.

"Bernstate, answer the inquiry, and do not play trivial games with me."

Immanuel glanced around the sanctuary looking for allies but found only cold stares. He looked directly back into Birmingham's eyes.

"The truth is, I am not sure."

Lord Birmingham snapped at Immanuel, "Not good enough, Bernstate. This is not a country club you're joining! We and our fathers have labored for nearly a millennium to achieve our form of social justice and world peace. We will not allow one mountain, valley, speck of sand...," Lord Birmingham hesitated slightly, "or one Jew, to ruin our plans."

Immanuel remained calm while Birmingham continued.

"You brag that you have the answer to our regional control difficulties. Of course, those difficulties mostly relate to the Islamic religion. Therefore, you must know that a Jew would never command the respect of the Arab world." Birmingham's palms began to sweat as his tone became more emphatic. "The money and power from those oil fields must be in our hands at any cost."

Immanuel reassured Lord Birmingham and the group.

"My plan—" he cleared his throat, "our plan will succeed. Allow me to address the Order at the end of the assembly, and I will enlighten you fine gentlemen on every phase of our strategy to bring the new world order alive onto the pages of history."

Immanuel had their attention, and he knew that the power of the underworld was on his side.

Far away, on an arid mountaintop overlooking the Dead Sea, General Blasphemy was in a meeting of his own. The Dead Sea was the perfect location for the demons to assemble. They were close to home, near the fiery pits of the planet. Bickering for the best view of Lucifer, thousands of fallen angels eagerly awaited orders for their next mission against the sons of Jehovah God. Their callous hearts yearned to go forth and evangelize the earth with religious deceit, hate, bigotry, and violence. The victories against their enemy, Jehovah God, had been limited and short-lived. Through the centuries, the sword of the archangel Michael had ripped their life's work to shreds.

The horde of creatures sneered in utter delight as hundreds of revolting demons announced Lucifer's arrival. His servants carefully placed a black carpet on the sand that led to his throne, straightening every wrinkle for fear of inciting one of Lucifer's infamous tantrums. Lucifer was known as the lord and Prince of the World as well as the supreme chieftain of the army of evil. At one time, he had been the most beautifully created being of Jehovah God. However, his twisted wisdom and colossal pride had convinced him to start a revolution against God. He saw Jehovah as a self-righteous God who thought more about faith, hope, and love than the essential necessities of life—power and personal fulfillment.

The self-made king and his swarm swooped downward and landed in front of the crowd. His servants bowed in forced submission as the devils jeered and hissed. He turned to the mob and raised both paws, rousing raucous clamor.

Miles away, on a mountain ridge opposite the Dead Sea, the archangel Michael scrutinized every move the rebels made. He and his group of angelic warriors had just received an order from the throne of God not to engage the enemy in battle.

Michael was God's most powerful angel. His enormous golden wings reached to the ground. With sparkling ivory hair, blue eyes, and hefty muscles, he appeared to be superhuman. His silken robe was draped over his ten-foot frame, and an often used sword rested by his side.

Michael had millions of troops under his command. He was a majestic creation, blessed with every attribute of goodness and truth. He executed every order with lightning speed and remarkable accuracy; therefore, his presence brought chills to his enemies. He served God unselfishly, never standing in the way of his Commander's mission. He turned and faced his holy army.

"My fellow friends and warriors, our faithful God has informed me that His blueprint for human history is approaching a climactic end. Our all-powerful God and Creator of the universe understands our concerns regarding His cease-fire order. His Holy Word has promised an end to all forms of suffering, brutality, and idolatry. To accomplish this miraculous feat, He requests our patience. The prayers of the saints will be answered in our Lord's timing. Have diligence for the faith, and be ready for battle when your loving God calls."

Michael hesitated, fondly gazing at Jehovah's devout followers. A wind rushed over the mountaintop and lifted him upward into the desert sky.

"Allow the enemy their moment of glory. We have the one true God on our side! Be patient, young soldiers, and the prize of obedience will be yours."

Resounding cheers echoed through the desert air. The entire group flew in circles around Michael as a sign of universal support. Michael joined the angels in their celebration as they sailed through the air, singing praises to their Creator, Jehovah God.

Meanwhile, Lucifer was seated on his throne high above his servants. He could see his enemy on the opposite mountain engaging in a festive celebration. The spectacle made him fidgety. He turned his focus back to the group of demons and summoned Blasphemy to approach him.

"General Blasphemy, draw near to the throne of the almighty," stated the egotistical Satan.

Blasphemy crawled on all four legs, keeping his head and eyes facing the ground. He despised the submission that he had to display; however, he had firsthand experience of Lucifer's wrath. Wanting to avoid an embarrassing and possibly deadly confrontation, he paused a few feet from Lucifer and bowed in forced allegiance.

"What news have you brought me?" questioned Lucifer as he basked in his own conceit.

"I have word from our intelligence branch, sir," responded Blasphemy, daring to glance into the haunting eyes of Lucifer.

Lucifer hissed, sending drool in all directions.

"Who gave you permission to stare into my soul? Learn your place, or face the consequences of your folly!"

Blasphemy instantly lowered his eyes.

"My deepest and sincerest apology, master, but—"

"Shut your mouth, you peon, or I will charge you with high treason and throw you into the abyss!"

There was an awkward silence in the congregation. Nobody dared speak or even breathe for fear of Lucifer's stinging wrath. Satan scanned his army for any sign of rebellion.

"Continue with the report," commanded Lucifer.

Blasphemy cleared his throat.

"I humbly present the latest spy data regarding our enemy. Reports have confirmed that they have been weakened by our—I mean, your—superior forces." Blasphemy paused. "The foe appears to be softening. Jehovah God has ordered a cease-fire."

The demons went ballistic. Blaring barks of egotism and conquest polluted the air as the demons pranced in delight. Their momentary bliss was abruptly suspended as Lucifer stood to assert his authority.

"That will be enough!" he screamed.

The spontaneous party came to a screeching halt.

"May I continue, master?" questioned Blasphemy.

"What are your sources?" sneered Lucifer.

"Last Sunday night, the adversary's defenses surrounding the throne room of Jehovah God were light, so I ordered our finest spies to investigate immediately. We overheard Jehovah ordering Michael to stop resisting our forces. He told Michael to remove their troops in some key areas all around the globe. Unfortunately, Christians will continue to be protected by their prayers; however, some generals who protect Christianity's doctrines will retire permanently from the global battlefield."

Lucifer jumped in joy. He hated evangelical Christianity but adored a lukewarm religious substitute. This was his golden opportunity to cunningly drag millions away from Jehovah. It was payback time for God's kicking him out of heaven.

"Sir, may I have permission to analyze this data and speak about its implications?"

"Your permission to speak is granted, but make it short. If this information is true, I do not have time to waste!"

Lucifer leaned forward on his throne, anticipating an opportunity to rebuke Blasphemy.

"The enemy's withdrawing from strategic positions concerns me. They must be up to something. Jehovah is very cunning. Remember Jesus Christ on the cross? Our biggest victory turned out to be our greatest and most humiliating defeat. Jehovah has been vigorously warring your forces for over seven thousand years and has never left so many significant posts unguarded. He may be luring us into a trap. Passages in the Bible prophesy—"

Lucifer lunged out of his seat and wrapped his claws around Blasphemy's neck.

"Don't ever quote the Bible to me again! That trash is the propaganda book of the enemy and has done more to destroy my life's work than any archangel, church, or saint put together!"

Blasphemy pleaded for mercy as Lucifer tightened his grip.

"Mercy is not in my job description!" Lucifer was inches away from Blasphemy's face. "So, you have been reading that garbage again, my dearest Blasphemy?"

The assemblage was struck with fear. Many of the devils had secretly scanned Jehovah's Scriptures after Lucifer's edict had been set forth banning any reading or even thinking about the Bible.

Blasphemy was gasping; his face was red and his eyes were bulging.

"Master, I had meditated on the babblings of Jehovah before your order was ordained almost two thousand years ago. I felt it was a clever notion to—"

Lucifer terminated the conversation as he growled at Blasphemy.

"I will tell you what is wise! I will tell you what to think! You are nothing without my guidance. You followed me during the great civil war of the heavens eons ago and walked out of Jehovah's presence. You chose my ways over that dictator's ways and made me your lord and savior! If it were not for me, you would still be bowing to Jehovah! Obey or die a coward's death!"

Lucifer relaxed his lethal grip.

"Master, it will bring me great joy to obey every command that proceeds from your lips. My motivations have always been in accordance with expanding your kingdom." Blasphemy gulped for air. "I thought it was wise to read the enemy's book, so that we could exploit His weaknesses. A weaker Jehovah is a stronger Lucifer. All hail, Lucifer!"

The troops joined in the praise. "All hail, Lucifer! All hail, Lucifer!"

Lucifer released his stranglehold, and Blasphemy quickly disappeared among his colleagues as he took a seat in the hot sand. Lucifer returned to his throne.

"The war of the ages will soon end with our swift victory over Jehovah's forces of hate, bigotry, and arrogance. Our rebellion for control of the heavens is a battle that must be won! The hypocrites of righteousness would love to make the world believe that we are the evil force destined for the fiery pit of hell. Listen to me, my sons. Truth is a term dreamed up by our archenemy for those who disagree with His abstractions. Jehovah God is a liar!"

The demons cheered.

Lucifer rose from his kingly seat and fearlessly stared into heaven's hot, burning sun.

"This retreat is a sign from Jehovah that His opinions cannot stand the test of time. Jehovah's kingdom will fall with a thunderous crash, and my kingdom will endure for eternity!"

The noise from the camp escalated to an earsplitting roar.

"He knows time is limited. His power base is crumbling around Him. He will have nowhere to hide. When we find Him, we will show no mercy!"

Satan motioned for his top general to step forward. Blasphemy glided over his comrades and sat down across from his boss.

"How can I assist you, sir?" beguiled Blasphemy.

"Take complete control of every bank in the world. Begin to apply political and monetary pressure on all governments to facilitate a new world order, using any means at your disposal. I will provide you with an arsenal of spiritual weapons. The power is with you, Blasphemy. Go forth and conquer in the name of Lucifer! The time has come to begin our countdown to Armageddon."

Blasphemy saluted his boss and called many of his high-ranking officers forward to accompany him on this critical mission.

"My fellow devils, I need your undivided attention for a moment," asserted Blasphemy. "I will maintain direct contact with Immanuel Bernstate, our spokesman on Earth. No one else is to initiate any subliminal transactions with him. Any violation of that order will bring charges of treason and swift judgment."

Blasphemy stared at the demons, searching for any trace of insubordination.

"A conference is now in session in Switzerland with some of the most affluent men in the world. Your job is to persuade these fools to unequivocally endorse our plan for world peace and harmony. Get ready for an exciting afternoon of supernatural seduction!"

Blasphemy and his cohorts jetted toward the north and vanished in the clouds.

Meanwhile, in the distance, the archangel Michael wept.

———————

Lord Birmingham called the international bankers' meeting to order. All these men were active members of the Order. They were conspirators who indirectly controlled the world through their careful placement of political contributions. They had the connections to alter interest rates, money supply, and everything else that made a nation tick financially. In their perverted minds, the world was a chessboard, and they moved the pieces.

"My father taught me the best way to kill a snake is a fatal blow to the back of the head," began Lord Birmingham. "Gentlemen, the Asian Federation is that serpent. Our first problem is to figure out how to fatally wound that monster. Second, the banking system is in terrible danger of collapsing, especially in the United States. When the banks collapse, how do we maximize our profits without destroying the very system we feed on? Finally, how are we going to unite all the governments when the world seems to be destabilizing all around us?"

He continued, "We need every bank in our control, every world leader feeding from our trough, and every world citizen on our side. No human being on the face of the earth has ever accomplished such a feat. What we really need now is a god!"

Immanuel's heart began to race as he imagined the world bowing at his feet. He would make sure Birmingham was the first to fall on his knees and worship. He knew he needed reinforcements from the underworld to persuade his companions that he had the key to unlocking their dreams.

Lord Birmingham sat down and was silent for a moment, waiting for his words to have their full impact.

Then he spoke. "Theodore, here is your big chance. The goals are simple. The barriers are insurmountable. You have been bragging in private about your workable blueprint for the new world order. Although I'm afraid your intellect could never match the size of your ego, I challenge you, sir, to prove me wrong."

Theodore loosened his tie and gulped some water. His hands began to shake. His demeanor was speaking louder than his words. Blood rushed to his face, and his breathing became sporadic. Something was terribly wrong.

"Are you all right, Gentile?

"I'm fine, Lord Birmingham," lied Theodore. He was desperately trying to concentrate on his speech.

The men openly snickered.

Theodore buttoned his jacket and stumbled to the podium. He forced a smile as he looked around the table. He could not focus on anything except Immanuel Bernstate's hypnotic eyes. Theodore looked as if he had just seen a ghost.

"Mr. Gentile, would you like a ten-minute recess to get your thoughts in order?" asked Lord Birmingham.

"No...no...thank you, sir. Once I get into the details of my plan, I...I should be...fine."

Immanuel was becoming fidgety. He needed Blasphemy's help in fully derailing this speech. Blasphemy was late. Immanuel stood up without the approval of Lord Birmingham.

"I would like to say something. As you suggested, Lord Birmingham, let us take a ten-minute break to gather our thoughts. Theodore is obviously stressed, and we certainly would not want to risk his health for this speech."

Lord Birmingham concurred.

"Theodore, how about a quick recess to calm down and get yourself together?"

Theodore's arrogance was stirred at their tone. He couldn't understand what was happening, but he was not going to let this opportunity slip away. The anger surging through him cleared his mind.

"I feel wonderful. My mind has never worked better, and I take offense at Immanuel's insinuation that I am not in control of myself. Let's move on with the show!"

Immanuel was desperate. This was supposed to be his moment of glory. He knew that Theodore had received crucial information from one of Blasphemy's bigmouthed agents. He also knew that Theodore would use it to make himself look good. Immanuel searched for a way to take credit for these new ideas himself, so that he would be given power over this project. Not certain how to derail Theodore's speech, Immanuel decided to remain silent and put his faith in Lucifer and Blasphemy.

"Lords of the Order," Theodore began, "I would like to take this opportunity to thank you for the chance to speak to this honorable group of world leaders. My purpose today is to give you information that will change your lives forever. The world needs our resources and ingenuity to make it to a new age. We have already mastered the skills of creating wealth out of thin air. We have learned the subtle art of paying for political favors. We have even discovered ways to reprogram the human mind through television, music, and rewriting history. But we have neglected one crucial part of this mysterious equation, and without it, we will never achieve our one-world order."

The members of the Order began to whisper among themselves, which made Theodore pause for a moment. Regaining his confidence, Theodore continued.

"I recognize that I just indicted everyone present, and that my remarks are not popular, but I beg you to allow me just five minutes that will change your lives forever!"

An irritated Lord Birmingham took control of the situation.

"You have five minutes out of respect for your dearly departed father and my close friend."

Immanuel was meditating. He was focusing all of his mental and spiritual energies on Blasphemy.

"I need your power. I request your presence and weaponry to further our domain on Earth," prayed Immanuel.

Theodore asked, "Why do people believe certain things? Why are people of all nations willing to die for their principles? What universal doctrine tends to divide the nations rather than bring the whole world closer together? What causes most wars?"

Theodore paused, surprised at the Order's ignorant contempt. He knew history would recognize him as the first world citizen to usher in an eternal period of peace and prosperity.

Suddenly, the ground began to shake. One of Lord Birmingham's prized elks fell from the wall. Immanuel's selfish prayers had been answered. Blasphemy and a full battalion of sinister spirits invisibly invaded the chamber. He began shouting commands to his soldiers and to Immanuel.

"Demons, I want all one hundred of Company Delta to take possession of Theodore's body and destroy him! Company Alpha, begin chanting praises for Immanuel and his profound plan for a new world order. Saturate their stubborn mortal minds with visions of an earth under their command. Brainwash them into embracing Immanuel as their fearless leader. Don't allow any brain wave to be unaltered by your influence. Make Lucifer proud."

Blasphemy was enjoying every opportunity to frighten his unsuspecting prey.

Lord Birmingham skyrocketed from his seat as he shouted for everyone to stay clear of the broken beast.

Meanwhile, the fainthearted cowards were huddled under the table, assuming an earthquake was in progress. Immanuel was the only one enjoying the chaotic spectacle.

Birmingham snatched the elk's head from the floor. He summoned Lord Winchester to follow him to his office.

"This meeting is adjourned for fifteen minutes. Get the servants to clean up this disgusting mess!"

Theodore, along with the rest of the men, picked himself up off the floor. The bankers noticed that Immanuel was the only one who had remained calm during the fiasco.

Lord Birmingham and Lord Winchester were in the adjacent room, huddling over the elk's head. Winchester was Birmingham's most trusted friend.

"I know you have a sentimental attachment to that elk, but you almost went off the deep end. What's happening to you?" questioned Lord Winchester.

"What I have to show you cannot leave this room!"

Birmingham placed the dead elk upside down on its antlers. He lifted some fur from the back of its neck to unveil a keyhole. He snatched the keys from his wool-lined pocket.

"Are you superstitious, my friend?" asked Lord Birmingham.

"I believe luck is for the foolish," snickered Lord Winchester.

"Ah, but there is a difference between simple luck and supernatural power," retorted Lord Birmingham.

He placed the key in the hole and turned the mechanism. He mumbled as he slowly opened a large panel concealed in the side of the elk's neck. He held his breath as he reached inside for the treasure. Lord Winchester was flabbergasted. He wondered what could be inside that would cause a billionaire to tremble. Birmingham carefully pulled out a stone tablet. His breathing became more normal as he discovered that the tablets were unscathed. He immediately reached inside for the other tablet and extracted it seconds later.

"What in the world are those?" inquired Lord Winchester.

"These are one of the catalysts to our new world order."

Blasphemy stormed into the room to see what they were doing. His eyes bulged as he realized what was there. He had been searching for those rock tablets for thousands of years. Should Lucifer be informed of this find? No, he would handle this on his own without Lucifer's meddling. He could now seduce Israel into a satanic trap, and do it his way.

Lord Winchester was still mystified.

"I must be missing something. Two worthless stones with chicken-scratched engravings will change the world forever?"

"These are the stones that Moses received from God." He waited for the truth to penetrate Lord Winchester. "These are the original Ten Commandments!"

Excitedly, Lord Birmingham grabbed Winchester by the shoulders.

"These are the Ten Commandments that the Jews lost so long ago and have been searching for since resettling the nation of Israel. My people found them while excavating under the temple in Jerusalem. The Commandments were inside the ark of the covenant! The ignorant government at that time knew it was a political hot potato, so they told me to make them disappear. I eagerly obliged. The Middle East has always been a thorn in my side. With these ancient stones and the ark, we can bring Israel in line immediately."

Lord Winchester was puzzled.

"How?"

"Leave the details to me. For now, the secrecy of this discovery is imperative."

Lord Birmingham cautiously placed the relics back into their unusual safe.

"I trust you more than anyone else, Lord Winchester, but all faith has its limits. Do you understand?"

"Certainly. Your secret is safe with me."

Lord Birmingham and Lord Winchester joined the other conspirators.

"Men, take a seat so we can resume what is left of this meeting," instructed Lord Birmingham.

As the men were seated, Theodore approached the podium. Immanuel closed his eyes and signaled Blasphemy. Blasphemy hovered over Theodore and attached his oversized claws into Theodore's cranium.

"Men of the Order." Theodore grabbed the podium. "I am pleased to announce the solution to all of your dilemmas concerning the new world order."

Blasphemy began to envelop Theodore's mind and spirit as he took partial possession of his body. Theodore's facial expressions turned erratic. He was strangely silent and struggled to breathe.

"My purpose on Earth is to destroy," blurted Theodore in an alien tone. He fought to regain his identity. "I mean my purpose in the world is to further the goals of Lord Bir—" Blasphemy tightened his hold on Gentile's dying spirit. "I mean, Lord Lucifer."

Birmingham jumped from his chair.

Blasphemy's monstrous wings began to encompass Theodore as he gained control over him. Theodore scowled at Lord Birmingham.

"You incompetent misers will never succeed. I will take your money and power and send you straight to hell."

Theodore lunged across the table and started choking a stunned Lord Birmingham. Seizure after seizure gripped Theodore's body. The bankers were filled with fear as they watched the horrific scene. Immanuel "bravely" dove across the table at the exact time Blasphemy released his deadly grip on Theodore's body. Immanuel grabbed Theodore and wrestled him to the ground. His body lay unconscious.

"Someone call the physician!" shouted Immanuel, who took control of the situation.

Lord Birmingham appeared unscathed as he pulled himself up from the marble floor where he had fallen. Immanuel crouched over Theodore and took his pulse.

"Let him die like the animal he is," whispered Lord Birmingham.

"I can't do that," responded Immanuel with faked compassion.

"I think he is too far gone to be of any use," sighed Lord Birmingham. "I wonder if he really did have the answer to our predicament."

Immanuel was somber in his performed reply.

"To be honest with you, he did."

The ears in the chamber perked up. The men gathered around Immanuel.

"Theodore and I had a private meeting last week. I had accumulated years of painstaking work in discovering the solution to world peace and wanted to compare notes with Theodore. I was anxious to hear for myself the ideas that he had been bragging about. Regrettably, his conclusions were based on faulty information. When he heard my information, he desperately wanted to take the credit for this plan himself," lied Immanuel.

"Theodore stole some papers from my desk that I had been working on. I had collected a great supply of knowledge on the history of world empires and the reasons for their collapse. I knew history would be our teacher. We could use the mistakes of the past to bring us into a glorious new future. Theodore was prepared to present this intelligence as his own. Apparently, the gods have sown his destiny for him."

The men encircled Immanuel as he took Theodore's pulse. Theodore's eyelids were tightly shut, but his eyes were wildly darting.

Blasphemy hung from the crystal chandelier.

"You can trust Immanuel. He should be your heroic leader. He has your best interests at heart. Immanuel has the attributes the Order needs to bring the world to your feet. Believe in Immanuel. Immanuel...Immanuel," chanted Blasphemy.

Blasphemy's transcendental signals were penetrating the iron will of Lord Birmingham.

"Tell us more about your research and conclusions," pleaded the lord of the Order.

Immanuel was about to begin when Theodore began to regain consciousness. He was struggling to mumble some kind of accusation about Immanuel. He was saying something about a plot to destroy Mother Earth. Immanuel was determined to be the Good Samaritan.

"He doesn't know what he's saying. He took a numbing blow to the head. It sounds like he is calling for his mother."

Immanuel was convincing.

"Get that doctor down here on the double! This meeting must continue at any cost," bellowed Lord Birmingham.

Theodore's eyes burst open, and he panicked at the sight of Immanuel and Blasphemy.

"It's Satan! Oh, my God, it's Satan! Get away from me, you hellish devil!"

Immanuel and Lord Winchester struggled to hold him down.

"Finish him off," whispered Immanuel to Blasphemy.

"I will be delighted to."

Blasphemy dove off the sparkling fixture and stretched his massive paws high in the air. His demonic comrades followed his example and stormed their way onto the feeble prey. Theodore went into convulsions as Satan's troops violated his body. He screamed in anguish as he took his final breath. Suddenly, his body lay motionless, and fear gripped the would-be rulers of the world.

The elevator doors swung open as the doctor rushed to Theodore's side. As he placed his hands on Theodore's neck, he searched for a pulse.

"This man is dead," pronounced the physician. "What on earth happened?"

Immanuel stepped forward.

"Apparently it's a drug overdose."

"What was he taking?" asked the bewildered doctor.

"Cocaine and who knows what else," responded Immanuel.

The physician summoned his assistant to remove the corpse.

A shaken Lord Birmingham patted Immanuel on the back.

"Son, I owe you my life. Let's try to leave this tragedy behind and return to the business at hand. Take the podium, Immanuel, and let's reconvene."

The men tried to regroup as they took their seats. Immanuel took an unusually deep breath and closed his eyes.

"Are they ready?" prayed Immanuel in his spirit.

"They have been reprogrammed as you desire. For world leaders, their minds were amazingly powerless to defend our attacks. The only obstacle we may encounter is Lord Winchester."

Blasphemy zoomed over to Lord Winchester and sat on his shoulders.

"Immanuel, are you okay?" asked a concerned Lord Birmingham.

"I'm fine."

Lord Birmingham was firmly focused on Immanuel.

"There's an ancient but accurate proverb that applies today more than ever. 'One man's trash is another man's treasure.' For the past several centuries, the Order has done a masterful job in manipulating the world's resources. You have brilliantly convinced the people to believe that there is an urgent need for a new world order of peace and justice. I congratulate the efforts of Lord Birmingham for the recent media blitz that popularized a one-world government by the people and for the people."

Immanuel began to clap, starting a chain reaction of applause, beginning with Lord Winchester. They simultaneously stood to their feet to pay homage to their astute commander in chief. Lord Birmingham courteously bowed. He directed their attention back to Immanuel, who began to speak.

"Let me first give a brief historical illustration. The Roman Empire was conquered by what outside intruder? None! The downfall of this once mighty kingdom was internal corruption and eventual anarchy. Why was the French Revolution a cancer in history's microscope? The only unifying principle was freedom, which soon led to national chaos and an ungodly bloodbath.

"We are all aware that the American experiment has miserably failed. The political and economic systems are disintegrating. All of these empires attempted to take control of the world with their differing systems of dictatorship, totalitarianism, freedom, and democracy. They have all been swept under the rug of time because they lacked one essential ingredient.

"The world will never become unified by pure socialism or pure capitalism, or even a mixture of both. Democracy alone will eventually lead to citizens draining the public treasury until it finally goes bankrupt. A dictatorship will lead to a peasant rebellion and social lawlessness. Socialism eventually drains the spirit and will of the masses, and fosters uprisings that bring industrialism to a halt. Socialism will most assuredly drain the economy as well. Capitalism creates class envy and pits the rich against the poor. Each of these man-made systems has its benefits. However, gentlemen, every ideology has errors that multiply with time."

Immanuel placed both hands on the podium.

"My friends, history has taught us an invaluable lesson. The world will never obtain peace and political harmony with the same old political doublethink."

He pounded the stand more for theatrics than passion.

28

"For the new world order to function in our favor, we will need an influx of fresh ideas and proven beliefs. We must change the way people think, the way they eat, even the way they breathe. There must be a quantum leap, a new age, and a noble purpose for living as a world citizen."

Immanuel stared at his notes, then took another deep breath and closed his eyes.

"Should I continue? Are they ready for this?" communicated Immanuel to Blasphemy.

"All but Lord Winchester. He has a mind of his own and will not budge an inch," Blasphemy reported.

Immanuel lifted his head as he opened his eyes. A smile spread across his face.

"We must coax all the countries into adopting a universal code of belief and conduct. I respectfully request you to withhold judgment on my initial draft until I have presented all the details of my plan."

The men nodded in agreement. Only Lord Winchester abstained.

"Our new world order will be a smashing success if, and only if, we devise a new universal religious system."

Lord Winchester's face showed his lack of support.

"This will be the catalyst to bringing the minds of the world into a workable harmony. For example, we now have Protestants, Catholics, Jews, Buddhists, Muslims, atheists, humanists, and a host of others who believe that they possess the truth. This causes lesions and splintering to Mother Earth. We cannot heal into one dynamic unit if parts of the body are at war with one another. This new religious system will be built on the principles of a god of love and brotherhood. It must be palatable to the majority of world citizens. The voices of the minority speaking against our idea will be silenced in order to assure a peaceful transition to our world order. This new creed will take pieces of each major world religion, along with new revelations from an appointed man of god, and bring them together to form the World Church. This man of god will create a democratic religious system based on principles that the citizens desire. Anyone who poisons the minds of our brothers with heresy will be quickly eliminated. They must die for the good of humanity.

"The new world political system will bring the three spheres of the world into partnership. The Asian, American, and European communities will work together for change. Democratic elections will be held to elect the leaders of the world. They will closely work with a president of the World Federation. The Order will decide who the president will be and give him the authority he needs to implement our goals. His power will be unlimited, but we will be pulling the strings behind the scenes. We will take command of the economy, media, politics, and Church. That is only a cursory look at my blueprint. I'm sure you gentlemen have some questions."

Lord Winchester bolted out of his seat.

"Immanuel, you are one smooth character. I don't buy any of it! I oppose you and your solutions, which are based on fantasy. Your motives are suspicious, and your methods are untried. It is a supernatural scheme that would make a great Hollywood movie. I do not believe in God or the miracles of this so-called unseen world. This man of god idea will never work. The only way he would capture the hearts of the world—the only way he would persuade *me* is if I would witness firsthand some supernatural miracles that I can see, touch, and feel."

Winchester sat back down again. The chamber ignited in conversation, with advocates on both sides.

"Gentlemen, gentlemen. Lord Winchester believes actions speak louder than words. I happen to agree," interrupted Immanuel.

"Blasphemy, I need you to use your powers," Immanuel prayed silently.

"I will send Lord Winchester on a roller coaster ride to hell!" boasted Blasphemy.

The chair Lord Winchester occupied began to shake. Then it slowly began to rise. Lord Winchester was paralyzed with fear, and his muscles froze. The other men jumped away from the table and glued themselves to the walls. Only Immanuel remained calmly seated. Lord Winchester and his chair remained suspended near the top of the twenty-foot ceiling. Blasphemy was effortlessly levitating the two-hundred-pound billionaire.

The chair then smoothly descended from the ceiling and returned to the marble floor. Lord Winchester trembled as he tried to stand on his own two feet.

The gentlemen slowly encircled Lord Winchester. They consoled their comrade. Each man glanced at Immanuel, who remained strangely to himself. Immanuel had made his point.

Two

Spiritual Warfare

Stephen pulled the reading glasses from his face. Rivers of sweat steadily flowed down his cheeks and neck. His body was overheating. For the fourteenth day in a row, the indoor thermometer had exploded over the one hundred degree mark. He was a large-framed African-American man with brown eyes and an honest face. A genuine individual, he had many friends willing to go the extra mile for him or his family. Stephen stared at the cranky AC, dreaming of the good old days when comfort was a given, not a luxury.

Only the very rich and influential enjoyed air-conditioning in the present days of economic depression. America, once the "home of the strong and brave," had been cursed and humbled to America, home of the weak and desolate. Rioting and lawlessness consumed the great eagle like spreading cancer. *Economic justice* and *greedy capitalists* were the newest buzz words in the newspapers and television news shows. American society had splintered into a multi-ethnic, religiously diverse culture with no discernable compass. It was known as a melting-pot society. Unfortunately, the components in that pot were now highly flammable.

Countless cities had been transformed from magnificent metropolises to towering infernos. The police and national guard were helpless as rioters ignored their weapons. The rioters' hopeless attitude had a sad basis in truth. They felt it was better to die than live with no savings, no hope, no justice, and no food. Tens of thousands were being murdered as racial hatred and class envy fed the flames of social injustice.

As Stephen reviewed the disturbing current events, his mind returned to happier times. He remembered the day he had asked his wife, Sabrina, to marry him. His heart fluttered as he recalled the blissful feelings of love and security they had had as they started their life in a country that allowed them to pursue their

31

dreams. He recalled the birth of their only child, Stephen, Jr.; the baseball games in the park; and the family camping excursions to the mountains. He sighed as he realized that the good days were over. He struggled to understand the Lord's purpose behind such national carnage and despair, but he was convinced that there was a reason for it all. He returned to the letter he was writing to his former boss.

"Dear Sir, I hope this letter finds you well and in good spirits. I have always enjoyed my job at the *St. Louis Herald Times*. I wish your newspaper success as we enter this new era of American history. I would be lying to you if I didn't admit the personal devastation I feel from being fired. I hope you will reconsider your decision."

Stephen struggled to find the right words.

"I know that you believe that I cannot be an objective journalist because I am a Christian. Unfortunately, that seems to be a common attitude. The notion that all Christians are judgmental bigots or preachers of apocalypse and lies seems to be spreading faster than I can comprehend. I recognize that numerous crimes have been committed in the past five years by those who profess to be Christians, but these actions are not characteristic of true disciples of Jesus Christ. There seems to be a small, well organized gang of vigilantes who publicly claim faith in Christian doctrine. I cannot emphasize enough that they do not follow His principles and would be denounced as hypocrites by Christ Himself.

"Sadly, I was present when an 'outsider' wielded a gun and murdered an abortion doctor and nurse. This assassin was not a member of the pro-life movement or associated with me or any other member of our organization. I believe this man was a plant whose plan was to destroy our peaceful movement. I abhor this act of cowardly violence! I will never support the notion that 'two wrongs make a right.'

"I pray that you will reconsider your decision.

"Yours truly, Stephen Wallace."

Tears formed in his eyes as he thought of Christ's words to "count it all joy" when persecuted for His sake. He printed the letter and placed his signature at the bottom. His wife Sabrina knocked gently on the door.

"Honey, are you all right in there?"

"Everything's fine," Stephen said.

He scanned the letter searching for mistakes. The heat and lack of sleep began to take its toll on his overtaxed mind. The words and sentences began to run together as the script turned fuzzy. He gradually fell asleep...

"Honey, I was let go from work last week," muttered Stephen.

Sabrina gave him a scolding look of betrayal.

"Why didn't you tell me sooner? You've been home for three days acting like your dog just died and ignoring me at any cost. Don't you trust me anymore? What are we going to do about the bills? We are going to be kicked out into the streets without a shirt to put on our backs! Don't you care about me? Don't you—"

Stephen awoke from the nightmare and vaulted out of his seat as Sabrina lightly kissed his neck.

"I'm worried about you, Stephen. You don't seem yourself lately." She glanced down at the table where the letter lay. "Is this your latest news piece?" She smiled excitedly as she went for the letter.

"No!" yelled Stephen.

He barely intercepted the letter from her hands. Sabrina was startled.

"What's wrong, Stephen?"

She looked into his brown eyes searching for a clue. He quickly looked away, embarrassed at his deceptive behavior.

"You've been depressed since the weekend. Is everything okay at work?" asked Sabrina.

He stared into her eyes.

"Honey, sit down. I have some bad news."

"What is it?"

She gently caressed his hand. Stephen's eyes fell to the ground, unable to meet her gaze.

"I've been deceiving you," muttered Stephen.

She squeezed his hand as a sign of support. There wasn't a trace of condemnation. Stephen was surprised at her reaction.

"The newspaper fired me on Friday for insubordination."

Sabrina had been expecting this for some time. She reached to hug her husband.

"Why?" asked Sabrina.

"The murder at the pro-life rally along with my politically incorrect writing did it," said Stephen. "This letter is my last attempt to save my job."

His mood was heavy as he handed the letter to his wife. As she read the words to his former employer, a sense of peace settled his apprehensive spirit. The nightmare he had feared never materialized. He could sense the Holy Spirit comforting him.

Sabrina placed the letter on the coffee-stained desk.

"It's perfect. You've told the truth with love. God will show us the reasons behind this adversity."

Timothy was seated on the baking rooftop of the city's leading newspaper. He was lonely and distraught. He had been unemployed for a meager three days and had no clue what to do next. He wondered where his next assignment, if any, would lead him. Timothy was three feet tall and holding. His white wings were petite and laced with golden ruffles. Last time he checked, which was yesterday, his top speed was a meager eighteen hundred miles an hour. Timothy was crowned with the rank of private first class in Jehovah God's heavenly army. His job was to wait for prayers from his saint. He then would fly to a command post in the clouds and relay the critical prayer to a captain. Occasionally, he would be forced into combat with one of Lucifer's conspirators. The amount of strength and power he displayed was not determined by him, but by the faith and prayers of his saint. Sometimes, he would be blocked by an evil cloud of demons who would try to steal his saint's prayer. His job was tough, but rewarding, and he loved it.

Suddenly, he realized he needed to make some big decisions, and fast. Should he leave his camp and search for his saint Stephen? Maybe he should report to headquarters regarding Stephen's absence. No, he would never disobey Jehovah God. His orders were perfectly clear. He could leave his strategic position in only one circumstance. He was allowed to travel from the newspaper office to the command center to relay prayers. Nothing more, nothing less.

"Where did that abhorrent thought come from?" pondered Timothy, as he began to search for an unwelcome intruder.

"Don't bother searching for me, you big baby; go after your sniveling saint. I can hear him whining for you all the way across town."

Timothy's adrenaline raced as he looked around. He anxiously pulled his weapon into open view. He looked everywhere but saw nothing.

"Na-na-na-na-na," mocked the invisible creature.

Timothy concentrated his vision in the vicinity of the noisy air-conditioning vent. A phantomlike creature immediately ducked out of sight.

"Bart, is that you? Come out and fight like a demon," demanded Timothy. Timothy tiptoed toward the dusty shaft. "I know you were trying to fill my head with trash. Why don't you find someone else to tempt who will foolishly listen to you?"

Timothy dove headfirst into the steamy pit. Bart panicked. He lunged through the pipe and into the newsroom. Timothy was hot on his trail. He chased the ghoul through offices, desks, and populated hallways.

"You won't get away from me!" shouted a tiring Timothy.

"You pip-squeak! You'll never catch me with those wimpy wings of yours," barked Bart.

Bart blasted through a wall and onto the hustling streets of the city.

"Come on, slowpoke, I'm over here," mocked Bart.

Timothy launched his angelic engine into overdrive as he jetted toward the ghost.

"I've had enough of your charades. You're history!" spouted Timothy.

He swung his dagger wildly in Bart's direction. Bart annoyed Timothy by not ducking until the last second. Timothy inadvertently sped past a laughing Bart but performed a lightning fast U-turn.

"That's it, buster. I'm really mad now."

Timothy threw his sword at the evil heart of the demon. Bart dodged the projectile and zoomed toward the clouds.

"Come and get me, you blockhead," mocked Bart.

Timothy was about to leave when he paused to remember his orders.

"Come and get me, you big chicken!" shouted Bart.

Timothy drooped like a flower deprived of its spring rain. He had been made a fool of once again. He watched Bart fly into the distance.

"Lucifer is king!" boasted Bart. "Lucifer and Bart rule the world."

Bart watched Timothy fade from his sight. Suddenly, out of nowhere, something grabbed him by his scrawny neck. He pleaded for mercy as he was catapulted back down toward the polluted city.

"Ouch! Help! No! What's happening?" panicked the helpless demon. "Lucifer, master, I need you," moaned the battered felon.

"What you need, young fellow, is an attitude adjustment," retorted Alexius, colonel and commander of the metropolitan area of St. Louis.

Alexius relaxed his stranglehold on the disoriented spirit.

"You devils just never give up. Your smoke screen will soon have the light of Christ shining through it. I can't wait to see you run when every evil deed is exposed. I will never understand a third of you angels forsaking the teachings of your childhood. Your Creator Jehovah God still mourns your betrayal."

Alexius was in no mood for back talk, especially from a low-ranked demon.

"Sir, I unequivocally apologize for my multiple sins and shortcomings. I was just having some fun with the little guy. No harm done. If you let me go, I'll promise never to be mean again."

Alexius turned a deaf ear to his prisoner. Bart was persistent.

"I really didn't intend to hurt anyone. Honest! Let's just forgive and forget, okay?"

His unrepentant suggestion bounced off Alexius's armor. Bart tried a fresh approach.

"Why would someone as powerful and prestigious as yourself want to detain someone as insignificant as me?" pandered Bart.

Alexius fired Bart a look that would melt a diamond.

"You tried to tempt one of my troops. How dare you twist this into a playground brawl. I refuse to allow this act to go unpunished. Unfortunately for you, your superiors are mobilizing their soldiers for a historic global campaign of death and deceit. They won't have time to rescue you."

"What...what are you going to do with me? Are you going to send me down to the great abyss? Please, I beg you. Don't send me to that awful dungeon!"

Alexius stared at the trembling spirit.

"No, I'm going to do something almost as bad. You will get on your knees and apologize to Timothy. To make this event more exciting, I will summon all the angels in the vicinity to witness your humiliation. Any questions, Mr. Big Shot?"

Bart turned psychotic. All at once, he jerked one paw free from Alexius's vise. He mustered superdemon strength and rocketed his fist toward the face of his tormentor. Alexius was caught off guard.

Bart's fist slammed directly into Alexius's jaw. Alexius, stunned by the blow, accidentally released his prisoner. Bart was no fool. He took off for the stars.

"I will never bow to the likes of you or one of your inept inferiors," bellowed Bart.

Alexius regained his senses. He effortlessly narrowed the gap between Bart and himself.

"Stop, if you know what's good for you!" commanded God's angel.

Bart instinctively disobeyed. He soared through the stratosphere in the opposite direction, performing loops, curves, and nose dives in his attempt to lose Alexius. Bart's mind began to crack under the pressure. The deviant demon knew it would only be a matter of time before he would be in the clutches of Alexius.

"It's useless to run. Give up now, and I may show you some mercy," ordered the officer.

Bart ignored the offer and concentrated on maximizing his speed and agility. All at once, Alexius overtook the ghost. He fastened his hands around Bart's throat.

"Let go of me, you overgrown, judgmental bigot!" screamed Bart.

He squirmed, spit, and bit. Bart battled with all his available fury, but he was no match for the colonel.

"Your doom awaits you in St. Louis. You have freely chosen your path of destruction and will receive the consequence of your decision. You have denied yourself the opportunity for mercy."

Alexius unfastened a clip on his belt and disengaged a small metal-like container from its holder. The size of a golf ball, it was purple and blue, and sparkled with silver rays of light.

"Lord Jehovah God, Maker of the heavens and the earth, send this hardened and unrepentant criminal to his rightful place of captivity," prayed Alexius.

Bart's voice accelerated into a high-pitched frenzy of unintelligible squeals. His atoms mutated and shifted as the energy beam from Alexius's weapon geared into action. His spiritual body was slowly vacuumed into the isolated cell inside the contraption. Alexius fastened the vaporizer to his belt. A refreshing repose spread upon the scene as Bart's presence was removed.

Alexius grabbed onto a gravity wave and floated downward to the bustling community. Timothy spotted the angel.

"Sir, First Class Timothy Butler ready for reassignment."

Alexius glided to the earth's surface. His wings smoothly folded into place as he examined the soldier.

"I hear you've been having some harassment problems," said the concerned elder.

Timothy remained at attention.

"Yes, sir," the angel admitted reluctantly. "Nothing I can't handle, sir."

"I want to commend you on our most recent effort with your Christian saint, Stephen. You have done an outstanding job protecting him and bringing his prayers safely to heaven. At ease, soldier," directed Alexius, as he patted him on the shoulder. "I have a surprise for you."

His eyes gestured toward his belt. Timothy was confused, then hopeful.

"You're going to let me try your sword out? I've been waiting eons for the chance to—"

"No, son. I witnessed the temptation and tongue-lashing Bart put you through. You did the wise thing by not abandoning your post. I am very proud of you, young angel. You may be interested to know that Bart hit a roadblock in the clouds. I found him rushing from the Earth for his home base. Unfortunately for him, he encountered an unwelcome visitor. Me!"

Alexius once again alluded to his belt. Timothy caught on.

"You zapped him, didn't you? What are you going to do with him? I have some great ideas of my own."

"Timothy, Timothy, Timothy. Remember God's perfect, unchanging Word. The book of Jude records that the archangel Michael was fighting Lucifer for Moses' body. He did not rebuke or pronounce judgment himself, but he left judgment to the Lord, who judges fairly. When Jehovah God judges the mortals, He, along with the Christian saints, will judge the angels also. Be patient and fight the good fight according to the rules, not the imaginations of your heart!"

Timothy dropped his head in repentance. Alexius fired off into the sky but came to a halt above Timothy. He reached for a golden trumpet masked under his weighty wings. Multitudes of apparitions from across the rolling prairie responded to the battle blast.

"My colleagues for Christ, I welcome you to this most exciting yet solemn of occasions."

Alexius searched the crowd for Timothy and fastened his eyes on him.

"As you know, Jehovah God has ordered a cease-fire for certain units of our militia. Most of us remain unaffected by this omniscient decree and are busy maintaining the public peace. A recent event may shed some light on our enemy's battle strategies. A low-ranking demon in Lucifer's army has actually tried to tempt one of our very own!"

The angels began to mumble to one another. Most wondered why the devils would waste their time trying to tempt angels. The enemy had been exclusively taunting mortals since the Creation. Was this just a fluke occurrence, or was this a new policy to search and destroy men and angels alike?

"Gentle angels, I have captured an enemy agent. This demon was caught tempting one of our finest agents, Timothy Butler. My first instinct was to believe that this was an isolated incident, since this disciple of the Devil has always been a shady character. But the end times are fast approaching. Lucifer knows his time is coming to an end. I would not be surprised at anything he or his demons might try."

Alexius tapped a button on the incinerator. A spectrum of lights and sounds gushed forth in every direction. The show danced throughout the star-filled sky. A cloud of ions sprinkled around Alexius and then conglomerated into a massive ball of charged energy, which began to spin around a central point. Specks of light broke orbit and darted toward assigned spots. The angels could discern a head, then a chest, arms, legs, and finally, the scaly wings. Bart's eyes opened. His body was stiff. The only signs of life in him were his bulging eyes and the steam from his nostrils. Bart realized he was not in control. He was miserable.

Alexius descended to eye level with Bart.

"Bart, welcome back to the real world."

Bart's mouth was trapped shut. A black fog of anger and contempt oozed from the spirit as he watched the angels encircle him.

"Timothy Butler, please step forward," requested Alexius.

Timothy nervously looked around at the audience. He appeared frazzled as he neared the spotlight.

"Timothy, thank you for your presence during this critical interrogation." The angel was firm yet gracious. "We are here to determine the motives of this demon who tried to tempt our associate, Timothy Butler."

"Bart, as you know, this is not a court of law. Jehovah God is the only true Judge in the universe. He will exercise that right at the end of the age. However, I warn you, don't take this situation lightly. You may end up trapped in a time warp."

Bart ignored the angel. He was busily sending SOS signals to his overseer. Alexius strolled toward the prisoner and forced eye contact. He was inches away from the tyrant's face.

"Bart, the way I see it, you have three choices. You can remain stubbornly silent and continue to hope that someone strong enough comes to your rescue." Alexius smiled at the possibility. "Someone of your insignificant stature and unreliable past could rot in prison before reinforcements arrive. Those phantoms consider you a disposable pawn."

"Your second choice is to receive your freedom by adhering to one simple decree: drop to your knees in repentance in full view of my angels and publicly apologize to your victim, Timothy."

Alexius's words sliced Bart's haughty heart. His bony cheeks swelled as unrighteous, vile passion boiled over. The mere thought of public humiliation caused his face to take on the color of an over-ripe tomato.

"Your final choice is to explain why your high command would want you to tempt spirits who are on the side of Jehovah God. I want accounts of the secretive meetings. I want indisputable evidence to confirm your statements. I want the battle tactics Satan is devising to launch a second civil war of the universe. I want dates. I want times. I want the *truth!*"

Alexius's eyes were locked onto the Devil as he reached around his belt for his demon demoralizer. He depressed the sensor on the side of the contraption. The force field that had zippered Bart's mouth released its clamp. The ghoul's eyes flared with excitement. He slowly and quietly began to flex his tightened jaw muscles. Then a screeching bark vibrated through the heavens. His howl for help could be heard hundreds of miles away.

Alexius's patience was wearing thin. He placed his hands around Bart's throat.

"It's time to decide your fate. I'll tolerate no further delay. What is your choice?" questioned Alexius.

Bart's brain was working overtime. He longed to see the day when Satan would smash the powers of heaven, especially Alexius. He said nothing.

"Bart!" roared Alexius. "Speak now, or face a future out of your control."

The villain sarcastically cleared his throat.

"I will never, ever, bow to any self-righteous, legalistic animal who falsely claims angelic status!"

Bart was just getting started. He could not remember the last time he had an audience of this size.

"I will never allow myself to be imprisoned in that repugnant, tortuous time machine."

Alexius was shocked at the demon's response. In a voice that sounded like a ten thousand-watt speaker system, he said, "A follower of Satan chooses treason over humility or judgment. Lucifer's kingdom must fall with a mighty crash. Jesus' words remain true: 'Every kingdom divided against itself is brought to desolation, and every city or house divided against itself will not stand.'"

The angels flew in all directions. Shouts of joy rocketed through the air.

Bart wanted to vomit. He watched as God's servants streaked across the sky, singing praises to their Maker. After a while, Alexius calmed the crowd.

"Bart, you have apparently chosen to give away internal secrets. In my eyes, your choice is most unwise. Satan will be outraged when he gets word of your treason. I certainly would not want to be in your shoes."

The angels applauded. Bart's demonic eyes were inflamed with contempt and hatred. He used every ounce of available strength to tear loose of the force field.

"We will see who the foolish ones are when Lucifer takes control of the globe!" The Devil's acidic spit boiled over and dripped down his whiskered chin. "Don't worry, Alexius, I will give you the truth. You see, we demons are capable of good and bad. We have the choice. You bunch of pests act like you don't. Always doing the right thing. How boring! You're mindless robots obeying your God, no matter if it makes sense or not. Even with all the spy data in the world, you and your bunch are not smart enough or strong enough to affect our plans."

The crowd was stunned at Bart. In a no-win situation, the ghoul continued to spew off at the mouth. Alexius grabbed his shining sword and placed it on Bart's shoulder.

"Spill your guts. And remember, the slightest twist of the truth could be an eternal blunder. First, I want to know if Satan ordered his demons to entice angels of the Most High. I want to know his motives, and his long-term plan."

Alexius probed the private's eyes, looking for credibility.

"The answer is no, absolutely not! Satan did not order me to tempt your precious little angel," answered the rebel.

"Then I assume you decided to tempt Timothy on your own, without outside interference?"

"I did not say that."

Alexius decided he would play along.

"Then who ordered you to entice my comrade?" asked a very patient Alexius.

Bart paused. He wanted to watch his enemy's faces when he released the truth.

"Blasphemy, five-star general of Satan's army, issued the order."

A light flickered in Alexius's head.

"Did Blasphemy get permission from Lucifer to order angelic tempting?" asked Alexius.

"I don't have a clue, and I couldn't care less about their embattled relationship!"

Alexius was convinced that the demon was being truthful. A rare occurrence indeed.

"Why does Blasphemy want you to waste your time tempting spirits?" inquired Alexius.

Bart shot a scolding look his way.

"Blasphemy is too smart to waste his time or mine. That is the problem with you angels of the Almighty. You don't give your enemy the credit they deserve. That will be the catalyst to your final defeat!"

The slur bounced off Alexius.

"Blasphemy said we should be gracious and give the enemy a chance to jump ship before it sinks. He said there is a short time remaining before we will break the powers of self-righteousness and so-called absolute truth. After that period of intense conflict, we will rule the evolved universe forever. Through our tempting, some of Jehovah God's angels may actually come to their senses and join the side of prosperity and power!"

"One question, young devil. When have you known the Evil One to be gracious?"

"My dear Alexius, graciousness is a tool for us, not an order. Graciousness is an eloquent deception. It's used for personal power and influence. Graciousness is neither good nor bad; it's a concept. You see, we sons of the darkness use good to further our individual agendas. But we also have evil at our disposal to accomplish our goals. We are smart enough to use whatever works! The doctrine is simple. Do good so that evil may prosper!"

Alexius was astonished. He had never heard the dogma of demons so eloquently stated.

"Your words have taught me much about the seductiveness of Satan," admitted Alexius. The colonel appeared somewhat puzzled. "Why are you classified as only a private? If evil is prospering, as you say, you seem to have been left out."

Bart bowed his head in embarrassment. He had no answer.

Alexius scrutinized the demon and sensed his confusion. He put his hand on Bart's shoulder. "Perhaps the Father of Lies is lying to you," he offered.

Those words sliced through Bart's spirit. He did not want to believe such a thing. Bart felt as if he were a wolf cornered by hungry lions. He responded the only way he could to alleviate the pressure. He dove headfirst toward the sleeping city.

"You are lying! How can you lie like that? Don't ever lie to me again. Liar! Liar! Liar!"

Bart was miles away before he began to hope that this was all just a miserable nightmare. The shaking spirit panted as he searched for an asylum. He spotted a solitary place and made a dive for freedom. In no time, he had concealed himself inside a transformer at the edge of town.

Just as he regained his composure, a strong gust of wind shook his safe haven. The fury sent shivers down his spine. Suddenly, a loud cracking whip ripped open Bart's fragile hideout. The phantom was knocked out. When he regained consciousness, his eyes rested on Alexius. For the first time in his life, he wondered if he was on the wrong side.

"Bart, your crimes against humanity, angels, and God are too numerous to list," proclaimed Alexius. "By your actions, you have proven that you are unworthy of future clemency. My heart weeps at your chosen misfortune. You are hereby sentenced to isolation until the time of judgment."

The demon tightly closed his eyes to the outside world. How he wished he could do the same with his ears. He had acted like an animal from the beginning of time, and now he was being treated like one. Justice had swung its icy pick in his direction. Suddenly, a wave of thunder howled from heaven. Sheets of lightning blanketed the midnight sky. Alexius hoisted his hands into the sky.

"Prepare to meet your Maker!"

Bart was horrified. He instantly flung open his tearstained eyes and watched helplessly as Alexius cued Timothy. The adolescent angel located the black button labeled "Deep Dungeon." He scanned the sensor with his finger. With eyes closed, fists clenched, and heart hardened, Bart was transported to his holding cell, his last home before the fires of hell.

Three

A Few Good Men

The call letters of the St. Louis news station hung over the anchor desk. WLIB TV 5 was the only television station left in St. Louis since the other stations had filed for bankruptcy a few years before. Following the national rebellion, the government had taken tight control over the news outlets nationwide. Those who broadcasted news other than the government's version were severely fined and occasionally imprisoned.

At WLIB, producers were finalizing their politically correct stories. Directors were hovering over their shoulders, awaiting their final scripts. Several reporters were in sound booths, taping the news stories of the day. Editors were combining the video and sound to make the news blurbs complete. As the deadline for the 6:00 P.M. news grew closer, tension in the office increased.

"Thirty seconds to air," yelled a camera operator.

The broadcasters shuffled through their papers.

"I'm missing the lead story in my lineup," panicked the male prima donna.

"Twenty seconds," shouted the floor director.

An intern scrambled from her seat, grabbed the script, and lunged toward the anchor desk. The anchor was saved from another disaster.

"Five seconds. Stand by!"

The news room chaos was instantly replaced by an air of professionalism.

"You're on," mouthed the cameraman as he pointed toward the anchor's camera.

"Coming up next on Channel 5 at six o'clock, the money problems continue. We'll have the latest figures and the government's response," reported Ken Action.

"As the Middle East edges closer to war, one European official says he has the answer to a peaceful compromise," added Sally Winter.

"And tonight, in our special feature, America's bloody civil war. Signs of peace in a republic that has gone mad," announced Ken.

"The news of the day that will change your life is coming up next," Sally recited as the lead-in to the commercial.

"All clear," said the director through the studio sound system.

The mood instantly changed from professional to informal, as good friends conversed about their weekend escapades.

Meanwhile, in a corner of the newsroom, the news director, Ben Stanwick, rested in his plush office. Ben was a middle-aged man with rapidly graying hair. He casually observed the drama outside his office.

Turning back to his newest executive producer, Ben said, "As you can see, Mr. Wallace, my news organization runs about as smoothly as our country."

Stephen Wallace smiled.

"Mr. Wallace, I need a man of strong moral fiber in this critical position." The news director paused to gather his thoughts. "I have the utmost respect for you, Stephen. You took a tough stand, and I admire that."

"Thank you for giving me this opportunity. I thought I would be out on the street begging for bread. The Lord has been good to me," admitted Stephen.

Ben appeared embarrassed as he lowered his voice.

"I must ask a favor from you, even though I wish I didn't have to. You cannot share your Christian faith with your coworkers."

Ben hoped Stephen would understand the circumstances. Stephen was wise enough to expect this as a condition of employment. He remained silent as he watched his new boss struggle for words.

"I have a friend who was sued by the Equal Employment Opportunity Commission because he shared his faith at work. They told him he was creating an unhealthy work environment. Their ears are everywhere. I've placed my job on the line by hiring you, so please, don't let me down!"

Stephen grinned.

"When do I start?"

Ben glanced out the door at the outgoing executive producer. The producer's feet were on his desk, and he was munching on a candy bar. He appeared not to be interested in the ongoing live newscast.

"The EP will be leaving on Friday. Show up bright and early Monday morning."

The men stood up and walked toward the door.

"Thank you, really," said Stephen. "How did you get this job?"

Ben smiled.

"Let's just say my boss is like-minded."

Stephen was elated. He was convinced that God had everything under control, even his firing at the newspaper.

Ben placed his arm around Stephen's shoulder, and said, "I'm glad that the Lord sent you."

The tranquility of the moment crumbled when they opened the door to the lions' den. Following Ben through the turbulent newsroom, Stephen silently prayed, "Jesus, please help me to make a difference here."

———————

Stephen Wallace's humble request floated unhindered toward the throne room of God Almighty. Timothy, who had been reassigned as Stephen's chief guardian angel, caught the prayer in midflight. As he intercepted the heartfelt words to the Lord, adrenaline flooded his system. He excitedly looked over at his new companion, Daniel.

Daniel had been assigned the angelic rank of private. Shorter than Timothy, Daniel had ocean-blue eyes, curly hair, and a small nose. The petite angel also had a contagious smile.

The anxious private had just been reassigned from book work detail to battlefield preparedness. His simple life had always revolved around safe tasks, such as recording and filing the prayers of Christians in the Missouri area. Day after day, Daniel would sort the requests that were received from the Central Prayer Agency, better known as the CPA. With many changes rapidly approaching, Jehovah God was ordering transfers of 30 percent of the processing personnel into field training. It was obvious to Daniel that a battle of biblical proportions was certain in the near future.

"Daniel, the most important duty of a guardian angel is not to guard, but to communicate. Your primary duty will be to pass on prayers to the CPA." Timothy raised his voice to get the recruit's undivided attention. "You must be on guard twenty-four hours a day. A prayer can be uttered with sincerity anytime, anywhere. Many inexperienced angels let down their defenses, especially when their humans sleep. Stay alert at all times. You can never be sure when your appointee may awaken."

Timothy fed Stephen's prayer into a spatial decoder. Daniel was watching his every move.

"What are you doing now?" asked the inquisitive angel.

"I'm capturing the message from our saint. Once you've finished this, you then feed it into this central computer system. This delicate information is automatically sent to the CPA. Once retrieved, it's automatically delivered in the speed of light to the very throne room of God."

The private looked perplexed.

"Why do you travel to the CPA if this gadget does all the work?" inquired the puzzled angel.

"I'm surprised that someone who worked in the CPA doesn't know the inner workings of the agency," commented Timothy.

Daniel was crushed. Tears welled up in his eyes.

"No one ever explained it to me. I didn't think I was supposed to ask."

Timothy felt horrible.

"I am sorry I hurt your feelings. Your job must have been strictly regimented. On the battlefield, your knowledge of fighting, communication, evangelism, and a host of other things is critical. Please accept my sincere apology."

"So why all the extra work and hassle?" asked Daniel.

Timothy's disposition turned bitter.

"Satan's army of troublemakers," responded the spirit.

Daniel was still confused.

"You see, young soldier, the Evil One's technical spies have devised a scheming system to jam the airwaves. The prayers are gobbled up by an immense black hole of reverse ionized energy. Simply put, the prayers are lost in space. Lucifer's troops have enough of these machines to block out about 10 percent of the petitions."

Daniel's righteous passion flared as he soared around Timothy.

"Why would the King of the universe allow such a thing to occur?" questioned the private. "It makes no sense at all!"

Timothy's patience was depleted. Daniel's maneuvers were making him dizzy. With one swift sweep of his arm, Timothy clutched onto one of Daniel's wings.

"Get back down here and listen to me," ordered Timothy.

"I'm coming! I'm coming!" blurted Daniel.

Timothy unhooked his catch. He watched as Daniel willingly flew to his side.

"There are some truths so deep and so hidden that only God Almighty knows the answers. We must keep the faith and recognize that we will be given all the facts at the second coming of Jesus Christ."

Timothy rocketed toward heaven, with Daniel following. As Timothy gained speed, the less agile Daniel was left floundering in Timothy's exhaust. Within seconds, the two were miles apart.

"Wait for me!" cried the humiliated spirit. "I can't go that fast!"

The distance between the spirits widened to ten, then twenty miles. A feeling of betrayal began to overwhelm Daniel as he realized his friend and teacher had abandoned him. Daniel slowed to a jet's pace and gave up on Timothy. Daniel was hovering above a broken cloud deck where there was no pollution, no noise, and no human in sight. As he looked southward, the Mississippi River appeared as a blue snake slithering its way through the green landscape of the Missouri forest.

Daniel had never had the chance to witness such splendor. His position as a clerk had relegated him to a humble office at the Central Prayer Agency. Daniel was like a curious puppy, investigating everything as he floated from cloud to cloud. However, he was completely unaware of the danger lurking in the distance. A wave of ghouls rapidly descended toward him. They bickered over which one would be allowed to sacrifice the angelic lamb. As the black vapor of demons advanced toward their naive victim, Daniel mistook them for a dark cloud. Suddenly, his worst nightmare became reality.

Razor-sharp paws pounded him. The violent power of the blows abused his body and hurled it through the air. Daniel landed inside a growing cumulus cloud. He was shielded from their sight for the moment.

"Split up! Scour the region. Don't leave a vapor streak unturned," dictated the demon in charge.

The angel was in a state of fright. Fortunately, the expanding cloud perfectly camouflaged his petite body. He knew the demonic dogs of the underworld would eventually sniff him out. What should he do? Run? Stay hidden? Fight? Where was Timothy when he needed him? He closed his eyes and quietly cried. He could hear the search party nearing his position. Why had Timothy left him in this mess?

A demon pointed to Daniel's hideout.

"Troop movement in the upper sector of this cloud," howled a nearby devil to his commander.

The team of troublemakers instantly converged on the cloud that masked Daniel. The angel huddled into the foggiest corner.

"Charge!" shouted the demonic leader.

Daniel remained silent and as still as a statue. The demons dove headfirst into the misty blob. In near zero visibility, one could only hear the grunts and groans of the creatures as they mistook one another for Daniel.

"I found him!" hollered one as he bit his comrade.

"Ouch! You imbecile! That's my arm!" squealed the injured demon.

Demons, in their frenzy, collided headfirst into one another. Devils body-slammed devils; spirits cursed spirits. After several minutes, Daniel noticed a transformation in the sound of the battle. The foulmouthed devils stopped cursing one another. Instead, they directed their verbal garbage toward Jehovah God. Then the hidden angel heard only demonic wails of pain. A demon flew just inches above his head. Suddenly, Daniel realized that the demon wasn't flying. He had been picked up and thrown like a bale of hay. Then the thunderous war ended, and a strange silence followed.

"Daniel! This is Tiberius, captain in God's holy army. All is clear. You can come out now."

The inexperienced soldier did not budge. He thought that this was some satanic trick.

"Daniel! This is Timothy. Come on out."

Daniel kept quiet. Those rats were not going to trick him. Whoever that devil was, he sure was good at his job.

"Listen to me, Daniel. I left you behind to teach you an invaluable lesson. The atmosphere surrounding the planet is controlled by hostile forces. In the Bible, in Ephesians 2:2, God says Satan is 'the prince of the power of the air.' Therefore, the first rule is, Never stop in enemy territory." Timothy was interrupted by the overzealous rookie.

"Why didn't you just tell me that in the first place," yelled Daniel. "I'm not a dummy!"

"I know that. I also know you don't know everything about global warfare. You must believe me. I was looking out for your best interests. I don't want you caught off guard on the battlefield.

You were never in any great danger. The angel soldiers and I were tracking the enemy's every move!"

Daniel sailed in the direction of Timothy's voice.

"I'm coming, Timothy. I'm sorry I didn't believe you."

Timothy was the first to spot the young angel. He raced to meet Daniel halfway.

"It's good to see you in one piece," said Timothy.

His smile brought tears to Daniel's eyes.

"I thought you had left me for demon meat," confessed the shaken spirit.

Tiberius checked his atomic timepiece.

"I hate to leave on this joyous occasion, but my team of angels is needed immediately in Kansas City."

Timothy checked his altimeter, and said, "Come along, buddy. We have a long trip ahead of us."

"Where are we going?"

"The CPA. We have a prayer to deliver!"

Stephen Wallace maneuvered his Oldsmobile into the parking lot of WLIB TV 5. A thunderstorm was pounding the St. Louis metroplex. The deluge was assaulting the entire city on this gloomy Monday morning. As he slid into his new parking space, he flung his electric razor to the rear of the car and grabbed his umbrella. As he sprinted toward the door, a sudden gust of wind swept the umbrella from his hands. Within seconds, he was soaked.

Stephen lunged toward the door. As he passed the receptionist, her attention was diverted to the squeaking sound from his water-logged shoes.

Stephen opened the door to the newsroom.

"Welcome aboard Noah's ark," teased Ben.

"Thank you, sir," responded Stephen, leaving a water trail.

He wiped the water dripping from his face, as Ben showed him to his new office.

"You have ten minutes to dry off and put yourself back together. Your morning meeting should begin no later than 9:15, sharp."

Ben shook Stephen's wet hand and disappeared out the door.

As Stephen unpacked his briefcase, the Lord spoke to his heart.

"Stand up for truth, in and out of season."

Goosebumps surfaced all over his saturated skin as he realized the Holy Spirit of God was near.

The moment was interrupted as several members of the staff walked in to introduce themselves.

"Mr. Wallace, hello. I am Camelita Rodriquez. Everyone calls me Cammy. I produce the six o'clock news. Boy, do we need your help around here."

Cammy was in her late twenties. The stress of the news business had caused some premature graying in her dark hair.

"It's nice to meet you, Ms. Rodriquez." They cordially smiled at one another.

A slender man entered and introduced himself.

"I'm Bubba Taylor. I'm your five o'clock producer."

Bubba wore wire-framed glasses that regularly slid down his nose. He had a high-pitched voice that could rise above newsroom noises. It was obvious he was in his late thirties, but he dressed like a kid fresh out of school.

The men shook hands. The power in Bubba's grip shocked Stephen.

"Nice to meet you, Bubba," said Stephen as he pulled his hand from the grip and massaged it.

Cammy laughed under her breath.

Stephen reviewed his notes.

"Why don't you both have a seat," said the new executive producer.

Before he had a chance to speak, the two anchors of Channel 5 came into his office. Stephen stood up to greet them.

With a deep, polished voice, the lead anchor introduced himself.

"Hello, Mr. Wallace. Ken Action."

When Webster made his dictionary, he should have placed Ken's picture next to the adjectives arrogant, flashy, selfish, and cocky.

"Well, Ken, it's a pleasure to meet you in person. Please take a seat."

Stephen's lack of enthusiasm after meeting the celebrity of St. Louis bothered Ken's insecure ego.

"Hello, I'm Sally Winter. I'm glad to make your acquaintance."

Sally was a needle in the media haystack. She was an uncorrupted piece of authentic gold that shined from a heap of fool's gold. Even with her star status, she was a genuinely humble and caring individual.

Sally Winter and Ken Action were due to marry the next October. This puzzled her closest friends. They couldn't fathom why this popular, sweet lady from Georgia was engaged to such a pompous man.

Stephen graciously extended his hand.

"Sally, it's a pleasure to finally meet you in person. I've heard so many wonderful things about you."

Sally blushed. Sally and Stephen sat down as they exchanged smiles.

"First of all, I want to let you know some things about myself. I have been a member of the media for twenty years. I think I have seen just about everything this business can throw at one person."

Stephen paused to get Ken's attention.

"Ken, would you care to join our meeting?"

Ken was shaken out of an oncoming nap. He abhorred these meetings and wanted to express his disinterest.

"My apologies. My shift normally begins at three in the afternoon, not nine in the morning." Ken's tone was more apathetic than apologetic.

It was obvious to everyone that Ken was testing Stephen.

"I understand, Ken. The purpose of this meeting, though, is to communicate, not sleep. Everyone is expendable if he or she becomes a hindrance to the progress of this department."

Sally flashed a scolding look at her fiancé. Ken kept quiet.

"I don't know if I can speak for everybody here," she said, "but I want to say that I am fully on your side."

Everyone except Ken quickly endorsed her view.

"Thank you, Sally. I knew that I could count on you to be a team player." Ken bit his tongue. Stephen smiled at Sally, and then at Ken.

"The first order of business is to institute a code of conduct around this television station. I'm concerned about strengthening our position in the ratings. In short, people want the truth. I plan on insuring that they get just that. Ben and I have decided your personal view of politics should be left at home. Whether it is conservative or liberal, it's not welcome on the six o'clock news. I am tired of seeing a blatantly pro-constitutionalist story followed by an obvious pro-nationalist piece. This television station is not to be used as a vehicle to indoctrinate citizens into a particular person's worldview. We should be offering an unbiased news report—not a propaganda machine for the left or the right."

No one said a word. They all knew that many of the more militant reporters and producers would consider this a declaration of war.

Stephen nervously smiled as he leaned forward.

"I know this sounds impossible, but my plan is quite simple. Step number one, we become journalists—not social activists. I want to see both sides of a story presented, no matter what the cost. Those who decide not to comply with this mandate will promptly be suspended. Step two, we will agree never again to take sound bites out of context. When people talk to our station, they need to feel that they will be truthfully quoted. Step three, all stories will be submitted to me before they cross the airwaves. Those not following that mandate could face immediate termination."

Ken's eyes were fast closing.

"That goes for editors, producers, reporters, and anchors."

Ken's slumbering eyes popped open. Was he being threatened? He could take his talent and go elsewhere. Without him, this news department would be nothing.

"Let's say I'm typing a story at 10:30 P.M. for the eleven o'clock newscast. How am I supposed to get confirmation for my script when you are asleep at home?" mocked Ken.

"You pick up the phone, dial my number—which will be posted at your computer terminal—ask for me, then read your script," instructed Stephen with more patience than Ken deserved.

Ken was strangely silent.

Stephen grabbed the local section of the newspaper. He read the boldly typed headlines of the day.

"'City of St. Louis slashes welfare budget.' 'Illegal gun possession sparking more violence.' 'Local church preaching message of hate will soon be shut down.' 'Spiritual love seminar receives praise from local leaders.' 'Local death toll in civil war hits 2,000.'"

He folded the newspaper and neatly placed it in the trash can.

"What did you do that for?" questioned Bubba. "There's some good stuff in that section."

Stephen shook his head in disbelief.

"Good stuff? Four out of five of those headlines are biased. I really believe the writers don't even recognize their own partiality.

Folks, we need to be responsible journalists who report the entire news. We cannot just report the news that fits into our worldview. I want fact, not cleverly disguised fiction!"

Ken Action abruptly interrupted. "Give us a break! You're starting to sound like one of those right-wing religious fanatics!"

"I'm not a right-wing extremist, but I am a Christian," he responded.

"Oh, great. Talk about biased," grumbled Ken.

"The problem is that liberals have not put themselves in conservatives' shoes. They don't attempt to understand the other side of the political spectrum. The same can be said of the Conservative movement, as well. At this time in American history, the obvious bias in the local and national media is Liberalism. It's the modern ideology of today's Nationalist movement," explained Stephen.

Ken rolled his eyes in obvious contempt. Stephen overlooked his antics.

"Stephen, do you think we are predisposed to the left or to the right?" asked Cammy.

Stephen folded his hands together on top of his desk. He leaned back into his chair and deliberated on whether to answer the question.

"My opinion is that there's a 90 percent bias toward the Liberal or Nationalist point of view. That is certainly understandable, with our government suing stations for pro-constitutionalist stories."

"Okay, with that out of the way, let's look closer at these headlines. 'City of St. Louis slashes welfare budget.' Any problems here?"

No one said a word. After some awkward silence, Sally meekly spoke up.

"The word 'slashes' has a negative connotation."

"Bingo!"

Stephen reached for the dictionary to look up the meaning of the word.

"It's only a word," said Bubba.

"Bubba, words mean things. We are supposed to be good journalists and good writers. We should be careful to use words that say exactly what we mean." Stephen found the word moments later. "'*Slash*, to criticize cuttingly. To cut, lash at, or hit recklessly or savagely.'" He closed the book and placed it in the middle of his desk. "Obviously, a person who thinks it's cruel, reckless, or savage to cut transfer payments would use this word. That is the Liberal slant. Now, let's think how Conservatives or constitutionalists could make this headline say something they wanted."

Stephen waited for suggestions. Everyone was stumped.

"How about this one? 'Welfare budget trimmed for the good of the country.' Could someone tell me how to write this headline with some resemblance of journalistic credibility?"

Cammy raised her hand.

"How about this: 'Welfare budget reduced by 40 percent'?"

"Good!" exclaimed Stephen. "How about the next piece? 'Illegal gun possession sparking new violence.' Do any of these words slant this news?"

Cammy, Bubba, and Sally unanimously shook their heads in the negative. Meanwhile, Ken remained in his defiant, statuelike pose.

"You guys are absolutely correct. The words are fine all on their own. It's the message that is one-sided. Some may even label it manipulative. It seems to say that more violence is occurring because there are more illegal guns. What it does not say bothers me. It doesn't say that violence had increased 300 percent after all guns were banned by the government. These crucial facts were conveniently absent from the story."

Sally remembered reporting that story the evening before.

"I wish I had known those statistics before airing the piece. Where did you get those?" asked Sally.

"Research!"

Ken rolled his eyes again. He decided to grunt to spark some attention. No one responded to him.

"We rely solely on the news wire for all our news stories and information. That has to stop. I plan on hiring two new employees this week whose primary responsibility will be to collect facts. With this critical knowledge, we will be poised to present both sides of the story."

Stephen took his pen and reviewed the next headline he would dissect.

"'Local church preaching hate will soon be shut down.'"

Stephen tried desperately to remain poised and detached. He took a deep breath and prayed that the Lord would take control of his tongue.

"How about this headline? Any difficulties with it?" asked Stephen.

"I would use the word 'spreading' rather than 'preaching,'" observed Ken.

"The word 'hate' bothers me somewhat," spoke up Cammy. "Maybe another term like 'deceit' or 'violence' would work better."

Stephen managed a stiff smile as he pondered his next move.

"People, the media seems to be on a witch-hunt against religion."

Ken interrupted his new boss.

"If that's the case, then why did the newspaper do a story on this spiritual awareness seminar? That appears to be a positive story on the side of religion in our community."

Sally nodded her head in agreement, and said, "Stephen, I can see your point on all these other stories. But I must admit, there does seem to be a balance on this religion issue."

Stephen stared at his drying shoes as he tapped his pen on the desk. He silently muttered a prayer.

"Lord, please grant me the wisdom needed to explain Your position. Open their eyes to the truth."

At that moment, Timothy and Daniel entered the room. They were just returning from the Central Prayer Agency. Timothy spotted Stephen's prayer from across the room. He apprehended it in his prayer decoder.

"Daniel, you stay here while I deliver this request. Watch for more prayers from our saint!" Timothy sped away. "Keep a sharp lookout for those rebels," he called.

Timothy's voice echoed from a distance and faded as he rushed toward heaven. Daniel settled into the corner of the office near the feet of Sally Winter.

"This church in the headlines 'preaching hate' is my church!" offered Stephen.

Sally's eyes widened, Cammy's jaw dropped, and Bubba became restless. Ken folded his arms, leaned back into his chair, and smirked.

"Why is the newspaper saying your church is preaching hate? I have friends who work there, and I don't believe they would intentionally lie," asked Sally.

Stephen knew the spiritual war had just begun.

"There's a small but vocal minority in this country trying to destroy the Christian church. As objective journalists, we need to sift through what is fact and what is fiction. When I first read this story in the newspaper, it was painfully obvious to me that the reporters did very little background work into this touchy subject."

Stephen's face was flushed and moist as the blood rushed to his head. "A reporter from our city newspaper showed up on the scene. He talked only to the activists picketing us—not the pastor or any of our members. People, that is shoddy journalism."

Sally appeared confused and somewhat upset. "So why is the government shutting down your church? It seems unfair!"

Stephen shook his head.

"I would use the word *criminal*. About half a year ago, the FBI was ordered by the Justice Department to crack down on churches. The first thing they did was threaten all Bible-believing churches across the country with a loss of their tax-exempt status if they continued to preach the entire Bible. Within a month, they made their threat a reality and served us with a $30,000 tax bill. We did not have that kind of cash. They are repossessing the property today."

Sally was enraged.

"I think we should do a three-minute piece on this."

"Okay, Sally. If you're serious, I'll get you the pastor's phone number. You may want to interview a few of our members, as well. Also, I can put you in contact with one of the hundreds of people we took care of when they were in need." Stephen paused to gather his thoughts. "Contact the IRS and the congressional office for their rebuttal."

"If you want this for the six o'clock show, I'll need to leave here immediately," spoke Sally. She quickly stood to shake Stephen's hand. "Thanks for your honesty. I'm looking forward to working for a boss that I respect," complimented Sally.

"You're welcome."

Stephen was encouraged by Sally's willingness to see the truth and fight for it. He jotted down a few notes before resuming the meeting. Ken mumbled about a lawsuit from the government and the station not being around in six months. Stephen ignored him.

"Okay, this last headline is interesting. 'Spiritual love seminar gets praise from local leaders.' What do you guys think of this?"

Ken decided to dive back into the conversation. "It just so happens that I attended that seminar. It was fantastic! Everybody I spoke to agreed with the philosophy. Such great ideas like peace on earth through spiritual harmony were discussed."

Stephen chose his words carefully.

"This sounds like one of the New Age groups."

"They are," responded the news star. "In fact, they are the main New Age group. They said the Earth will soon be entering the new age of Aquarius—no war, no hunger, no strife, just peace and love."

Stephen knew this was not a biblical religious movement. He decided to change the direction of the potentially explosive conversation.

"Is there anything in this headline that disturbs you all?" explored Stephen.

Silence permeated the air. Stephen patiently waited for a response.

"The way I see it, we have a fantastic view of one side of the story," said Stephen.

"What in the world do you mean by that? What other side is there to the story?" questioned the anchor.

Stephen stopped to measure his next thought.

"An acquaintance of mine was thrown out of this peaceful event. It is said that he questioned the religious doctrine of the master host."

Stephen opened his mouth to continue his thought when Ken interjected.

"The guy was clearly a troublemaker. He had the nerve to stand up and openly insult this fine group of ministers," countered Ken.

"My friend told me his statement was not well received. According to him, he stated that Jesus is God, and wanted to know what they thought about that. This group promptly threw him out."

Stephen quickly raised his hand to stop the next verbal assault. "Listen, Ken, my purpose is not to align myself with any particular religion. What I want to do is pursue the truth."

Ken remained obstinate.

"This seminar was a good thing. The religious right, which you're obviously a card-carrying member of, could learn a thing or two from these peace-loving people."

Stephen prudently ignored his statement.

"We have a newscast to deliver in about eight hours. Cammy, Bubba, what are your thoughts?"

Bubba proceeded first.

"I think we should ignore these religious stories. It's not something we have generally messed with in the past."

"I tend to agree with Bubba. I think we should stick to politics, the war, and crime," voiced Cammy.

Stephen was flustered by their opinions.

"Did you guys know that two-thirds of the American people consider themselves religious?"

Cammy and Bubba appeared perplexed. Ken casually checked his watch and stood up. "Sorry, I've got to go. Dental appointment in twenty minutes. Hopefully, in our next meeting, we can get off this religious crap."

Ken left the office. Stephen did all he could to maintain a professional posture.

"I understand your concerns about injecting religion into our newscast. I must tell you that the civil war has its roots in religion. Cammy, choose a reporter to cover the pros and cons of this religious seminar." Stephen shuffled through some news releases. "The rumors of a new American currency seem to be intensifying. Let's do a piece on how this could affect the average American. Also, see if you can find any connection between the United Nations and this new dollar idea."

Cammy and Bubba diligently scribbled some notes.

"The United Nation's proposal for peace has just been issued. It appears they want to put their troops on American soil. Let's do a poll to find out people's reaction on this matter. It seems like this idea could turn our constitution upside down. Let's do a story with a local lawyer's opinion about foreign troops on our land. Make sure we have conflicting opinions so we can see the diversity on this issue."

"What are the latest numbers on St. Louis's unemployment rate?" Stephen asked.

Cammy scanned her notes. She shook her head in despair.

"It's up another full percentage point. It now sits at 24 percent."

Stephen's mood turned somber.

"Instead of reporting the raw numbers, let's do a more in-depth look, with personal stories describing the real-life effects of losing one's livelihood. We should do a weeklong series highlighting one out-of-work person each day. We can discuss why their job was eliminated, what effects the depression and civil war had in its eradication, what plans they have for the future, and what kind of emotions they are going through. A human interest series with a touch of politics would work perfectly."

Cammy and Bubba were impressed.

Stephen stood to adjourn the meeting.

"Thanks for your time and valuable input. Let's get the ball rolling on these stories."

Cammy and Bubba quickly returned to their desks in the newsroom. Stephen sat down and pulled out a notepad.

"Dear Sally, my wife and I would love to have you and Ken over for dinner this evening. How about seven o'clock, right after the news? Please respond ASAP. Thanks!"

The red Corvette sliced its way through the rush-hour traffic, tempting fate at every chance.

Inside was Ken Action, comfortably situated at the helm of his newest toy.

"Ken Action, you'd better slow down and drive like a sane human being!" screamed Sally as she pressed her heel on the ebony carpet.

Ken ignored her as he flashed a smile her way.

"Watch this, honey," bragged Ken as he accelerated into third gear.

The car went from seventy to ninety miles an hour in less than three seconds. The traffic in the lanes surrounding the Corvette appeared to stand still.

"Feel that force. It's like the car and I are one! Ah!"

"The way I see it, you have two choices. You can slow this car down and act like an adult, or you can stop at the nearest exit and let me out!" threatened Sally.

He wisely eased off the accelerator and tapped on the brake.

"I'm sorry, honey. I was just having some fun."

"I have one thing to say to you: Grow up! I know you were trying to have fun, but don't put our lives in jeopardy." Sally's voice lowered. "I'm looking forward to spending the rest of my life with you. It may take me that long to straighten you out!"

Ken nodded his head in agreement.

"If anybody can, it's certainly you."

Ken made his way to the far right-hand lane and began to exit.

"I'm not looking forward to this dinner. Stephen gives me the creeps. He's a self-righteous troublemaker who wants things his way or no way."

"Ken, he is your boss. Need I remind you that he has the power to fire you?"

Ken laughed so hard that he almost lost control of the wheel.

"They're not going to fire Ken Action. I'm the person people turn to when they're looking for real news. I'm the most recognized face in this area. If it weren't for me, they would be a third-rate station facing bankruptcy!"

Sally ignored Ken's arrogance as she had thousands of times before. She knew that his conceit was just a thinly disguised cover. His insecurity made her love him even more.

As they turned the corner, Ken's attitude turned sour.

"I don't want to go to this dinner. I promise I will be miserable no matter what happens. I—"

"Shut up, Ken! If you love me, you will be considerate to Stephen and his wife."

"I'll behave, unless he gets on that religious kick again."

Ken carefully pulled into Stephen's driveway.

"I mean it. Behave," warned Sally.

As they walked to the door, they held hands in silence.

Stephen's house was a modest brick ranch in the suburbs. A bountiful array of flowers lined the sidewalk.

As Ken followed Sally up the sidewalk, Stephen opened the door and enthusiastically greeted his guests. He was surprised to see Ken. He wondered what Sally had done to coax him to attend.

"Well, hello, Sally."

Stephen graciously shook her hand. Sally smiled without uttering a word. Stephen's focus quickly shifted to Ken.

"Ken, I can't tell you how much this means to us that you could take time from your busy schedule and have dinner with us."

Stephen was excited to see Ken. The positive energy rubbed off.

"Thank you for the invite. Sally tells me your wife's cooking puts most chefs to shame," responded Ken.

Stephen's wife Sabrina overheard the compliment as she exited the kitchen.

"Well, thank you for that vote of confidence," said Sabrina as she welcomed her dinner guests. "Ken and Sally, it's nice to meet you. I really enjoy watching you both on the evening news."

Sally blushed.

"Thank you for those kind words."

Sally followed Sabrina toward the kitchen. Sabrina raised her voice as she rounded the corner of the living room.

"You men stay in there and get better acquainted. Dinner will be ready in five minutes, so don't you guys touch that dessert on the table!"

The ladies quickly disappeared behind the kitchen doors. Ken glared at Stephen. Stephen immediately tried to break the ice.

"Please, have a seat," said Stephen.

Ken made his way to Stephen's recliner and sank down into its soft cushions. Ignoring Stephen, he pulled the lever on the side of the unit. The chair locked into the recline position. Ken stretched his muscles and stared at the ceiling. He hoped to annoy Stephen. To his chagrin, Stephen became more friendly. Stephen sat on the sofa and tried to relax.

"That's a great chair, my friend. The thing literally sprouts arms and holds you in. I wind down in it each night. It's the next best thing to heaven."

Ken forced a smile. The silent treatment didn't deter Stephen.

"When you were growing up, did you plan to be a news anchor?" questioned Stephen.

"Nah, I was going to be a jet fighter. I wanted to use my superior talents to save the universe. I used to watch those old Star Wars movies over and over again, pretending I was Luke Skywalker. When I found out how scarce jobs were in the piloting field, I majored in communications, with the dream of being a news star."

"Why—" Stephen was instantly interrupted.

"My first television job was in Montana—the state where the air is cold, but the women are warm."

Ken chuckled to himself. Stephen smiled out of politeness. He tried to get a word in, but Ken continued to brag about himself.

"After Montana, I received a job offer in Birmingham, Alabama. Of course, I was an instant hit."

Stephen decided to sit back and relax. He would ride out this exhibition in cockiness.

"Oh, let me tell you about those Southern women. They talk like queens from heaven. Sweet, seductive, yet snappy. That's one reason I'm marrying Sally. She—"

"Did I hear my name out there, Ken? Don't you be making up stories about me! Stephen is too smart to believe those tales of yours, anyway."

Everybody laughed except Ken.

"Dinner is served," announced Sabrina.

Stephen and Ken rushed to the table. Ken playfully passed by Stephen and was the first to sit down. Ken grabbed a spoon and reached for the piping hot lasagna.

"Do you mind if we say a blessing first?" asked Stephen.

Sally slapped Ken's hand.

"Where are your manners, young man? In the South, we always offer a blessing before the meal."

"I'm sorry guys, please go ahead with your prayer," apologized Ken.

Stephen prayed.

"Lord Jesus, we thank You for the blessings of life. Thank You that Ken and Sally could be here tonight. We ask that You would touch all our lives. Nourish our bodies with the food, and nurture our spirits with Your presence. In Your name we pray, amen."

Stephen quickly opened his eyes and lunged toward the spoon resting near Ken's hand.

Without hesitation, Stephen dug into the food.

"Check out those reflexes," laughed Sally.

"You see, I'm a gentleman. These fine, hardworking ladies should be served first," Ken retaliated with a smile.

Ken reached for the carrots and placed the vegetable on Sally's plate, while ignoring his own.

"Thank you, Ken. I knew you had manners; I just never know when or where they might pop up," kidded Sally.

The dinner continued without any further verbal sparring. When dinner ended, Stephen did not hesitate to help the ladies with the dishes. Ken begrudgingly followed his example.

"Would you guys like some coffee?" asked Sabrina.

Ken was the first to speak up.

"You bet. Fully loaded with fattening cream and sugar, and an extra dose of caffeine, if you please."

Sabrina looked at Sally.

"Yes, thank you. That would be very nice."

Sabrina walked into the living room with the tray of coffee in her hands. Her bright, cheerful eyes illuminated the room. She placed the tray on the coffee table.

"I hope you all like this. It's a specialty coffee blend. It has cocoa, nutmeg, and a touch of Irish mint."

Sally quietly clapped her hands.

"I love chocolate. I dream about chocolate. I live for chocolate! In fact, I would rather be indulging in chocolate than be stranded on a lush, secluded island for a week."

Everybody laughed, including Ken. It was apparent that Ken was having a splendid time, even if his arrogance would never allow him to admit it. He looked at his gold-plated watch and nudged his mate.

"We will have to be leaving soon," said Ken as he tapped on his Rolex.

Sally only glanced at her watch.

"Oh, hush, you party pooper. We have another hour to enjoy their company."

She looked at Stephen for his approval.

"Cammy is a big girl. She can write most of the show. Sit back and relax," ordered Stephen casually.

Ken sunk down into his seat.

"Are you guys attending any of the churches in the area?" asked Sabrina.

Ken ignored the question. Sally grinned as she shrugged her shoulders.

"Not really. Don't get me wrong. I believe in God, and I know I should be going to church. I just haven't gotten around to it since moving here last year."

Sabrina smiled.

"You guys should come with us this Sunday. Our church is a Christian church, not affiliated with any denomination. It is just Bible-believing people gathering to hear the Word of God," said Sabrina in her soft, nonthreatening tone.

Ken bounced up to the edge of his seat.

"I'm sorry, guys. I, for one, am not interested. If you like this religious stuff, that's great for you, but don't force it on me!"

"I have a feeling that getting Ken to church would be like sending a hog to the slaughterhouse. He will only go kicking and squealing," bantered Sally.

"Sally, you certainly are invited to come yourself," said Sabrina.

Sally stared at Ken, gauging his feelings on the matter.

"Thank you for the invitation, but I don't think so."

Sally's conscience was causing butterflies in her stomach.

"I do feel as if I'm a Christian. You know, a person doesn't have to go to church to call herself a Christian."

Sabrina scooted to the edge of her seat.

"Let me ask you something, Sally. What makes a person a Christian?"

Ken rolled his eyes as he fell back into his seat.

Sally carefully thought the question through.

"Well, I guess it's being the best person you can be. Loving people and doing what is right. Obeying the Ten Commandments." Sally stuttered as she gathered her remaining thoughts. "It's believing in God!"

Sabrina smiled at Sally and grasped her hand. Stephen could sense that Ken's temperature was rising. Without anyone realizing it, Stephen silently prayed to the Lord above.

"Lord Jesus, I ask but one favor. I don't want wealth, fame, or even health. I just want the wisdom to speak Your truth of salvation with patience and love. Please, Lord, help Sally and Ken see the fact that You died on the cross to set people free from sin. Open their hearts so they can have a personal relationship with You. Amen."

The newsroom at Channel 5 was almost empty. Nearly everybody was out on dinner break. Timothy and Daniel, the spiritual soldiers of God Almighty, were seated on the edge of the TV station's rooftop. Their feet were dangling over the edge of the building. Timothy was lecturing Daniel on the finer points of angelic warfare.

"When one of those smelly, vulgar demons tries to violate your airspace, throw this one-two-three maneuver right in his ugly face."

Timothy hopped up and flexed his muscles. He slowly contorted his angelic body. Just for theatrics, he screamed at the top of his lungs. He spun like a whirlwind out of control. His arms and legs were spinning wildly, like a hacksaw preparing to devour a tree.

"Wow!" exclaimed Daniel. "That's the neatest move I've ever seen."

Timothy tried to remain humble.

"You see, it takes years of rugged training and—"

Timothy stopped. He looked toward heaven.

Daniel was clueless as to what was happening.

"What's going on? Do you hear something?"

Timothy remained silent.

"Why can't I hear what you're listening to?"

Timothy focused on the orders that he was receiving.

"It's our saint. He is asking for guidance and the power of the Holy Spirit. He wants the Lord to convert nonbelievers to Christ. They will need backup support to pull off this dangerous operation!"

Timothy tried to cover all his bases as he analyzed this delicate situation.

"Daniel, remain at your station. Guard our post with everything you have. The battle at Stephen's house could travel back here." Timothy placed his quivering hand on Daniel's shoulder. "Practice those moves I showed you. Keep a sharp lookout for enemy troop movement!"

Timothy thundered off into the sky and headed to Stephen's house. Daniel stretched his muscles and searched the horizon. He was hoping for peace but preparing for war.

"I think your definition of a Christian was right on the nose in an outward sense," said Sabrina.

"What do you mean?" asked Sally.

Sabrina looked at Stephen. Stephen gave his wife the signal to continue the conversation on her own. He believed Ken would be more open to Sabrina than to him.

In the spiritual domain, a dozen demons were having their way with Ken and Sally.

Sabrina was heartbroken over Ken's lack of interest in God. Ken sat, staring out the window.

"The neat part of Christianity is not the rules, but the relationship," she said to Sally.

"Oh, yes. Friendship is so very important."

By that statement, Sabrina was sure that Sally was blind about God. The lies of the Evil One were growing into a mighty obstacle in her life that only God could uproot.

As the demons continued their relentless assault on Sally and Ken, a devil scout rushed into the room in a state of utter hysteria. He saluted his commander, who was directing traffic.

"The salvation squad is fast approaching from the north. Estimated time of arrival is two seconds!"

Damien, the commander of the demonic coup, barely had time to gulp.

"Secure your positions, especially around Ken Action. We need him for our future plans."

Before he could belch another order, the captain of the salvation squad kicked him square in the buttocks. He sailed through the air, and landed on the kitchen stove. Seven highly trained angels ambushed the room. The warriors from heaven were clearly outnumbered, but not out-skilled. The ghouls attached to Sally held onto their positions.

They chanted, "You're a good person. Good people go to heaven. Don't ever become a Jesus freak."

Their satanic advertisement was bothering the young, Southern lady. Two heavily armed angelic sergeants attacked their position. Their swords of gold glittered as they successfully overcame their adversaries. One swift swing dislodged the pests infesting Sally. Without hesitation, the terrified demons fled. Damien flew from the kitchen, where he had just been force-fed a dish of humble pie. He realized the battle plan had to change before it was too late. A defeat would mean losing the souls of Sally and Ken, which would invite the wrath of his superiors. He chose to sacrifice the eternal fate of Sally in exchange for Ken.

"Demons, all on deck!" shouted Damien.

The demons quickly huddled into the corner of the room.

"Surround Ken Action. Forget about Sally. I want four devils encircling him, one on each side. Four more reinforce their positions from the air. The rest of you perform offensive maneuvers to distract the enemy. You must keep the opposition busy and away from Ken Action. Our reputation is at stake. Fight to the death!"

The devilish horde took their positions. As they girded their lines of defense, Timothy exploded into the room searching for action. Timothy jumped in the chimney shaft and awaited his orders.

Titus, the lieutenant of the guard, wisely revised his battle plan.

"Angels, I want a canopy of protection around Sally. She must be saved from the wiles of the Devil."

Titus scanned the room and spotted Timothy.

"Timothy, I want you and Demetrius to break through the armor vexing Ken Action. Give it all you have!"

Timothy was the first to dive into the ring of fire. He brilliantly executed his spinning, punch maneuver. The demon guarding Ken's northern flank was hurled on the roof. He was instantaneously replaced by a devil who showed no mercy. He smashed Timothy in the head with a paw of iron. Timothy collapsed on the floor.

Stephen, Sabrina, Ken, and Sally were unaware of the violent warfare surrounding them. Sabrina was loving, gentle, and patient as she continued to share the Gospel.

"The relationship I am talking about is with God Himself. Jesus Christ takes precedence over all earthly alliances."

Sally was bewildered by the new light of truth shining in her path. She was confused, yet open to Sabrina's message.

"How can one have a relationship with God? He's in heaven, and we are on the earth. It just doesn't make sense to me," admitted Sally.

Ken interrupted.

"I'll tell you how! You go to a church every Sunday that preaches hate, jump up and down in the aisles letting the Spirit move you, talk to the walls with blind faith, shout at the heavens in different tongues, and claim that everybody who doesn't see it your way will burn forever in hell!"

The devils guarding Ken danced with delight. Everything they had fed him was gushing out of his mouth. Stephen dove into the conversation.

"Let me give you an example. Sabrina and I have a relationship. The way we nurture that bond is communication."

Sally blushed as Stephen and Sabrina stared into each other's eyes. Sally was jealous of their obvious commitment to each other. The demons were sickened. In their perverted minds, selfless love was disgustingly childlike and guileless. The demons wondered how anybody could enjoy life while not getting his own way.

Sabrina picked up on the delicate explanation.

"Relationships are watered by communication. That is exactly how we maintain our relationship with Christ. Don't you see? We talk to God through our prayers. He talks to us through His Word, the Bible. If we did not communicate with God, our relationship with Him would suffer. Just think what would happen if you and Ken did not talk. Could you even hope of having a lasting marriage? Of course not!"

Sally remained silent, trying to absorb it all. Ken intentionally interrupted her thinking.

"Sally, please don't be swayed by their empty words. I couldn't bear the idea of being married to a born-again bigot!"

Damien's devils continued their inexorable offense on Ken. The demons were infecting Ken's spirit with a mind-altering trance.

"Their God is not real. He is an illusion devised by the down-trodden. All Christians are bigots. Christians have no right to talk about their hateful, nonexistent, impotent God. If Sally becomes one of them, you will lose her forever," chanted the demons.

"How do you get this relationship?" asked Sally.

Ken Action was horrified to hear those words come from her mouth. He pondered his next move. Even Ken, with all his moral flaws, recognized the limits of his brazen behavior. Sally was an independently minded woman who could not be pushed around. Ken was helpless.

Stephen opened the Bible on the coffee table. He flipped through the pages and stopped in the book of John.

"Before I read this, I want to explain the importance of this Book. This is the mind of God. This is God's letter to humanity. Literally speaking, when we read the Bible, we are hearing God talk to us." Stephen quoted the Lord's Word. "'The grass withers, the flower fades, but the word of our God stands forever.'"

"Oh, I believe what the Bible says," responded Sally. "I always have. I just haven't taken the time to read it. I always thought it said that you should be a good person, and then God will let you into heaven."

Damien snickered as his devils guarded Ken. The spiritual barricade was insurmountable for Timothy and his two angelic companions. The warfare had settled into a stalemate.

Sabrina took the Bible from Stephen's lap.

"God's Word will change your life forever," said Sabrina. "You know, it's like we are computers. The Bible is a kind of floppy disk. We pull out the old floppy disk, with all its errors, and we insert a new, perfect disk into us. With that new, godly information inside of you, you are a new creation!"

She looked down at the Bible and read from John 3:3.

"'Most assuredly, I say to you, unless one is born again, he cannot see the kingdom of God.'"

Sabrina placed the Bible on the table.

"These are Jesus' words. He was speaking to a deeply religious man named Nicodemus. Jesus was telling a religious leader how to get to heaven. You see, Sally, religion does not promise you entrance into heaven. A personal relationship with Jesus Christ gives you the keys."

Ken appeared to have ants in his pants; however, the others ignored his theatrics.

"Nobody has ever described Christianity to me like this before," confessed Sally as she set down her cup of coffee.

"If you don't have to be a good person to get into heaven, then can you do whatever you want? It doesn't make much sense to me!" admitted Sally.

"Sure it does!" interjected Ken with sarcasm in his voice. "These Christians go out and murder abortion doctors all the time, and all in the name of their religion! I'm sure that Book says something about murderers not getting into heaven!"

An eerie silence filled the room. Sabrina glanced at Stephen. Stephen took charge.

"The Bible does command us not to murder under any circumstance. These people who have butchered abortionists will have to answer for it. I seriously doubt the true salvation of these violent, irresponsible people. You know, just because they label themselves Christians doesn't necessarily make it so. God will be the ultimate Judge!" He rubbed his hands together, releasing some nervous energy. "The Bible has an answer to your question. Here it is." He turned to Romans, chapter three, verse twenty-eight, and read, "'Therefore we conclude that a man is justified by faith apart from the deeds of the law.'"

Ken leaned over Stephen's shoulder to get a look at the words for himself.

"Sounds like a lot of lawyer mishmash! What point are you making, anyway?" spewed Ken as he hardened his heart.

Stephen ignored Ken as he turned a few pages further in his Bible.

"Chapter eight, verse one, spells it out the best. 'There is therefore now no condemnation to those who are in Christ Jesus, who do not walk according to the flesh, but according to the Spirit. For the law of the Spirit of life in Christ Jesus has made me free from the law of sin and death. For what the law could not do in that it was weak through the flesh, God did by sending His own Son in the likeness of sinful flesh, on account of sin: He condemned sin in the flesh.'"

Stephen gently closed his Bible and smiled at Sally.

"Christianity is much more than a religion. It is a relationship with the God who created the world. He wants us to talk to Him, and He wants to talk with us. Only forgiven people get to heaven!"

"You people are crazy!" Ken mumbled as he headed toward the car. "You have five minutes, Sally, or you can take a taxi home!"

Sally was visibly shaken, yet, miraculously, her mind was beginning to change from years of mistaken beliefs.

"You are forgiven by saying the sinner's prayer, but you must mean what you say. It must come from the heart," instructed Stephen.

"What should I say?" asked Sally.

"Just tell Him you're a sinner, a person who does not always do what's right. Tell Him, from the bottom of your heart, that you need Him in your life, to guide you, to talk to you, to be your Lord and Savior," directed Sabrina.

Sally bowed her head.

"Lord Jesus, I am a sinner. I want to go to heaven to be with you." Tears welled up in Sally's eyes. "Please, save me from my sins. Come into my life. Help me to become the best Christian I can be." Tears flooded her face. "Forgive me for not doing this sooner. Amen."

Sally embraced Stephen and Sabrina.

"Thank you so very much!"

"We love you," sniffled Sabrina.

The salvation squad jumped for joy. Their mission was complete. Heaven was rejoicing. The leader's joy faded to anguish, and a gloomy expression filled his face.

"What's wrong?" questioned one of the angels.

"It's wonderful that Sally is now saved. It's not so wonderful that she is going to marry Ken Action."

Four

The Great Mystery

S atan stood on Mount Zion and glared at the stone city below. His X-ray vision scanned beneath Jerusalem. He raised his eyes to the sky and watched his demonic troops wage war around the city. Suddenly an idea came to him to alter his plan. It would be brilliant. He would be worshipped there as God Almighty; he would rebuild the temple and dedicate it to himself.

He knew that the time was not at hand. His biggest thorn was the Christians. Throughout history, the power of their prayers had demolished his plans for a new world order. Nebuchadnezzar, Caesar, Napoleon, Hitler, and Stalin were men after his own heart. Unfortunately, those right-hand men had only managed to grab part of the world. Satan was a glutton. He wanted it all.

The Devil studied the landscape. He knew it well. He lusted after this city and its unsuspecting citizens.

"Lucifer, Prince of Darkness," a voice thundered.

Satan nearly jumped out of his slimy skin. No one sneaked up on him and lived to tell about it. He slowly turned his body, only to face the archangel Michael. Satan was surprised to see Michael's sword firmly in its holster.

"You coward!" cursed Lucifer. "What do you want?"

Michael ignored him. His job wasn't to judge sin, but to relay a message from his Master, Jehovah God.

"Our Father in heav—"

Lucifer abruptly interrupted him.

"He may be your Father, but not mine! Never!"

Satan's eyes were aflame with hatred.

"Jehovah God wants you to repent of your wickedness," relayed Michael.

The Devil smiled sadistically.

"Repent? Of what? Good is evil and evil is good! He is the One in need of repentance! He is the One who can't handle His kingdom. Look around you. The Earth's in shambles. His ways don't work!"

As Satan took a step forward, Michael drew his sword. Satan stopped and chuckled in amusement.

"I have much more important things to do than to play cat and mouse games with you," mocked Satan.

Lucifer floated closer to the archangel. A tear trickled down Michael's cheek as he watched his adversary.

"Lucifer, you will be given the keys to all the earth. This opportunity will be a witness against you that evil will not prosper for eternity. When you fail, a dungeon awaits you. Prepare to meet your doom and your Maker!"

Satan said nothing. Those were powerful words, even for an archangel, but he took none of them to heart. He stared at Michael and read his every move. The archangel had never lied, which was a weakness, thought Lucifer.

"Are you telling me that I will rule the Earth?" questioned Satan, as hot saliva oozed from his parched lips.

"God's Word has been predicting this for some two thousand years," responded Michael. "You should train your dark heart to believe the Bible. Your top aide, General Blasphemy, reads it daily, and against your orders. His knowledge exceeds yours, but don't worry, his arrogance never will."

Satan hissed like a python trying to intimidate its prey.

"Am I also to believe that the Christians will be raptured from the Earth?" asked Satan.

Michael responded, "If God has said it, then you can count on it!"

Lucifer methodically lifted his aged yet agile body toward the stars.

"Then your God has sealed your fate for all eternity. With the prayers of the Christians eradicated, and the Holy Spirit's power broken, nothing and no one can stop me from ruling the entire universe—not only for seven years, but forever, forever, forever!"

The Devil's gloating faded into the night as he sped off toward the north. His work had just begun.

———————

"That's the news for tonight," Ken Action said as the broadcast came to a close.

"We'll see you tomorrow with more news that affects you and your family," added Sally Winter.

The anchors smiled on cue, looked down, and began to shuffle their cheat sheets. They continued the charade until the red light died.

"Good show," said the floor director. Sally returned the professional etiquette with a touch more sincerity.

"Thanks, guys. Have a good one."

Ken ignored their trivial banter. In a silent rage, he rushed into the green room to scour the makeup from his face. Sally followed closely behind him, dejected, confused, yet ready for battle. She hoped that no one had noticed the tension between them. As she entered the room, Ken ignored her. She was struggling to control her emotions.

"Ken, would you at least acknowledge my presence?"

He was carefully rearranging his hair. Sally slammed the door. Without a word, she locked the door and moved to Ken's makeup counter.

"You have exactly two seconds to tell me why you're treating me like a dog that just peed all over your new Corvette!" she shouted.

Ken was stunned. He was smart enough to know that the silent treatment was a bad move. He tried talking but wound up babbling.

"There's nothing wrong. I mean, I'm fine. I just can't understand," he sighed. "It's useless."

Sally's mood shifted.

"What's useless? Everything will be fine if you will just tell me what's eating you."

Ken shook his head in despair.

"Listen, Sally. Sometimes I just don't understand where you're coming from. It's like you're from another galaxy. I'm planning on marrying you next year, and look what happens. You go and become a born-again bigot!"

Her tone was soft and gentle.

"I think you know I am not a bigot. Not all Christians are like that. I know your deep hatred for religion. And why not? Your father drank and cursed six days of the week and played church on the seventh. I know he beat your mother when she didn't agree with him. But your problem should be with him, not God."

Ken turned away from the mirror and looked in Sally's direction. His pride prevented him from looking into her eyes. It was evident that her words had hit home.

"Look, if you want to be a Christian, that's great. If it works for you, then more power to you. Just make me one promise."

"What's that?"

"Promise me that you will never try to force that stuff on me."

She gave Ken a bear hug.

"Have I ever tried to change you or any of your many flaws?"

"Many flaws?" retorted Ken.

"Would you like a list?" Sally answered with a smile.

Ken fidgeted.

"Let's go grab some potato skins. This conversation is going nowhere."

———————

Rome was bustling with activity. It was early Sunday afternoon. Families were returning from church, and tourists were hustling about hoping for that perfect picture.

Immanuel was seated in a chair dating from the fifth century. He had spent the previous months mesmerizing political partners all over Europe. National borders had been dissolved by a simple stroke of the pen, yet obstacles remained. The United States of Europe needed a face-lift.

"He'll never fall for such an idea," Dominic Rosario, the senior cardinal to the Pope, was saying.

"A noble goal such as this must surely find some endorsement in the Vatican. Peace should be your ultimate goal on earth," warned Immanuel.

Immanuel's words cast a spell on the suddenly weak-willed, faithless cardinal. He had the backbone of a jellyfish when he was around Immanuel.

"Some may agree with that statement, but many would say upholding God's laws is our most sacred duty," admitted Dominic.

He began to stutter, which was unlike the suave cardinal.

"I, I personally abhor their 'holier than thou' attitude. They put so much emphasis on God's laws and their tradition. I believe that the Bible is interpreted differently from generation to generation, and the idea of absolute truth went out with the Stone Age. However, the Pope will fight you because his doctrine cannot be affected by political expediency."

Dominic was a hippie-turned-priest who hoped to rule one day. His lofty aspirations were not motivated by patriotism, duty, or honor. He wanted recognition. God had shed many tears watching this self-made man ascend from priest, to bishop, to archbishop, to cardinal. Outwardly, he was deeply religious, loving, charitable, and an integral part of the Vatican hierarchy. Inwardly, unlike the Pope, he was a wolf. Dominic wanted to become Pope of the Catholic Church, no matter what the cost. His cunning words soothed Immanuel's mind.

"I would certainly want to follow your noble goal of peace on earth over any religious doctrine."

Immanuel folded his hands and placed them on the ivory table.

"I know your heart yearns to be the head of the Catholic Church," concluded Immanuel. "Your aspirations are noble, yet shortsighted."

His cutting words made Dominic angry yet curious.

"That's a most interesting statement. How could someone of your intellectual caliber suggest I am being shortsighted?" questioned Dominic.

"My thoughts and dreams are on a totally different level. Your goal is only the tip of the iceberg."

Immanuel's eyes were ablaze with fury.

"How would you like to rule the world?"

From a distance, they appeared as a swarm of locusts. They were black, haunting, and ready to destroy. Their insatiable hunger was not for plant life, but for human life, the souls of mankind. Thousands of senior-ranking demons were dancing to the sound of tribal drumbeats. Blasphemy, who was poised like a lion, inspected his troops. In his warped mind, he was determined that his demons look up to him. He would never forget the humiliating ordeal with Lucifer when he had to crawl on his hands and knees in front of his army.

His officers were in their best uniforms. General after general marched past the platform. They saluted their chief, bowed, but cursed under their breaths. In the distance, a black speck appeared on the rising sun. It grew larger by the second. Blasphemy took note of the unusual phenomenon.

"Incoming object," warned a lookout, who had been careful not to interrupt the parade unless absolutely necessary.

Blasphemy raised his paw into the dense morning air. The devils quickly halted.

Blasphemy's paw remained suspended over his body. It was his symbol of authority, similar to the Nazi salute during World War II. He followed the object with his telescopic eyes. As the object came into focus, his anger flared. Suddenly, he dropped his arm in disgust. A general near the platform spoke up.

"Enemy troops, sir?"

"No!" roared Blasphemy. "It is a demon, one of our own! He is in deep trouble. He has shunned orders and has disturbed my parade."

Blasphemy didn't care about the parade. He only wanted his moment of fame and glory.

The demon approached them.

"What are you doing? You have ruined the mood of this moment!" thundered Blasphemy.

The shock waves from his roar nearly caused the demon to have a nervous breakdown. He struggled to regain his composure as he neared Blasphemy's restricted airspace.

"Master, urgent news!" announced the breathless devil.

"The news is, you're dead!" barked the general.

He lunged at the youngster's throat, but the young devil ducked in the nick of time.

"Sir, my fear of Satan, King of the Air, must supercede my fear of you and your edicts," replied the messenger.

Blasphemy froze.

"What does Satan have to do with this?" questioned Lucifer's left-hand demon.

"He wants to see you, immediately. He says to drop everything and report to him at his headquarters."

"Good job, private," praised Blasphemy.

Blasphemy addressed the crowd.

"Return to your posts, my fellow demons. I will return before the sun makes its round in the sky."

Seconds later, he blasted off. His destination was Israel. Checking his watch, he figured that it would take him thirty-five seconds to cover the six-hundred-mile distance. That was just enough time for him to formulate a plan. He forced himself to re-engineer his thought processes. Ego was out; humility was in. As he reached the border of Israel, he began his descent over the thirsty land of the Dead Sea. In times past, he had never understood why Satan chose this place to call home. More recently, his

Bible reading had revealed some possibilities. He figured it could stem from the fact that the Word of God was always symbolized by water. Satan hated God and His Word. Therefore, Satan should hate water. If one were to disdain water, then one would surely feel most comfortable where the sight of the water was forbidding and even its effects were null and void. The Judean desert was Satan's home sweet home. Satan's cave overlooked the Dead Sea.

As Blasphemy descended into Satan's subterranean pit, his mind strayed. He was dreaming of the day when he would be worshipped as God. He had figured out Jehovah God. And why not? He had memorized the Bible from cover to cover. He was also beginning to understand the inner workings and weaknesses of his nemesis, Lucifer. His resolve to overthrow Satan grew daily.

Blasphemy found the cave and followed it downward to the center of the earth. He was as agile as a bat. His spiritual body defied the intense heat and pressure from the planet's core. The hot air from the bowels of the earth was refreshing to him. The cave resembled a city. It was six miles high, long, and wide. Fashioned in the shape of a crystal ball, the center of the chamber was a crystal mountain that peaked at 6,666 feet. It stood above a river of lava, which flowed around the base of this superstructure. The magical mountain resembled a medieval castle that was laced with gold and silver.

Blasphemy slowed his speed as he approached the throne room of Satan. The throne was located at the geographical center of the earth. Blasphemy had been in the Devil's dungeon on only one other occasion. He clearly remembered the details of that day. They were burned into his mind like a brand. It was approximately two thousand years ago—on the day that Jesus Christ was crucified on the cross. What they had thought was the greatest battle plan Satan had ever devised was crushed without a fight. During the third day of their victory, all of hell had been turned upside down. Jesus had raised Himself from the dead. He had defeated death! Of course, Satan had lied about it to the ignorant troops under him, but Blasphemy and many of his closer colleagues knew the truth. But those memories faded as he approached Lucifer's throne.

The Master of Evil was glued to the dark, marble chair, reviewing his battle plans for the conquest of the universe. His head was immersed in paperwork, and only his horns were visible. His eyes rose from beneath the intelligence information.

"Blasphemy, where have you been?" berated Satan. "You know what I do to recruits that keep me waiting!"

Blasphemy remained calm as he landed. He instantly dropped to his knees and bowed. The five-star general thought that he would rather gouge out his own eyes than perform this routine of ignominy.

"My apologies, most wise one," pandered Blasphemy.

Satan didn't buy the act. He became more irate.

"Don't try to shove that humility crap on me! I know you hate my guts as much as, if not more than, you hate Jehovah God!"

The general did not flinch. The Devil pointed his long, bony finger at him.

"Just remember who your boss is. I have the power to destroy your soul!"

Blasphemy remained on his knees. He remembered the number of times Satan had threatened him and others with his power to atomize. Nobody in hell had ever tested his resolve to use this mysterious power. That would be sheer suicide.

"What can I do for you?" smiled Blasphemy.

"You can start by wiping that asinine grin off your face," chided Lucifer.

It disappeared at once.

"Enough of the theatrics! There is much work to do. I don't know how much time we have before the battlefield will be re-aligned, but it can't be long."

Satan tossed Blasphemy a few maps of the Middle East and the new Europe.

"We will need to increase our troop strength sixfold in these areas."

Satan was annoyed when Blasphemy did not react to the maps in front of him.

"Get your nose off the ground and look at these maps, you fool!"

Blasphemy obeyed without a word.

"Get the extra devils you need from North and South America, eastern Asia, and Africa."

He circled Europe with a blood-filled pen.

"This area must be brought under our control first. The rest of the countries will fall in line once those idiots buy my plan."

Satan watched his reflection in the crystal floor. The pride of his heart was running amuck. He loved looking at himself.

"What idea are you referring to, master?" questioned Blasphemy.

Satan returned to the task at hand.

"My plan on Earth can be achieved only through a chosen human. Our agents must work in concert with him and his religious guru."

"I take it you are referring to Immanuel. But who will this religious man be?"

Satan welcomed the question.

"Yes, Immanuel will take care of the political deception. A man named Dominic Rosario will handle the religious side. You'll find him in the Vatican."

"The Vatican!" exclaimed Blasphemy. "Brilliant plan! They have the infrastructure we need to capture the globe!"

Satan's mutated fingers tapped out a devilish tune on his rocky throne. His eyes were wild with poisoned excitement.

"We must marry the two into one," prophesied Lucifer.

The words went right over Blasphemy's intellect. He paused to ponder the idea, trying to piece his words together carefully.

"I do not follow your analogy, O masterful one."

Hot saliva dripped from Satan's fangs.

"Of course you don't follow my analogy. Since the day I hired you to lead my coup, you haven't followed me in your heart. You're a self-serving, pigheaded, dim-wit who's biding his time. You're as blind as those shallow humans who worship Jehovah God!"

Lucifer rose to his feet.

"Without me, you will never inherit the earth! Without me, you would wallow like a worm in your own excrement. You're not capable of ruling any kingdom, except the one in your own fantasy-driven imagination!"

When the Devil was finished releasing his bottled anxiety, he plopped down on his throne and relaxed. He enjoyed watching Blasphemy squirm.

"Blasphemy, your job will consist of melding political and religious deception into one beautiful global beast. The brain-dead human population will not follow a one-world politician without a value base that entices their hearts and spirits. My prophet and king must work together."

Satan laughed.

"You will ensure my success by planting seeds of euphoria. I want everything that reeks of Jehovah God to be uprooted and burned. Seduce them with visions of bliss, enroll them with promises of peace, and conquer them by the iron hand of economic ruin."

Blasphemy was flabbergasted. It was like a script from the Bible. Did Satan really read God's Word? Did Jehovah God really have the power to predict the future?

"I will carry out your every whim with diligence and servitude," soothed Blasphemy.

Every word sliding off Blasphemy's tongue cut at Satan.

"Get your two-timing butt out of my castle! Come back with a victory, or I'll come for your head!"

Should he tell Satan about the ark and Birmingham?

"Nah," rationalized Blasphemy, "Lucifer would just foul things up."

Blasphemy bowed. His face disappeared beneath his oiled body.

Dominic wondered if he was dreaming? Rule the world? How? The world was such a large, diverse place. Was he just an overly ambitious madman? Life returned to his eyes as he addressed Immanuel.

"The only men who have tried such a thing are dead, failures, or villains to planet Earth. They used every method of evil to accomplish their agenda of destruction. I am a man of the cloth, a man of God!"

Immanuel blew away the smoke screen, to Dominic's chagrin.

"Don't give me that lip service. Drop the facade. That God crap will get you nowhere with me! You know as well as I that God is impersonal and He indwells each one of us. The Christian God has caused more war and poverty than all pagans combined! We need something new, different, and strong!"

Immanuel's zeal spread like wildfire through Dominic's soul, but he continued the game of innocent bystander.

"Certainly, you must know the theology of the Catholic Church. God the Father, Jesus the Son, and the Holy Spirit, and don't forget Mary's importance."

Immanuel was careful to rattle, but not provoke, Dominic's pride.

"Don't sling that bull on me, man! I came to you so that you would change the Catholic Church and build an empire of a one-world religion."

A dazed, clairvoyant expression blanketed Dominic's face.

"Those who have attempted to rule the world have possessed one great, insurmountable flaw," said Immanuel. "The church was not behind them, nor could it be. The churches in the world have never had the power to control the thoughts and morals of the planet. Their power base has always been splintered into denominations. Protestants, Catholics, Muslims, Hindus, Jews, and Buddhists have never seen eye to eye. Without their endorsement, the only thing that we will achieve is another world war!"

Dominic was spellbound.

"The dictators in the history books managed to capture the hearts and minds of one, or maybe two, of these creeds, but never all of them. Instead of destroying or subduing the church, we must build it into a world empire!"

Immanuel's dirty heart was racing. The veins in his head were pulsating. Neither man said a word. They stared at each other, like poker players in a championship match. The magnetism swamping the room would have sent the world's best compass for a spin.

"You're talking about a one-world Pope?" reasoned Dominic.

"Yes and no," muttered Immanuel. "One world, yes. Pope, no!"

"Then why are you courting my influence?" asked Dominic, now highly energized.

Immanuel smirked, making Dominic antsy.

"I want you to head a world religion that combines all the major world religions into one mighty, evangelical, political machine."

Dominic appeared more perplexed than ever.

"It sounds great, and I'm sure that it looks great on paper, but how in the world are we going to persuade those religious zealots to jump on the bandwagon? I would have to be a god to do that!"

Immanuel patted him on the knee.

"Yes, you would."

———

"I want to protect Sally. She's so sweet and gentle, and so unlike that brute Ken," bemoaned Daniel.

Timothy tried to ignore his student's whining. Daniel was not deterred by his lack of response. He was like a barking puppy that demanded his master's undivided attention. Daniel proceeded to fly around Timothy, who was seated on a newsroom supercomputer. Timothy felt the urge to swat at the angel, but resisted the temptation. He continued reviewing the plans submitted to him by the high command of Missouri.

"I just don't have my heart in it. Ken Action belongs in a pit of snakes, with his own," spouted Daniel.

Timothy placed his pen on the table.

"If you love the Lord, and you love Sally, you will carry out her prayers. She has been praying unceasingly for protection and enlightenment for Ken. Your duty is to obey God and to deliver that prayer."

Daniel hung his head. He was ashamed of himself, once again.

"I'll tell you what," coaxed Daniel. "I'll guard both of them. I need the experience, and you need a vacation. You work way too hard, day and night."

Timothy stared at the younger comrade. He didn't have to say a word. Daniel received the message loud and clear.

"I'll guard Ken," sighed the youthful angel.

"Good," said Timothy. "I knew you would see it God's way. Do your best to keep those demonic pests out of his mind. Without you, they would infest every brain cell in that grubby little head of his."

"Some would call that blasphemy," responded Dominic.

Immanuel was prepared for the predictable line from the cardinal.

"Let me ask you a question. Was Jesus Christ God, or was He man?"

Dominic was slow to answer. He weighed his response, being more concerned with politics than the truth.

"Biblical scholars have been grappling over that controversy for centuries. Now, the official position of the Catholic Church has been in cement for fifteen centuries. He was both."

"What do you believe?" catechized Immanuel.

The cardinal frantically observed Immanuel's body language. He needed to tell Immanuel what he wanted to hear.

"It's obvious to those of us who have been enlightened. He was a human, with godlike potential. He was not God, but He did perfect His godhood."

He had captured Immanuel's attention and was not about to let it go.

"All of us have the potential to achieve godhood, as long as we bond with the Mother of all creation, which is the earth. We must also get in touch with our inner beings, allowing spiritual, healing energies to permeate our spirits and souls. Jesus knew these hidden truths and used them to the fullest to claim godhood."

Immanuel was pleased.

"That is not standard Vatican theology, Dominic."

The corrupt cardinal would say whatever was needed to achieve his goals of power and prestige.

"I received my master's degree in India. We could learn a lot about God from their religious system. Achieving godlike powers through meditation is more acceptable than worshipping God through a bloody death."

Immanuel stood to leave.

"The plan is set in stone. You will be my right-hand man."

Dominic's bushy eyebrows stood on end.

"Plan? What plan?"

Immanuel walked toward the door.

"My associate will be in touch."

"When?" shouted the frazzled cardinal.

"Tonight, but don't wait up for him," quietly laughed Immanuel.

For Sally, staring in the mirror was a chore. She could see only one thing, Ken Action. Prince Charming was fast becoming the Devil incarnate. Christianity and Ken Action did not mix.

The door to the green room burst open. In a frenzied state, Ken hustled to prepare for his thirty minutes of glory. It was as if there was a complete stranger in the room. He completely ignored her. Words were useless when hearts were hard. Sally begged herself not to make the first move and prayed that Ken would have the character to apologize for being a total idiot. Her luck ran dry. Nothing materialized except some occasional snorts. She could no longer stand the silence.

"Ken, how are you feeling?"

Daniel and Timothy were floating through the room like a couple of free-spirited, tropical fish.

"I can't believe it," sighed Timothy. "I haven't seen even a shadow of a demon today."

"I guess they have better things to do," lamented Daniel.

He glided toward Ken, observing his reaction to Sally.

"Say something nice, you overgrown gorilla," whispered Daniel.

"I feel better," obeyed Ken.

The tone of his voice sent a smile across Sally's face.

Daniel sniffed the air. It reeked of sulfur. Suddenly his thought process was severed by a storm of demons, too numerous to count. Before the angels could lift a sword, they were flattened like a pancake. They lost consciousness, not knowing what had hit them.

"Let's talk about last night," urged Sally.

"It will be a cold day in hell before I succumb to that garbage!" barked Ken, suddenly switching gears.

His vile retort was like a knife in Sally's soul.

A production assistant poked his head in the room without noticing her reaction.

"Five minutes to air."

"Okay," faked Sally.

Her tears had made streaks in her makeup. She prayed to the Lord for peace. Miraculously, the flood of tears was dammed. She quickly patched up the damage and headed for the news set.

Dominic was relaxing in his plush Vatican apartment. He was snuggled in his armchair, channel surfing through his international cable system. His tired eyes glanced, for the thousandth time, at the crystal clock resting on the mantle. It was eleven at night, and no special guest had arrived. He rubbed his puffy eyes, punched the power button on the remote, and headed for bed.

The archangel Michael paced the golden floor outside the throne room of God. Just minutes before, he had received orders from Christ Himself. They contained instructions to assemble outside the trumpet hall at 11:55 in the evening, Jerusalem time.

Moments later, the light in the throne room magnified into a blinding avalanche. Jesus Christ was approaching. The archangel instinctively dropped to his knees in humble allegiance.

The King of Kings and Lord of Lords entered the hallway. His eyes blazed with fire, yet were gentle and kind. He appeared as a man, yet possessed the presence of God Almighty. There was no need for blaring trumpet calls, flowing red carpets, or burly bodyguards. Christ did not need any human signs of deity to prove His Godhood. He was who He was.

"Michael, my friend. It's good to see you. I have been watching you carefully over the centuries. You have served My Father and Me most admirably. Well done, good and faithful servant!"

Jesus' words soothed Michael.

"From the depths of my heart, I thank You for allowing me to serve You."

Michael remained on his knees.

"Please stand, Michael."

Jesus' request was the archangel's command. He leaped to his feet. Jesus smiled, causing tears to fall down Michael's face.

"The time is at hand," ordained Jesus. "Embrace the golden trumpet reserved for this occasion and follow Me into the heavens."

Michael rushed into the beautifully decorated trumpet room, grasped the perfectly tuned instrument with both hands, and followed Jesus.

"Michael, as soon as heaven's clock reaches noon, sound the trumpet. I will greet My flock as they follow Me home."

The archangel smiled apprehensively. History was about to be made, and God's Bible prophecy fulfilled.

———

Dominic squirmed underneath his body-warmed sheets, unable to coax himself to sleep. His mind was restless, but he was too proud to pray for God's peace. Instead of counting sheep, he counted faces, faces of people who would look to him for guidance, deliverance, and even salvation. Before long, an hour had crawled by. Dominic's mind faded into the dark night.

"Dominic," thundered an unfamiliar voice.

"Dominic, answer me, you superhuman!"

The tongue was furious, violent, yet deliciously inviting. Dominic panicked as he realized that he was not dreaming. He lunged out of his bed and onto the hardwood floor.

A gray nine-foot phantom glared at the shivering mortal, staring right through him. A light seemed to radiate from the center of the ghost, who remained motionless and silent, the only sign of life being his roaming, haunting eyes.

"Who, who are you?" muttered the dumbfounded priest. "Are you good—or—or evil?"

The image seemed unwilling to respond. The silence unleashed butterflies inside Dominic's stomach.

"Why, why have you come here?" stuttered the cardinal.

It seemed as if an eternity had passed before the spirit broke its icy silence.

"I am Jesus, to whom you pray irregularly," acted Blasphemy.

Dominic's hand searched for his reading glasses. His luck evaded him. He managed to spill the vodka near the night stand. He rubbed his bloodshot eyes.

"I have been watching you from heaven," invented Satan's right-hand demon. "I have been well pleased to see your devotion to self, religion, peace, and equality."

It took all the willpower Blasphemy could muster not to laugh. He tried to maintain his poise.

"How do I know that you're really Christ?" questioned the squirming cardinal.

Blasphemy was totally prepared for his reasonable unbelief.

"I and the Father are one," lied Blasphemy. "You have been chosen because you possess the talents to bring all of the world into our kingdom of light. I need you now to take the next step of spiritual evolution. You will, with our help, take Mother Earth on a spiritual journey of epic proportions! I need you to rule with me. I must have your talents to lead the greatest religious revolution the world has ever seen!" pronounced the demon.

Dominic raised his clammy hand.

"Speak, my special friend," spoke the ghost.

"How will I be able to accomplish all of this? You sound just like Immanuel. There are too many cultures, too many religions, too many divisions. Everybody has an opinion but nobody has proof. People need to be able to feel, even touch, God to radically alter their stubborn beliefs. How will I—"

Blasphemy made a sudden move toward Dominic.

"The answer to all your questions is with me," responded the deceitful demon. "Place your hand in the holes of my hands."

Dominic feigned bravery as he met Blasphemy halfway across the room. Before second thoughts took over, he placed his quivering hands inside the counterfeit nail scars. He sensed nothing but air. There was no flesh or blood. He was being promised the world, and then some. Christianity did not compare to this experience of a lifetime.

"I believe," whispered Dominic.

His eyes were wild with passion. Standing in front of what he thought was the master of the universe had erased any unbelief.

Blasphemy raised his right hand, placing it on Dominic's forehead. His left hand grasped the cardinal's hand.

"You will be blessed with the same miraculous powers that Jesus—" he quickly cleared his throat and adjusted his script, "that I possessed when walking the earth two thousand years ago. You will use these miracles as a sign to the unbelieving nations that Christ's consciousness lives inside of you. Use this power as I—I repeat—as I direct you."

Blasphemy closed his eyes. He began to chant a tune in some alien tongue. It sent shock waves down Dominic's spine.

"Close your eyes and repeat after me," directed the demon. "'I hereby give my heart, soul, and spirit to the prince of the air, to the one who longs after peace for the nations, to the great one himself who is the master of his own destiny.'"

Dominic wholeheartedly repeated the vows of allegiance to his new master. His conscience was numb.

Blasphemy was pleased with the capture of another soul. Dominic would be the catalyst to making all his dreams come true.

"Continue to repeat after me. 'I will make every effort to further the goals of my master. I will obey the commands, precepts, and wishes that emanate from his holy tongue. I hereby recognize the inalienable fact that I am a mere human and that he is a god. I will defend his kingdom to the death, if necessary. I pledge to carry out his all-knowing orders, no matter how unorthodox they may appear. I wholeheartedly agree to set aside my personal beliefs and follow him, so help me God.'"

The soul-slurping serpent, disguised as an angel of light, finished his deposition. Dominic repeated the damning oath.

Sally plowed headfirst into the newsroom.

"How much time?" she mouthed.

"Just under thirty seconds," responded the flustered production manager. "How many times will it take before you anchors learn it takes us time to set these shots? You're supposed to be here five minutes before the open!"

"I'm sorry. It won't happen again," she sighed.

"Ten seconds to air," barked a camera operator.

Sally hurriedly popped in her earpiece and placed the microphone on her beige blouse. She didn't have time to notice Ken next to her, smirking through the painful fiasco.

"Stand by on camera two."

"Just ahead on your six o'clock news," voiced the aloof, polished Ken Action, "a one-world, cashless currency. We'll have the ups and downs of such a project coming up."

"We'll take you to one local church that has been forced to close its doors. Is it justice or political correctness? We'll have both sides of this drama coming up."

Sally turned toward Ken.

"We will also have the latest on the new breed of supercomputers. Is it moral to merge man and machine?"

Ken paused and turned to Sally.

"All that plus sports and weather coming up in a moment."

The camera light died just milliseconds before their smiles did the same.

"Okay, people. Two minutes before the opening news block," said the production manager.

Sally glanced in Ken's direction. She wanted to say so much, but the gloomy fog of reality had set in. His heart was as hard as stone.

"Are we still having dinner tonight?" whispered Sally.

Ken picked up on her anxiety.

"I'll think about it," kidded Ken.

He smiled through the pent-up anger that was eating him.

"Remember, Sally, bring a change of clothes for our getaway on the river this Sunday morning."

"Ken, is it all right if we make it in the afternoon? I want to go to church in the morning," she said, with the thought that if he truly loved her, he would understand.

The icy smirk plastered on his face spoke volumes about their future. Ken acted like a jackass. He refused to acknowledge her, choosing to review his script for the upcoming show.

"Thirty seconds," announced cameraman one.

Sally gave up trying to break the stone wall separating them.

It was seven minutes past six. Sally's piece on religion was next in the lineup. She was off camera, mashing newly applied lipstick between her dried lips. A camera person cued her to get ready.

"The freedom of religion has been the capstone in America's precious Bill of Rights. Since the birth of this great nation, our country has weathered the storms of foreign wars, civil wars, and great depressions. Today, the tide seems to be turning. Churches all across the fruited plain are fighting for their very lives as—"

Ken was buried in the script of his upcoming news story, barely realizing that Sally had not completed her sentence.

"Oh, my God!" screamed a cameraman.

Ken couldn't believe his ears. How dare he shout at the top of his lungs while the newscast was live on the air. He jerked his head from the news copy. His heart sputtered. He rocketed out of his chair in shock. She was gone, vanished, disappeared. Her blouse, slacks, shoes, and jewelry were still on her chair. It appeared as if her body had carefully slipped out of its garments and disappeared.

The quick-thinking director pulled the plug on the historic telecast. No one said a word. Shock clouded the studio. Everybody's eyes were glued to the chair. Panic seized Ken. He could find no reasonable explanation. He desperately tried to take control of his breathing.

"Where did she go? Is this some cruel trick? I want answers, now!"

Ken's outburst was met with dead silence.

"Look! Stephen and Ben are gone, too! I know I saw them there, in the office, just seconds ago!" shouted Cammy.

The producer was trembling. Her hand was violently shaking as she pointed to the evidence.

"Look, there are their clothes!"

Ken tried to take charge of the insane situation. He barked at a nearby producer.

"Go to the news wires and see what they are saying!"

He looked around the newsroom. Everybody was staring at him. It was his time to be the hero.

"Let's go back on the air, pronto!"

Ken brushed the wrinkles from his Italian suit. He seated himself at the anchor desk, fighting the temptation to look at the remains of his fiancée. He masterfully numbed his emotions.

"Can we get up in thirty seconds?" Ken asked the floor crew.

They looked at each other in bewilderment. They all wondered how he could turn his heart on and off like a faucet. After a brief conversation with the producer, they flashed a thumbs-up sign his way. He straightened his tie, wiped his teeth with his thumb, and cleared his throat.

Without warning, an earsplitting crashing sound shook the ground and their nerves.

"What the hell was that?" cursed the frazzled anchor.

The newsroom staff abandoned their positions and flocked toward the windows. Panic and horror jarred them.

A few blocks away, near their favorite after-hours pub, everything was destroyed. Their eyes followed a two-hundred-foot flame of fire that danced through the blood-littered streets, dangerously close to the studio.

"M...my God, what happened?" stammered a male producer.

Ken scanned the debris. It was impossible to make out what had happened. He looked away from the flames. A quarter mile away, he focused on a piece of metal lodged inside a razed building. He noticed the inscription "797."

"It was a jet!" said Ken.

His voice was strong, yet strangely void of human feeling. He turned from the horrid landscape, walked toward the news desk, then did an about-face.

"Get back to your posts! This is the news event of the century for this area. We need to get this on the air, right now!"

Ken was shouting at the top of his lungs.

"Charlie and Doug, get your camera gear in tow. I want pictures, reactions, humanity!"

Ken Action's order was ignored or never heard. Everybody's eyes remained fixated on the human tragedy.

"Charlie, Doug, are you listening to me?"

"What did you say?" asked Charlie.

Charlie was evidently annoyed at Ken's tone. He had always hated his egotistical personality and was envious of the money that he made.

"Don't you ever order me around again, you egomaniac! You are not, and will never be, my boss!"

Ken was aghast by his coworker's emotional outburst. Ken remained detached from the scene.

"You say you want pictures of humanity? *There is no humanity left!*" roared Charlie.

Ken avoided the confrontation by focusing his eyes on the group.

"Listen, people. The executive producer and the news director are gone. Heaven only knows where. By the bylaws that are printed in our employee handbook, that puts me in charge, at least for the time being. We need—"

Ken's speech was halted by a series of robust explosions. The sonic shock waves shattered the windows. The lights flickered and died. Seconds later, they reappeared as a secondary generator kicked into life.

Ken continued.

"We need to remain focused. We must get this catastrophe on the air as soon as—"

Charlie jumped at Ken. He was eighty pounds heavier and six inches taller. The cameraman placed his finger within biting distance of Ken's face. He grabbed Ken by the collar.

"Listen, pretty boy, those people out there need help, and I'm planning to give it to them. To hell with the ratings! To hell with you!"

Charlie looked at his friend, Doug, and said, "Get a group together and find every fire extinguisher and first aid kit in the building. Station a few people on the roof and in front of the building to protect it from the fire. That wind could send those flames our way at any time!"

He released Ken. With no one following him, Ken gave up his bid for leadership.

"You're right. We need to protect the building from catching on fire so we can get this news on the air! Someone call the fire department!"

———

Timothy and his sidekick Daniel hovered over the charred wreckage of the Boeing 797. Their spiritual antennas searched for any signs of a prayer. It was painfully obvious there were no survivors. It was impossible to identify the blood and flesh as human. Both grieved over the misery saturating their sight.

"I can't believe these human spectators aren't offering up prayers to our heavenly Father," commented Daniel.

Timothy nodded.

"This is it!" exclaimed Timothy.

"This is what?" asked Daniel.

"The Rapture of the church, the bride of Christ," explained Timothy. "A couple of minutes ago, we witnessed a ton of spirits disassociating themselves from their human bodies. Remember seeing Sally, Ben, and Stephen pass right through the roof? They were floating right into the heavens! You thought it was some satanic deception. It wasn't! Remember the trumpet call? It was the archangel. It was Christ calling up His disciples, the Christians of the Earth! Don't you see, we are now in the seven-year Tribulation!"

Daniel's excitement faded quickly as he watched buildings burn and people weep. He turned to his teacher.

"What does it all mean?"

Timothy wrapped his arm around the inexperienced recruit.

"It means the Christians of the earth are now in heaven. That's the good news. The bad news is, they took their prayers with them."

"So we are out of work," deciphered Daniel.

"Without their prayers, we have no power to work! We can't intervene without the requests of our saints!"

Timothy smiled at Daniel.

"Jehovah God predicted all of this. Let me show you."

He took his Bible from underneath his robe and turned to the book of First Thessalonians, chapter four, verses sixteen and seventeen. His hands trembled as he read God's Word out loud.

"'For the Lord Himself will descend from heaven with a shout, with the voice of an archangel, and with the trumpet of God. And the dead in Christ will rise first. Then we who are alive and remain shall be caught up together with them in the clouds to meet the Lord in the air. And thus we shall always be with the Lord.'"

Timothy took a deep breath and turned to another text, Second Thessalonians, chapter two, verses seven and eight.

"'For the mystery of lawlessness is already at work; only He who now restrains will do so until He is taken out of the way. And then the lawless one will be revealed, whom the Lord will consume with the breath of His mouth and destroy with the brightness of His coming.'"

He closed his Bible and placed it back under his robe.

"You see now? Christ has come to bring the Christians home with Him. The 'lawless one' is Satan himself. 'He who now restrains' Satan is the Holy Spirit, through the prayers of the Christian church. When they are gone, their prayers are gone, and the power to hold back evil is gone!"

Daniel appeared dazed by Timothy's technical explanation. He dragged his feet along the gravel roof.

"So, what are we to do for the next seven years, twiddle our thumbs?" asked Daniel.

Timothy shook his head.

"No, no, no! No angel will be unemployed with Jehovah God at the helm. We were created for a purpose, and that is to serve the Creator of the universe. Listen, who are we to question God? Who are you to suggest that God is not in control of this situation? Who are you to be downcast about your position? God has you right where He wants you."

Daniel straightened the curves in his spine as he stood at attention.

"Jesus is the Head of our government," Timothy continued, "if one could call it that. Nothing imperfect will ever trickle down to us. Sin is a human and demonic phenomenon. Unemployment is a product of a sinful society. Our jobs will just change."

Daniel looked convinced at his explanation. Timothy only wished he was as sure as he sounded.

"So, what is our next move?" asked Daniel.

Timothy approached his angelic brother and placed both hands on his shoulders.

"We need to wait on the Lord!"

At that very moment, a trumpet call sounded from deep in the heavens. The sound filled the air with a spiritual electricity that set their hair on end. Every angel around the earth heard the blast.

"We have an invitation to the outer throne room of God. A very big announcement is about to be made."

Timothy motioned to his comrade.

"Let's move! I want a good seat for this!" shouted Timothy.

———————

Ken was seated at his desk with his hands folded, in deep reflection. His mind played back the fatal event from just hours ago. One minute, Sally was reading the news, the next minute, gone! Where? How? Why? He would be willing to sell his soul to the person who could explain it. How he wished he had treated her better. He looked around the newsroom, hoping to see her walk in and give him one of those wonderful hugs.

The entire newsroom had jumped ship to help out with the plane crash. The news wires were suspiciously quiet, yet they were functioning just fine. He had inspected them an hour ago. That was the eerie part of the puzzle. He had called the Associated Press to find out what the problem was, but the phone had rung off the hook. That doesn't happen either. They weren't sending news, but there was news, and big news at that.

"Hey, Mr. Hollywood, you'll be glad to know we saved at least a dozen lives," said Charlie cuttingly, as he reappeared from outside.

The others quickly followed behind him. Some were bloodied; others were covered head to toe in oily dust.

One of the producers approached Ken. Her eyes were bloodshot from the smoke.

"I know how hard this is for you," consoled Cammy. "We all loved Sally, too. Even though you didn't always show it, I know deep down you loved her."

Ken ignored her mercy. His mind was glued to the memory of Sally playing with his puppy, Rambo. Cammy tried to make eye contact with Ken, but was waved away. She walked away from the human statue. She understood.

Suddenly, Ken snapped out of his heartbroken trance. Life had returned to his veins. "Let's get this stuff on the air," said the anchor.

Thumbs-up signs were exchanged by the fellows. They headed for their battle stations. Ken's mourning was over.

"One minute to air," announced a floor crew member.

Ken nodded. A familiar humming sound returned to the newsroom. It was the sound of printers spewing out the news. Cammy rushed to the printers, hoping to retrieve additional information about their local tragedy.

"Pass any information to me, live on the air," ordered Ken.

"Thirty seconds, Ken," said the floor manager.

Ken looked at Cammy with an annoyed frown.

"Can't you get me something, anything, from that blasted news wire before I go on the air!"

Cammy looked at the printout, and then at Ken. She slowly pulled the paper from the clutches of the printer. Her hands were shaking as if she had just seen a ghost.

"Stand by. You're on," waved cameraman one.

Ken nodded to the camera.

"Good evening, ladies and gentlemen."

Ken's poise was flawless, his delivery smooth and controlled. It was quite a performance for a man who had just lost the love of his life. He looked down at the desk. There was no script.

"I wish it was a good evening in St. Louis," voiced Ken. He paused to look for Sally. "You see, just hours ago, many of you witnessed the disappearance of Sally Winter." He wiggled in his seat.

"To me, she was a fiancée, a friend." A tear drifted down his cheek, surprising everybody, including himself. "I want to level with you," said the anchor. "Something very strange has occurred."

A news release appeared on the desk.

"This just in. Reports are being received all over the country, and around parts of the world, of massive fires engulfing whole towns, mysterious disappearances of people, sometimes entire families. Hundreds, if not thousands, of planes have crashed. Highways all over the globe are littered with wrecked cars, trucks, and motorcycles. Apparently, many of the drivers have fled the scene with no explanation of where they have gone." A gleam was returning to Ken's eyes. He lived for news stories like this. "Many disturbed people are claiming that they have seen God's face in the clouds. Electricity is reportedly out in over 50 percent of the United States."

Ken had nothing else to read.

After an awkward pause, he continued.

"As many of you witnessed, my fiancée, Sally Winter, disappeared before our very eyes," stormed Ken. He picked up her clothes, which were resting on the chair beside him.

"Why have half a dozen others in our television family evaporated in the exact same way? Their clothes, jewelry, all of their earthly belongings remain behind. Only their bodies disappeared! This cannot be a hoax. I have witnessed it with my very own eyes!"

Ken carefully placed Sally's clothes on the news desk. Even when she was alive, he had never treated her as tenderly as he was treating her clothes just then. Another update was thrust in front of him.

"This just in. The St. Louis Police Department is reporting that most of the roads in and out of the city are impassable. One spokesman guesstimated that there were over ten thousand accidents. Many observers have reported that cars all over the city suddenly veered out of control for no apparent reason. Many of those vehicles were found to be empty, with no signs of human life. One emotionally strained observer was quoted as saying, 'My God, I have been left behind! Hell is right around the corner!' Obviously, that comment is from a deeply disturbed young man."

Ken tried to catch his breath. He placed his hands underneath the desk and cracked his knuckles.

"Pandemonium has broken out on the streets. Citizens have been running up and down neighborhood roads, breathlessly calling out for loved ones. Reports continue to pour in about uncontrolled fires slicing through subdivisions. Residents are urged to remain calm."

Ken placed the news copy on the desk and looked seriously into the camera.

"I firmly believe that we will discover the reason behind the disappearance of so many people in St. Louis and in the world."

The director began to run the video of the plane crash.

"This was the scene only a couple blocks from our news tower."

Ken shuffled through a mound of papers that had accumulated on his desk. He unbuttoned the top of his shirt, loosened his tie, and rolled up his sleeves. The heat from the lights was causing his face to sweat. The human eye could not see, nor would it want to fathom, the creature hovering over Ken. Blasphemy's fiendish sidekick Judas had entered the news station. He began brainwashing Ken with Satan's side of the story. Judas was assigned to slant and twist every godly idea that might begin to come from Ken's mouth. Ken passed this perversion of the news along to his audience.

Five

The Great Merger

The skyline in Frankfurt, Germany, glistened as the sun crept over the forested hills. It was the morning after. Most of the world was hung over from the supernatural overdose of the Rapture of the church. Germany was only grazed by the storm that swept through civilization.

The country continued to crawl its way through a recession. A job was harder to find than a diamond in a coal mine. Germany's citizens blamed America, Japan, Russia, and the Islamic Fundamentalists who were illegally invading their borders in record numbers.

Immanuel Bernstate was an unknown figure to the average German. He was the behind-the-scenes giant only to the politically elite. The average man or woman believed the newly elected chancellor possessed the power to change Germany, yet those enlightened knew the true, ugly picture. The power the politicians coveted always descended from money.

Immanuel strolled into Helmut Blitzkrieg's office. The new chancellor had the political savvy of a snake and the personality of a bull. However, behind his bulldog image was a forty-nine-year-old man who would suck up to a pig if it meant money for his campaign war chest. Immanuel was the queen of the sows, and Helmut was his most faithful piglet.

Helmut had rolled into office on the heels of economic panic. The populace was so fed up with the status quo that they would have elected Satan himself to purge the establishment of greed and lies. With the unadvertised help of Immanuel's underground network of banking villains, Helmut took 72 percent of the popular vote.

Mr. Blitzkrieg's personal secretary greeted Immanuel.

"Hello, Mr. Bernstate," voiced a monotone Helen Stawlinski.

She anxiously flipped through her boss's—and lover's—calendar. She studied the daily planner. One hand sorted its way through the day's planned events, the other hand steadied her reading glasses. Immanuel stared out the large oval-shaped window at the long shadows swaying with the trees.

Helen nervously fidgeted in her seat. It took all her energy to look in Immanuel's direction. She was afraid to look into his eyes.

"Mr. Bernstate, I can't seem to find your appointment in his schedule. I'm sure that it's a simple mistake...a...uh...scheduling error. Let me just double-check."

Immanuel's tone wrecked Helen's world.

"He will see me, right away. You are to tell him that I have arrived and that I demand a face-to-face meeting, immediately!"

Immanuel left no room for compromise.

"Yes, sir, right away," winced Helen.

She picked up the phone and rang her boss. She was in a no-win situation.

Helmut picked up the phone.

"I told you never to bother me when I have someone in here, especially when it's Lord Birmingham. Do it again, and I'll have you working on an assembly line!"

Helmut Blitzkrieg slammed the receiver down, partly in disgust, and partly for show.

"You'll never get on her good side by treating her like a dog," observed Lord Birmingham.

Helen attempted to speak. Immanuel casually placed his finger in the air and shook his head.

"Don't bother explaining your lover's arrogance. If I were you, I would find a man with some backbone."

Immanuel readjusted his tie as he headed for Helmut's closed door. He stormed through the door. Helmut, who was leaning back in his executive recliner, nearly fell backward. Immanuel's sadistic smirk faded.

"Hello, my friend," said Immanuel in his best cocky tone. He looked at Helmut as a drone who was disposable. Lord Birmingham had his back to him. Immanuel reversed to a more graceful, businesslike demeanor.

"Lord Birmingham, it's so good to see you. What great timing! I can kill two birds with one stone."

Both men stood to shake hands with Immanuel.

"It's good to see that you're still around," smiled Lord Birmingham as he patted Immanuel on the back. "I thought that you might have disappeared with the other rebels of the world."

Immanuel merely smiled and weighed his next response. Should he tell them the truth about the global disappearances or his version of that truth? He looked the two mortals over. He decided to wait and let them hear it on the nightly news. For the moment, his mind was on money.

"Fortunately for you gentlemen, I am alive and well!" crowed Immanuel.

Lord Birmingham abhorred Immanuel's almighty attitude, but not as much as he feared his psychokinetic powers. One example was enough for a lifetime.

"Yes, we are certainly thrilled to have you on our team," pandered Lord Birmingham.

Helmut rushed to the other side of his office suite to fetch a chair. It was the piece of furniture that his great grandfather had used to entertain royalty.

"Have a seat," coaxed Helmut as he placed the relic directly behind Immanuel.

The men sat down, but only Immanuel was relaxed.

"What can we do for you this fine morning?" asked Helmut.

Immanuel fed on the royal treatment.

"It is time to move on with my plans," stated Immanuel in a matter-of-fact way.

It was apparent to both men that he wasn't asking for their support; he was demanding it.

Immanuel opened his leather attaché.

"What plan might that be?" ventured the chancellor. Immanuel played the part of the surprised party.

"Oh, I didn't tell you, did I?" acted Immanuel.

Lord Birmingham decided to play along with the game.

"No, you didn't," said Lord Birmingham. "But I'm sure whatever it may be, it will be brilliant."

Although Immanuel could not read the thoughts of a person without the aid of Blasphemy, he was still a master at discerning motives.

"You are correct," stated Immanuel.

He stood up and walked around the room with his hands poised behind his back.

"My plan is called Operation Money Grab."

Lord Birmingham's ears perked up. Helmut's hands perspired.

"Hear! Hear! A subject that always soothes my soul," chuckled Helmut.

Immanuel removed a document from his leather case. He placed it at the center of Helmut's desk. Then he pulled a pen from his shirt, leaned over the escritoire, and began scribbling on the contract.

"This is the plan, gentlemen," directed Immanuel.

"Lord Birmingham, direct your friends to pull all their fortunes out of the stock market, and out of government bonds. Place the money into gold, silver, and platinum."

Lord Birmingham flew out of his seat without considering the consequences.

"My God, Immanuel! Do you have any idea what that would do to the world economy?"

Being the politician that he was, Helmut sided with neither man.

"What will this mean for the political climate in Germany, and around the world?" asked Helmut.

His self-centered statement was expected and admired by Immanuel. Immanuel knew his plan would mean disaster for any politician holding office. When the bottom dropped from the world economy, everybody would blame the politicians.

Helmut Blitzkrieg was only a part-time idiot. He knew that he would be blamed for an economic disaster, even though the controls were in the hands of the bankers.

"How would this plan affect my job security and my power base?" maneuvered Helmut.

Immanuel turned away from Lord Birmingham and stared at Helmut.

"Your job is in my hands. If you cooperate with me fully, I will guarantee you power beyond your wildest dreams." Immanuel looked away, choosing to stare out the window. "If not," vowed Immanuel, "my formula to control the world's currency will proceed without you."

Helmut knew who buttered his bread, but he worried that Immanuel's plan might backfire.

"I see your point," stretched Helmut. "I am anything but a financial genius, and I don't understand the full implications of such a move, so I trust that you will do the right thing."

Immanuel was pleased.

"However, I do know this much. The nine other political leaders in this ten-nation Confederacy will be a great deal more difficult to persuade than me!"

Immanuel rubbed his bottom lip. He strove to be authoritative yet political. He had the power to destroy these men, but preferred that they join the bandwagon. Things would progress more quickly and smoothly with them in his pocket.

"You let me worry about that! If I were you, I would concentrate on Helmut, and Helmut only."

The German leader rolled his dice.

"I'm in," announced Helmut in a halfhearted manner.

Immanuel transferred his attention to the more formidable foe. The lord was seated with his legs crossed, and his hands folded in his lap.

"Lord Birmingham, I fully understand and can sympathize with your burden for the future of mankind," conned Immanuel. "Allow me to fully explain my blueprint for success."

The billionaire motioned his agreement. An observant person would have seen him gritting his teeth.

"The world must become one in thought, deed, and action. Since the dawn of history, man has striven to unite his fellow brothers under one umbrella. Time and time again, he has miserably failed. The right people have not tried it up to this point. Many leaders allowed the power to get to their heads. They became irrational, letting their emotions run their minds. I will not allow for that weakness. Emotion is a sign of failure!"

Immanuel had their unequivocal attention.

"I need a one-world currency, one-world government, and one-world moral system of laws and values. To foster this objective, a universal currency must be established. The technology for this transformation has been in place for years. However, technology has always raced ahead of the human intellect and will. That, my friends, will change. The wealthy countries have resisted this because it would naturally force them to lower their lifestyles to accommodate the Third World countries. A one-world currency would literally drain the money from the rich countries into the poor ones. So, the question is, how do we persuade these rich countries to join our team? Who would be willing to give up such unilateral power? No country in its right mind would do such a thing."

He paused.

"It's easy. We make those rich countries poor."

"Do you have even a shred of human decency in those veins of yours?" attacked Birmingham.

Immanuel's plastic smile mutated into a sadistic scowl. Lord Birmingham's hypocrisy would have made the Pharisee in Jesus' day envious. He would sell his mother's soul to acquire another international conglomerate or two.

"Of course I do. But, it's long-term decency. Any short-term discomfort for our fellow citizens can be tolerated when we think about their long-term good."

It was clear to Immanuel that these men didn't care about the poor, unless, of course, they were suddenly going to be made one of them. This was where he must offer assurance. They needed to know that in the turmoil ahead, they would maintain their comfortable place of wealth and power.

"My plan is simple and will cause only a slight and momentary interruption. I assure you, you'll barely feel it." He discerned their fear.

"Each of you is to take your fortune and buy bulk bullion. Everybody in our inner circle does the same. The stock markets around the world panic as they see this massive sell-off. The exchanges plummet from Tokyo to Wall Street. The psychological reaction will take over as investors see gold and silver as the place to invest. Since you have bought the brunt of the supply, the demand increases. People fearful of losing their shirts will retreat from stocks and gobble up the precious metals. You will make a fortune, legally! As interest rates soar, the governments around the world will realize they don't have enough money to finance their debts. They will print the money, make it worthless, and send themselves into a world depression."

Immanuel smiled and sat down. "You see? A day's work. A blink of an eye and, poof! Like magic. Hyperinflation. The world economy is destroyed, and the rich and resistant nations silenced."

Though Helmut appeared dazed by the onslaught of information, his mind grasped one thing. When the economies crumbled, the German mark would be buried beneath the rubble.

"The American dollar will be dead, the German mark will be mauled, and the Japanese yen will sink into the sea," forecasted Immanuel.

"You should have been a poet," quipped Lord Birmingham.

Immanuel ignored the minor stab. He focused on the German leader, who looked as if all the blood had been drained from his body. "No, no, no," muttered Helmut, as the shock gave way to anger.

"Helmut, listen to me!" warned the stern-faced Immanuel. "The German mark must fall. The only way we can capture the world market is through this plan. My spiritual masters helped me devise this scheme, and I promise you, it will not fail!"

"What happens after the collapse?" shouted Helmut. "Starvation? Pandemonium? World War III?"

Immanuel was rapidly losing Helmut. He had to do something fast. He had nine other meetings planned with the European heads of state. Helmut was supposed to have been a pushover. Reinforcements were needed, with no time to spare.

———

Ken Action was hungover in bed. He was partly watching the television and partly watching a fly on the ceiling. He wanted to scan the morning news shows, hoping to find some answers.

Sally was gone, probably forever. His performance yesterday evening started out brilliantly but ended dismally.

Ken began to skim through the national and international news programs. The PNN, or Planetary News Network, was his uncontested favorite. Eighty percent of the news anchors were females. Eighty-five percent of the ladies were gorgeous. To Ken, the easiest way to forget a woman was to replace her. The beautiful anchors would keep him company, thought Ken. He turned his attention to the woman reading the news.

"The United States, much of South America, and much of South Korea are reporting the highest percentages of casualties from yesterday's historic event. It has been sixteen hours since that 'hour of infamy,' and people everywhere are still asking the same nagging questions. Where did they go? Why so many people—both young and old? How did they simply disappear off the face of the earth? Why did this happen? Who, if anybody, is responsible?"

Ken broke free from the bed and sat up against his pillows. He turned up the volume.

"Standing by right now are three people who claim they can shed some light on this mystery. Before I introduce our guests, I want to remind our audience that we here at PNN do not endorse any of the views of our panel."

"Our first guest is Dr. Herbert Stain, one of the leading biological scientists in the world today. Sir, we will start with you."

The science nerd nervously smiled as the camera panned his way. Herbert Stain was a meek, thin gentleman with thick bifocals that veiled his gray, darting eyes. He wore a brown tie with bright orange dots. It was irregularly small and tilted like the Leaning Tower of Pisa.

The anchor casually glanced down at her cheat sheet, looking for the questions that her producer had written for her.

"Mr. Stain, do you believe there is a reasonable scientific explanation for this?"

The camera closed in on the self-proclaimed expert. The shot was so tight, one could see the nose hairs waving in his nostrils.

"Yes, madam, there is a perfectly plausible and scientific justification for the events that transpired yesterday. I believe I have the answer. Allow me to elaborate."

The anchor just stared at him. She had trouble conversing with a nerd.

"I'm sure that you have heard of spontaneous combustion. It is the principle that describes a person who literally burns up into a ball of ashes. It all happens in a matter of seconds. After much research and painstaking testing, I have discovered the catalyst that triggers this spontaneous reaction."

The news anchor tried not to laugh.

"Mr. Stain, I am a little confused. What does this have to do with these victims vanishing?"

The science wizard continued his prepared speech as if the anchor had said nothing.

"I am reasonably sure that the mechanisms for spontaneous combustion in human beings are one and the same as what I will call 'spontaneous disappearance.' Though many might cite the lack of an ash trail left in the wake of this disaster as proof negative, my theories have explored this further. Atomic structure could play a part, negative ionization of the life force could be a key, or even intense isothermal deterioration could offer us some clues. A host of plausible theorems are available to research, and I might add, I will be working around the clock to discover the answer to this perplexing mystery."

As the scientist continued to rattle on, the anchor wisely ended any further torture to the viewing audience.

"Well, we thank you for joining us this morning. We will let you get back to working out your theories."

The split-screen interview ended. The anchor reappeared. Once again, she paused to glean more data from her script sheets.

Ken Action wiped the mucus from his eyes. He steamrolled his fingers through his hair. He was now hoping for some real news.

"We now turn to the Rev. Horrace Darden. He is a pastor for the Church of England. Welcome, Rev. Darden."

The electronic eye zoomed to a plump, jolly-looking man. He was dressed in a traditional black uniform. He appeared to be in his late fifties and wore a large cross around his fleshy neck. He blinked uncontrollably.

"Thank you for allowing me the opportunity to share my beliefs with you on this tragic morning after," orated Rev. Darden.

His image seemed to put the lady at ease.

"I understand that you believe this event was actually predicted some two thousand years ago. Could you explain that view with our audience of millions? It is quite interesting, from what I understand."

"Jesus Christ predicted in the New Testament that a time would come when some people would be 'raptured,' that is, caught up in the air with our Lord. They would leave this earth suddenly, all at once, just like what happened yesterday. In fact, it says two people would be working in a field; one would be taken by our Lord, and the other would be left behind."

The Reverend's reddened eyes began to fill with tears.

"Reverend, I think everybody can see that this is provoking a deeply emotional response from you. Why is that?"

"It's because of the meaning of those verses that I just quoted to you. The Scriptures are incontrovertible. When you rightly divide the Word of God, something that I haven't always done, you will quickly discover the truth. The people who have left the earth were the true children of the Most High God. The people left behind are not."

She quickly interjected. It appeared to her that he had just condemned every person viewing the program, which didn't go over well with her because she was one of them.

"If that is so, Reverend, then how is it that you are here to talk about it? Shouldn't you have been taken by God, too?" mocked the anchor.

Her words were like a double-edged sword piercing his inmost being. The overflow of tears rolled down his quivering cheeks.

"Miss, that is why I am so very upset. I have been living a lie! I have pretended to be a Christian, a child of God, a saved soul, for over forty years. I never truly gave my heart, or my life, over to the Lord of the universe, Jesus Christ."

Ken grabbed two pillows and stuffed them over his ears to try to block out the man's words.

"You see, I was playing a religious game rather than living a changed life."

The anchor didn't believe her audience was interested in the confessions of a bad apple. A little voice in her head insisted that she end this interview as quickly as possible.

"We sympathize with you, sir. We will allow you to collect yourself while we proceed to our next guest."

Rev. Darden desperately tried to get in a final word.

"Please, please, if you have not given your heart to Jesus Christ, the Son of God, the Savior of the world, do it now before it is too late! The Bible says that—"

His mouth continued to move, but the sound was abruptly cut off. The network had turned off his microphone, and his chance to share the truth. In a blink of an eye, the camera was pointed back at the anchor.

"Thank you, Rev. Darden, for joining us." Her eyes brightened as she found the name of the next guest. "Our last guest is a professor of history for Harvard University in Boston, Massachusetts. His name is Dr. Thomas Hurley. Thank you for taking the time to be here."

"It's a pleasure to be here, especially after the cataclysmic episode of the past twenty-four hours. To be alive and well on planet Earth is a blessing we may never take for granted again!"

The doctor sported a stylish beard. A toupee covered his baldness. No one had the nerve to tell him that it looked as if a rodent had died on the top of his head. The doctor embraced the view that there were no absolutes in this ever changing world. Equally keen people could read into almost any historical period and arrive at differing opinions.

"Dr. Hurley, as a history professor at one of the most respected universities in the world, I understand that some of your opinions are unorthodox."

The doctor chuckled.

Ken yawned.

"Since the beginning of time, man has been obsessed with the idea of the vastness of space, and who may occupy it. I'm here to tell you today that there is life on other planets, that I have concrete proof of it, and that this is the piece of the puzzle that is missing in our search for the truth. You see, they have been visiting our planet ever since the beginning of time. They have remained behind the scenes up to this moment. However, they cannot and will not stand back and watch us destroy ourselves!

"Nuclear warfare is one button away from atomizing our very existence! We have already witnessed, in horror, what several modern nuclear bombs can do. Did you know that one drop of certain highly toxic chemicals could pollute our water supply and kill millions, all in a matter of hours? Look at our overpopulation predicament. It threatens to starve much of the Third World. Trust me, Western civilization will not be far behind. The aliens recognize the dilemma and want to help. Remember, they are highly advanced thinkers. They know the answers to our problems."

Ken was glued to his television. A spell was cast over him. He believed every word that he heard.

"I'm here to tell you that they have already helped us, and we don't even know it."

"How have they helped us?" the reporter asked.

The doctor smirked as he pictured himself being applauded for uncovering the great revelation.

"These aliens are responsible for the vanishings. They are attempting to create a safe and livable Mother Earth that we all can enjoy—not dread. Hundreds of millions, maybe a billion or more, are gone, relieving our planet of its overcrowded conditions."

The reporter loved the idea of peaceful and loving extraterrestrials.

"Okay. That sounds logical, but what concrete evidence do you have of this?"

Ken hadn't flinched in over three minutes. He was frantically searching for the meaning of life.

The doctor pulled out a collection of secret NASA photos. He had obtained them from a friend of a friend of a friend.

"Here's your proof!" gloated the professor.

He placed the first one upright on the interview desk.

"The first image that you see is an aerial view of an object deep within the Atlantic Ocean. We now have the capability to take a semiclear photograph through the ocean water and view the bottom of the sea. Your viewers can clearly see a real UFO." He used a pencil to point out the features. "Indeed, this alien aircraft is spherical in shape. Here are what appear to be five or possibly six engines that are located on the downward sides of the spaceship. The ship appears to be made out of some kind of unidentifiable metal alloy that is resistant to the corrosive effects of sea water. Certainly, this was not manufactured by mankind!"

Ken moved closer to the television.

"The picture looks blurry," said the anchor as she squinted. "I'm curious; what are those objects surrounding the saucer?"

Dr. Hurley was enthusiastic.

"Those appear to be pieces of the ship. The tremendous pressure beneath five miles of water probably caused them to implode, forming balls of metal."

He snatched the photo from the view of his audience, and replaced the image with another satellite photo of a desert.

"Now I want to move on to some historical evidence of alien abductions from the great Egyptian Dynasty. Notice this wide line in the sand dunes between these two mountain ranges."

He pinpointed each of the features as if he were leading a classroom discussion. "My nearest estimate is that this line is fifteen miles long and a mile wide. Nature could never have produced this detailed highlight."

The anchor leaned forward for a closer look.

"What do you propose this may be?" asked the lady.

"Well, I know this may sound unlikely, but I believe it is a landing strip for alien aircraft. Let me show you how I came up with that conclusion."

He held up the next picture for the camera.

"This is a much wider view of the same landing strip. As you can see, the naked eye can clearly see this alien airport from outer space. What a perfect place to land if you wanted to hide your existence from the human population. It's in the middle of nowhere."

"I must confess that I have always been intrigued with the idea of life on other planets," confessed the anchor who was quietly tapping her nails against each other. "But what definitive proof do you have of yesterday being an authentic alien abduction?"

The doctor seemed flustered at her lack of belief. He cautiously picked up an image and lifted it high into the air.

"Get on with it!" barked Ken.

He slowly turned the picture into the light.

"This masterpiece of modern technology was completed on my computer a couple of days ago."

The camera zoomed in on the doctor's work. It appeared to be a digitized map of the Earth that was taken from space. Red streaking dots filled the atmosphere around the Earth.

"A NASA satellite took this spectacular photo of our planet. This is top secret information that I shouldn't be showing you; however, desperate times deserve desperate measures. I have high-level connections in that space agency who agreed to track meteorite activity for me over the past several years. I told them I needed to know how many of those rocks were impacting our atmosphere each day.

"However, I lied to them. I had something else in mind. You see, the equipment in the satellite has the capability to distinguish the makeup of this space debris. They never really used it to its full potential. They always assumed that what they were looking at were meteorites, but they were too smooth to be meteors. They were UFOs!"

The doctor continued his next sentence before the anchor could object.

"Over the past several months, these so-called space rocks have become more numerous. In fact, the sightings took on an exponential increase. This was indeed a major event!"

The anchor was speechless. Days ago, this man would have been labeled a nut, a kook, and a dreamer, but times had changed.

"The blips on that photo, are they really alien aircraft?" questioned the leery reporter.

"I invite any reputable scientists to analyze the data," challenged the doctor. He had no idea of the impact that he was making on the future of human civilization. He immediately showed an animation sequence from the space camera.

"This is a map from last January. Approximately thirty non-meteorite, or UFO sightings, are displayed here. After that first sighting, I noticed more and more showing up, almost daily."

He switched pictures.

"This map was compiled just before yesterday's event. The total elapsed time for this data is only a week. Look, hundreds of streaking red dots passing by our lens and into our atmosphere. Every last one of these had the patterns synonymous with logical design, in other words, alien spacecraft! The vast majority of these objects seemed destined for the African continent. It's quite likely that they have landed in the exact location that I showed you minutes earlier."

Ken hadn't missed a word. He was quickly putting the pieces of the puzzle together. He jumped off the bed, grabbed the phone, and quickly dialed the television station. Cammy answered.

"I quit!" shouted Ken, as he packed his suitcase.

Six

Incomprehensible Patience

The Master of Evil streaked like a meteor across the pale blue sky. Closely behind him were his most intimate confidantes and greatest enemies.

Satan, also known as Lucifer, the Devil, the Prince of Darkness, the great dragon, was on a self-appointed mission from hell. His desperately wicked heart longed after wealth and power. Much of that was his for the taking, yet he wanted more. Money, prestige, and influence only whet his unquenchable thirst for meaning and joy. In his twisted thinking, his latest plan, *the* plan, would finally give him what he had always wanted and deserved. He wanted to be worshipped as God Almighty by every man, woman, and child on the face of the planet.

Satan gazed at the Earth below, searching for the city where he would set up his religious empire.

"Our destination is just ahead," shouted Satan to his high-level coconspirators.

The King of Deceit peered over his shoulder and glared at one of his generals who was mumbling.

"I will not tolerate anything less than 100 percent compliance with my orders! Got it?" warned Satan.

The foolish general repented. The train of demons followed the Devil to a rocky hill in the center of Rome, Italy. It was the site of the old Roman ruins.

Satan swooped down and landed on top of the partially crumbled religious temple where the goddess Diana had been worshipped. This was to be the most critical meeting of his life.

In succession, each demon landed, bowed to its master, folded its black wings, and stood at attention. Satan reviewed the troops. As they seated themselves, they formed a perfect circle around their leader.

Satan did not waste any time with his normal theatric displays of dominance and nobility.

"My fellow demons, the clock is now ticking. I have discovered a way to stomp out the enemy. We will not be defeated!"

He raised his freshly sharpened claws high into the midnight air.

"Each one of you will be reassigned to a strategic command post. For most of you, your duties will change significantly. The Middle East and the United States of Europe will now be our primary targets for demonic propaganda of the most wicked kind."

Satan hissed.

"I will increase our troop strength threefold in those regions. You must trust me or risk death. I have decided to concentrate on three fronts. First, on the one-world religious movement that will sweep the world with paganism. Second, the world peace movement must be propelled to center stage. Finally, I want the global media outlets saturated with globalists. Prune the people who think their nation should be loved more than their world. I want every human who refuses to follow our vision to be labeled as unpatriotic rebels."

Suddenly, a devious thought passed through the hollow crevices of his skull.

"Millions of people will oppose our efforts, even with Jehovah God's presence waning. The world will not accept the death of these people, so I want them secretly disposed of in the most cruel, inhumane way possible!"

The demons cheered in delight.

"Our friend Adolf Hitler did an absolutely superb job of concealing his classified killings from the world's eyes. I want the same three generals who formulated the German's plan to oversee this campaign of terror."

Lucifer grabbed the orders and motioned for his troops to receive them in the usual, servile fashion. Like clockwork, each officer slowly glided to its feet, crawled on all fours to a designated point beneath their leader, and bowed until their faces were coated with dirt.

Satan's soul relished these moments.

The ceremony lasted half an hour.

"Your orders are clear. Anyone caught questioning or disobeying any of these directives will be severely reprimanded."

The Prince of Darkness sailed into the sky.

"Onward, Satan's soldiers!"

Like a throng of locusts coveting a field of fresh crops, the troops of darkness wildly marched toward their posts with mayhem on their minds.

"'After these things I looked, and behold, a door standing open in heaven. And the first voice which I heard was like a trumpet speaking with me, saying, "Come up here, and I will show you things which must take place after this." Immediately I was in the Spirit; and behold, a throne set in heaven, and One sat on the throne. And He who sat there was like a jasper and a sardius stone in appearance; and there was a rainbow around the throne, in appearance like an emerald. Around the throne were twenty-four thrones, and on the thrones I saw twenty-four elders sitting, clothed in white robes; and they had crowns of gold on their heads. And from the throne proceeded lightnings, thunderings, and voices. Seven lamps of fire were burning before the throne, which are the seven Spirits of God. Before the throne there was a sea of glass, like crystal. And in the midst of the throne, were four living creatures full of eyes in front and in back.'"

Timothy took a deep gulp as he closed his Bible. His heart sputtered at the sight of the heavenly host surrounding Daniel and himself. He was shaken by the words from the last book of the Bible. They came from the book of the Revelation, chapter four. Prophesies from Scripture were unfolding right before their very eyes. Daniel was in total awe.

"Where are we in the Bible right now?" wondered Daniel.

"Well, we must be somewhere right in between chapters four and five of Revelation," deduced Timothy.

He pointed out the four living creatures surrounding God. Then Timothy guided Daniel's darting eyes to the twenty-four elders seated around God's throne. Both of them were having difficulty seeing. Millions upon millions of angels, many of them taller than they, were huddled around the throne.

"The Bible says those four creatures have always been alongside God Almighty, announcing His holiness," explained Timothy.

Daniel's size was beginning to upset him. He didn't want to miss any of the action. Timothy smiled. The more mature angel was glad to see Daniel's enthusiasm. He grabbed the young angel and slung him onto his shoulders. Timothy guided Daniel's eyes toward the elders who were the representatives of the Christian church.

"There's the proof that we are between chapter four and chapter five. Elders in heaven don't appear until chapter four in the book of Revelation. We must be at the beginning of chapter five, because there is the Lamb of God! The Lamb is Jesus Christ," whispered Timothy.

Just as the Bible predicted, Jesus Christ approached the Father of Creation, Jehovah God. Right in the middle of heaven's climactic ceremony, the angels' attention was diverted by a weeping human. The huge crowd was distracted by the crying. Jehovah God motioned for one of His elders to calm the man's fears.

"What is a human doing up here?" implored Daniel.

Timothy opened his Bible to chapter five, verse four, in the book of Revelation. He gave it to his comrade.

"That's the apostle John, who wrote the book of Revelation. God had supernaturally transported him through time so that he could write the book from firsthand experience," accounted Timothy.

Daniel nodded his head. He kept his eyes transfixed on the elder who was speaking to the apostle John. The wailing immediately ceased.

Timothy placed his finger on the next verse in the Story of stories.

"Read the next verse."

"Oh! He is upset that no one is worthy to open God's scroll," realized Daniel.

Daniel squinted.

"What's the big deal with that scroll?" he asked.

Timothy pulled Daniel off his shoulders.

"The scroll is God's judgment upon the earth. Jesus Christ is the only Man who ever lived a perfect, sinless life. Therefore, He is the only One who can rightfully open the book of judgment and pronounce sentences on His subjects. He earned the right to condemn the people of the earth and the angels for their evil and lack of repentance."

Their glimpse of heaven's treasures was a dream come true. Evil and sin could never be present in this spectacular showroom of power and grandeur. The crystal sea stretched to the corners of heaven. The brilliant colors of God's rainbow would send waves of awe into any human.

Every angelic eye was watching the movements of Jesus Christ. God's Son began to approach God Almighty. A peace that transcends all understanding glistened from the faces of both Jehovah God and Jesus. God the Father was grasping the book with both hands as He gently handed it to Jesus. Though they possessed separate bodies, it was evident that they were one in mind, emotion, soul, and spirit. The only imperfections one could discern were the holes in Jesus' hands and feet. These were the nail holes from Jesus' crucifixion two thousand years ago.

Jesus reached His hands out and grasped the book from God Almighty's hands. Anyone else would have been instantaneously incinerated by God's holiness. In the blink of an eye, the four creatures transferred their attention away from God the Father and onto God the Son.

The twenty-four thrones surrounding God's throne were vacant as the elders gathered around Jesus. Each elder held a golden harp. In perfect harmony, they dropped to their knees to pay homage to their Maker and Savior. The pristine music and song were extraordinary.

Timothy and Daniel were mesmerized.

The heavenly choir could be heard throughout the universe.

No one noticed a tiny, dark blot appearing from the earth's surface. Satan had just concluded his strategy session and was destined for the sun, his favorite place in the galaxy. The praises to God and His Son pierced Satan's dark heart. The evil Prince of the World choked as he flew toward the sun.

————————

As Dominic was being introduced to the crowd, his mother's words of wisdom were playing in his mind.

"You will not answer to anyone except yourself on the road of life. Determine your own destiny. If the purpose of your actions is for good, then the end will always justify the means," his mother had indoctrinated.

The sound of applause overwhelmed him. He realized that the remainder of the congregation that had not been raptured were standing on their feet as a tribute to his life in the ministry. It was his time to shine.

He rose to his feet and meekly walked to the podium. He held his hands together in a ball. As he stared out at the crowd, he noticed their eyes were filled with tears. They were putting their hopes and dreams into his hands. They were staring at him as if he were the savior of the world.

"My fellow friends in Rome and around the world," began Dominic.

Hundreds of television cameras from every country were there. Dominic Rosario was smooth and believable.

"My sincerest desire is to see our world at peace."

It was hard to tell if the crowd was cheering or crying.

"We want a peace that is strong, fervent, and built on solid rock. It must have roots! Peace is our only solution for our continued existence!"

Dominic had to raise his voice over the crowd.

"We either will die in endless wars or compromise to have peace! I want a world that will work together, yes, together, for your dreams and the dreams and safety of every man, woman, and child around Mother Earth. I want a world where you can turn to your neighbor for assistance without expecting a cold stare of indifference or hate!"

Dominic's words penetrated their hearts. He made a concerted effort to focus on the cameras. Immanuel had enlightened him on the finer points of television intimacy. Treat the camera as if it were your closest ally, Immanuel had taught.

"Today, we lament those who have passed away, such as the Pope himself in all his glory to the choir boy in the pew. I want to offer my condolences and sincerest thoughts to all of their family and friends."

A tear trickled down his cheek.

"At this point, I would like to take this opportunity to offer a moment of silence. I want us to ponder the memories of our missing loved ones, and dream of a new world free from war, crime, and poverty."

The new successor bowed his head and the crowd followed. A heavy silence swept through the crowd.

Like a spider descending from its cobweb, Blasphemy slowly dropped from the ceiling.

Dominic sensed his presence. Years of resisting the true Spirit of holiness from Jehovah God had left his soul in ashes. He was capable of responding to only one kind of spirit, and it wasn't the Holy Spirit.

"Allow my words to enter the very center of your being," cooed Blasphemy.

Dominic responded in his spirit. Verbal words were not necessary.

"Speak to me, lord. Use me to further your kingdom on earth," prayed the False Prophet.

Blasphemy descended inches above Dominic's head. A smirk shined from his face as he uncurled his four-inch-long nails. He rubbed them across his face as he enjoyed his own touch. He raised his claws into the air and plunged them into the False Prophet's head. Blasphemy massaged the ends of his spiritual antennas, making sure that his spirit was connected to Dominic's mind. He brought his mouth close to Dominic's ears.

"Immanuel is God," chanted Blasphemy.

"Immanuel is God," repeated Dominic.

Dominic raised his head. He felt a new form of energy flowing through his veins. His mind was flooded with unbelievable quantities of knowledge and wisdom.

"War has been a way of life for the human race," he told the people. Something is drastically wrong not only in our society, but in the churches of the world. History teaches us that thousands of wars have been waged since the beginning of modern man. The end result is the useless and barbaric slaughter of millions upon millions of innocent people, all in the name of freedom. We can no longer afford to remain silent and let this continue. The church must take a stand. We must take back the world!"

The people sprang to their feet in one accord. It was time for the good and moral people to make a difference. They applauded as the seeds of Dominic's lie settled into their hearts.

A multitude of demons invaded the hall. There were six demons for every person, as ordered by Satan's high command in Rome. Each phantom was positioning itself around preselected people. They were directed to capture and destroy any thoughts that were not useful to Satan's objectives. Spiritual nighttime had fallen on the crowd. The applause had faded and only echoes of enchantment remained. Blasphemy was in the driver's seat of a steamroller with no mercy. Dominic was literally possessed by the demon.

"Religion offers the world the hope it needs to revive it from the deathbed of insanity and selfishness," exclaimed Dominic, raising his hand into the air. "Politics is the vehicle we need to get us to the promised land. I hereby propose that the world put aside its religious differences that so easily entangle us. The divisive nature of differing religions creates the bitter fruits of hatred, violence, and wars! A world religion built on the common beliefs of all the world's great religions can usher us into a new world order. It can be a new millennium of heaven on earth!"

Utopian fever engulfed the people as Dominic's sermon enchanted their imaginations. He was the spark that would set the world on fire.

"A tree does not grow overnight; a skyscraper cannot be constructed in a week. Neither will our dream appear tomorrow. You can make a difference in the eternal struggle between good and evil. No matter if you live in Hong Kong, Bangladesh, Tokyo, Berlin, London, Los Angeles, Montreal, or Mexico City, you have the power to change the world."

Blasphemy gave a cue, and the demons assigned to the cameramen went to work. They began chanting for them to zoom into a close shot of the religious leader. Televisions worldwide could literally see the steam rising from his nostrils.

"What I have to say is not just for those in this medieval hall. My vision of a new world order can positively affect every human being listening to my voice!"

Blasphemy was proud of his newest creation. Dominic's sincerity could not be denied, even by the staunchest atheist or Nationalist.

"What you believe affects how you act; it affects how your nation's government acts. Please, begin to think globally and act locally. I know you have heard that divine theme for years, but this time I want you to act upon it! Press your government officials to reinstitute morality in the legislatures, the courts, the churches, and the infested streets."

The False Prophet glanced at his notes. He nibbled at the dry skin on his lower lip and closed his eyes. He took a deep breath.

Blasphemy almost cried as the charade unfolded beneath his hands. The leader of the demons had plowed a field of fear in Dominic's head. From that fear, he was able to plant the most sinister of seeds. He planted the seeds of "good is evil, and evil is good."

Dominic grabbed his notes in a controlled rage and crumbled them in midair. The crowd was mystified and began to mumble.

They were accustomed to their leaders being more reserved and pious.

"My friends, I am struggling intensely in my inner spirit. God has anointed me, but I am scared! You see, I have received a message from God Almighty, but I do not understand its implications!"

Sweat dripped from his forehead.

The crowd chanted for him to share his revelation with them.

"Speak, O enlightened one!" shouted the congregation.

"My heart is heavy because I know the truth!" exclaimed Dominic.

He looked around the sanctuary, waiting to see if they would nibble at the bait.

"Tell us the truth!" shouted a man standing in the back of the hall.

"We trust you," yelled another.

Dominic raised his hand at half-staff. He tilted his head slightly forward. His body was now poised like a religious man, yet his mind was possessed by a devil.

"The truth will be difficult to swallow. In fact, I am having difficulty dealing with this revelation myself. It hits so close to home that it can tear you apart."

He had no idea of the power that he had tapped into.

"The mass exodus of our fellow friends and family yesterday was ordained, ordered, and carried out by God!"

The crowd became silent. It was the kind of silence that made you think and fear. His comment raised the hairs on their backs and questions in their minds. Why would God snatch up so many people, young and old, including the Pope? Why would He leave millions of families longing for loved ones?

Dominic appeared confident, inspired, and above all, credible.

"My fellow citizens of the world, God has a divine purpose in the sweeping Rapture of the Earth's population. He has two reasons, but one central purpose."

He leaned against the podium.

"He wants more than anything else to see our world at peace; after all, He is a God of peace. The missing people were judged as unworthy of existence. He created them, and He has every right to get rid of them! Our dear Pope was obviously not one of them. God also wanted to call some of His patriots home. As for the others, they used God as a weapon of war. God watched from heaven and wept over their arrogance and judgmental ways. They preached about a mean-spirited God and a God who punishes people for thinking the wrong ways. If you did not agree with one of them, then you were set in stone as a worldly humanist or a follower of the Devil!"

The black cloud of demons had completely drained God's spiritual light.

"They were separatists, resisting to the very death the realities of a world uniting for peace. They opposed everything that our God stands for because their master was the Father of Lies, Satan himself! They condemned all the other great world religions with a judgmental attitude that was complete blasphemy."

Blasphemy was delighted to hear his name.

"We know that these wonderful religions, like Buddhism, Hinduism, and Islam follow the same God as we do, just in a different way. But these religious bigots were hatemongers who held to a rigid interpretation of their Bible while destroying the faith of their neighbors. They didn't realize that to love their neighbors, they needed to compromise their beliefs for the good of all humanity. They were two-faced exhibitionists hoping to brainwash you and your children."

Dominic took a sip of water. Without his guide's help, he would have been drained.

"They murdered abortion doctors in the name of life! There are over six billion people on the face of the earth. Millions are starving as I speak, and they championed saving a fetus over a malnourished child in Africa or India. They were blind, not out of ignorance, but out of willful pride. Most were capitalists who wanted to protect the rich at the painful expense of the poor. How could somebody support the greedy over the helpless? Is that what our God stands for?"

The crowd roared in one accord, "No!"

"They believed in converting people to their ideology by using merciless intimidation, fear, and guilt. We didn't need to get 'saved' from ourselves, but we needed to get 'saved' from them! I thank my God that He did just that. They were psychotic followers of a bloody, violent, warring religion that has no place on God's earth. They played with words, and I thank God that their days of toying with the world are over!"

More cheers followed. The worldwide network of demons was making every attempt to bring as many people as possible to their televisions.

All around the world, Satan's army had free reign to deceive the Earth's gullible people. Throngs of tantalizing demons, hundreds of millions of them, baptized every sector of the earth. With all the angels and Christians before God's throne in heaven giving reverence to Him, the demons could easily attack and brainwash the people of Earth. Satan was sure to make the best of this opportunity.

The ruckus in the aging cathedral reminded one of a rock concert. No one was seated. Pandemonium ruled as the religious, political fervor carried the people into a near riotous climax. Every lost soul in the sanctuary was wooed by Dominic's sermon of social justice and world peace.

Television rating companies worldwide were reporting astronomical numbers. Nearly half of the planet was watching the staged event. Blasphemy was pleased.

"Dominic Rosario for world president!" chanted the spellbound audience.

The newly ordained religious leader was flattered yet fearful. He knew Immanuel was vying for the position of world leader. The temptation was inviting but the consequences would be toxic. He would never forget what Immanuel had revealed to him in their private meeting a few days ago. It had changed his life forever. He feared Immanuel more than death itself.

Dominic tried to recapture the crowd's attention. He placed his lips within inches of the microphone.

"May I speak?" Dominic asked kindly.

The commotion from the fanfare subsided. Dominic jumped at the opportunity.

"This is important, my friends," shouted Dominic.

Not a sound was heard.

"God's final message to me made my heart jump with joy. The Bible has always predicted that the Savior of the world would come down to Mother Earth and save the planet. God has confirmed that this prophetic event will soon take place. He did not reveal the exact hour or day that He would appear, but He told me that it would be soon, very soon!"

Seven

Fleeting Peace

A white private jet glided toward the runway of a small deserted strip on the African continent. The sun had risen only an hour earlier, yet the heat index was already one hundred twenty-eight degrees. As the plane's wheels bonded with the earth, one could hear the rubber tires screaming on the parched runway. Inside the immaculate airliner, Immanuel was sleeping in the master bedroom suite. The inside of the plane resembled a posh Manhattan apartment, complete with multilevel accommodations, three luxurious bedrooms, gourmet kitchen, and two full-time chefs: one Eastern and one Western. His personal engineers, who had originally developed the plane exclusively for him, had refused to budge on the aerodynamic principle that he could not have tons of gold and ivory adorning his living space. Immanuel fired those engineers. He then found suitable scientists who designed and built his fortress in the sky. Gold, silver, ivory, leather, and jewels saturated the living quarters. The value of the furnishings outweighed the multimillion-dollar cost of the jet.

A buzzer awakened the sleeping giant. Immanuel's eyes instantly opened. There was no time for slumber or coffee. Immanuel sighed. For the first time in his life, he had to deal with the fact that he was no longer in total control. Blasphemy, his spiritual master, was now calling the shots. A critical meeting, where Immanuel had planned to meet with the European heads of state, had been abruptly cancelled at the last second. Blasphemy had directed Immanuel to this pit of sand, dust, tribal warfare, and poverty. The billionaire's trust in Blasphemy was slowly winning out. He knew that the next move on the chessboard of life awaited Blasphemy's instruction. The pilot's voice spoke over the intercom.

"Sir, the limousine you ordered has arrived. The driver tells me that the trip will take exactly 2.5 hours, not counting time for sandstorms and camel drives. Oh, by the way, would you like breakfast, sir?"

"No," said Immanuel.

He couldn't stop reviewing his predicament. He didn't remember getting on the plane. He had no idea where he was or where he was going.

Immanuel noticed that his hands were shaking as he rearranged the knot on his Arabian silk tie. Had his spirit guide betrayed him? He closed his eyes. He tried to regain his composure. He quickly opened the bedroom door and headed for the exit.

At the bottom of the sun-warmed stairs, an airport concierge offered him a turban. The head covering was a necessity in this sweltering wilderness. Immanuel ignored the man and stepped into the stretch limousine.

He would occupy his time by focusing his energies on phase two of the plan. In the exact moment that he signaled for his spirit guide, Blasphemy appeared from across the desert floor. The eccentric general carried a scroll in his hand. As he entered the vehicle, Immanuel's heart began to race. The billionaire tycoon closed his eyes and raised his hands in the air. It was Immanuel's way of worshipping his shepherd. Blasphemy's teeth emerged as he smiled at Immanuel's submission.

"You have passed your first test of faith, my friend," congratulated the demon. His tone turned sour. "Your heart, though, is deeply divided. I was listening to you question our relationship. Remember, human, I can read your every thought, and I can sense your waffling emotions," scorned Blasphemy. "I have the ability to transcend time, to be everywhere at the same time," blasphemed Blasphemy. "To make you a great leader, the strongest and most courageous the world will ever see, I will require unwavering devotion. You have a long way to go before your armor is capable of bearing my other tests!"

With surprising servitude, Immanuel begged for the chance.

"Allow me the privileged opportunity to be tested again. Fill me with your ageless wisdom, omniscient understanding, and omnipotent insight. Use me, master."

The chauffeur was having trouble driving the limousine on the desert road. He got goosebumps as he stared at Immanuel worshipping the ceiling. "The richer they are, the crazier they get," thought the driver.

After a twenty-six year drought, Immanuel began to cry. Like a child denied his dessert, Immanuel was determined to have everything or nothing at all. Partial power had already corrupted him. It was anyone's guess what absolute power might do. Immanuel feared nothing except failure to obtain his dream of world conquest.

"I need more. Please. My appetite is insatiable," pleaded Immanuel.

Groveling was not common for the banker; he only did so in extreme emergencies.

Blasphemy stroked the fur on his elongated chin. Submission pleased him more than a good battle with one of Jehovah God's angels.

"Very well, your status will be maintained for the moment. See to it that you submit to my authority, or I will crush you like a roach caught in the light!" threatened the phantom.

"Your wish is my command," positioned Immanuel.

"Good. Today, you will meet the man who will help your media image. I have been grooming him to be your spokesman. He has the media connections necessary to make you a household name."

Blasphemy placed the scroll he carried onto Immanuel's lap. Immanuel's eyes were still closed when he smelled the nauseous odor. It smelled like burning flesh and rotting fish. The rank scent caused Immanuel to jerk his eyes open. His natural reaction was to check outside the carriage. As he contorted his body for a view of the road, he felt something shift in his lap. Immanuel glanced around and discovered an ancient scroll. He was hypnotized by the supernatural appearance of the scroll.

Blasphemy was amused. It was rewarding for him to watch humans experience the power that he possessed. This was only the beginning. The demon picked up the scroll. It appeared to levitate on its own. Immanuel was wise enough to realize that it was Blasphemy.

"My power is as limitless as the sun's energy," deceived Blasphemy. "This scroll is my plan to lure the world into following the true provider of wealth, wisdom, and armistice. Ingest its wisdom. Obey me and live!"

"I have some ideas about our new world order," eagerly offered Immanuel.

Blasphemy was not interested in Immanuel's input.

"Don't waste your time and mine with your own plans. I want you to spend every minute of your day trying to sway, and eventually changing, the hearts of people who have the position and power to aid us in our quest for the prize. Go seek the rich and powerful.

Find those individuals from the four corners of the earth who will help us reach the promised land. Trust me. I will be there to guard against anyone who may attempt to impede our mission."

The limousine driver had been entranced by the floating scroll. His priorities were sadly misplaced because he never noticed the oncoming car that was fast approaching from the east.

Satan was lounging on his throne, using a toothpick to remove pieces of human souls from between his ghastly fangs. He had stolen nearly ten thousand of God's humans in the past hour, gobbling up their souls and spitting out their pieces into his hellish pit of horrors. The sting of death was sugar to Satan. His sweet tooth was never satisfied. He had one of the keys to death, and he thirsted for the other. Jehovah God had outsmarted him some two thousand years ago with the death and resurrection of Jesus. Satan would never forgive God for that. He was bent on destroying anything God loved, especially the human population.

Satan's dream was rudely interrupted by an unwelcome intruder. He barely had time to adjust his focus before the archangels Michael and Gabriel were directly in front of him.

Their swords were drawn in a defensive position.

"Lucifer! God Almighty wants you to drop your devious plans to take over the earth!" relayed Michael.

Satan couldn't hold back the laughter, though he didn't really try.

The archangels were accustomed to the hollow spirit's behavior. They looked at each other with pity in their eyes.

The dragon sat up in his throne in an attempt to look more kingly.

"Let me see if I got this right. Jehovah God wants me to stop before He loses? He wants me to lay down my arms and come home to Him, like that sickening story about the prodigal son? Doesn't He have any backbone? You fellows are great warriors with misplaced loyalties. I have fond memories of sparring with you. Why don't you renounce your allegiance to Jehovah, or better yet, be a spy for the side of strength and vigor?"

Righteous anger surfaced in them, yet the angels remembered to leave judgment to the Lord.

"I will not waste my time answering your questions," Michael continued. The clock is now ticking; the fuse has been lit. You have less than seven years before the judgment. I am sure that you re-member when Jesus Christ pronounced you and a third of the an-gels guilty of high treason two thousand years ago. You mocked Him because you foolishly thought that He didn't have the guts or power to carry it out."

Satan interrupted God's archangel.

"Jehovah God is a racist and a tyrant. He doesn't believe in equality or achievement. He thinks we should all be happy wor-shipping at His feet, saying, 'Thank you, your holiness; bless you, your majesty; we adore you, our Creator; honor and power and blah, blah, blah,'" mocked Lucifer.

Michael and Gabriel were always astonished at Satan's twisted attitude. They wondered how one of God's creations could have turned so sour.

"Our purpose is to warn you of your impending judgment. Lay down your weapons of war, or Jehovah God and His angels of righteousness will do it for you! This is not a threat; it is a prom-ise!"

Satan sneered as he drew his sword.

The archangels repositioned their weapons. They would use them only if necessary. Each of the mighty angels waited for Luci-fer to flinch. He chose to back down. Michael resumed the message from God.

"In the book of Revelation, God has clearly outlined your strategy, motives, and final doom in the upcoming years. If you only had the humility to read it and believe," exhorted the angel.

They slowly backed away from the Devil of devils, watching his every move with scrutiny. When they were a safe distance away, they turned toward the wormhole exit. Satan was the type to get the last word in, no matter what the circumstance.

"When I'm finished, there will not be a Bible in print on that planet. I will make certain of that!" shouted Satan.

The chauffeur's eyes nearly jumped from their sockets as he realized he was driving in the wrong lane with another car ap-proaching. The vehicles were less than one hundred feet apart when Blasphemy looked up and grabbed the wheel. His plan did not include the death of his two most important stars in the play of the millennium. Blasphemy knocked the driver unconscious with one swift punch and swung the wheel to the left. As he slammed on the brakes, he caused the limousine to skid into a screeching halt. He flew into the other car, punched the driver in the stomach, and stopped the rental car only inches away from the limousine.

Immanuel cursed as he shook his head. He opened the window that separated him from the driver. The chauffeur was out cold.

Blasphemy was carefully observing Immanuel's thought waves. Immanuel's heart was proving to be loyal to the demon. The thought of Blasphemy engineering this fiasco never entered Immanuel's mind. He was more concerned about how he would make it back to the plane.

Immanuel ventured out of his comfortable nest to investigate the damage. For the first time in years, he opened his own car door. He was instantly bombarded by a burst of untamed heat. He ripped off his jacket and tie, and tossed them into the cool car. His outrageously expensive cotton shirt, which had boasted of its breathability in sunstroke weather, offered little resistance to the muscle of the African desert. Immanuel made his way to the front of the limousine. He casually took note of the other vehicle with a blind eye to its occupant. His concern was with his chauffeur's ability to serve his needs. He slowly opened the driver's side door.

"Forget that loser," chastised Blasphemy. "There's someone I want you to meet."

Immanuel patted the chauffeur on the cheeks, expecting a response. He quickly searched his neck for a pulse.

"Forget about that ingrate!" shouted Blasphemy at the top of his tarfilled lungs. "There's something for you in the other car. Get over there, now!"

"Message received," sighed Immanuel.

He rushed across the road and knocked on the tinted windows of the car.

"Are you injured?" asked Immanuel.

There wasn't any response, although he could see some movement inside. He banged on the window again. Sweat rolled down his cheeks to his lips. Suddenly, the door latch on the blue sedan clicked halfway open. He could hear someone moaning from within the car. Immanuel's adrenaline mushroomed as he gently opened the door.

"This man will be your media mongrel," unveiled Blasphemy.

As he opened the door, the man's face looked strangely familiar.

"Excuse me, are you okay?" asked Immanuel.

"Yeah, I think so," said the man, slowly emerging from the car.

"Ken Action, from St. Louis, Missouri," he offered, as he shook hands with the banking giant.

"Immanuel Bernstate. Glad to make your acquaintance."

Blasphemy flew to the rental car and began tinkering with the engine. Ken got back into his car.

"Why don't you sit with me in the limo for a while. I have a story that could make your career," tempted Immanuel.

Ken was startled by the statement. Though enticed, this strange man was making him uneasy.

"No, thanks, I already have the story of a lifetime. I couldn't handle another one, at least not this week!" Ken nervously offered.

Ken closed the door and turned the ignition key. Nothing happened. Immanuel smiled at the enthusiastic reporter as he opened the door for him.

"I guess that story will have to wait, won't it? Why don't you wait in the air-conditioned limousine while I check my driver's condition."

Somehow, Ken felt he had no choice. He obediently got into Immanuel's limousine. Immanuel walked around to the side of his vehicle and found his driver badly shaken.

"Can you drive us back?" questioned Immanuel.

"Yes, sir, but I think I'll need a few more moments."

Immanuel politely smiled as he closed the man's door.

He walked to the back of the limousine, searching for Blasphemy's wavelength for wisdom and direction.

"Offer him the job at a salary that he cannot resist. His one love in life, other than himself, is money!" whispered the demon.

Immanuel opened the door and sensed a welcome rush of cool air.

"The driver will be ready in a few minutes. He's a little queasy after our mishap," said Immanuel.

Ken appeared more relaxed. If Ken Action knew who was courting him, he would be on his knees, thought Immanuel.

"I am very interested in hearing about your story of the century," initiated Immanuel. "Is that why you are in the desert?"

Ken didn't want to talk.

"You can trust Immanuel," Blasphemy repeated over and over. "He will buy your ticket to fame," brainwashed the demon.

Ken didn't normally open up to strangers, especially about secrets that could be worth millions.

"Spill your guts," sang the demon.

Ken obeyed.

"You may find this hard to believe," Ken prepared him, "but I have concrete proof that alien creatures are visiting this planet, and are planning to colonize!"

Immanuel remained pleasant on the outside, but inside he wondered of what possible use this man could be.

"Trust me, Immanuel. Don't fumble the ball. I will lead you," preached Blasphemy.

"What proof do you have of this?" searched Immanuel.

"It's a twenty-minute drive from here," said the reporter.

On Wall Street, a huge sum of money had flooded the market. Nobody had a clue as to where it had come from, and nobody really cared. The market was skyrocketing with what appeared to be unlimited fuel. By early afternoon, the Dow Jones Index's value had launched into orbit. Immanuel's closest allies had bought nearly every stock imaginable at the opening of the trading day. Less than five hours later, the worth of those companies had increased by almost 50 percent.

Lord Birmingham was ready to sell. The market was like a jet liner reaching its cruising altitude with only a few drops of fuel remaining. Alternately puffing on a Cuban cigar and inhaling a martini, Birmingham looked and felt in control. He was on top of the world. Centuries of work and sweat were about to reap their just reward. The reclusive banker was comfortably reclined in his black leather chair. His elegant office was filled with television screens, computers, and a bearskin rug that greeted visitors with a snarl. Twelve television monitors were arranged in a semicircle around the front of his desk. Each monitor was linked to one of his banking gurus, who stared out of the screens at their ringleader with envy.

One enlarged computer screen displayed the ongoing stock rally shaking America. Lord Birmingham casually sat up in his chair and took one last look at the manufactured numbers that he had helped to create. The 50 percent increase had steadied at that rate. He took one last puff from his cigar and then stuffed it in the ashtray.

"Gentlemen, I believe our moment of glory has arrived! Any dissenters?" questioned Lord Birmingham, as cigar smoke chugged out of his nostrils.

He reached over to a telephone control panel and placed his finger on the sensor. He took one last look at his lifelong friends in the television monitors. Each exchanged the look commanders give before going off to war.

Lord Birmingham brought his eyes around to the phone. He pushed the button.

"Sell!" ordered the financial wizard.

"How much, sir?" asked the nervous voice on the other end of the phone.

"Everything!" commanded the chief.

He carefully diagnosed the reactions of his friends. Each man reflected the same maddening, unemotional glaze of greed. Lord Birmingham was waiting for a response from his personal broker.

"Sir, did I hear you say, everything?" wondered the shocked voice.

Lord Birmingham was not accustomed to his dogs disobeying or even questioning his commands.

"Did you have a problem with that?" chided the conspirator.

"Well, no, sir. But I do believe you shouldn't put all your eggs in one basket. Diversity is always wise. The market has been undervalued for years because of that pathological civil war. But if you sell everything in your and your partners' portfolios, that could devastate the market! We're talking about tens of trillions of dollars! Where would you put your profits, and how long would it be before they crashed right along with everyone else's?"

Lord Birmingham leaned forward, stuffed a shot of caviar in his mouth, and began to laugh. It was the kind of laugh that would make an educated person uneasy.

"I couldn't care a rat's ass about the market. There are times when money is not my main objective! After all, we have just made about four trillion dollars in less than five hours!" blew the lord. He deepened his voice while raising its level. "Sell everything! Buy gold, silver, and platinum. Within days, we will practically own the earth!" bellowed a man not to be messed with.

Lord Birmingham snapped his fingers. At once, a middle-aged man dressed in a servant's tuxedo approached with another Cuban masterpiece.

"May I cut it and light it for you, sir?" asked the generously paid man.

The royal banker nodded his approval.

Lord Birmingham turned his attention to his accomplices.

"Gentlemen, you know that I had my reservations, deep reservations, about our friend, Immanuel."

The modern-day gangsters chuckled under their breaths.

"I must say, though, that his plan is making us richer than any of us could have possibly dreamed. His ideas are brilliant."

He raised his hand-sculpted, crystal glass to the television images.

"A toast, to the man who taught us how to make money the easy way."

The men shared his cheer. It was a deeply moving experience for the Wall Street warlocks.

As the group's broker punched the return key on his computer, he felt a lump the size of a bullfrog in his throat. The electronic transfer took less time than a blink of an eye. The order to sell was nothing more than a simple dot of computer language. It was incapable of good or evil, but it was destined to cause grown men and women to jump from high-rise buildings all over the country.

On the floor of the New York Stock Exchange, a broker was neck deep in trade orders. It was the most exhilarating day of his professional life. He was busy with buy orders when, suddenly, an alarm screamed from his computer terminal. A fifty-point drop zapped the computer. Simple profit taking, thought the broker. Suddenly horrified, he dropped back in his seat and watched the market take a nosedive in a matter of seconds. As each second was lost to time, another ten points were eaten up. The Dow Jones was diving into the great abyss like a sky diver who had no parachute. The 50 percent gain had vanished into the wind. In less than an hour, the created wealth had turned out to be a cruel hoax, a mirage in the desert.

Lord Birmingham's sell order sent the market into a tailspin. It was the simple law of supply and demand. The supply of the stocks increased as he sold them, causing the demand to decrease. When there is little demand for a product, the price drops.

It took less than ten minutes for the American market to lose an additional 6 percent of its value. The clock stopped at six minutes past two o'clock. Trading was halted for the day.

The news shows called it the "Wall Street roller coaster." The media reported that the early closing was caused by a computer problem. The majority of investors bought the lie, some with their life savings, but the more astute investors knew the computers on the exchanges had been upgraded using the most advanced technology. The world was told the computers could not handle tens of billions of shares being traded. Many who were rookies of the financial market had trusted their money managers. Now the news of the decline caught everybody completely off guard. It had made sense to buy, even if you had to take out a loan.

There was more bad news. The bonds that governments sold to finance their irresponsible debt had not been selling. With Lord Birmingham unloading that debt earlier in the day, and with people swarming to the stock exchanges, treasury officials all over the world had been getting nervous. They were concerned about having to raise the interest rates to attract investors. The market downturn at the end of the trading day made them feel better. The rule was simple. If everybody was putting his money in stocks, there wasn't enough money to buy bonds. National debts could explode if interest rates went too high. A worldwide financial meltdown haunted their thoughts.

Immanuel looked at his watch and frowned.

"What has you in such a quandary?" dissected Immanuel.

"Alien creatures on Earth is a shattering news story, wouldn't you say?" countered Ken.

Immanuel was not satisfied.

"That's not a big deal. Governments have been covering up those facts for years."

Immanuel's eyes seemed to be X-raying Ken's soul.

"What else is on your mind?" forced Immanuel.

Ken tried to circumvent his question.

"Why do you think that there is something else bothering me? This discovery raises a ton of red flags. Where are they from, why are they here, are they friendly, do they want us for dinner?" Ken was bordering on the ludicrous, a sure sign Immanuel had hit a nerve.

"What else is on your mind?" repeated Immanuel.

Ken's face turned pale.

"I may not have a job to go back to in America. If I have been dumped by the management at my station, nobody at the networks will touch my story. They won't take me seriously. They'll conclude that I'm making it up to get another job," vented the broken man.

Immanuel felt uneasy being a shoulder that somebody could cry on.

"Why didn't you bring video equipment on your trip? Obviously, you were expecting to find something big," questioned Immanuel in a nonthreatening tone.

An agitated smirk crept up on Ken's face.

"I did! Nobody bothered to inform me that the circuitry in my camera couldn't handle the heat." Ken paused to swallow a lump in his throat. "You see, I stopped for some gas and a snack. I had left the car windows up and I wasn't gone five minutes, but when I returned to the car, it must have been one-hundred-and-fifty degrees inside. It felt like an oven in there! Anyway, I didn't even think about the camera. I was worried about myself. I didn't think too much about it until I tried to turn it on."

"Don't worry. I'll help you. I have connections."

"What do you mean by that?" proclaimed Ken in an abrupt manner.

He was threatened by people bearing gifts that he hadn't earned. It reminded him of Sally giving her life to Christ. She had claimed that the gift of eternal life was for everybody, no matter what his or her past was, and that no one could earn it. Free gifts were for those who believed in Santa Claus, thought Ken.

Immanuel was able to diffuse the explosive situation with ease.

"I need a young handsome journalist who knows the ropes, who can handle the wolverines in the media," dealt Immanuel.

"Are you making me a job offer?" played Ken.

"If what you say is true, yes, I am," trumped Immanuel.

"Can you match my three-hundred-thousand-dollar salary in St. Louis?" bluffed Ken.

"One million is the starting salary, not including benefits or monthly bonuses," replied Immanuel.

Immanuel's generosity stunned the news jock. He was accustomed to brutal bickering during contract negotiations. Immanuel's offer was a welcome departure.

"Your offer is more than tempting," began Ken. He had trouble holding eye contact with the forbidding billionaire. "I find it hard to believe you would offer a seven-figure job to someone whom you have just met!"

Ken swung his eyes around the cabin as his heart began to sputter.

"I take a great deal of pride in surrounding myself with the kind of people who will help me build my empire. Only self-motivated, highly intellectual, extensively qualified applicants are considered."

Immanuel's tongue was razor sharp.

"You have shown me that you will go the extra mile when pursuing your dreams. Your demo tapes have reached my office several times."

"I've never sent you a résumé tape," corrected Ken.

A smirk emerged from Immanuel's lifeless expression.

"My people tape television newscasts from the top twenty-five television markets in America and around the world. They have been conducting a grueling six-month search for the perfect spokesman for my cause. Your name has been near the top of every list that they have presented to me."

Ken's objections seemed like stubble for the flame. He stretched out his hand to cement the deal.

"You've made me an offer that I can't, in good conscience, refuse," smiled Ken.

Immanuel was pleased. Money was the oil that made his political machine churn.

"That's the smartest decision that you've ever made, Mr. Action. My team always comes out on top!"

Both men looked around at the barren landscape speeding past them. Ken suddenly recognized a landmark. A lonely palm tree marked the entrance to a dirt road.

"Take a right at that tree," directed Ken.

His attention quickly returned to his new boss.

"Right over that sand dune," pointed Ken, "is the spot where I saw it all happen."

Ken's apprehensive behavior was offset by Immanuel's relaxed state.

"Ken, how do you feel about a one-world government?" inspected Immanuel.

———————

Israel's newly elected prime minister had his head buried in his trembling hands. Tears were useless, fear was rampant, and war was imminent. The deeply religious politician was a rare breed of leader in Israel. A long string of prime ministers had avoided the marriage of politics and Judaism ever since the country had been granted life after World War II. David Hoffman had quietly used the growing friction between the flourishing religion of Judaism and the politically correct socialist movement, to sweep into office. He promoted himself as a moral man who was sick and tired of political compromise with the Arabs and the United Nations. He knew the Arabs would not stop their press for land until they acquired Jerusalem. Blood would flow as high as the bridles of a horse before that happened, thought David, remembering the biblical prophecy.

He was not easily swayed. He used his mind first, then his heart. He followed a narrow course that had led to sweeping social, financial, and political reform. He was popular among the Jews, and despised among the Arabs. He had the unique ability to scare the Arabs into some forms of submission. He did not hesitate to threaten Middle Eastern countries with swift and damaging military repercussions, if they invaded an ounce of his territory. State-sponsored terrorism had been quickly extinguished under his rule. No Middle Eastern group had the will to claim responsibility for the actions of their defunct members. Car bombs were common; a braggart claim of ownership was not. They sincerely believed that Prime Minister Hoffman had an itchy trigger finger and a shrewd mind. He was the kind of leader that caused fortresslike roadblocks for globalists dreaming of a one-world government and a world void of war.

Hoffman was a descendant of the tribe of Judah, and a distant relative of King David himself. People voted for him because they embraced the fantasy that he was their modern-day King David. His frame rose to a stunning six feet, three inches. His build was firm but aging.

His philosophy of life was centered around the Old Testament. Treat people as you would want to be treated, discipline in love, and laugh often.

His poll ratings were in the mid-eighties—his highest approval rating ever. A couple of strategically placed bombs in neighboring countries had boosted his popularity. The man had an iron fist but used it sparingly.

"What is your report showing us today?" David asked his intelligence advisor. "Any more signs of troop movements?"

The advisor glared at his notes. The news was obviously disturbing.

"The Russians have amassed nearly one hundred thousand men, along with hundreds of tanks and the latest antiaircraft weaponry, on their southernmost borders. I have reason to believe that Iran, Iraq, Jordan, and Syria may cooperate."

The military advisor dug his nose deeper into the paperwork. David knew he wasn't reading; he was hiding.

"How about the United Nations?" tossed out David.

His advisor didn't budge a muscle, except for his upper lip, which tended to twitch when stressed.

"They're claiming to be neutral, peaceful bystanders who want peace at any cost. But, of course, their talk is not matching their walk. Nothing new there," concluded the strategist.

"One would think they would hide their lies better," vented the prime minister.

His advisor laughed.

"When you listen to their lies long enough, you start believing them yourself," he observed.

"What are those globalists up to?" asked David.

"My insiders are telling me they are trying to unlock our northern and eastern borders. They want to see us go down!"

David placed one end of his glasses in his mouth, and bit down on the edges.

"What recourse do we have?" searched David.

Unfortunately, he already knew the answer. He was praying for some miraculous revelation from heaven, hoping his security advisor would be the prophet.

"We are being cornered, sir. Our only defense is a strong offense. We must bite down hard and not let go until they stop kicking!"

President Colt slammed his hand down on the oval desk. Seated across from him was his longtime school buddy, Patrick Bonney, the Secretary of the Treasury. The treasurer of the United States looked like a dead man waiting to be buried.

"You don't understand, Mr. President. Eighty percent of our short-term bonds have been sold at a highly reduced value. There is absolutely no doubt in my mind that we will have to offer astronomically high rates of return to attract investors."

The highly emotional, yet intellectual, plea fell on clogged ears. The president seemed totally uninterested in the numbers game.

"So what? Let's offer a great rate so that people can make some money. We have social programs for everybody else; why not help those who go bankrupt on Wall Street?" shot back the figurehead.

"Sir, with all due respect, that would cause our debt to spiral out of control. In less than a year, we will be in financial, and probably social, chaos," announced his friend.

The president cringed.

"We own the printing presses; we'll just print the money we need."

"Printing the money will be a different kind of death. The inflation rate will skyrocket! We call that hyperinflation!"

President Colt picked up a pen and threw it toward his nemesis.

"I know what hyperinflation is, you idiot!"

"I'm sorry, sir," appeased Patrick. "I love my country, and I want the best for it. If hyperinflation creeps up on us, people will see that the dollar is worth less and less. The media will crawl all over the story like vultures over a carcass. This administration will be that carcass! People will believe it! Perception is everything on the economic front!"

President Colt slowly rose from his seat with a presidential facade. His rubber smile made his friend uneasy.

"I want you to print just a little, let's say one trillion. Hide it from the market any way you can. When they do eventually find out, initiate a public relations blitz. Persuade them that printing this money was the best long-term move we could possibly have made. Paint a picture of stability, and leave the hurricanes for those constitutionalists."

The Secretary of the Treasury wore a look of horror. The president was passively awaiting a response. Patrick Bonney quickly stood to his feet and stared at his lifelong friend as if he were a stranger.

"I don't know you anymore!" Patrick began.

President Colt was taken aback.

"You don't mean that, Patrick."

The top treasury official was aghast at the mutation of character that had occurred in his friend.

"You only think about yourself and how you can stay at the top of the pyramid. Your priorities are messed up! Don't you remember those long nights at the fraternity house when you talked about wanting to change the world? You said that you would stand in front of a bullet if it would help this country."

"That's still true," insisted the president.

"I wish it were! You are more concerned with merging this once great country into the United Nations. Everybody on Capitol Hill knows that you are being led around by the nose. You may become the first President of the World under the United Nation's veil of democracy, but you will have to destroy this country to do it. I know that we will never agree on the true intent of the proposed one-world government, and I know that my opinion is in the minority inside the beltway, but I will hold true to my conviction that the United Nations is not the answer!"

The Secretary of the Treasury walked to the door, without asking to be dismissed.

"I refuse to sell my soul for power. I find it disgusting that you would enslave your countrymen for a utopian dream that is destined to fail!"

President Colt was boiling over. Friend or no friend, he had no right to speak to the president of the United States in that tone or manner. The problem was, President Colt knew that he was right. He admired him for having the guts to tell him this to his face.

"I can't believe that you would watch a tempest swallow us and call it a lamb!" slapped Patrick. "When our currency crumbles, and my country dies, at least I can stand before my God and say that I refused to be part of it. I hereby resign my post as Secretary of the Treasury!"

Patrick Bonney opened the door. President Colt lunged out of his seat. He was hyperventilating.

"You're making a tragic mistake, Patrick. Nobody crosses me!"

Immanuel and Ken were standing beside the limousine. Sweat was cascading down their bodies. They were carefully watching the mirage, wondering if it were real.

"You see that water or mirage in that valley between those two large hills? That's where I saw the ships landing," remembered Ken.

Immanuel wanted to believe his new employee. After all, who would want an unbalanced person working on presenting his image to the world's masses?

Like a flea on a dog, Blasphemy was sticking to Immanuel. He knew it was time for the fireworks to begin. He reached into a dark pouch. A square, hollow box the size of a child's walkie-talkie appeared from the darkness. Blasphemy tapped on the device six times. The space in the box filled with distorted faces. The faces appeared half human, and half extraterrestrial. They miraculously resembled a cross between a mortal man and the character "E. T."

Blasphemy had often communicated with some of the top producers in Hollywood. He had fed them information about his special agents. In reality, the supposed creatures from other worlds were simply demons with the power to materialize into the visible spectrum. But the general's plan had gone like clockwork. People had become accustomed to the idea of aliens who are cute and cuddly, but who are smart enough to lead us into a new age of peace, love, and harmony.

"What exactly did you see here?" asked Immanuel.

Ken Action pointed toward the valley.

"Well, they were round, and were made out of a strange kind of metal that I've never seen before. They didn't spin; they just hovered! And they didn't make any noise at all. It was kind of eerie. Uh, they, uh, were kind of, well, I mean, it was like they just, and when they landed I saw these things, you know, uh, like."

Ken was moving his hands in all directions, trying to draw a picture.

Blasphemy eyed his atomic time crystal, closed his eyes, flexed his fingers, and chanted a spell. Electrostatic energy bounced from his fingertips to the square capsule, and then into the eastern horizon. The transfer of ions took a few seconds.

Suddenly, six ships appeared over the horizon. Ken Action was the first to spot the capsules.

"Look, over there, to your left!" panted Ken.

The ship quickly approached the men. Ken Action felt vindicated, yet mildly threatened. Immanuel grabbed Ken's arm.

"Well, Ken, I thought you had a screw loose!"

Ken didn't hear a word he said.

"What do we do now?" uttered Immanuel.

Ken began to make his way through the deep, crusty sand. The saucers landed two hundred yards away. Immanuel followed Ken, keeping a good distance away from the courageous anchor.

The six ships were exactly as Ken had described them. They couldn't hear, smell, taste, or feel them, but they could see them. The UFOs landing pattern appeared to be a ragged circle. There were no signs of life.

Without thinking, Ken took off at a full sprint. Immanuel picked up his pace, but still chugged along at a slower speed. Ken shifted into first gear as he approached one of the ships. He reached out his shaking hand to the metal giant. Just as he was about to make contact, Blasphemy stormed in Ken's direction, and knocked him twenty feet backward. He sailed through the air and landed square on his back in front of Immanuel. The sand cushioned his fall, but not his nerves. Immanuel froze. Ken was at his feet, gasping for air. He didn't appear to be seriously injured, only shaken.

"I don't think I would try that again!" observed Immanuel with little emotion.

The obstinate anchor picked up his frazzled body and knocked the hot sand from his shirt.

"I guess there must be some kind of force field protecting them from outside attack," guessed Ken.

The towering demon giggled. Blasphemy knew the ships were merely spiritual projections that had no mass. They could never be touched. The unidentified flying objects did show up on radar, but only because Satan's spirits could alter computer codes. They were only a masterful mirage of a demon. Thousands of people had witnessed this phenomenon, though no one knew the true origin or purpose behind it. Satan had assigned a detail of demons, headed by Blasphemy, to familiarize the world with creatures from other planets.

A door began to silently slide open on the ship nearest them. Ken's heart pounded against his chest.

"It's opening up," faltered Ken.

Immanuel wondered how this all fit in. It was not his time to die. He hadn't tamed the world yet. His goals were still unfulfilled. He shook his head and focused on the alien aircraft.

Blasphemy dashed inside the UFO. When he reemerged, both Ken and Immanuel took two quick steps backward. Blasphemy was limping on one leg as if he had been injured. However, what Ken and Immanuel saw wasn't Blasphemy, but an alien. The alien began to float above the cabin of his star machine.

Ken and Immanuel dropped to their knees. The hologram appeared real. They looked at each other like two boys who were about to enter a haunted mansion. Immanuel's attempt to stand proved fruitless. One of Blasphemy's buddies was jumping on his shoulders as if he were a trampoline. The extraterrestrial began to float in their direction.

The face of the creature looked peaceful. Immanuel had never seen such contentment. It seemed unaffected by the harsh conditions of the desert. Blasphemy's deceptive performance was spectacular.

Neither Immanuel nor Ken dared to say a word, or even flinch a muscle. Their mouths were hammered shut by fear. As Blasphemy approached his specimens, his baseball-sized eyes radiated a spiritual message.

"Do not fear. I come to bring good news to your earth. Your wishes have been heard and answered. My people have sent me to usher in a new world, void of war."

His transcendental signal registered with their hearts.

Immanuel stepped forward.

"I represent the United Nations of the world. How can I assist you?"

The creature stared through Immanuel. It appeared to be processing some form of information. Immanuel hoped it wasn't his thoughts. The ruthless banker tried to return the intimidation but with zero success. He had no idea that Blasphemy was up to one of his pranks.

"I represent the United Worlds of the universe. Your planet is at the brink of collapse, and I have come to help," stated the coy, cunning demon.

Ken's eyes began to tear at the thought of benign life from outer space.

"How do you plan to help us?" probed Immanuel.

"Earthlings are a stiff-necked people!"

Blasphemy's disguise fooled the men into submission.

"The people of Mother Earth must come together into a family. Every man, woman, child, and animal must look at their neighbors as if they possessed the same bodies. After all, the earth is one. We are all connected to a universal spirit of goodness and peace."

144

The alien paused, as if it were picking up a signal. Immanuel watched the creature's every move, searching for weaknesses.

"Your nemesis, Lord Birmingham, has a gift from the gods that you must possess. You are the only one with the intellect to know what to do with it."

Ken appeared confused, but Immanuel was intrigued.

"Your spirit guide will tell you what to do. Don't mess it up!" warned the imposter alien.

Blasphemy instantly sensed Immanuel's doubt.

"We are a highly advanced species. The majority of the universe is light years beyond Earth in its evolutionary track to godhood. Earth is the cancer that needs to be cured or eradicated. The people of planet Earth are the stumbling block to the rest of the universe's inheritance."

Blasphemy glided dangerously close to the mortals. Ken quickly crawled away from the extraterrestrial. UFOs, spirit guides, and this Immanuel character were more than he could handle. Immanuel held his position, daring the creature to adjust his attitude. Blasphemy had had enough of Immanuel's pomposity. He reached for a crystal that he kept for times like these. The globalist squinted, hoping for a better look at the hidden rock. The creature placed it between two fingers. It crushed the crystal into sand, and tossed the particles toward Immanuel. Each particle had a mind of its own. They quickly entered Immanuel's system through his nose, ears, mouth, and eyes.

It took less than six seconds before Immanuel began hallucinating. He was in the pit of hell. It was the real McCoy. It was a place that God had revealed to every angel, good or bad. Ken watched in horror as Immanuel gnashed his teeth, clawed at his face, and whined like a wolf in heat. As soon as the crystals had produced their desired effect, they exited. After reassembling on the alien's palm, they disappeared from sight.

"To those who trust in my wise ways, I am a friend. To those opposed to my solutions for the world's illness, I am a foe," terrorized the ghost as it closed in on Immanuel.

The heat was melting Ken's body, and Blasphemy was melting his will.

"Are you going to make your presence known to the people of this world?" interjected Ken.

The alien was void of emotion. He turned to the reporter.

"We will make ourselves known if and when we deem it necessary. Until then, I expect full cooperation from the United Nations!"

Immanuel raised his hand, not in objection, but for permission to speak. The spirit signaled his approval.

"I look forward to working with you in the very near future," sucked up Immanuel.

Blasphemy ignored his pandering as he slowly glided back to the ship.

"Release the prisoners," ordered Blasphemy in his spiritual voice.

The demons obeyed, though they were sorely disappointed that they couldn't use their dummies for target practice.

Immanuel took the lead and stood up. Ken Action quickly followed.

Blasphemy reached the ship and turned to face his serfs.

"Remember, you are a mere parasite on the evolutionary ladder of the universe. You must learn your place in the body before you can be of any use. We never use force except when we have to discipline. War begets war! He who is against us is truly against himself, and doesn't recognize it because he is spiritually blinded from the truth. Ignorance of the natural laws of the heavens invites despair and destruction!"

His words pierced their souls. His message would live in their minds for years to come, echoing its poison over and over again.

"It's now day two of the 'stock market slaughter,' or 'money meltdown,' as some have called it," reported the attractive anchor at the Global News Network.

The terms *meltdown* and *slaughter* were an editorial decision to hype the news. This calculated decision caused more people to watch, which led advertisers to buy commercial spots, which meant more money for the news outfits. The accurate dissemination of information seldom stood in the way of making a buck.

The American market had lost less than 10 percent of its value, hardly a "meltdown" or a "slaughter." The media's mauling of the English language was translating into a self-fulfilling prophecy of gloom and doom. The distortion was perceived as truth, which led to action based on falsehood, which caused the lie to become reality.

"Stock exchanges around the world are reporting a second day of record transactions and horrendous declines. The New York Stock Exchange plummeted an additional 8 percent before being forced to close down six hours early. The public perception of the market's early closing is weighing heavily on investors and the United States government. World markets are responding to the crisis by selling dollars in record amounts."

Lord Birmingham snickered like a bobcat ready to devour a helpless rabbit. The bad news for the world economy was good news for him. He guzzled a Bloody Mary as he glanced at his time-piece. A frown emerged on his face.

"Well, gentlemen, our friend Immanuel Bernstate seems to be running behind schedule. I'm sure that whatever is delaying him must be of the utmost importance. Before we begin our official meeting, I'm curious if anyone has thought of a way to bring the politicians in Europe in line? Of course, this will be strictly off the record," announced Lord Birmingham.

The eleven banking bigwigs pondered his question. Douglas McSwath, CEO of one of England's monstrous investment firms, cleared his throat.

"Lord Birmingham, our plan is right on schedule. I see no need to be concerned about these stray dogs. We have warned these politicians that the end of paper money was right around the corner. It's time the chicken was plucked and fried! These politicians need to be taught a valuable lesson about who controls their economies. All we need is time. They either join the team or get kicked off the playing field!"

"Time may ripen six, maybe seven, of the ten," predicted the lord. "England, Switzerland, France, and Germany are nagging question marks at this point. My hunch is, these men will go to their graves before relinquishing power to our cause. Their sovereignty is more important to them than food and water."

"That may not be a bad idea," considered McSwath. "We could easily muster some kind of economic revolt in those nonconformist regimes. During the revolutions, we simply pluck those tumors away.

"I have a list of hired hands that could do the job flawlessly, with zero trails."

The men were stunned at his openness. They had all committed murder in the name of free enterprise, but had never spoken of it in such barbaric terms. To them, it was "the greatest good for the greatest number," a concept that Lenin had mastered under the communist system. He murdered tens of millions so that hundreds of millions could supposedly be better off. It was an unwritten rule never to speak of murder; just do it and sweep it under the carpet.

"Listen. We blame it on some right-wing, fringe fanatic. We promote class warfare, soak the media with our version of the truth, and present their savior on a golden platter."

McSwath measured the attitude of the men in the room. Maybe he had been too candid and gone too far, too fast. He decided to protect himself.

"I must tell you that this idea isn't mine," lied McSwath.

"So what! I like it! It makes sense!" declared Lord Birmingham. "We should go with it, as long as Immanuel doesn't find any holes in the logic."

McSwath caught his breath and began tapping his smooth, unworked knuckles on the desk.

"Immanuel will surely like it, since it was his idea!" admitted McSwath. "I was just passing it on because he's not here yet."

Laughter burst forth from all four corners of the office.

"Good thing you told us. Immanuel would probably call down a lightning bolt if he knew you took credit for one of his ideas."

McSwath forced a grin.

A light silently blinked on Lord Birmingham's private phone. He put the call on his speakerphone.

"Birmingham, it's Immanuel."

Lord Birmingham's expression turned dark and cloudy.

We're ready to start," commented the tycoon.

"Listen, I have a slight rearrangement in my schedule that will prevent me from attending the meeting."

A look of relief landed on the group's faces. Immanuel had a way of intimidating these high rollers.

"I've just hired our new media spokesman who will be responsible for our public image. By next week, the world will be in fiscal ruin! You know some of the right-wing media will be putting two and two together. It will be a circus. We don't need that scrutiny to go unchallenged. This man has the kind of talent we need for the situation."

Their leader's announcement eased some of their fears.

"Where can we reach you if any unforeseen circumstances develop?" asked Lord Birmingham.

"I'll be in Israel. Contact the prime minister's office if you encounter anything that demands my immediate attention."

The phone line abruptly went dead. Immanuel was not one for etiquette.

Immanuel punched his phone sensor again. A low voice answered the other end of the line.

"Yeah."

Immanuel chewed on his lip.

"I have a job for you."

"Great," said the American.

"You'll need plenty of men."

"How many?"

"At least fifty," said Immanuel.

"No problem."

"People will die," predicted the Antichrist.

"Good!" mumbled the hit man.

———————

The exceptionally attractive aide eyeballed every feature with scrutinizing detail. Everything had to be in impeccable condition. Her long, delicate hands reached out to straighten the tie. She moved it a tenth of a centimeter to the left.

"That's better, Mr. President. Very handsome," seduced the woman.

President Colt tried to attend to his speech, rather than his in-house call girl.

"Thirty seconds to air," bellowed a voice from behind the camera.

The president repeatedly cleared his throat.

"Ten seconds, and stand by."

President Colt adjusted his demeanor. He looked distinguished, yet middle-American. The red light above the camera began to glow.

"Good evening, my fellow Americans. I have called this special news conference for two very important reasons. My purpose tonight is to set the record straight about some ongoing events. The first issue is the financial uncertainty that has surfaced in the past several days. I want to applaud those who have their life savings in our strong stock markets and our treasury bonds. The United

States of America is a ship that has weathered many storms. We have always emerged stronger and more secure. Sometimes one must go through trials to test one's strength and agility."

The president leaned into the camera.

"You know, if a growing tree was never confronted with a strong gust of wind or a storm, the first gale to come along would topple it to the ground. But let a maturing tree go through continuous storms, and let its branches bend and sway with the currents. When the killer typhoon blasts in, it will stand! It's been tested and proved. We are being tested like that tree! Our history is replete with the storms of life, and this great country has always weathered them."

He settled back into his seat.

"The United States of America is as solid today as it was last week. In fact, I believe her foundation is stronger! Nothing has changed to make our markets react as if the world is about to end. What has changed is our perceptions, our beliefs. If everybody wants our financial system to collapse, then sadly, it will. Yes, you heard me right. If America wants to self-destruct, she will! But why would anyone in his right mind want to see such a thing happen to the greatest nation that has ever graced this planet?"

The president's acting lessons were paying enormous dividends. He looked at his notes, visibly shaken by the idea. Hundreds of millions of people watched as the president fought back his rehearsed tears.

"All we need to get back on track is confidence! We need faith that can move mountains! I believe that every American will not panic and will do the right thing."

He pointed a nonthreatening finger at the camera. The press hounds furiously scribbled on their note pads.

"Effective today, I have fired my Secretary of the Treasury. I believe that his policies are partly responsible for the fiasco we are now in. Don't get me wrong. I am not the type of person to shift blame. I am not a coward. I am Commander in Chief, and I accept full responsibility for the actions of my staff. I believe the coming weeks offer hope and encouragement for our monetary system and our way of life."

He glanced down at his notes.

"Second, I am proud to announce that the United Nations has agreed to send two hundred thousand troops to help facilitate the end of our civil conflict. I fully understand why many of our brave men and women in the military refuse to fire on their fellow countrymen. They won't have to now. Let me warn you constitutionalists who refuse to lay down your weapons: the United Nations will have no pity on your misplaced nationalistic fervor! Give up now! Within weeks, I believe that our conflict will be history. Our markets will once again be thriving, and our hearts will be at peace! Keep the faith, and God bless America!"

A few hours later, Immanuel stood outside the prime minister's office. It was located in the heart of Jerusalem.

The stone city was divided by religions and time. The old city center, which was razed by the Romans during biblical times, bore testament to the unrelenting spirit of the Jewish people. Modern-day Jerusalem was a bustling city of half a million people. For years on end, the deeply religious Jews and Muslims had desperately tried to live in harmony. As time steamed along, tensions continued to build. Both groups claimed exclusive rights to this historic city as a center of worship. Many were willing to die for this tiny piece of real estate. It was their religious fortress, their heaven on earth. In their minds, compromise was for cowards. It was a miracle that war hadn't already obliterated this country.

This year, the balance was changing. Thousands of Jews were fleeing the increasingly totalitarian land of Russia every week and finding refuge in Israel. Many were Orthodox Jews who were dedicated to their God, and they shunned material wealth as a way to happiness. They sincerely believed that the secular mind-set was the reason that the prophets of old had condemned the Jews of their time. Secular Jews saw the Orthodox Jews as a bomb with a short fuse. They thought of them as backward and simple.

Meanwhile the Muslims were increasingly agitated by the Israeli governmental policies favoring the Jewish citizens over the Muslim inhabitants, giving preferential treatment to these settlers. Muslim land was being confiscated for a fraction of its value and being given to the immigrants. Like thorns crackling over an open flame, it was only a matter of time before the nation blew up, sending thistles of violence catapulting throughout the land.

Immanuel was meditating with Blasphemy when Prime Minister David Hoffman greeted him with a firm handshake.

"Mr. Immanuel Bernstate, it's a pleasure to make your acquaintance," lied the primed politician.

Immanuel sensed the masquerade, yet played the game.

"I'm a fond admirer of your unparalleled rise to power. Very impressive, indeed!" followed Immanuel.

Israel's leader hustled the United Nation's representative into his office. He didn't want to be seen allowing the enemy on Israeli soil.

"Please have a seat, Mr. Bernstate," invited David.

Immanuel agreed without a word.

David looked at his watch, which Immanuel took as an insult.

"I know that your time is important, Mr. Prime Minister. I believe it would be in your country's best interests not to take what I say lightly," warned the master politician.

David nodded his head, not to agree, but to acknowledge that he had heard the globalist. He remained uncomfortably silent.

Immanuel clicked open his black leather attaché and removed a contract. He handed it to Israel's leader.

"Mr. Hoffman, this is a peace treaty that the United Nations is graciously offering to your people."

David didn't bother looking at it before he threw it into Immanuel's lap.

"I have no use for such a document. You need a war before a peace treaty is necessary."

Immanuel's temper was dangerously close to erupting. The slightest tremor could set off the dormant volcano.

"My country is a sovereign nation ruled by God. You people in the United Nations get your cheap thrills out of playing God with small countries. You bureaucrats are simple bullies trying to pick on the seemingly weak and defenseless. We are neither."

David slammed his hand on the table.

"Let me assure you that we are determined to fight the entire world if necessary to retain our God-given land. Every square inch of our homeland, from the Dead Sea to Tel Aviv, is off-limits to you and your cronies!" David paused as he stared Immanuel down. "I know that you have given Russia the green light to take care of this thorn in your flesh!"

Immanuel stopped the prime minister.

"This peace treaty guarantees United Nations protection against everybody, foreign and domestic," recited the suave internationalist. "That includes the Muslims!"

The prime minister continued frowning, unfazed by Immanuel's speech.

"The only way to have peace in this region is to disarm the citizens, arm the United Nations, and rebuild the temple of David!" disclosed Immanuel.

David Hoffman couldn't believe his ears. This offer would mean the Muslims would lose one of their sacred temples, the Dome of the Rock.

"That's insane! The Muslims would go to their deaths fighting before they allowed such a thing!"

Immanuel didn't appear deterred by his logic.

"Mr. Hoffman, the United Nations has already extended an olive branch to the Islamic people. We have negotiated their deed for the Dome of the Rock for something even more valuable to them. They will not stand in our way, I can assure you of that!" He spoke to the Israelite like he was a brother. "The United Nations will provide the funds—under the table, of course—to rebuild the temple that your people have been longing for. We want to see the Jewish people joyfully worshipping their God!"

The prime minister stared like a hawk at the apparent peacemaker. He was rightfully suspicious.

"I'm curious about something," began David as he shifted in his seat. "Why do you and the United Nations care about my Jewish nation? Your history teaches me that we are a stench to your objectives," poked David.

Immanuel didn't hesitate in his answer. He was expecting a barrage of skeptical inquiries.

"We hate war! It is demeaning to the human spirit. The United Nations wants to bring in a new era of peace to this frail planet," positioned the globalist.

"Don't give me that trash! I know your agenda! Any nitwit out there knows what your game is. We all want peace, but the question is, at what price? My gut tells me that you lust after power, not peace!"

"It's obvious, sir, that you are the one who covets conflict," answered Immanuel. "I have tried in good faith to offer you a gift with no strings attached."

The prime minister snickered at Immanuel's stretching of the truth.

"I'll be honest with you," exclaimed Immanuel, "we do have an ulterior motive! Many countries are balking at our world peace plan. They all seem to believe that we are not capable of producing lasting peace in the world. I don't blame them! We need a testing ground. The Middle East has been a bed of hostility for nearly two thousand years. If we can do it here, then we can do it anywhere!"

Immanuel's tone changed from that of a diplomat to a chum. "World peace is achievable if, and only if, the Israeli-Arab conflict can be smoothed over. In short, world peace rides on your backs. If we can persuade you to resolve your differences, a lasting peace can then be achieved!"

The banker's candor didn't sit well with the prime minister. Something was missing, such as the truth. He played the game, hoping to discover the fine print.

"So you're willing to tear down the Dome of the Rock and re-build our temple, and you can guarantee no bloodshed?"

Immanuel seemed more cautious with his words.

"I cannot assure you that some lone religious zealot won't do something rash, but I can vouch for the Muslim governments. They are getting their bread richly buttered."

Immanuel didn't dare speak of the ark or the Ten Command-ments with the prime minister, who would give his right arm for the religious treasures.

Immanuel continued speaking. "They will control their mem-bers to the best of their ability. Remember, Mr. Hoffman, they use torture against anybody who disagrees with them, even their stray members!"

The prime minister still didn't trust Immanuel, though his words were inviting. David found it humorous that Immanuel thought he could make him believe that he could control the Arab governments.

Immanuel thrust the peace treaty back in David's face.

"Signing this guarantees a rich future for your country and your career! It also is the catalyst to world peace, which I know your God desperately desires for His people!"

David placed it back in Immanuel's briefcase, unsigned.

"My opinion of you and your entangling organization cannot be changed overnight!" fired David Hoffman.

Immanuel was not deterred.

"Do you believe in God?" probed Immanuel.

David looked at him.

"A question like that is not worthy of my comment!" refired the man of God.

Immanuel grabbed his briefcase. His face turned deadly serious.

"At midnight tonight, prepare to meet your Maker," said Immanuel calmly.

The prime minister's tongue sizzled.

"How dare you make a death threat to a head of state!" fumed David.

Immanuel swung open the door.

"That wasn't a threat!"

Satan sailed in from the southern horizon, with the stench of death trailing him. His plans for a new world order were ripe for the picking, though a few pieces of the fruit were rotting on the vine.

He had just made a personal appearance at the United Nations, where he had laid spiritual seeds of seduction.

His scarlet eyes peered from their dust pits, searching for Blasphemy on the Swiss landscape below. Lucifer let out a shriek so earthshaking that birds a hundred miles away lost their feathers.

Blasphemy, who was lounging on the roof of a New Age church, nearly jumped out of his spiritual skin. He knew that he was in trouble. The Lord of Darkness had spotted his second-in-command from twenty miles away.

"Blasphemy, what are you doing?" pounced the dragon.

Satan took a nosedive toward his lackadaisical general. The five-star officer didn't have time to think. Instead of getting on his knees and pleading for mercy, he made a dash for the nearest planet. His body sputtered as it lifted off from the church beam. Satan kicked into high gear and latched his poisonous grip onto Blasphemy's charred hair. The treasonous demon yelped. Satan's fist fastened even more tightly to his hair. He took his other hand and wrapped it around Blasphemy's squirming neck. The Devil didn't understand mercy. His overpowering stranglehold tightened around Blasphemy's neck.

"I gave you specific orders to shadow Immanuel. Because of your insubordination, that pigheaded Israelite snubbed our peace contract!"

Satan continued to sap the spirit from Blasphemy. The tardy general's voice was reduced to a high pitched, erratic whisper.

"I didn't think that he—"

The Evil One pummeled him as if he were a punching bag.

"That's right! You didn't think! I have less than seven years to make my case against our caustic Creator, and you have set us back by months or even years!"

Blasphemy wisely dropped to his knees as a sign of his acquiescence. Satan refused to move downward with him. It left the demon dangling in midair. He was seconds away from unconsciousness.

"Jehovah God has always protected Mr. Hoffman with the archangel Michael," calculated Satan. "You'd better hope that I can break enemy lines and get to him before it is too late!"

The great dragon dropped Blasphemy like he was a bag of trash. He flew off in a fiery rage, heading toward Jerusalem.

The clock on the New York Stock Exchange's wall read 9:21. At the beginning of day three of the "great reckoning," the market shocked analysts by plunging an additional 12 percent in a measly twenty-one minutes. The bell blared its disapproval as trading was prematurely halted for the third day in a row. History was in the making. The bears on Wall Street were being hunted by the bulls, and were being given a tongue lashing. In reality, it was the bears that had the bulls hanging on their walls, stuffed with their own pride.

Much of the money leaving the market was finding its way into precious metal funds, especially gold. That benchmark had just toppled the thousand-dollar mark in New York. Investors lined up to buy gold, and Lord Birmingham and his agents held nearly 95 percent of it. The value of the pure alloy was sure to zoom out of this world. The European bankers held five aces in their stacked deck.

Lord Birmingham stared at the computer screen. He was analyzing numbers. Everything from mutual funds, to stocks, bonds, dividends, and precious metal figures appeared on his screen with a mere click of a button.

"When do you gentlemen believe the word will get around that they are printing money like there is no tomorrow?"

Lord Birmingham paused to take in the reactions of his money maggots, his pals for life. The head of Germany's largest bank began to speak.

"I give it two weeks! It should take that long before some of the more keen dogs out there sniff out a rat. By that time, gold should be selling at five thousand dollars an ounce! Once the truth comes out about those overactive printing presses, most people will have their entire portfolio in gold. They will follow the pack right over the edge of the cliff, no questions asked! I figure that government bonds will have to triple overnight, sending a plethora of suckers investing in worthless paper. Hyperinflation should steamroll most of them. The world system should collapse, just as Germany's did in the 1920s! My only concern is, what do we do with all that gold? Do we support the European common currency with it?"

The German looked toward Lord Birmingham for direction. The lord shrugged his shoulders.

"I'm not sure how Immanuel envisions the use of all that money and power," retreated Lord Birmingham. "I, for one, would prefer not to second-guess him."

David Hoffman stared at the ceiling, with visions of nuclear annihilation attacking his mind. He was tucked into his king-sized bed, covered by a down comforter. Snuggled beside him and sleeping soundly was his loving wife of thirty-five years. Instead of counting sheep, he was numbering enemy tanks on Iran's border.

Suddenly, a ghostly form materialized on the ceiling directly above him. David thought he was having a nightmare. He pinched himself, but to no avail.

The grandfather clock in the hallway began to gong. It was midnight, and the witching hour was at hand. The cloudy shadow mutated into an angel of light. It resembled the patriarch Moses, with beard, staff, and sandals.

"When I called your forefathers out of Egypt, I did it peacefully. I, Moses, beseech you to seek the way of peace! I have come to show you the good road paved to heaven. Immanuel has shown you the way to peace, but you have spurned him. When you rebuke him, you rebuke our Father in heaven."

Satan was laying it on thick. David Hoffman rubbed his eyes in disbelief. He glanced at his wife, who was fast asleep.

"Immanuel is a devil. He should be executed," dramatized the prime minister.

The image of Moses lifted its staff into the air.

"You are just like your fathers before you! You desire to kill the prophets who come to bring you truth. It bites at your soul because your father is Satan!"

David's once finely tuned conscience was filled with static. The ghost was right. Many of the prophets had been executed by their fellow countrymen for proclaiming God's will. They were mischaracterized by the people of the day so that they didn't have to repent. Could he be so badly mistaken?

"If what you say is true, how could Immanuel be involved with such a sinful organization?" questioned the prime minister.

A red glow welled up in Moses' eyes. Pain shot up David's nervous system like tongues of fire.

"The Word of God says that an Anointed One will come to bring peace. The lion and the lamb will play together. Why do you think Immanuel is offering to rebuild the temple of David? Trust him, and it will go well with you!"

The dragon's twisted theology was sticking like superglue. David had always wanted to follow God with all his heart. The Prince of Darkness sensed David's doubt.

A black tornado with the voices of a thousand demons descended into the room. Inside the vortex appeared deceased friends and family, begging him to listen. Their disjointed, burnt faces appeared one at a time. Their appearance sealed David's fate. He closed his eyes and bitterly wept. Satan's dart had punctured his heart.

"All right! Enough! I'll do it! I'll sign the damn peace treaty!"

Lucifer disappeared without a trace or a thank-you. David's view of God, and Immanuel, would never be the same again.

Eight

The Coming Conspiracy

Wall Street was busted. Stock markets around the globe closely followed the United States into the recession of recessions. Like a herd of wild pigs, they followed the leader of the free world into the mud pit of despair. The American dollar was the foundation of the world's economy. Trillions upon trillions of dollars of investments had vanished without a trace. The only things left were the tears and the blame. The middle class of the world was fast becoming the impoverished class. The ruling elite crushed them into poverty without a trace of reservation.

Money was the blood that kept the world's heart beating. Without this lifeline, a catastrophic heart attack was imminent. Open-heart surgery was the only logical solution. Of course, Immanuel would be the lead physician. The world needed somebody to give them hope, a reason to live. The staples of everyday life, food and clothing, were not enough for the average human. Prosperity was expected. It wasn't considered a luxury. The planet needed a "god" who could make things better. Immanuel planned to fill that order, whether they wanted it or not.

The world was fractured. It was in desperate need of repair. Many people who had lost loved ones during the Christian Rapture were still hurting. People were fearful of nuclear attack or biological warfare. Rampant viruses that outsmarted modern medicine plagued many. Unemployment was showing signs of skyrocketing, life savings were evaporating into the wind, and hearts were faint.

Everybody seemed uglier, less hospitable, and more prone to violence. The love of many was waxing cold. The Bible verses from 2 Timothy 3:1–5 were becoming reality: "But know this, that in the last days perilous times will come: for men will be lovers of themselves, lovers of money, boasters, proud, blasphemers, disobedient to parents, unthankful, unholy, unloving, unforgiving, slanderers, without self-control, brutal, despisers of good, traitors, headstrong, haughty, lovers of pleasure rather than lovers of God, having a form of godliness but denying its power."

Ken Action busily unpacked moving boxes in his swank office in Geneva, Switzerland. The move from America to the new Europe had been short and sweet. At his television station, there had been many good-byes but few tears. His new home was the sixth story of the United Nations building. Ken had a team of sixty-six employees at his beck and call who were responsible for public opinion surveys and news coverage trends. Their purpose was to make Immanuel look like the only hope for a dying world.

This public relations branch could be compared to the S. S. arm of the Nazi propaganda machine. Their mission was to gauge public opinion, acquire the means to twist it, and mold people's minds. Their power base reached to the stars, figuratively and literally. Immanuel would formulate policies and then make the leaders of nations believe that these policies were their ideas.

"Tina, I'm finished unpacking," called Ken. "Get someone to take these empty boxes out of here! I have an important meeting in less than an hour!" he demanded of his executive secretary.

She fumbled for the sensor on her telephone. Her scratchy-sounding voice was distraught but obedient.

"Yes, sir, right away!" agreed Tina Marie.

The executive secretary frantically looked around the room for a bookmarker for her Bible. Reading a Bible in public was considered religious harassment. It was an unwritten rule that carried hefty social penalties, including job discrimination. Tina was deeply considering some of the prophesies of the Bible. She nervously placed a pen in the book of Daniel and closed the contraband book.

Instead of calling housekeeping, which was notoriously slow, she rushed into his office to do the work herself. The lady from Salina, Kansas, quietly knocked on one of the bronze double doors.

"Yeah, come in!" yelled Ken.

Tina quickly placed her sweaty palm on the scanner at the side of the entrance.

"Scan positive," announced the female computer voice.

The door clicked open, and Tina poked her head inside.

"If you don't mind, I'll get those boxes for you now. No sense in gambling on what day housekeeping will show up," joked the attractive brunette.

Ken waved a hand of approval at her statement. As she reached down to pick up the cardboard containers, Ken pretended to be reading some highly valuable material. His eyes dodged her glances as he scanned her features from head to toe. Tina Marie was petite, with large eyes. Her attractive features masked the independent and sometimes selfish side of her heart. She was a lonely lady in the midst of a real-life nightmare. She had lost her fiancé to the Rapture of the Christian church. She was bitter at God, yet envious of her onetime love because she knew that he was in heaven. Her fiancé had exhaustively presented the message of Jesus Christ to her, but had encountered a stone wall at every turn. She came from a family that believed that good people went to heaven. She had believed there was a heavenly scale that measured the number of good deeds versus the bad ones, but her vision of God had been shattered when her fiancé had disappeared before her very eyes. One minute, they were cooking lasagna together. The next, he was gone, without a trace. Her dreams had been swallowed up in the time it takes an eye to twinkle.

"You're quite an efficient worker," complimented Ken.

Tina Marie played hard-to-get. A quick smile flashed on her face.

"I know you may consider this forward, but I was wondering if you would show me around town this weekend? I don't have a clue what kind of fun one could have around this mountain village," inquired Ken.

Tina was coy with her response. She batted her eyelashes like a teenage girl being courted for the first time.

"Mr. Action! I am surprised by your forward proposal. I'm not that kind of girl!"

Ken rolled his eyes in disbelief.

"What kind of girl do I think you are?" tossed back Ken.

Tina hesitated with her response.

"Well, not the kind of girl who goes out with a complete stranger!"

Ken looked at his watch in despair.

"Next week, I won't be a total stranger, now will I?"

Tina thought about it, but didn't know what to say.

"We'll finish this conversation at another time," smiled Ken.

Tina cast the last of the boxes into her office and exited without a word.

———————

The United Nation's Council of Churches was in a brainstorming session in Paris, France. Most of the religious leaders of the world were present. Only a few born-again Christians were missing. The Council had always been made up of every major religion. Christianity, Islam, Hinduism, Buddhism, and Judaism were represented in a kind of democratic, spiritual boot camp. God never had veto power in this humanistic seminar of so-called saints. The only participants who had ever rocked the boat were the born-again Christians and a few Orthodox Jews. Past leaders had displayed an open hatred for anyone who believed his way was God's way. To the past leaders, God was who you wanted Him to be. Truth didn't matter, as long as everybody got along. Peace at any cost was the "divine" United Nations mandate for the church body.

Dominic Rosario had been invited to their meeting as a possible candidate for Council leader. Most had wept with relief as they had listened to his speech to the Church and to the world several days before. He was what they needed to finally have an influential voice in the politics of their world organization.

Dominic was comfortably seated on stage as he was being introduced to the crowd. The counterfeit humility that lined his face fooled everyone except the God of the heavens. As the speaker read his impressive résumé, the energy in the room seemed to build.

Several thousand demons were attending the religious harem. They were special field agents trained in the latest techniques of Bible bashing and Scripture twisting. They were flying through the auditorium like an army of bats in the early evening. Sixty-six of the night owls attached themselves to Dominic.

"I am pleased to introduce the next leader of the Council of Churches, Dominic Rosario," announced a leading spiritualist from India.

The devils sneered in delight; the humans cheered. Dominic quietly rose from his seat and meekly walked to the microphone. His six-page speech was promptly edited by Blasphemy. When the spirit general was through correcting the script, the only thing remaining was the "thank-you" at the end.

"Thank you for your warmhearted greeting. I have come before you today with a radical agenda from God Himself."

The crowd broke into applause.

He raised his hand for silence.

"I love every one of you! I want the best for you, your children, and your children's children. I love Mother Earth with all my heart, mind, and soul. I say that to prepare you for the way. The way is not easy; it is not flat, nor is it without danger!"

The demons formed a circle around the building. The ghosts held hands as they chanted their allegiance to Dominic. Their demonic devotional slowly sank into the dark crevices of the religious leaders' minds.

"Trust Dominic with all of your mind! He will lead you down a path you have all prayed for!" caroled the devilish choir.

"God wants Mother Earth at peace, but that peace can be achieved only through the 'threat of war'!" continued Dominic. "Our God has shown me the answer to this age-old dilemma. As a part of the United Nations, you should know that our mission is to bring the world under one umbrella of humanity. Everybody in this great organization has concentrated his efforts in the political arena. That is a good start, but we must move further, much further."

He looked down at his script. "All nations on Mother Earth must disarm and hand over their weapons of war to the United Nations. No individual nation will then have the resources to threaten the united peoples of the world."

The world's spiritual bellwethers bought the lie.

"How will we persuade the national leaders to hand over their bombs, planes, and guns? We must, and I repeat, *must* become one in spirit and purpose! We must be a united front for good, and oppose evil at every dark corner. Up to this point, we have accepted our differences with dignity and respect. Today, I say to you that we must relinquish any differences! We need a single, feasible, workable theology. A house divided against itself cannot stand! Although we say we are one, we are not!"

A few calculated groans sent a nervous chill up Dominic's spine. His demonic accomplices saw his faith waver. They quickly gave him a burst of demonic strength. He leaned forward and scolded the dissidents in the crowd. "Don't judge me until you have heard me through, and I will give you the same respect!" He pointed at each of the pirates with no fear of reprisal. "When we believe something that opposes our neighbor's belief, we promote disunity. That friction can turn into a deadly infection. Don't you see?" pleaded the False Prophet. "The world needs to see our organization as an extension of God. They need to see God! We must form a set of critical beliefs that we all can agree on. Peace can be achieved only when we form a one-world Church, dedicated to a core set of values and laws. Those laws will be introduced to every man, woman, and child on Mother Earth as God's precepts. If the World Church can unite the people's spirits, we can unite their minds! When we start thinking like a family, we will start acting like a family. Everybody needs to give up some of his freedoms for the good of humanity. The governments of the world will follow our lead. They will gladly hand over their weapons as their part in doing the will of God. Once the United Nations has control over the very weapons that threaten to destroy us, we can guarantee peace."

Dominic was expecting an extended period of applause. Instead, silent stares confronted him.

"The plan is simple. Number one, we bring our views of religion into one core set of ideas, and decide what we will keep and what we will toss out. Number two, we present this dogma to the world's people, especially those in power, as God's authoritative will. Number three, we sit back and watch the political wing of our organization go to work. Evil weapons will be handed over to the United Nations' police force. This will create peace. Religion will no longer divide anybody! Instead of separating us, it will bring us together. People will no longer have the choice to be members of the church. It will be mandatory for a peaceful and prosperous Mother Earth!" Most of the religious cads applauded. A few, though, were as stiff as a corpse. They wanted his head on a platter.

The man of perdition stared at the plush, purple carpet. He was 99 percent sure he could trust his highly paid minion. That 1 percent could not be left to chance. That is what separated him from the pack. World conquest was a "take it or leave it" proposition. It started with his employees. He either had a monopoly on his employees' wills, or he hung them out to dry. He left nothing to chance. That was for the Las Vegas gamblers and the weather prognosticators.

Suddenly, he looked at his slave. The time was at hand.

"Ken, what kind of man do you think I am?" explored Immanuel.

Ken Action was caught off guard by the question. Surprisingly, he thought before he spoke.

"Well, you are a man with a high degree of skill in what you do," sugarcoated Ken. "You are a perfectionist who doesn't put up with incompetence. I believe you love your job and take it seriously."

Immanuel smiled genuinely at Ken. He was beginning to like him. He patted himself on the back for his intuitive decision to hire him.

"If I can be perfectly candid, you're the kind of man I wouldn't want to cross."

The son of Satan laughed out loud. If Ken Action played his cards right, Immanuel would make him more than a highly prized employee, but a personal friend. Immanuel had no personal friends. He had had some in the past, but all had crossed him in some way. Needless to say, they were no longer breathing. Ken took advantage of the positive response to lay it on thicker.

"I believe you are the one man who can bring our world into peace. From what you have shared with me, your plan is brilliant. Your leadership skills are a combination of military genius, suave politician, and savvy priest. You are the first person in the history of the world to merge those into one palatable person."

Immanuel wasn't listening. The crocodile turned his powerful, laserlike stare to Ken's moistening eyes.

"You must understand who you are dealing with before you can be an informed employee," whispered Immanuel in a ghostly tone.

Ken's spine felt a cold wind move across it. Immanuel had closed his eyes and placed his hands together as if he were praying. Ken was spooked, but not enough to give up the money, the prestige, or that secretary he had just lusted over.

A dark cloud descended from the ceiling. It wasn't water vapor, but it was a sweet-smelling gas that was foreign to Ken. The cloud enveloped the room. The light coming in from the stained glass windows was obliterated by the evil vapor. All sound from the outside world had disappeared in the vacuum. A purple, effervescent light glowed from the darkest corner of the satanic mist.

A few of Blasphemy's special effects wizards were behind the shenanigans. Satan had given Blasphemy his personal magicians of mayhem. Previously, these spirits of seduction had been kept inactive by Jehovah God. However, Jehovah God had significantly decreased His troop strength, which left Satan open to do what he wanted. Satan didn't know why God had done this, and he didn't care. He knew the ability to perform miracles was the key to his kingdom on earth. The last time he had such control was in Egypt over four thousand years ago.

Ken wanted to run, but felt some kind of force hindering his escape. A large, nasty looking spirit stood between Ken and the exit. Ken's eyes did a double take as Immanuel started chanting to the hazy shadow.

"Show him the truth, show him our power, show him his destiny," crooned Immanuel.

Suddenly, the apparition began to encircle Ken, who was shaking. It began to rotate in a cyclonic pattern. The purple mist began to contort. It evolved from a round ball of energy into a paper scroll with writing on both sides.

Immanuel placed his hands into the electrified air.

"Go," commanded Immanuel with a militant tone.

Ken was trapped. Every muscle in his body was scared into submission. Even his tongue was under the spell.

The minityphoon continued to speed up around Ken. His eyesight began to fail him as Immanuel's cruel trick gained its emotional and psychological hold. The scroll slowly glided toward Ken. It appeared as if the globalist were directing the scroll, but in reality, a demon was carrying it. The scroll floated toward the homemade hurricane and began to rotate in its wind field.

Ken vomited.

"Feed him with manna from heaven," ordered Immanuel.

The scroll was quickly caught up in the eye wall of the storm. Ken was barely conscious.

"Take it, and eat of it, for it will soothe your soul," decreed Immanuel.

Ken's last memory was of a rolled piece of paper lying on his face.

President Colt's aide patted him on the back. The television camera was off, and so was his political smile.

"Do you think I pulled it off?" the president asked his senior advisor.

"You bet you did! The polling data is painting a home run for us, sir," informed his most trusted ally.

The president yawned. He hadn't had a good night's rest in over a week. The tumultuous period of the nation had just been fixed, according to the administration. Unfortunately, it was a quick fix.

"Mr. President, I think you should know something," interjected the Assistant Secretary of the Treasury.

President Colt shook his head in disbelief.

"You people just don't get it! I am dead tired. I am going to bed. I don't want to hear any more bad news tonight. I want to pass out on a good note!"

"But, sir, you do not understand the importance of what I have here," insisted the official.

"I don't care if a nuclear weapon has been fired our way. I am going to get some shut-eye!"

The Treasury official was trying to get a word in, when one of the president's bodyguards quickly placed his hand over the man's mouth.

"You heard the president, man. Shut your trap, or I'll do it for you!"

The official was taken aback by the ruthlessness of the secret service agent. President Colt chuckled as he left the room.

The number two man at the Treasury looked at the National Security Advisor with an alarmed expression.

"That was probably the biggest mistake of his career!" said the Assistant Secretary.

The National Security Advisor looked confused and concerned.

"Why don't you meet me in my office in, let's say, twenty minutes," said the National Security Advisor as he looked at his watch.

Still staring at the president's exit, the treasurer's face was pale and ghostlike.

The economic squeeze that Lord Birmingham had directed was having its desired effects. The Dow Jones market had lost another 20 percent of its value during the past week. The only thing that was keeping it from plummeting further was the flickering hope of those who said it could never happen. Psychology ruled the market, and fear ruled the people.

"So, what the hell do I do now?" shouted the German chancellor. His temper was flaring like a campfire that had just had gasoline sprinkled on it.

Lord Birmingham didn't fall prey to his emotions. His eyes said it all. He cared more about tea in China than he did about Helmut Blitzkreig's political future.

"Listen. What is happening to our financial markets was bound to occur. We facilitated it so that we could control the power of the explosion. Immanuel gave you a choice to join our movement or be left in the cold. It sounds to me like you have chosen Siberia," snickered Lord Birmingham.

Helmut Blitzkrieg wanted to wrap a crowbar around the Englishman's neck.

"What do you want from me, blood?" barked the German.

Lord Birmingham slammed his fist on the table.

"Grow up! Let me put it this way for your pea-sized brain. You cannot turn back now. You must move forward. You have no choice!"

Helmut jumped out of his seat.

"I have worked my way to the top with sweat and blood! I am the guardian of the German people. I will not stand by and watch you take over our country."

"Whatever," mocked the banker. "You have one week to see it our way, or I can promise you the German mark will be destroyed."

Lord Birmingham walked out the door humming an English folk tune.

Helmut Blitzkrieg grabbed a portrait of himself and Immanuel at a political function and slammed it against the wall. His nostrils were flaring like a bull. He screamed at the shattered picture as if it were alive.

"I will get even with you, Immanuel! You don't even have the guts to threaten me in person. You have to have one of your cronies do your dirty work for you!"

He dropped to his knees, dangerously close to the fractured glass. He picked up one of the sharp pieces of his past and crushed it against his wrist.

He cried out in misery.

"You will pay! You will pay!"

The signing ceremony was a sight to behold. Dignitaries and politicians from all over the world were present. The Israeli flag and the Arab flags swayed in the hot, desert breeze. The United Nations flag stood boldly between them. The location was the valley of kings, deep in the heart of one of Israel's mountain valleys. Immanuel had every major media outlet in the world covering the event. This was his day to shine.

Trumpets announced the beginning of the festivities as two dozen multinational jets streaked across the blue sky. Thousands of United Nations troops appeared over the hill, accompanied by hundreds of tanks and armored vehicles. The show of global force was stunning yet foreboding.

Immanuel walked to the platform. The man of damnation approached the microphone. His guests competed to see who could welcome him the loudest. The applause lasted a full two minutes, and was followed by the singing of the new world anthem by a Russian woman.

As the song faded in the wind, Immanuel walked to the edge of the platform. He placed his hand on his heart.

"I come today to proclaim peace!"

A well-timed applause ensued. Billions of people were watching the event on television from every corner of the sphere.

"We have reached a critical turning point in history. The people of Earth are fed up with a few evil people controlling them. We are sick and tired of the dark forces of this world manipulating our lives and our futures! We have put up with war for thousands of years, but today, I am pleased to announce that war as we know it is over!"

Immanuel's smile covered his diplomatic face. The audience stood to their feet, showing thanks for the work that he had accomplished. He tried to talk over the accolades, but the praise was overwhelming. It took several gestures for them to settle down. He was honored by their display of affection, yet, at the same time, annoyed at their "kissing up."

"Today, right before your very eyes, we are entering the dawn of a new age. It will be a blissful period, in which we will not have to worry about nation rising up against nation. It will be a time when everybody will be equal. This era will be the turning point in history. I promise peace, prosperity, justice, and harmony to everybody who joins our crusade."

Immanuel paused to await the ovation that was sure to follow. It did.

"The wonders of science have taught us that all life on our planet is interdependent. The Amazon rain forest is linked to the survival of the Japanese people. The thoughtless dumping of hazardous waste off the American coast can destroy the fish population in Europe. The selfish overuse of fossil fuels can destroy future generations. Our actions affect those around us, and the children of our wombs! Life is intricately connected on this earth. When part of Mother Earth is damaged, it hurts the entire planet. That brings us to our problem. This wonderful body called Mother Earth is divided, and can never be healthy until it realizes the oneness of its being."

Immanuel realized his words were too symbolic for his listeners.

"I know I get excited about the future of our precious planet, and I speak in terms that may confuse you. The problem has always been man! We are selfish, and have left Mother Earth gasping for life. Man must change and work to keep our frail planet alive."

His words sank in like a long awaited spring shower. Once again, the leaders of the world jumped to their feet in admiration.

"Man's abuse of technology and science has brought humanity to the rim of a very large and dangerous cliff. Our civilization is at the brink of ecological and social catastrophe. The only way to prevent our world from falling apart is to create a world united in purpose, belief, and government. That unification begins with this peace treaty."

Immanuel waved the treaty in the air.

"Many of you believe that your military gives your nation the protection it needs. Those who have tried this way are broken, and their environment is destroyed! There is a better way! A world united under one democratically elected government, possessing all the military might, would make war a plague of the past. It's a simple concept that a child understands, yet the proud are blinded to it. I am here to give the world sight! I am here to proclaim that peace can be achieved. This treaty is only the beginning of what we can do if we are willing to give a little so that we can gain so much!"

The spiritual world was buzzing with activity. It was the Woodstock of the demon warlocks. There were literally billions of little devils, big devils, ugly devils, and uglier devils partying at the treaty signing. Their mission was to drain every morsel of decency and goodness from the inhabitants of the world.

Satan was present, receiving praise from thousands of his devils. They were on their knees, chanting their allegiance. This signing was the event that would kick off Satan's and Immanuel's rise to power. He would leave nothing to chance.

"Before we have our friends from the Middle East sign this monumental document, I want to offer my vision for the future of the world," enlightened Immanuel.

The spirits pushed all the dignitaries, politicians, and friends of Immanuel to the edges of their seats.

"I propose a World Federation of United Peoples be established to supersede the United Nations. This Federation would be democratically elected, and would have the power to make international law the supreme law of the lands. There would be no more war because a world guardian would possess all the instruments of destruction. Crime would be reduced to a trickle because we would possess all the firearms. A world police force would end international terrorism, drug trafficking, and Mafia-related crime.

This government would spend one trillion dollars a year for environmental cleanup. This government would guarantee that the earth's resources would be equitably shared to help us live every day in safety and joy. Every person would have food on the table, a roof over his head, clothing on his back, health care, and safety to walk the streets at night! Imagine a world where there is no heaven or hell, no rich or poor."

The Devil's disciple changed from politician to preacher in the blink of an eye. He had the ability to be all things to all men.

"I'm not a religious man, but I must say that all the great preachers of the past dreamed of this day. I know that God is on our side, and that He will lead us into the land that is flowing with milk and honey!" lied Immanuel.

Daniel and Timothy kept hidden in a slow-moving cumulus cloud about thirty miles away. Thousands of guardian angels were doing the same, most at a considerably farther distance than Timothy and Daniel.

As Immanuel turned his fiery vision to religion, Timothy quickly opened his Bible and silently wept. Daniel didn't understand Immanuel's blasphemy or Timothy's reaction to it.

"Why are you so troubled?" questioned Daniel. "I thought you were pumped up about our new assignment."

Timothy wiped a tear from his eyes.

"I thought we would have some time before the spiritual deception would kick in with such force."

He opened his pocket Bible and turned to 2 Timothy 3:5.

"Listen to this," said Timothy. "The Bible says that they will have a form of godliness but deny its power. That is exactly what that beast is now doing. He is appealing to their moral side, while denying the source of all of morality. Unfortunately, it will get much worse."

"What does it all mean?" wondered Daniel. "Is there going to be out-and-out war, or are we just going to play around with a few battles here and there until Armageddon comes?"

Timothy was astonished at Daniel's tone. He pushed his finger into the younger angel's chest.

"You should show more respect for the war of the ages! This isn't some human video game! This is the war between the God of Creation and His first created being, Satan! He is the strongest angel in the heavens!"

Timothy looked under his feet toward the enemy celebration.

"True spiritual warfare," sighed Timothy, "isn't pretty! It's the scariest thing you'll ever go through. Humans think their petty warfare is hell, but let me tell you, it is nothing compared to this! It's nothing compared to what's to come."

Nine

Evil Is Good, and Good Is Evil

Okay, let's hear it!" said Jim Smith, the National Security Advisor to the president of the United States. His job was to guard the United States' national security and sovereignty against all enemies, foreign and domestic.

Bill Thomas hesitated, wondering if the National Security Advisor could handle this kind of information.

"On second thought, I'm not sure if you're the man I should be talking to," acknowledged Bill.

Jim lifted his hands in a broad gesture.

"If you're talking national security, after me, there's the president. You tried it on him, and he blew you off, so come on. What's got you all bent out of shape?"

"Okay, okay. I'm just not sure what you can do about it," admitted Bill. "The United States as we know it is ending!"

Bill's gloomy statement was uncharacteristic of the Harvard graduate. He had always been one of the most respected economists on the White House staff.

"Coming from somebody like you, that scares me, a lot," said Jim. "Back up a little bit. Where's this coming from?"

Both men stared at each other. Bill was still tentative.

"My boss resigned because he had some very damning information about something that will probably destroy our economy," confessed Bill.

Jim's reaction surprised Bill. He sat and listened as if he had expected something like this.

"We are going to be sold out to the United Nations. Our currency will be transferred into ECUs. The dollar is dead, and its burial is only a matter of time, most likely weeks, not months, and certainly not years!"

Jim was not ready for the fall of the American empire.

"I have the greatest amount of respect for you, Bill, but I must be honest with you. I know the stock market is down hard, and that there are rumors of a collapse. However, that's a long way from being gone in just a few weeks," offered Jim.

"The facts are undeniable. About ten days ago, the big players in the world market decided to hang the entire system out to dry."

Bill paused to read Jim's eyes.

"I know you know who I'm talking about. The problem is, I don't understand what their motivation would be. When they destroy the market, they destroy themselves!"

"The rich may not have only money on their minds," said Jim, who was starting to get the picture. "What do they want? How is the president involved?"

Bill knew he was taking a huge chance by talking to Jim.

"I hope you're not suggesting that the president..." scolded Jim.

Bill knew the cat was out of the bag. There was no turning back now.

"My boss knew that the power people in Europe sold off all their notes, which caused the Treasury to panic. He knew that the money supply would have to be increased twofold, but he also knew what to do to avert a disaster. The president at best wanted the easy way out. At worst, well, I know this is hard for you to believe." Bill stopped and looked Jim in the eyes. "At worst, he's part of it."

"And the Secretary of the Treasury told you all this?" checked Jim.

"Yes, he did."

They both stood and looked at each other, letting the truth settle around them.

A knock rattled the door.

"Who is it?" said the flushed Security Advisor.

"It's Eileen. Turn on the television! Big news on Channel 9!"

Responding to his secretary's words, Jim stretched across his cluttered desk and grabbed the remote. He quickly turned on the television.

A plane had crashed, and there were no survivors.

The prayer lines at the Central Prayer Agency were once again beginning to light up, which pleased the archangel Michael. The phones had been dead for more than two weeks because most who had prayed in faith were gone and in God's presence. The mega-angel was hopeful that the prayers would increase so that his power to fight evil could begin again.

Those who had recently become Christians had similar stories. Loved ones who were devout Christians had disappeared during the Rapture, leaving their families and close friends stunned. Many of these godly believers had been telling their non-Christian family and friends that they might one day vanish, as the Bible states. Once their loved ones were gone, the people left behind read the Bible and believed. The sight of these newly born-again Christians greatly pleased the archangel.

Michael moved down the assembly line to review the prayers. With his wings folded behind his white cape, and his powerful arms by his side, he walked down the ten-mile line of workers. The angels gasped at the sight of the majestic creature. As the archangel interpreted the prayers, he realized he had to call several battalions forth. The final battle was just beginning.

Immanuel felt energized by the demonic force indwelling him. Was it time to reveal the big surprise?

"Tell him, 'No! The people are not ready,'" Satan told his aides.

His messenger demons instantly delivered the commandment to Immanuel. Immanuel could feed the people crumbs, but not the full loaf.

"Today marks the beginning of the World Federation of United Nations!" proclaimed Immanuel.

Immanuel scanned the crowd with a fine-tooth comb, watching the leaders of the world murmur.

"I know many of you are wondering about the United Nations and its role in the World Federation. Their heart is in the right place, but they don't have the tools to put their vision into action. Today, I propose to abolish the United Nations and institute the World Federation of the United Nations!"

Immanuel's comments were like a meteor slamming into the United Nations' enclave. It was sudden, unexpected, and terrifying for those whose lives revolved around the global wish tank.

Satan read the minds of the people and ordered a demon runner to deliver his message.

Immanuel sensed the unrest.

"Let me assure you. Everybody involved with the United Nations will be hired by the World Federation."

The mutiny had been averted, but some of the world leaders had questions, and many, at that.

"In the next several weeks, I will be laying out the blueprint for a peaceful world under the World Federation. It will be an all-encompassing, unique approach to controlling the evils that plague us, while retaining the freedoms we all cherish."

Immanuel knew they now needed some bits of information to ease their minds. He needed to finish painting a picture of future hope for them to absorb.

"An incentive system will be set in place so that those who are first to get involved with the World Federation will reap the most benefits," he calmly offered. "As we all know, a financial crisis is now gripping the world. Stabilizing each of your country's currencies will be an impossible task, and could do more harm than good. My revolutionary approach will redefine how we live our everyday lives, all for the better. I need your countries to turn in your value-less monies for the world standard of money, which is the European Common Currency. I believe the world is now ready for a one-world currency!"

Satan was beside himself at the intelligent decision he had made in choosing this sly banker. The Prince of Darkness lounged on a flown-in throne, cleaning his nails. In fact, Immanuel was so good at deception, Satan didn't need to rely on Blasphemy to provide the script anymore.

"I also believe that we eventually need an advanced, cashless society. The advantages of such a move are limitless. Think about the billions in drug trafficking profits that will be halted, overnight! Tax evasion will be a thing of the past, so that everybody will have to be honest and contribute his fair share to help society thrive. This will increase the tax revenues of the World Federation, guaranteeing a stable inflation rate and low interest rates. The cost of printing money will be nil, and the cost of collecting taxes will be a fraction of what it is now. All this extra cash flow will be used not on bureaucrats, but instead on you, to enrich the lives of people all over the world!"

Immanuel's demeanor was prime time. He was believable, trustworthy, and charming.

"I make this plea to the leaders and the citizens of the world: Join the World Federation of United Nations! The nations who sign up within a week will be offered the best exchange rates for their currencies, the most democratically elected seats in the world congress, and the majority of monetary privileges. The sooner you join, the greater your reward!"

He didn't tell them what would happen if they didn't join. There was time for that later. First he would use the positive approach. The Antichrist shifted his focus to the television cameras at the base of the stage.

"You, the people of the world, have the inalienable right to control your own destiny, and the destiny of the world! You should not be a political pawn. Don't allow your leaders to manipulate you or intimidate you. If your leader finds his political career a higher priority than your future, let him know about it in a peaceful but powerful way. The World Federation will be there for you! You, a citizen of the world, have my word on it!"

Immanuel's contagious smile and enthusiasm was a hit with the television audience. However, many of Immanuel's political acquaintances were now sharp critics of his behavior, although their criticism remained unspoken. He knew this would occur. He had entered the court of public office without their consent. He had passed them by, galloping straight to the people as a knight on his white horse. It was a brilliant, well-planned power grab.

Anybody who had the guts to stand in his path would be booed out of the bleachers by public opinion. Immanuel had the ball and was prepared to run with it until every last opponent gasped for air and died. What did weigh heavily on Immanuel's mind were those countries who did not democratically elect their leaders. Rabid dogs were easier to control than desperate dictators. They were a special problem that Immanuel looked forward to dealing with.

With the speech of a lifetime behind him, he invited the prime minister of Israel and the Arab leaders to stand, shake hands, and sign the peace accord before them. The sinister blueprint was sealed.

Dominic Rosario was relaxing in his historic, plush office, caressing his lips with a worn pencil eraser. He was considering the dream that he had had a few hours ago, wondering what it all meant. He was not one to dream, but in the past several weeks,

Dominic had had a vision every night. It was spiritual suicide to ignore such messages from God, thought Dominic.

Every dream he had involved the future, and his part in the creation of an omnipotent Church. Was God going to physically inhabit the planet? Would the Bible prophesies really happen under his command? What form would God take? Dominic's thoughts excited him. One of the visions suggested that Immanuel would be the man whom God would physically indwell. Another vision painted a picture in which he himself was being worshipped as God.

He slowly wiped his weary eyes, and placed his glasses on his face. He reached for his Latin Bible. The dreams seemed to weaken him, as if something were physically entering his body and robbing energy from it. Outwardly, he was searching for God, but inwardly, he was molding God into an idol that his prideful imagination would accept. He closed his eyes and prayed. The prayer was intercepted by Blasphemy. Dominic's prayer wasn't exactly the most difficult to intercept. After he voiced his wish, the prayer just floated near the chandelier. Jehovah God wasn't interested in this self-centered, arrogant prayer. God Almighty longed for the prayers of the humble, meek, and brokenhearted. Even Blasphemy had trouble stealing those petitions. The demon watched Dominic's one-sided plea sink to the floor like a fattened pig in quicksand. He slowly scooped it off the floor and gobbled it whole.

Dominic thumbed through his Bible with his eyes closed. He was waiting for a lightning bolt from heaven to stop his fingers. Blasphemy grunted, then belched, as he helped Dominic's fingers stop at Isaiah 11:6. Dominic began reading there.

"The wolf also shall dwell with the lamb, the leopard shall lie down with the young goat, the calf and the young lion and the fatling together; and a little child shall lead them. The cow and the bear shall graze; their young ones shall lie down together; and the lion shall eat straw like the ox. The nursing child shall play by the cobra's hole, and the weaned child shall put his hand in the viper's den. They shall not hurt nor destroy in all My holy mountain, for the earth shall be full of the knowledge of the LORD as the waters cover the sea. And in that day there shall be a Root of Jesse, who shall stand as a banner to the people; for the Gentiles shall seek Him, and His resting place shall be glorious."

The religious leader closed the ancient but divine prophecy. A dim lamp clicked on in his clouded mind. God was planning to usher in a period of eternal peace. The entire earth would have the knowledge of the Lord. God needed somebody to pass on that knowledge. Would he be that man? thought Dominic.

The False Prophet, once again, closed his eyes. He leafed through his Bible, continuing into the New Testament. He didn't feel the urge to stop until Blasphemy slammed his paw against Dominic's hand at the book of Revelation, chapter eleven, verse three. Dominic excitedly opened his eyes and stared at the words on the page. He started to read.

"'And I will give power to my two witnesses, and they will prophesy one thousand two hundred and sixty days, clothed in sackcloth.' These are the two olive trees and the two lampstands standing before the God of the earth. And if anyone wants to harm them, fire proceeds from their mouth and devours their enemies. And if anyone wants to harm them, he must be killed in this manner. These have power to shut heaven, so that no rain falls in the days of their prophecy; and they have power over waters to turn them to blood, and to strike the earth with all plagues, as often as they desire."

Dominic's hands began to shake violently. He dropped the Bible in his lap and shouted hallelujah as he threw his arms in the air. He vainly thought that he and Immanuel were the two witnesses. He was the world's spiritual leader. Immanuel would be the world's leader. Had he read the verses in context, his joy would have quickly wilted. However, truth didn't matter to Dominic—or Blasphemy. They were the perfect couple.

They would have the power force of God behind them! He would be able to perform miracles, dreamed Dominic.

A swift look at the clock brought him out of his seat. He needed a private meeting with Immanuel.

"We will turn the world upside down with this kind of power!" spouted Dominic. "I will be like God!"

———

News shows from around the globe were singing the praises of Immanuel's plans. Opinion polls found Immanuel to be a magnetic personality, with approval ratings of 95 percent. That number sent shock waves through the leaders who wanted to hold on to their power. A few came forward to protest, making accusations of conspiracies and cover-ups. The media had no tolerance for such individuals.

The elitists in the media were in their own glory. Liberal political policies were masked as conservative, commonsense solutions. People shouldn't turn to God, but to government, for the help they needed. Socialism was caring. Truth was relative. God was whatever or whoever you wanted Him to be. Immanuel's slick sales message was blaring from every demon roaming the earth.

Television stations agreed to suspend normal operations for six days, in an all-out effort to facilitate the new behemoth government. They knew that they were in a position to help change attitudes, which, in turn, changed governments. Times were too critical for showing both sides of the story. They would show only the side that mattered to bring the world together.

Ken Action had his feet propped up on his desk. His eyes were glued to the entertainment center housing sixteen television sets. He could monitor world opinion as it was displayed on the network newscasts from every major country in the world.

He was watching the news shows from America, Europe, and the Orient, the key areas that Immanuel had asked him to target. He was amazed at the common thread of reason that was being woven among the communities of the world. A newscast in Europe was sounding strangely similar to its distant cousins in America. Historically, attitudes about government, and life in general, had separated cultures into warring factions. Today, they were miraculously coming together. With different religions dotting the earth like measles on a child, Ken was shocked at the global agreement.

Ken glanced away from the barrage of smiling newscasters. He noticed a red light blinking on his phone.

"Yeah, what is it?" answered Ken.

"Do you have a second?" asked Tina Marie. "I have something to discuss with you."

He quickly pulled his feet off the desk and placed them back into their proper position.

"Fine," smiled the lady-killer.

He opened his desk and grabbed a small tin tube from underneath a note pad. He blasted two squirts of the breath freshener into his mouth. A nanosecond later, Tina walked through the double doors. She was dressed in a long, flowing, flowery dress. She was nervous as she took a seat. Ken's executive secretary managed to make eye contact. She wasn't being flirtatious, but she was being extra friendly.

Ken leaned back into his chair and grinned from ear to ear. He waited for her to speak. "Let her do a little squirming," he thought.

"Um, you mentioned wanting to be shown around town. Um, I'd be happy to do that."

Her tone sounded conditional.

"Before we go, I want to tell you again that I am not 'that' kind of girl!"

Ken played dumb.

"I'm not sure I understand?"

Tina blushed.

"Never mind. Come on. I'll show you around." The fly picked up her purse and exited, as the spider, wearing a smug look, followed her.

———————

A plume of black smoke towered out of Shenandoah National Park. The Virginia mountainside was littered with twisted debris from an Air Force plane. Hundreds of rescue workers were on the scene, picking through the strewn wreckage, praying to find survivors amid the torn metal. A few wildfires were hopscotching from hill to hill, as a valley wind began to kick into full gear.

The Federal Bureau of Investigation had dispatched dozens of forensic experts. The crash was less than three hours old, and the rancid smell of burnt flesh assaulted their senses.

Media from Washington's four news stations were already on the scene, choosing the most gruesome pictures to send to the viewers back home.

The National Security Advisor and the Assistant Treasurer were shocked. Both Jim and Bill felt their hearts drop into their stomachs as they listened to the grizzly facts coming from the television. It wasn't the blood or guts, but the political implication of one dead man. The television station was broadcasting aerial shots of the disintegrated plane that had been designed to carry high ranking politicians and military officials. A broadcaster's monotone voice gave the details.

"What we know right now is that eighteen people were on this Air Force jet, including the former Secretary of the Treasury. You may recall that President Colt had fired him for, quote, 'A dereliction of duty that could compromise the American economy.' When he was asked what he meant by that statement, President Colt said that the information regarding his firing could compromise, and, I quote, 'A serious breach of national security,' unquote."

Jim's hand was shaking as he reached for some water.

"As you can see," continued the news reader, "the plane exploded on impact, which apparently caused that thirty-foot crater. There must be tens of thousands of pieces of that plane over a five-square-mile area."

The veteran anchor hesitated, a sign that he was receiving additional details from a producer.

Bill and Jim waited, hoping they were not going to hear what their hearts already knew.

"I have just received this report from the Director of the FBI. There are no survivors!"

———————

At ground zero, Bubba Davis was running around the crash scene, desperately trying to get somebody's attention. Bubba, a homegrown mountain boy, was as tall as a tree. He easily weighed as much as a farm tractor. A high school dropout who worked on the family farm, he never forgot his father's favorite country saying: "When the going gets rough, it's better to be with an uneducated, commonsense kind of folk than an educated fool." The political population of Washington, D.C., was his father's prime example.

Though Bubba had a slight problem with stuttering, his mind was sharp. He spotted five men with orange FBI jackets.

"Sirs, misters, I...I...saw what happened! I...I seen it all! I...I can...can help!" he said, approaching the men.

The city men glanced over their shoulders, then turned back into their huddle.

Bubba picked up his speed, thinking that they were hard of hearing.

Suddenly, a startled investigator took Bubba's sprint as aggressive and drew his laser gun.

"Hold it right there, boy," said the agent.

He skidded to a screeching halt and stopped within spitting distance of the government police.

The country boy's tongue rapidly tied into a knot. "I...I...I...can...can help! I...I..." endlessly stuttered the shaken witness.

The national policeman laughed in the rudest of ways.

"Why don't you help all of us out by getting us some coffee."

Bubba smiled out of politeness but ignored the request.

"I...I was videotaping some birds when...when the plane blew up in the air!"

Their laughter cooled to a low rumble.

"You have film of the plane blowing up?" asked the agent.

"Yes, yes, sir! I have the camera back at my pickup. My family is guarding it for me."

The federal agents were enthused but cautious. One of the men radioed a message to the makeshift headquarters at the base of the mountain.

"Headquarters, I have an eyewitness who says he has a videotape of the crash. Planning on further investigation, out," transmitted the investigator.

As he placed the satellite communication device back in his vest, the commander of the operation barked at a fellow agent.

"Steve, go get the tape. Don't stop to look at it. You understand what I'm saying?"

Steve seemed irritated.

"But, sir, I—"

The commander promptly cut him off.

"What you don't know now will keep you alive." The agent had seen that look on his boss's face before. He obeyed without another word.

The commander turned to his team of detectives. "Take all persons involved into custody." He looked at Bubba.

Bubba wasn't stupid. He panicked as the men attempted to frisk him.

"I...I...didn't do...do anything wrong! I tried to...to help!"

An agent placed a red laser directly between his eyes.

"Get on your knees, and place both hands on top of your head, now!"

Bubba felt betrayed but obeyed. The five men called for backup support as they prepared to take the rest of his family in.

"Where's your truck, boy?" questioned the lead Fed.

Bubba was feeling faint.

"What do you want?" asked the president.

Immanuel, who had had only two hours of sleep in the past three days, was still as alert as a rattlesnake.

"It's time for your country to merge with the World Federation!"

Immanuel's eyes seemed to dissect every atom in President Colt.

The president squirmed in his seat. He feared Immanuel.

"I plan to keep my side of the bargain," said the president. "I'm sure that you are planning to do the same?"

"Are you suggesting that I may back out of my word?" questioned the Antichrist.

The president backtracked.

"Not at all! It's just that I love my country, and I want the best for it. My being a vice president of the world should ensure America's fair share of influence in world matters."

"What you love is power," Immanuel snapped back.

The president bit his tongue. He was no longer in control.

"We're printing money like there is no tomorrow. Hyperinflation should be only days away. Public opinion is firmly on our side," offered the president as assurance of his cooperation.

This was music to Immanuel's ears. The country that had put up the greatest obstacles to world dictators in the past two hundred years was about to be tamed. The great eagle was about to be willingly caged and defeathered.

"What are your spin doctors saying?" asked Immanuel.

The president tilted his head back and forth as if he were waffling. Immanuel ignored the trivial gesture.

"Will the public accept a transfer of the military into World Federation control?" interrogated the Antichrist.

The president gritted his teeth.

"If we can control the media spin, then absolutely! If not, we will need to do it in stages."

Immanuel's sinister smile appeared.

"I prefer the quick and painless approach," reminded the globalist. Now, how about the tax issue?"

"What tax issue?" asked the president.

He was caught completely unprepared.

"You heard my speech. The World Federation can't run properly unless it has the money. Each sponsor country must agree to transfer its tax base over to the world system."

Immanuel's point made sense, but the president didn't like surprises. Colt massaged the back of his neck, desperately trying to relieve the pain that had suddenly appeared.

"I don't think the press will buy that one," said the president.

The Antichrist remained calm and collected. His hands were neatly placed on the table as if he were about to pick up a fork and have dinner. Sadly for Americans, the sovereignty of the United States was his appetizer.

"I think the citizens of the U.S. will cooperate," announced Immanuel. "When the dollar goes down the drain, and your currency has been transferred into ECUs, I will agree to completely forgive your astronomical debt. Your crisis will be over only if you agree to join us!"

"We'd be fools to refuse such a generous offer," said the president, barely feigning enthusiasm.

Immanuel took a treaty out of his briefcase. He passed it across the table. "I'm glad you've seen the light," he said, pretending to care. The president signed the treaty.

Immanuel stood to leave. He had received what he came for.

"One of my assistants will be in touch with you in the next several days to iron out the details," finalized the Antichrist.

President Colt tried to keep Immanuel's attention.

"And the vice presidency?" reminded the insecure American.

The Antichrist turned his way as he opened the oval office door.

"It's yours, Vice President Colt. You'll be one of two hundred vice presidents that the World Constitution will allow."

President Colt was incredulous.

"What do you mean two hundred?"

"You shouldn't have assumed that the world constitution would be like America's. I think we can all agree that your system of checks and balances has failed miserably. The leader of each country that immediately signs up will automatically be given the post of vice president. In the future, you may want to read the fine print before signing such an important document. The limited powers of your post are all discussed in detail."

Immanuel snickered.

"You always find the Devil in the details," bragged the Antichrist as he slammed the door shut.

––––––––––

Bubba, along with his two brothers and sister, were handcuffed and cramped in the corner of an FBI truck. It was a mobile crime unit with the latest state-of-the-art technology. The only witnesses to the crash were on their knees, and had been threatened with torture if they got out of line.

The assistant director of the new FBI watched their videotape. He was not a man to mess with. During the latest civil war, government agents were instructed to use brutal techniques on criminals. The new, relaxed rules had pleased the assistant director and turned him into a murderous warlord. He was credited and applauded for brutally executing over one hundred leaders of the constitutionalist movement, and all this with the stamp of approval of the United States government.

He watched the plane blow up on Bubba's videotape. "What we have here is a small difference of opinion," he casually commented.

He pushed the off button on the television and slowly made his way over to the hostages.

"You didn't really see that plane blow up in the air, did you?" asked the assistant director, a little too close for comfort.

Bubba was shaking. He looked at his brothers and then his sister. He was more distressed than at any other time of his life.

"Sir, I...I can't lie! It blew up a few hundred feet a...above the air! You just saw it on my...my tape!" stammered the farm boy.

The assistant director cocked his foot back into the air and then slammed it into Bubba's gut. The power behind his boots sent Bubba into convulsions.

"No!" screamed his sister. "Why are you hurting him? He didn't do anything wrong!"

The Fed ignored her plea, and he continued to pound Bubba's stomach until blood spurted from his quivering lips. His two younger brothers tried to run. A heavily armed Fed was just outside the van. He heard the ruckus and rushed in. A round of shots could be heard. When the smoke cleared, four teenagers from the mountains of Virginia were dead. It would have taken an act of God for this story to make the nightly news.

"President Colt announced today that the United States will be signing up for full membership in the World Federation. His press secretary has informed the Global News Network that America's decision was based on the long held dream of a world ruled by a government in tune with the wishes of the people. The news spread like wildfire through Capitol Hill, with much of congress saying very little. The conditions of the agreement are sketchy, but here is what we know right now," reported the anchor. "The financial crisis that has caused the stock market to collapse and the bond market to melt would end by having America trade in her dollars for the ECU, the currency that is traded in the United States of Europe. Immanuel Bernstate, the spokesman for the World Federation and the candidate for its presidency, has confirmed his willingness to forgive most of the United States' multitrillion dollar debt. In short, our entrance into the World Federation would pay huge dividends for almost every American. The only losers would be the rich, who would be forced to hand over their Treasury bills without getting their principal back."

The anchor seemed pleased.

"The president has agreed to enlist our armed forces into the World Federation's peacekeeping forces. No other details have been given, but a source close to the president has confided to the GNN that the president believes this is the best step to take for a United States that is deep in debt and cannot maintain its forces, and for a world deep in turmoil. In short, NATO and the United Nations will be expanded to cover the entire globe. A new GNN insta-poll says that a vast majority of patriotic Americans favor the concept of the World Federation, by a ten-to-one margin."

Her eyes dropped away from the camera. A message in her earpiece seemed to upset her. She stumbled over herself for a moment, then regrouped.

"This just in. A major earthquake has hit Japan. The magnitude was registered at 9.2 on the Richter scale. The center of the earthquake was located only six miles from downtown Tokyo. There are initial reports of collapsed buildings, including skyscrapers. We have no further information at this time, but Immanuel Bernstate from the World Federation has just been quoted as saying, 'An earthquake of this magnitude would not only destroy the city of Tokyo, but the entire Japanese economy.'"

The National Security Advisor and the second in command at the Treasury walked quickly out of the office and down the long, nineteenth-century hallway. They said nothing as they turned a corner and raced down a set of stairs. As they walked outside into the sunlight, they felt more comfortable discussing their plan.

"Where do we go?" asked Jim.

Bill looked at him and shrugged his shoulders. It was terribly clear that the president of the United States, their boss, was a traitor, and most likely a murderer. Jim wisely decided to keep his mouth shut until he was sure that no one was listening. His car was only fifty yards away. "We will have refuge there," thought Jim.

As the men reached the oversized car, both cautiously looked inside.

"What are we doing?" mouthed Jim. "If somebody was really going to get rid of us, it certainly wouldn't be low tech."

Bill stared at the lock on the car door.

"Really? I'm not sure. Anything's possible now," he muttered.

Jim couldn't believe he was having this conversation. What had happened to the America he grew up in? What happened to the Pledge of Allegiance? The joys of their pasts were now haunting memories.

"So, the door, are we going to try it?" asked Bill.

Jim was shaking the keys in his right hand, weighing the options. He placed the key in the door lock, held his breath, and slowly turned it clockwise.

Lord Birmingham clenched his teeth. He had just received the distressing news that someone had stolen the elk's head with its priceless tablets, as well as the ark and its contents. He was in no mood to meet with the most likely suspect. His eyes were fixated on the life-sized portrait of his great-grandfather. Would he have been proud of his great-grandson? pondered the banker. What would his idol think of Immanuel Bernstate? He put his thoughts on hold as he put on his best face for Immanuel. He was sure that the miracle man would have plenty of gifts, promises, strings, and threats to offer. Lord Birmingham looked down at his manicured nails, wondering what it would be like to work for a living. Physical labor was a cakewalk compared to the pressures of being around Immanuel Bernstate, rationalized the European.

A five-inch monitor broke the news. A man was staring directly into Lord Birmingham's security device. He could feel the power of his stare. Lord Birmingham didn't want to push the security button.

"Lord Birmingham, I don't have time to stand out here and waste time," sounded off the Antichrist.

Lord Birmingham opened the door. Immanuel sauntered in beaming from ear to ear, giving Birmingham cause for concern.

Ten

A Morality Void of God

P eace had completely covered the earth, yet the hearts of men remained evil. It was a manufactured peace, forced upon the people of the world by the iron claw of the World Federation. It was like spraying disinfectant on a decaying corpse. For a season, the rank odor would be covered by the pleasant smell. However, as time ticked away, the power and stench of death would overwhelm the man-made perfume. Immanuel had simply covered over the factions that divided men. The angels knew peace could never reign until the hearts of men were pure.

During the past fifty weeks, Immanuel's plan had been working without a hitch, at least publicly. Every nation had signed up into the world body, some happily, some begrudgingly. President Colt remained in the White House as the World Federation's vice president of American Affairs. Three of the ten leaders of the United States of Europe did balk. They were the first challenge to Immanuel's new world order. Each of these men wound up paying a hefty price for their insubordination. He destroyed them with a small but deadly weapon: the television sound bite. The media allowed Immanuel to smear each of the rebel's good names with lies. The false allegations sank each of the once-popular politicians. The power and prestige of a media controlled by the World Federation drowned their voices out. Had they read the seventh chapter of the book of Daniel in their Bibles, they would have seen this coming:

"After this I saw in the night visions, and behold, a fourth beast, dreadful and terrible, exceedingly strong. It had huge iron teeth; it was devouring, breaking in pieces, and trampling the residue with its feet. It was different from all the beasts that were before it, and it had ten horns. I was considering the horns, and there was another horn, a little one, coming up among them, before whom three of the first horns were plucked out by the roots. And there, in this horn, were eyes like the eyes of a man, and a mouth speaking pompous words."

Japan was another nation that had concerned Immanuel, but the earth-shattering earthquake in Tokyo had been the catalyst that had brought the small Asian country under submission. The quake was the worst natural disaster of modern times. The human impact had been devastating, with over half a million people losing their lives. Almost every structure within thirty miles of the epicenter had been demolished. The value of the real estate that had been destroyed was in the tens of trillions of dollars. The banks had always been bedfellows with the real estate market, so that when Tokyo fell, so did the banking and insurance industries. It was the perfect time for Immanuel to persuade the Japanese people to join the World Federation.

The one country that had offered the most significant impediment to the Antichrist's world government was China. Threats bounced off them like straw arrows, and propaganda was useless. Their economy had remained relatively untouched by the international depression. There was nothing that Immanuel could use to force the Chinese into his camp. He had no choice but to cut a deal with the ruthless and independent communist government. They joined the Federation, but only on paper.

The details of the deal were never made public. China was to receive all the benefits of participation in the World Federation if they promised to refrain from crossing any national boundaries. For that agreement, they were given billions of dollars in aid, a favorable currency exchange into ECUs, and Immanuel's guarantee that they would not be subjected to the World Federation's tax system. The Antichrist also agreed to allow the Chinese government to violate any rights of their citizens that they deemed necessary in order to subjugate them. Chinese citizens were denied access to satellite dishes, so that they would be kept in the dark about world affairs. In fact, anybody caught with one would be immediately put to death. Immanuel looked upon their system of injustice without even batting an eye.

The Global News Network, which was now the powerhouse in world news, simply repeated the World Federation's spin. Whether it was politics, economics, or morality, they toed Immanuel's line. One could liken Immanuel to the head of a poisonous serpent, and GNN as its mouth. The economic collapse from the previous year had silenced almost every other news outlet. When companies didn't have extra money to spend on advertising their products, these television stations had no source of revenue.

Without precious advertising dollars, most stations had been forced to close up shop. They simply went bankrupt, leaving the GNN, financed by Lord Birmingham, as the sole distributor of the World Federation's propaganda. It was the ideal opportunity for a world dictator to get out his brand of news without letting a simple obstacle, like the truth, stand in the way.

Technology had advanced beyond comprehension. Every phone in the world was bugged by a central computer network. The advances in science had placed a great deal of destructive power into the hands of a few. Immanuel had taken control of the nuclear weaponry; at least he hoped he had, because he found it difficult to control the spread of homemade devices.

The World Federation also boasted of its state-of-the-art planetary police force. Every local and national police unit was put under its direct control. The standard definition of a crime was written to include any act, voice, or thought that would hinder or impede the long-range plans of the Federation. Immanuel justified this dictatorial doctrine as a necessary evil to battle an even greater evil, which was world terrorism. He convinced his world subjects that what they lacked in freedom was a small price to pay for their continued safety.

During the height of the depression, the unemployment rate soared to 50 percent worldwide. To offset this, Immanuel ordered that every citizen be given a job working for the World Federation. It was a global job handout, similar to Roosevelt's New Deal policies of the 1930s. Five hundred million were recruited into the planetary police patrol. Five hundred million were assigned to an environmental cleanup force. An additional one billion were given jobs in the middle levels of the bureaucracy, so that the government could keep track of every individual on the planet. Each of these individuals was assigned a group of people to "protect." Immanuel's spin was that these monitors were assigned to people to act as their companions in times of need, want, or trouble. The additional billion people out of work were given jobs in manufacturing, construction, farming, and anything else that Immanuel and his elitists could dream up. The world economy no longer had open and free competition. The divisions that created competition had been wiped away. The grand result was a political Christmas for the World Federation. The people were left with a system that would feed them, clothe them, and treat them when they were sick. The new world order was a smashing success.

A central computer system, which was called the Beast, controlled the cashless currency system that had replaced paper money. Everyone had money in his account. It wasn't based on any tangible assets, but on microscopic computer blips. The problem was not money, but products to buy with it. Supplies at local stores were meager. Food was especially scarce in many parts of Immanuel's kingdom. The more people that the Federation hired, the less work was done.

The day that the World Federation officially obtained power brought more than a few surprises. Immanuel immediately ushered in a new calendar to mark this historic change. The Judeo-Christian calendar was replaced with the World Federation's timetable, which began at day one, year one. The laws of the world, which had been roughly based on the Ten Commandments, were junked.

Immanuel instituted the Ten Commandments of the World Federation. They were: "You shall not have any other allegiances than those of the World Federation. You shall not make with your hands anything that would profane or disrepute the new world order. You shall not take Immanuel's name in vain, nor shall you speak evil of the World Federation. You shall observe every day as a day to further the goals and objectives of your global leadership. Honor your local officials as a merciful arm of the World Federation. You shall not murder any citizen who has an active membership in the world community. You shall not have sexual relations unless you have made arrangements for birth control. You shall not take your neighbors' goods unless you are needy. You shall not lie unless you are trying to save the feelings of another. If you want your neighbor's wealth, you shall turn to your government to equalize the inequities of the world's resources."

Membership in the World Church was strongly encouraged. Those who did not attend the services of a locally approved Earth Church were considered third-class citizens. Church services reminded one of political rallies. The belief was promoted that everybody was a god and had godlike qualities. Dominic had also managed to persuade Immanuel to tithe to the Earth Church. Ten percent of the taxes were diverted to Dominic's beast of burden. The False Prophet promised spiritual, emotional, and psychological healing of the world's citizens. He guaranteed Immanuel that he and his church would produce the fruit that the Antichrist coveted. That evil fruit was the theology that every citizen of the world would look toward the Antichrist's government for their well-being.

Dominic's pact with the ruthlessly seductive leader was on shaky ground. Immanuel would prefer to lose his mother's love than part with his 10 percent of the pie. Those trillions could have been used to build up Immanuel's peaceful military. It was an abomination in Immanuel's eyes to give anybody a tithe of his bounty. The man of sin hated any religion that didn't have him as the sole savior of the world. He decided to allow Dominic to spread his religion as long as it served his vested interests.

A battered cross stood in a remote valley deep in the Idaho mountains. The April sun crept over the snow-covered mountain range. As it met the broken cross, an elongated shadow reached to the edge of the opposite mountain. Most locals called this God's country. It was one of the few spots in the world where the earth touched the heavens.

An underground group of what the World Feds called renegades were gathering in a cave nearby. People from as far as Spokane, Butte, and Idaho Springs had heard of the meeting through word of mouth. Any other means of communication were too risky. Electronic communications, such as the telephone, facsimile, or computer, were being monitored twenty-four hours a day by Immanuel's thought police.

These devout Christians who had gathered were serious about their commitment to God. They had been converted by reading the Holy Scriptures. Bill Thomas and Jim Smith were the ringleaders. Both had had godly families who were snatched up in the Rapture of the church. Before the Christians of the world were transported into heaven, Jim and Bill had been "fence sitters" about Christianity. They had attended church on most Sundays as long as something better didn't come along. They had occasionally scanned the Scriptures, and when times got tough, they would pray. They had been lukewarm in their faith, choosing to concentrate on the things of this world rather than the things of the next.

They found their escape from Washington to be easy, almost too easy. As they ate their evening meal in a quiet Chicago diner, they planned their next moves. A thief had had the misfortune of choosing their car to steal after they had arrived in Chicago. When he had put his foot on the gas, the car had exploded; it was reduced to a ball of flames in just seconds. President Colt thought that Bill and Jim were dead. They wisely did nothing to convince him otherwise.

"I would like to bring this meeting to order," announced Jim Smith, the former National Security Advisor.

He looked around the dimly lit cave with love in his heart. These people were his new family. A lump formed in his throat as he addressed the crowd.

"First, I would like to tell you all what you have meant to me. When the Lord took our loved ones last year, I had foolishly thought that I would never see my family again. Now I know that I will see my wife and children someday soon in heaven."

The Christians applauded.

"Before I continue, I would like to turn the floor over to my good friend Bill Thomas, who will brief us on our plan of action."

Bill graciously shook Jim's hand as both men stared at each other with admiration. They had gone through hell to get to heaven. Bill watched Jim take a seat on a rock near the front of the company.

"As most of you know, the Beast of the book of Revelation has made itself a secure home on our planet during the past year. I know that most of us here today are upset with ourselves. If only we had accepted Jesus' healing message earlier in life. If only we had put our pride aside and come to the Cross before the Rapture. But now we have to pay that price. The Antichrist wants us dead!"

Bill didn't cause a feather to ruffle. The flock was at peace with their destiny. Their minds were on heaven. Although their eyes were on Bill Thomas, their hearts were knitted to the Lord.

"We need a vision, a plan of action, that we can turn to when the Beast comes to devour us. Should we sit back and wait for the inevitable and be sent to the atom chambers like sheep to the slaughter? Should we fight fire with fire, and wield our swords and fight for what we believe in? Some have suggested that we infiltrate the enemy's defenses, but what would our strategy be once we make it into that darkness?"

He was unsure of the leading they should follow, and he hoped for some divine guidance. One could hear the water from melted snow seep through the caverns of the cave. The sound of the pure water filtering through God's earth was refreshing and relaxing. A hand in the back of the cave slowly raised, hoping to be recognized. He spotted the timid, elderly lady within seconds.

"Please stand," waved Bill.

"We have to do the right thing," vented the seventy-year-old woman. "I've lived a long life, and I've seen so many people do so many things terribly wrong, all for the right reasons. I've done stupid things in my past, which is probably one reason why I am here speaking to you today instead of being in heaven with most of my family. I know that I'm rambling on like an old lady, but I do have something to say about this predicament of ours. The Bible says in Ephesians that our fight is not with flesh and blood, but against the principalities and powers of this dark world. We are fighting the Devil, not the World Federation! I believe the best way to fight this Beast is through prayer. We should never raise the sword. Don't you remember that Peter cut off one of the guard's ears when they came after Jesus? Christ condemned his action, and He will condemn ours if we don't follow His will in our lives."

Bill was speechless. He had no doubt that she was right on target with her condemnation of violence, yet he was still searching.

"I would like to take a quick vote for those who side with this sister."

Bill was the first to raise his hand. Everybody unanimously followed his lead.

"How about infiltrating the World Federation? Do you believe the Lord would have us spy on them and possibly try to destroy them from the inside out?" wondered Bill.

The old woman didn't even hesitate with her reply.

"Let's send off missionaries to key areas in the country and maybe around the globe. Assign them to particular people who may have influence. Pray that God will keep them safe. He will not send us into battle without the armor we need to win the war."

The aged lady took a seat. Applause rang out from the musty cavern. Many seconds later, the Christian stalwarts settled down. All eyes were back on their leader.

"You are to be commended for your insight and humble walk before our Lord," commended Bill.

The mature woman shook her head. She appeared slightly annoyed.

"Don't say all those nice things about me. Say them about the Lord. He gives me my inspiration!" chided the woman.

"You're right again," admitted Bill who was embarrassed. "Here is what I would like to do. The main headquarters of the World Federation is located in Geneva, Switzerland. I would like to place 25 percent of the volunteers into the heart of the Beast. I would also like to place another 25 percent in Rome, which is the center of worship for the Earth Church. The other half should scatter themselves through the more influential city centers of the world. Our goal is to convert people to Christ. I warn you that this could be extremely dangerous! Be as wise as a serpent and as gentle as a dove. Don't be surprised to see the Antichrist perform miraculous signs and wonders. Remember that the Bible teaches that the Devil has the ability to perform all kinds of deceiving miracles. Be on guard!"

Bill paused to open his Bible. He opened to 2 Thessalonians 2:7 and started to read:

"'For the mystery of lawlessness is already at work; only He who now restrains will do so until He is taken out of the way. And then the lawless one will be revealed, whom the Lord will consume with the breath of His mouth and destroy with the brightness of His coming. The coming of the lawless one is according to the working of Satan, with all power, signs, and lying wonders, and with all unrighteous deception among those who perish, because they did not receive the love of the truth, that they might be saved. And for this reason God will send them strong delusion, that they should believe the lie, that they all may be condemned who did not believe the truth but had pleasure in unrighteousness.'"

Bill struggled to control his emotions. He placed the Bible against his chest.

"I believe every word that is in this Book. I believe that the 'lawless one' is Immanuel. He will pull this charade off because he will have powers that we can only imagine."

Bill walked into the middle of the group. He wanted to be face-to-face with as many people as possible.

"Don't be fooled. The world will buy his lie, and it will cost them their souls!"

Immanuel rolled his fingers against his marble desk. It was a nervous habit that he had developed during his days in the banking industry. The Antichrist's normal routine was as predictable as the sunset. If an individual failed to perform his duties for him, he was called into his office for disciplinary action. Immanuel would tap each of his fingers against his desk in rapid succession. He would stare at his hand until he was ready to pounce on his prey. The emperor of the earth patiently awaited Ken's arrival. The regeneration of the Christian church gnawed at his security. A soft knock on the door interrupted him.

"What?" uttered Immanuel in an eerie, soft tone.

"Ken Action is here," observed Immanuel's executive secretary.

"Send him in."

His mood sent shivers up and down her spine. Something was terribly wrong. His media manager walked through the door with sweat streaming down his forehead. Immanuel smiled.

"Mr. Action, come in and have a seat. I have a bone to pick with you."

Ken knew that he was in deep trouble.

"Yes, sir. I'm sorry I couldn't get here sooner. The elevator would have taken a couple of minutes to catch, so I took the stairs instead."

Immanuel didn't act on Ken's statement. He knew that Ken was craving a compliment for his physical gesture of allegiance.

"I wonder," began Immanuel as he looked at his fingers caressing the desk. "Why did I hire you?"

Ken was taken aback by his boss's inquiry. He knew he had to handle this correctly.

"Sir, you hired me to make you look good. I work day and night to further your power base. My complete loyalty is to you. You are like a god to me!"

He sounded sincere in his candy-coated reply. Immanuel's eyes were welded to his desk. The only emotion that he showed was in the hypnotizing motion of his flowing fingers.

"Did you know that there is a worldwide rebellion now occurring against my regime?" tested the Antichrist.

"I...I...w...wasn't aware—"

Immanuel interrupted Ken's stammering.

"What shocks me, Ken, is that you aren't aware of this critical matter."

His fingers began to tap the desk more violently.

"I have a revolution in my kingdom that could affect the security and well-being of every man, woman, and child."

Ken knew when to keep his mouth shut. Immanuel's fingers increased the speed of their assault on the stone fixture.

"You have let me down. You have let down every person on the face of the earth who wants to live in a world free from religious fanatics who cause pain and suffering. What do you think I should do about this?"

Ken didn't know if that was a question for him to answer.

"Sir, I have not taken my job seriously enough. I have allowed this critical information to slip through the cracks. I offer no excuse. I can only plead for your forgiveness, and pray that I will be allowed to stay under your wings to learn from the master himself."

Immanuel's fingers paused from their activity. His eyes shifted upward.

"Get on this immediately! I want the media to exploit these freaks as antagonists of the state. If you don't nip this in the bud, I'll be forced to remove some of those distractions that seem to be keeping you from doing your job."

"Distractions? Sir, there are no—"

"Tina Marie," interrupted Immanuel.

Ken was unpleasantly surprised.

"Yes, I know about Tina Marie," Immanuel smirked. "I even know about Sally Winter. I know that she was one of them. I hope your heart is in this because I don't take kindly to misplaced loyalties."

Ken was slowly backing away from this ruthless despot when he heard a sudden, loud crash. A six-foot statue of the sun god Ra had crumbled into a million pieces, only a foot from his feet. His eyes traveled from the shattered stone deity to the god in the Armani suit.

Ken looked at Immanuel, and then at the mess surrounding his feet. He was positive that the million dollar idol had been thirty feet across the room. How in the world did it get beside him?

"Did you...?" delved Ken.

Part of him didn't want to know. Ignorance was certainly bliss in this instance.

"Mr. Action, I could destroy you without raising a hand. Don't test me, or you could get burned, badly!"

Ken lowered his head and dropped his eyes to the ground.

"Yes, sir!" acknowledged Ken as he quickly exited the room.

Blasphemy winked at the demon who had done his dirty work for him. He glided over to Immanuel and took a seat on the top of his computer terminal.

"Soon, we will be performing signs and wonders to the entire world," bragged Blasphemy.

Immanuel's eyes looked as if they were blind.

"When?" interrogated the Antichrist.

Blasphemy didn't take kindly to the coarseness of his tone.

"When I say so, human," retaliated Blasphemy.

———————

"Do it, now!" yelled Timothy as he pushed Daniel toward the modest Swiss chalet.

"You're going to get me zapped into a billion atoms if you don't watch it!" whined Daniel.

It was his first expedition into enemy territory. His mission was to gather troop data on the adversary's home turf and bring it back to Timothy. Hopefully, he would come back in one piece.

"Listen, angel, Tina Marie is on the verge of making the most important decision of her life," lectured Timothy. "She needs our help to clear those cobwebs out of her mind. Satan's servants have her mind all tangled up. It is your responsibility to clear the air for her. Find out where their weaknesses are. Once you do that, I will get us the soldiers we need to bomb them back into the pit. The archangel Michael puts the Christian population at over ten million, and a hundred thousand are added every day. We now have the power we need to make selective strikes all over the globe!"

Daniel was not convinced. His last memorable encounter with Satan's snakes had left a lasting impression on his mind and a dent in his head.

"I thought that we were a team," defended Daniel. "If I were to get captured by the enemy, what would you do?"

Timothy smiled as he shook his head.

"I didn't want to tell you this, but I have backup support just in case you get stuck in a hole. I would have preferred not to have told you. I was just testing your bravery."

Daniel was embarrassed at his cowardice. He took an erratic plunge off the side of a telephone pole. Just before he reached the pavement, he spread his wings and quickly rocketed toward Tina Marie's house.

"Be discreet!" shouted Timothy as Daniel disappeared in the distance.

———————

Daniel noisily landed in some bushes near Tina Marie's house. From where he was hidden, he could see a large contingent of demons hissing at one another on top of her roof. He picked up a rock and hurled it toward the demon making the loudest boasts. Much to his surprise, the rock pounded the loudmouth squarely between the eyes. The demons scrambled like bees whose nest had just been raided. They took off in all directions, hunting for the spirit who had attacked their stakeout. Daniel didn't have time to laugh. He was horrified as seven or eight evil spirits flashed over his head. He had made a stupid move, and he knew it. He tried to camouflage himself by contorting his body into a tiny ball. Every few seconds brought another demon scanning the ground with its spiritual searchlights on high. Suddenly, he heard a noise from behind him, then all went dark.

A few miles away, Timothy was watching his radar screen with dismay. There were hundreds of devils, some highly armed and dangerous, flying through the full moonlight with reckless abandon. He knew that something big had happened at Tina Marie's. Daniel's friend didn't take any chances.

"Colonel, we have a big problem in sector gamma! I need at least two hundred soldiers and fifty officers. I think Daniel might be in trouble!"

The wireless communication reached its target in less than a second. The rapid response soothed Timothy's frayed nerves.

"You got it! We'll be there in less than a minute! Out," finished the officer.

Timothy wondered what Daniel had done to stir the pot so intensely. He looked toward the battlefield, and became increasingly alarmed when he spotted the entire company of demons swarming around Tina Marie's chimney. He recognized their movements as a tribal war dance. It was reserved for spies, traitors, and intruders.

"Daniel!" cried Timothy.

Daniel regained consciousness, but found himself encircled by crazed demons.

Suddenly, a burst of light exploded all around him. He had no idea what was happening.

"Attention, demons! You have seven seconds to release our soldier!" announced the colonel with a thunderous voice.

The demons were blinded by the light. They had no idea what to do.

"It's an ambush! Every demon for himself!" barked the devil in charge.

The demons fled to the nearby mountainside. Not a sword was drawn.

Inside the chalet, Tina Marie had decided to read her Bible. She had been so self-absorbed in her love affair with Ken that she had forgotten God. She opened her leather Bible and began to read the third chapter of the book of John.

"Jesus declared, 'Most assuredly, I say to you, unless one is born again, he cannot see the kingdom of God.'"

She continued to read, and then reread that text over and over again. She opened her heart to the Creator of the universe. Tears trickled down her face. Hundreds of God's angels stood at her side as she prayed for Jesus Christ to take control of her heart. The stranglehold that Satan had on her life had been ripped apart. Tina Marie opened her eyes and looked around the room. She sensed a peace that transcended understanding.

"This is cause for a celebration, angels! Another lost soul has been found," proclaimed the colonel.

Eleven

Flirting with Disaster

T he prime minister of Israel's eyes lit up. David Hoffman could not believe what he was seeing. Finally, after nearly two thousand years, the Jewish people had a place where they could worship their God in safety and peace.

"I know you never thought you would see the day when the Dome of the Rock would be demolished and your ancient temple rebuilt," exclaimed False Prophet Dominic Rosario.

"I still don't understand how you and Immanuel pulled this off," acknowledged David.

Their eyes gazed upon the stone temple. The eighteen month construction phase was ending today. The crowds, which numbered in the millions, were gathering for the opening ceremonies. There was rampant speculation about the world leaders' favoritism to the Jews. Nobody in his right mind dared to question Immanuel's or Dominic's motives. Political dissension always evolved into some kind of punishment.

Dominic leaned toward the Jewish leader and whispered to him.

"Immanuel would kill me if I told you this," began the religious baron.

The prime minister pulled back to get a good look at the Earth Church's leader. He trusted the Italian less than he would trust the Mafia. For political reasons, he masked his innermost emotions. After all, the rebuilding of the temple was the best thing that ever could have happened to his career. He had Immanuel to thank, though something told him that there would be repercussions in the future.

"Immanuel threatened to outlaw the practice of Islam if they didn't give in to his plans to rebuild the temple," revealed the False Prophet.

"Why would you tell me that after Immanuel swore you to secrecy?" questioned David with a hint of sarcasm.

"Listen, David. I am your friend. As one religious man to another, you must understand that Immanuel has risked life and limb to make sure that Israel thrives in the World Federation. He has given you complete sovereignty over the affairs of your country, which he hasn't done for any other vice president. Immanuel is your friend and ally, and so am I. Do you think that Iran, Iraq, Syria, and Jordan were calling him 'blessed' after he threatened their very way of life?"

"I know that he needed the Middle East's cooperation. I don't understand why they fell over and played dead when he threatened them. It's just not like them."

Dominic quickly changed the subject. Immanuel had given him permission to divulge a morsel of information but not reveal everything.

"Your neighbors will behave themselves! Take a look at the temple mount; isn't it a sight to behold?" pointed Dominic as he changed the subject.

David placed his hand above his eyes. The strength of the sun rendered his sunglasses useless.

"Is Immanuel planning to witness firsthand our form of worship?" asked the prime minister.

"Yes, he is. But I can't speak for the exact date. Today, I stand as his representative to consecrate your altar."

"We welcome your participation in our glorious event. Would you like to join me in the inner sanctuary?"

"Why, of course," reacted Dominic.

The men hurried into their individual limousines, which were parked on the top of the Mount of Olives. The cars slowly maneuvered their way down the snakelike road to the bottom of the holy hill.

As the limousines entered the outer wall, cheers from the crowds could be heard for miles. Television cameras from the Global News Network were everywhere. The cameras followed the men from the ivory gate to the entrance of the inner sanctuary. The top religious correspondent for the GNN, a close friend of Dominic Rosario, provided the commentary.

"The world is certainly witnessing religious history this fine Friday afternoon. The anointed prophet, Dominic Rosario, is on hand to offer the first sacrifice to God in nearly two thousand years. Jews from all over the world are here to share in the spiritual rebirth of the Israeli nation. They have converged on this holy site to thank God for Immanuel Bernstate and Dominic Rosario. The World Federation bankrolled the construction of this exact duplicate of the temple of David and Solomon. Immanuel Bernstate's spokesman, Ken Action, has said that the temple is a symbol of the World Federation's commitment to peace in every part of the earth. Today is the culmination of the peace process that the Federation has been painstakingly pursuing. Leaders from the World Church, as well as dignitaries from the World Federation, are expected to be here. I see Dominic Rosario approaching the altar, along with the newly chosen high priest of Israel. Let us pause to observe the historic events that are being made possible by the good graces of our World Federation."

Dominic, accompanied by a Jewish high priest, slowly made his way to the front of the altar, which was sixty-six feet wide. A hushed awe filled the air as the religious men picked up the golden tool used for lighting the sacrifice.

"God of our fathers, and Supreme Being of the heavens, we pay homage to you today by reinstating the daily sacrifice."

David Hoffman watched from a safe distance. His heart was divided between awe and anxiety.

To the surprise of many, Dominic began to speak to the crowd. The unscripted speech sent the television crew scrambling, and prompted the executive producer to make an emergency phone call to Ken Action.

"Before we offer up the sacrifice, I would like to take this time to explain the significance of this day."

Every eye and ear was cemented to Dominic.

"Christ, Mohammed, Moses, Ghandi, and Confucius were all prophets of God Almighty, and completely turned their worlds around. Today, in this great nation of Israel, we also have the opportunity, thanks to Immanuel and the World Federation, to turn the world around! This temple that towers all around me is not just for the people of Israel, but for all those in the Earth Church! Today marks the day when the great religion of Judaism accepts the Earth Church as its brother, whose objective is the freedom of all men, women, and children to worship God in whatever way that seems right to them!"

The prime minister couldn't believe his ears. He had never agreed to a merger between the apostate Earth Church and his forefathers' religion. This was a direct breach of the verbal contract that he had with Immanuel. What horrified him most was the reaction of his Jewish brothers and sisters. The crowd, which was crammed into the arena, cheered with delight at the False Prophet's cunning words. The high priest dropped his torch and fell to his knees. Immanuel was watching Dominic's treason from his penthouse in Rome. When the high priest bowed to Dominic, Immanuel hit the ceiling. Dominic was stealing his praise.

Dominic accepted the misplaced adoration with open arms. He raised his hands into the air as if to say he was worthy of worship.

"I have received a message from our God!" counterfeited the False Prophet. "God is pleased with our temple. He is overjoyed that the world is now one in mind and spirit. He has informed me that every world religion has worshipped Him, but that they called Him by different names. The Jews were the last people to accept His Church, the Earth Church, as His only begotten Son. The God of the heavens is planning to visit this temple in the not too distant future, and He invites all the world to bow down and worship Him in spirit and truth!"

Dominic reached into his white, flowing robe. He pulled out a pocket-sized book, and began flipping through its pages. Immanuel squinted at the television screen as he tried to make out what was in Dominic's hand. The False Prophet smiled and nodded his head as he found the spot.

"God gave me this verse from His book."

He glanced down at the holy pages, which tended to stick together from lack of use. Dominic cleared his throat.

The Antichrist was fuming as he realized his religious leader was reading from the Bible. Immanuel grabbed the television with both hands, lifted it into the air, and tossed it through his sixth-story window. He let out a frightening growl.

Dominic started to read from the book in his hands.

"In the great and mighty book of Isaiah, God predicted this time in history. I have found this passage from chapter nine. 'For unto us a Child is born, unto us a Son is given; and the government will be upon His shoulder. And His name will be called Wonderful, Counselor, Mighty God, Everlasting Father, Prince of Peace. Of the increase of His government and peace there will be no end, upon the throne of David and over His kingdom, to order and establish it with judgment and justice from that time forward, even forever. The zeal of the LORD of hosts will perform this.'"

Dominic gently placed the open Bible on the edge of the golden altar. He turned to face the crowd, which was hanging onto his every word.

"God has revealed to me that He will come to this throne in Jerusalem and rule the world in person!" said the False Prophet.

The Jews in the crowd looked at each other with joy. The concept of a God that they could see, feel, and hear was foreign to them.

"When He comes, He will continue our program of peace for all the world. The World Federation will be His instrument to use at His will. We have made the world ready for the coming of God on earth. He is well pleased!"

The crowd began to chant, scream, and wail. Pandemonium shattered their peaceful get-together. They wanted to know when God would make His visit. Many began to dance in the overcrowded streets, singing and shouting their praises to God Almighty.

The False Prophet attempted to take control of the rapidly deteriorating situation.

"People of Israel, listen to me. God loves a peaceful people. God hates confusion and disorder. He will not come to establish His home here if He senses a people who don't revere Him."

The crowd immediately settled down. The prime minister loosened his tie. Something deep down inside of him was churning. David Hoffman walked in a casual manner toward the fake prophet and whispered in his ear.

"We never agreed to join the Earth Church! I would like you to meet me in my office when this is finished! Also, I demand that you allow our high priest to make the dedications, since this is a temple for the Jewish people!"

The words were like weapons of war to the False Prophet. Dominic could never allow such blasphemy to go unpunished. Flames of anger shot out from his eyes as he stared at the politician. He spoke in a controlled whisper.

"You owe God much. I am God's spokesman on earth. Israel is God's, not yours! If you even consider crossing me or Immanuel, we will have you executed! God believes in the death penalty, especially for a corrupt politician with the heart of a Pharisee!"

As the noxious words flowed from his lips, he smiled at the startled prime minister. He knew the cameras were rolling, and he would not risk a public relations setback for the likes of a politician who thought he knew God better than Dominic did himself. As a grin settled on Dominic's face, a frown set on David's. A nightmare of biblical proportions was coming true right in the middle of the greatest celebration that Israel had experienced in thousands of years.

"What a paradox," thought the prime minister. The time when he thought he would have the greatest joy in his life was turning out to be the moment when he would experience the greatest pain.

"Your agenda, whatever it may be, will not survive, I assure you," admonished David.

Dominic ignored the rebuke as he repositioned himself at the altar. He grabbed a torch, lit the sacrificial animal, and looked toward the heavens.

"Today, in your city, O God, we recognize you as the God of peace, and the God of the Earth Church. Bless our endeavors to establish your kingdom on earth."

As the animal burned, a billowing cloud quickly formed over the assembly. It was as dark as night, and as foreboding as a nuclear mushroom. Lightning erupted from all around the city as the cloud grew to the troposphere. Thunder shook the ground. Hail, the size of baseballs, pounded down on the golden, charcoaled altar. Still receiving the praise of the crowd, the False Prophet was standing dangerously close to the burning sacrifice. Suddenly, a ball of ice slammed into his shoulder. The crowd, numbed by the awesome display of God, never noticed that he was hit. Everybody's eyes were fixated on the heavens and the storm that resided directly over the temple arena. Dominic pretended that nothing was wrong, though after several seconds, he began to feel faint. He could feel blood begin to soak through his silk garb and wisely decided to take cover. At that very moment, David Hoffman knew that Dominic Rosario was evil with the full power and fury of hell.

Switzerland was beautiful in the spring. It was a time for new life and lasting memories. Tina Marie's eyes matched the elegance of the blue sky. She blushed as Ken whispered into her ears. The lovebirds were relaxing on the hillside, enjoying a weekend retreat away from the pressure of the World Federation. An empty picnic basket was by their side.

"Ken, I know I haven't discussed my conversion to Christianity with you that much, but I want to tell you about somebody from America that I had the chance to meet the other day."

Ken's love for Tina Marie overrode his hatred for Christianity. Her prayers were slowly chipping away at his ingrained hostility.

"You know that whatever is important to you is important to me."

She hoped that he was telling the truth.

"I met a man who claims he was a high-level cabinet appointee of President Colt's back in the States. He was such a gentleman."

Ken's jealousy reared slightly.

"Another man, huh?"

Tina squinted, then frowned. She wasn't sure if he was joking. She snuggled up to her fiancé and gave him a quick kiss on the cheek.

"You know that you are the only man for me. He could have been old enough to be my father! Listen, this man had some very interesting things to say, and I think you should hear him."

Ken wasn't that interested, but he pretended to be.

"He has proof that Immanuel has done some very evil things. He believes that Immanuel is the Antichrist of the Bible!"

Ken's mind began to wander back to the time when Immanuel had played some cruel mind games with him. The vision of that tornado weaving in and out of the room captured Ken's mind.

"I never told you this, Tina, but I had an experience with Immanuel that I would rather forget."

Tina sat straight up.

"I don't know about all this Antichrist stuff, but I can tell you that the man is weird, very weird," confessed Ken.

Tina rubbed his arm as a show of support.

"Why don't you tell me what happened."

"Immanuel has powers," ruptured Ken. "He isn't just a man! He has the ability to make you see things that aren't really there, at least I don't think it was there. I mean it looked real and everything, but it couldn't possibly have been real. It just came down out of the ceiling and stalked the room. It was big and black and threatening! I really thought I was a dead man! Immanuel just sat there and watched me like I was some rat in his cage. It was as if he were experimenting on me!"

Ken knew that he was babbling. The memory of the experience was scorched into his mind. Tina hugged him.

"Ken, what powers does Immanuel have?"

"I'm really not sure. One time, not too long ago, he caused one of his priceless statues in his office to fly across the room."

"You saw it flying?" pried Tina.

"Well, not really. I remember that he was teed off about some religious thing. He took a bite out of me over it. I started backing away, wanting to leave, when I heard a loud crash. A statue that he had in his office moved over thirty feet and then crashed at my feet. I know that Immanuel didn't get up and do it; he never moved. You know, those statues always gave me the creeps anyway. It was like they were watching you, you know, like they were alive!"

Tina listened.

"All I can say is, the man definitely has some kind of special powers. He either made me see something that wasn't there, or he has the power to throw objects with his mind. Maybe he hypnotized me, and none of it was real. I don't know," lamented Ken.

Tina knew this was a perfect opportunity to talk to him.

"Ken, you know the Bible does predict that this Antichrist would control the world, and that he would have miraculous powers that would make everybody think that he is God!"

For the first time in his life, Ken took the Bible as something other than a glorified history book full of fairytales.

"Where does it say that?" wondered Ken.

Tina pulled her purse out from the picnic basket. She dug around inside it and pulled out a pocket Bible. Then she began to cry.

"What's wrong, Tina?" asked Ken.

"I just never thought I would see the day when I could read my Bible without you mocking me."

Tina's warm embrace surrounded Ken. She knew he needed her support and love more than anything else.

"I'm turning to the book of Revelation. It's the last book in the Bible. It's God's prediction for the last seven years on earth. Ken, we are in that seven-year Tribulation, and I think I can prove it to you."

Ken wasn't exactly open to religion, but he loved a good science fiction story. He didn't know that Tina had been praying for him for over a year, and that the angels of heaven were protecting him.

"I remember reading that stuff when I was a kid. I thought that it would make a great movie if somebody could make sense out of it."

"Well, I'm going to try to do that right now. I want to start with chapter thirteen, verse one. 'Then I stood on the sand of the sea. And I saw a beast rising up out of the sea, having seven heads and ten horns, and on his horns ten crowns, and on his heads a blasphemous name.'"

Tina glanced Ken's way. He was staring at the Bible.

"I'm not going to get into the horns, the heads, or the crowns, except that they represent power. The important part of this verse is that they have a blasphemous name, which is a name that curses who God really is. Ken, Immanuel is not your boss's real name. He adopted that name for a reason. Jesus Christ's name in the Bible is Emmanuel. It means 'God with us'! Immanuel will eventually announce to the world that he is God, like he did with you!"

Ken couldn't argue with that.

"'Now the beast which I saw was like a leopard, his feet were like the feet of a bear, and his mouth like the mouth of a lion. The dragon gave him his power, his throne, and great authority.'"

Ken was intently listening.

"Listen to the last part of that verse. 'The dragon gave him his power,'" repeated Tina Marie, with emphasis. "There is a Devil, who is called the dragon in the Bible. Immanuel's power is real, and it comes from the Devil!"

Ken felt as if a tidal wave had just crashed on him.

"Do you believe this?" questioned Ken.

"I do. There's more to life than what we can see. We may not be able to see the Devil, but we can see his effects. It's just like gravity; you can't see it, but you can see its effects. Ken, I see all this stuff happening in the world through the eyes of the Bible. These ancient prophesies are now coming true. You can see it. Open your eyes!"

"I can tell you this. I'll never accept Immanuel as my God. He can sign my paycheck, but I won't bow down and worship him."

"Take a look at this in verse five. 'And he was given a mouth speaking great things and blasphemies, and he was given authority to continue for forty-two months. Then he opened his mouth in blasphemy against God, to blaspheme His name, His tabernacle, and those who dwell in heaven. It was granted to him to make war with the saints and to overcome them. And authority was given him over every tribe, tongue, and nation. All who dwell on the earth will worship him, whose names have not been written in the Book of Life of the Lamb slain from the foundation of the world.'"

She quietly closed the Bible, keeping her finger in it as a bookmark. Another tear streamed down her rosy cheeks.

"Ken, this is the verse that really scares me. For three and a half years, Immanuel will bad-mouth my God, the God who created this beautiful field that we are enjoying. Do you remember when it said that he would make war with the saints?"

Ken nodded his head.

"It means that he is planning on killing every Christian that he can get his hands on. He will control the entire world. Have you noticed his intense hatred for anything Christian?"

Tina's tone was somber. Ken didn't have trouble putting the puzzle together. He now understood why Immanuel had hinted at his loyalty to Sally, and why he had brought up Tina Marie.

"I'm not saying I'm buying all of this, Tina. But I'm listening. I am listening."

Immanuel abhorred the people, religion, and poverty of the Middle East. His eyes peered out of his aircraft's oversized window. The plane was less than fifty feet above the ground when he started watching a group of Muslims gathering for their evening prayer.

"Fools!" snarled the Antichrist as he watched them bow toward the East.

"Your worry betrays your lack of trust in me," said Blasphemy, hovering over Immanuel's seat.

Immanuel had grown tired of Blasphemy. The spirit was becoming more of an annoyance than an asset, yet he feared what he couldn't see.

"I just don't see how they will get their people to stop protesting against the destruction of the Dome of the Rock. Our multibillion dollar payoff bought the politicians, but the majority of the Muslims have been boiling over, day and night, about Israel's temple. I don't think that I can hold the press back much longer. In the past year alone, I have ten thousand dead Jews and Muslims. They're fighting like cats and dogs over this pathetic thing. The GNN has vowed to me that they won't spread the news, but I don't know how long that will last. If this peace goes down in flames, so will our final thrust for power!"

It was the first time that Blasphemy had allowed the Antichrist to finish a thought without interrupting him, but it wasn't intentional. The demon general was watching a host of demons hovering near the cabin of the jet.

"Relax. It will work! I have the orders straight from the top!" soothed the dark demon.

Immanuel ignored the comfort offered. His plane had landed smoothly on the runway; the door opened.

An Arab suddenly appeared inside the cabin. Immanuel forced a smile.

"Abdul Mohammed, it is a pleasure to finally meet you," lied the Antichrist. I have a present for you."

He pointed to a large crated box.

What Abdul didn't know wouldn't hurt him. This "present" was stolen property. Several men had died in the robbery, an acceptable number to Immanuel. Abdul looked at it with curiosity.

"So you say that this will heal all our wounds that you have inflicted on my people?" questioned the Islamic leader.

His abrupt rebuttal caught Immanuel off guard.

"You will be pleased. Do you have a place for us to go to unveil my gift to your people?" asked the Antichrist.

"Ah yes! There is a secret spot below one of our most sacred temples. I take you there now, yes?"

———

It was the dark of night. The moon was on the other side of the Earth, making the evening sky thirst for light. A few lonely stars twinkled through the hazy atmosphere. Jim and Bill had joined forces in Rome. They were in the midst of a private meeting of Christians at a secluded location outside the city center. Nearly two hundred influential people had come to listen to them. All of these Christians were concerned about the future under the World Federation. Many had been personally led to Christianity by the efforts of Jim or Bill.

"Ladies and gentlemen, we must open people's eyes and ears to the truth. This world is under the control of the Devil. Peace is fleeting, and rumors of war are beginning to spread among my contacts all over the earth. The Global News Network is Immanuel's propaganda tool. Don't believe a word they say!"

A spotlight appeared from heaven. Bill looked up, hoping God was sending an angel. Nobody said a word. After a few seconds, the sound of helicopter blades slowly filled the air. Awe turned to dread.

"This is the Global Police Force! Put your hands on top of your heads and hit the dirt! You are all under arrest for treason!"

There was no place to run. They were surrounded by hundreds, perhaps thousands, of World Federation officers. They put their hands on their heads. As the armed mob slowly closed in on them, they quietly dropped to their knees.

"Any quick movement will be taken as an offensive action," said the voice from the air.

As Jim and Bill lay on the ground, they looked at each other with a sense of respect. They had done what the Lord wanted them to do. God was in control.

Ken looked at Tina Marie with admiration. For the first time in his self-centered life, he respected someone more than himself.

"What else did you want to show me from the book of Revelation?"

"Let's keep going in chapter thirteen."

She scanned the page for a moment, then placed her hand in Ken's.

"Here we go. Verse seven reads, 'It was granted to him to make war with the saints and to overcome them. And authority was given him over every tribe, tongue, and nation.' You see, Ken, he doesn't have complete authority, yet! But he will, after he gets rid of his nemesis, which is me and the millions of other Christians dotting the globe."

Ken seemed perplexed.

"Do you really think that he has it in him?" asked Ken.

"The Devil has been trying to kill Christians since the death of Christ. He had Christ killed. In the past two thousand years, history has recorded tens of millions of followers of Christ murdered. It's going to happen again, and it will be soon, very soon!"

Tina was serious. Ken was taken aback by her disposition.

"Immanuel is possessed by the Devil, literally!" continued Tina. "The man is dangerous! Our only hope is in Jesus Christ!"

Ken didn't argue. He began to read verse eleven.

"'Then I saw another beast coming up out of the earth, and he had two horns like a lamb and spoke like a dragon.'"

Ken stopped reading and began to think.

"You know what, Tina? That makes a lot of sense. When Immanuel is in public, he does speak like a lamb. He is always talking peace, but in private, he's evil."

"You're right, except this verse says that this guy is 'another beast.' Someone different, but just as sinister."

Tina was surprised to see that Ken didn't mind being corrected.

"The leader of the Earth Church, Dominic Rosario," she explained. "He is called the False Prophet in the Bible. His job is to make everybody think that Immanuel is exactly what they need, and to bring about a false religious revival. Satan has control over him, also!"

Ken appeared to understand. He continued reading.

"'And he exercises all the authority of the first beast in his presence, and causes the earth and those who dwell in it to worship the first beast, whose deadly wound was healed. He performs great signs, so that he even makes fire come down from heaven on the earth in the sight of men. And he deceives those who dwell on the earth by those signs which he was granted to do in the sight of the beast, telling those who dwell on the earth to make an image to the beast who was wounded by the sword and lived. He was granted power to give breath to the image of the beast, that the image of the beast should both speak and cause as many as would not worship the image of the beast to be killed.' There is the verse where he will kill those who won't follow him, which I assume will be the Christians!" interpreted Ken.

"Yes," said Tina.

"'He causes all, both small and great, rich and poor, free and slave, to receive a mark on their right hand or on their foreheads, and that no one may buy or sell except one who has the mark or the name of the beast, or the number of his name.'"

Ken began to tremble. God was getting to him in a very big way.

"'Here is wisdom. Let him who has understanding calculate the number of the beast, for it is the number of a man: his number is 666.'"

Ken's eyes began to water. He slowly closed the Bible and placed it on the sheet. He looked off into the distance. In his mind, the world around him was crumbling.

"Ken, are you okay?" asked Tina Marie.

Ken's eyes remained fixated on the far-off mountain range.

"Tina Marie, Immanuel has that number engraved in the back side of his desk. I saw it last week when I was reviewing some documents with him. I asked about it and he said that it was his lucky number. He told me that he was the sixth child in his family, that he was born on the sixth month of the year, and on the sixth of that month. He told me that it was the number of perfection."

Ken turned to meet Tina's eyes.

He appeared worn out, as if he had been fighting some mysterious force for years.

"You can trust the Bible! It gave this prophecy nearly two thousand years ago," noted Tina.

Timothy and Daniel were observing the conversation from a large tree some twenty yards away. They had arranged for an ominous shield of angelic warriors to guard their humans. In the guardian angel business, it was called prayer cover.

"What am I going to do now?" exclaimed Ken. "I can't go back to work for him."

"You have a bigger problem, Ken, and it's long-term. When you die, I want you with me in heaven!"

Ken Action lowered his eyes to the ground. It was hard for him to think about heaven when earth was becoming a personal hell.

"Why did God allow this to happen to us? It's hard for me to accept all this, and believe that all I have to do is say a prayer, and that's it."

"Ken, it's not the prayer that God wants. It's your heart! He wants a relationship with you. He wants you to talk to Him, and He wants to talk to you. It's so simple that a child can understand it."

Ken picked at a blade of grass. He thought of Sally.

"You sound like someone I knew a long time ago."

"Well, if she was telling you about how to get to heaven, then she was a true friend."

"Okay, I'm ready. If God wants me, He can have me."

At that very moment, the Holy Spirit enveloped Ken. Though just a moment before Ken had been an enemy of God, now he was His friend and son.

Timothy and Daniel could hear a choir of angels singing from a cloud above the valley. The battle was won, but the war had just begun.

Immanuel was gloating. He appeared relaxed as he sat across the table from Abdul Mohammed. The Muslim leader had the power to plunge millions of his people into a holy war. All it would take is a word from him, and they would die for their god, Allah.

The men were in a private chamber room underneath one of the Muslims' most sacred shrines. Only a few, privileged souls knew of this room. The room was dimly lit by bulky candles. Gold and silver lined the roof, walls, and doors.

"I have come to offer my thanks for your cooperation with the World Federation. Your people have suffered much, and I have come to bring a token of my gratitude," began Immanuel.

Abdul watched the Antichrist like a hawk. He hadn't forgotten what a close associate had told him about this European. Out of curiosity, he wanted to see those miraculous powers that he had heard so much about, yet he feared Allah more than he feared Immanuel.

"Indeed, we have suffered much," pointed out Abdul. "Israel's temple replacing the Dome of the Rock was the last straw."

Immanuel had little patience and less tolerance for this religious zealot. However, his future plans, devious as they were, were intricately entangled with the Middle East.

"My gift to you should stop all the fighting. Your people will be in seventh heaven, and you will be the talk of the region."

Abdul's eyes brightened.

"I am very curious what this may be."

"Abdul, God gave this to me several years ago for this very moment," lied Immanuel.

"Allah's will is sometimes very mysterious," responded the man, staring at the object under the white cover.

Immanuel's eyes descended toward Abdul's soul. He was staring hard at the Muslim.

"Allah has spoken to me! He wants me to give you a message," falsified the Antichrist.

Abdul Mohammed stepped away from Immanuel, all at once horrified.

"Blasphemy! Blasphemy!" shouted the devout Muslim. "Allah only speaks to those who have put their complete faith and allegiance into his hands. You are not a Muslim!"

Immanuel remained absent of emotion.

"I would never use blasphemy against you or your god. He told me that you would be suspicious, and that is why he gave me something that you would cherish more than gold or silver. Allah could have given this to you at any time, but he waited to give it to me so that you would trust me. It is his sign to you!"

Abdul remained defiant but curious. His eyes turned to the veiled object in the center of the room.

Immanuel quickly picked up on his overly active curiosity. He snapped his finger, and at once, his associate pulled the white sheet away from the mystery of the ages.

Abdul Mohammed's eyes glazed over with fear. His lips began to violently mutter a foreign phrase. The hair on his arms stood on end. His body slowly went limp at the sight.

"It has come home!" praised Abdul. "It has come home!"

Ken's hands gripped the wheel of his Mercedes. He and Tina Marie were heading out of the country. It was the weekend, so Immanuel would not notice his sudden departure until they were far away. Ken's eyes were transfixed on the windy road. His mind was reviewing plans for the future.

Tina Marie was just waking. She rubbed her face and looked around at the tranquil landscape.

"Where are we?" asked Tina.

Ken didn't respond. He didn't even hear her question. She looked at him with admiration. She hadn't had to persuade him to leave Geneva. It was his idea from the beginning. She reached over and began to stroke the back of his tired neck.

"Should we stop and get some sleep?"

Ken was adamant in his reply.

"No! Not yet! We have to make it to Britain before Monday morning! That is one of the few places that's still safe. The World Federation has control over every European region except Britain!"

"How are we going to use our world identification cards once he finds out we skipped town?" questioned the lady.

Ken flashed a smile her way. It was obvious he knew something that she didn't.

"When I worked for Immanuel, I had access to all kinds of classified information. One of the things I liked to do was play with the Beast."

"The Beast?" implored Tina.

"It was Immanuel's code name for the computer system that controls the wealth in the world."

Suddenly, Tina realized they could be tracked by their purchases. They were cashless.

Ken noticed her apprehension.

"Trust me. It will be okay. I will take care of everything."

Tina Marie suddenly screamed. Several dozen troopers from the World Federation's police force were blocking the road and holding laser guns in their hands.

Abdul Mohammed rushed toward the ancient artifact. Tears streamed down his bearded cheeks as he slowly rubbed the rectangular, gold-laced box. His hands delicately caressed the monument. The golden box was nearly four feet long, two feet wide, and just over two feet deep. The top of the structure displayed two angelic figures, made of pure gold. They were facing each other from opposite ends of the relic, with their wings touching on the ends.

"Praise Allah!" wept Abdul. "The ark of the covenant is all mine! This will be the final blow to the Jews!"

"Allah has given this to you as a sign to trust me," devised the Antichrist.

Abdul dropped to his knees. His joyful wails increased in intensity.

"Immanuel! You have brought the ark to its final resting place! God has chosen you to bring his good news to our ailing planet. Don't you know that your name means 'God with us,'" recognized the Muslim.

Immanuel smirked. Abdul was now putty in his hands.

"I need your support."

Abdul's heart was for the taking.

"Your wish is my command," hummed the Muslim.

Abdul turned his attention to the ark of the covenant. His hands began to explore the lid of the relic. He was hunting for a way to get inside it. The Antichrist carefully watched Abdul as he examined every nook and cranny of the ark. The Muslim's hands suddenly stopped. His fingernails slowly explored a crevice at the top. Immanuel quickly moved toward the ark.

"Don't violate the integrity of God's temple," roared Immanuel.

Abdul Mohammed was stunned.

"Immanuel! Allah would want me to see."

The Antichrist's temper was unveiled.

"I am God! You will listen to my commands or you will burn in the unquenchable flames of eternal hell!" thundered the psychotic liar.

Abdul was stupefied.

His ears wanted to reject Immanuel's proclamation, yet his eyes beheld the gift of the ages. His finger remained at the cleft in the ark.

He began to slide the top off the ark of the covenant. An uncanny glow encircled him.

"Don't!" yelled Immanuel.

Immanuel dove toward Abdul. It was too late. The energy from the ark blasted the Muslim across the chamber. Immanuel was knocked off his feet. He was dazed. He wanted to believe that Blasphemy had something to do with the display of power, yet he didn't sense his presence.

"Abdul!" bellowed Immanuel as he came to the Muslim's rescue.

The Antichrist slapped at the unconscious man's cheeks, hoping for a response. He didn't want this opportunity to slip through his hands.

"Wake up, Abdul! You have been called by God to proclaim the good news of His coming!" shouted Immanuel.

Abdul's watery eyes slowly creaked open. Everything was hazy.

As his sight slowly recovered, Immanuel's stern face replaced the murky mist.

"You have disobeyed my command! Let that be a material lesson for you! I have the power to alter space and time, to give and take away life! I will not hesitate to use my energy force to help you or to harm you!"

"Please, for...for...forgive me," stuttered Abdul.

He was flat on his back and in no position to question the powers of the Antichrist.

Immanuel had taken God's power and used it for his own glory. The fierce light that had radiated from the ark was the glory of the one true God's presence. It didn't take long for Immanuel to realize it. The Antichrist felt weakened by the force. Immanuel had been in the Lord's presence, but he was careful not to let Abdul see the fear that shook his being.

"You will be hearing from me soon! Until I call, use your gift to bring the Muslim people into submission," ordered the serpent as he headed for the door.

Twelve

Concealing Evil

The landscape was bleak and barren. Only a few deep-rooted trees could survive the harsh, waterless environment of the desert floor. Surrounding the camp was a barbed wire fence, with an electric current flowing through its veins. The camp was six hundred sixty-six miles in area, and had sixty-six lookout towers. It was a spot on earth where the climate left a seared stamp on one's mind, a spot where hell could lap away at a person's soul while he was still in the body. It was the perfect location for Immanuel's enemies.

"I don't understand why they just don't kill us and get it over with," sighed Tina Marie.

Her skin was dark red, a painful effect of the cruel desert sun. Her captors found it amusing to send groups of them out during the heat of the day, without sunscreen, clothes, or water to drink.

"They want to break our faith!" observed her new friend, Peggy.

Ever since the commander of this hellish city had divided the men from the women, the two had been inseparable. The order from Immanuel was to make life miserable for these dissidents of the state. Ripping up families was at the heart of his agenda.

Tina Marie hadn't seen Ken since their capture on the French border. Every night, she was assaulted by her dreams. In her mind, she replayed the global police blocking the road, and the razor-sharp pain of a laser blast grazing her ear. She could never forget the look on Ken's face when he realized that Immanuel had secretly planted a computer chip in his hand. He had been tracking their every move. She tried to squelch the memories of Ken's resisting arrest and being shot with a laser gun at point-blank range. She could only hope he was still alive.

"Death would be a victory for me right now," lamented Tina.

Peggy didn't want to hear that kind of talk.

"Try to keep your thoughts on Jesus. Remember Daniel in the lions' den?" comforted Peggy.

"Yes, I remember," vented Tina Marie.

Peggy smiled. Even in these dire circumstances she had a knack for looking on the bright side of things.

"At least we get water at the end of the day," observed Peggy.

Tina brushed a strand of wet hair from her eyes. She looked toward the opposite side of the camp. She thought about Ken.

Peggy placed her hands around Tina's worn shoulders as she quoted the Bible.

"'And He who sits on the throne will dwell among them. They shall neither hunger anymore nor thirst anymore; the sun shall not strike them, nor any heat; for the Lamb who is in the midst of the throne will shepherd them and lead them to living fountains of waters. And God will wipe away every tear from their eyes.'"

"That's in the book of Revelation," said Tina.

"Do you know what that means?" questioned Peggy. "It says that we will be in heaven very soon! All our suffering here will be like a dream from a distance."

"You think He is coming soon?" pondered Tina Marie.

"I hope so," said Peggy softly.

Tina stared at her before grabbing one of her thinning hands.

"I'm glad the Lord put us here together."

"What do you propose?" asked Ken.

"I can create some kind of distraction so that the other guards won't notice that you're gone."

Ken couldn't believe the Lord had brought this guard to help him.

"How do we get the keys to our cells, not to mention the inner and outer gates of the camp?"

"The only thing you will have to concern yourself with is one door, and the set of keys that go to it," whispered the guard.

"Which door is that?"

Suddenly, a loud clanging broke their whispers. It was a guard looking for trouble. He was using his laser gun as a club, banging on each of the jail cells.

The friendly guard pushed Ken against the cell wall and into the shadows.

The men stared at each other in fear. The sound grew louder. It wasn't even safe to breathe. Ken silently prayed. The guard watched with envy.

The news anchor appeared tattered and torn, as if she had been through a violent fight. Her hair was not groomed; her lipstick was missing.

"This just in. The former Republic of Russia has launched an all-out ground assault on the Middle East. The information is still sketchy, but a few people close to the northern border of Iran have confirmed that an invasion of their northern territories is now in progress."

The news reader glanced down at the news releases gathering on her desk. She was shattered and couldn't believe this was happening. Immanuel's man-made peace seemed to be crumbling.

"Officials in Moscow have just released a statement. I am now quoting. 'The Russian people have been treated like second-class citizens ever since we conceded to the World Federation's demands to relinquish our nuclear arsenal. The tax money that the World Federation has taken from our economy doesn't match what the World Federation is giving back. In short, our country hereby refuses to acknowledge the World Federation.'"

The news anchor remained professional, although most could see the emotion building inside of her.

"That is a direct quote from the vice president of Russia, who now claims to be the new president. There have been no reports of nuclear weapons being used. You might recall our report last week, suggesting that there may still be a few nuclear-tipped missiles not accounted for by the World Federation. Of course, that report is gaining new significance. So far, all we know is this: shortly before 2:00 A.M., Middle East time, satellite and intelligence data picked up hundreds of thousands of troops from the southern republics of Russia infiltrating the northern zone of Iran. Preliminary reports seem to suggest that the fighting has been intense, with possibly thousands having lost their lives. We will update you further when fresh details come our way."

Immanuel attacked the television with a priceless vase. The monarch of the world paced the floor. The peace had lasted three and a half years. He was almost to the point where he could claim victory.

"I need Ken Action. Death will be too kind for him," thought Immanuel, who hated him for deserting the cause.

"Get me the Commander of the World Federation Army," shouted the Antichrist to his secretary. "Also, I want the president of the Global News Network in my office immediately!"

The voice-activated intercom shut off. Immanuel's bloodshot eyes skimmed the room. The hair on his arms began to stand up.

"Is that you?" shouted the Antichrist to his invisible spiritual guide.

Blasphemy ignored his tone of voice. He didn't have time for petty theatrics. The demon wrapped his wings into his scaly body as he landed on Immanuel's desk. He had a message directly from Satan. The general cleared the bile from his black throat.

"Immanuel, you are to send a contingent of troops to the northern mountains of Israel. They are to number six hundred sixty-six."

Blasphemy paused to make sure that Immanuel was getting the message.

"You are to wait there until the armies from the Northern Kingdom are met by the armies of the Southern Kingdom."

Immanuel's body stiffened like a corpse.

"What southern armies?" reacted Immanuel in horror.

Blasphemy laughed in a pitch that sent shock waves through the leader. He disappeared through the ceiling before Immanuel had the chance to curse.

At that very moment, the president of the Global News Network knocked on his door.

"Come in," yelled the ruffled dictator.

The door opened to reveal a middle-aged businessman in a gray three-piece suit.

"Mr. Edwards, I hope you have an explanation for what you have done!" steamed the Antichrist.

Bob took off his reading glasses as he invited himself to a seat.

"What do you mean?" responded the longtime friend.

"You don't know, do you?" continued Immanuel.

Bob didn't fear Immanuel, though he respected him greatly.

"As I speak, my network is running coverage on the Russian invasion of the Middle East," spewed the Antichrist.

"Immanuel, calm down! There is only so much that I can do! It practically took an act of God to squash the battles between the

Jews and the Muslims. Your police had to arrest tens of thousands, who are still in detention, because they knew of the violence. There are some things that we can't ignore!"

Bob was one of a few who could speak to him in this manner and live to tell about it.

"If we do ignore them, then your power base will rot from within. You have to be very careful about holding too much back. Immanuel, you need the respect of your peers in the World Federation. If we don't report the truth, or at least some form of it, the World Federation will never last."

The Antichrist was already busy devising a public relations blitz condemning this attack as a cowardly act from a pack of apostates. His tone leveled out.

"You're right. Report it just the way it happens. Spin it in a way that vilifies the Russian attack as some sort of Christian conspiracy."

"No problem, sir. You know how much I want you to succeed, don't you?" soothed the television man.

"Get on it immediately," barked Immanuel.

"What kind of power do we have?" questioned the archangel.

The prayer technician counted the prayers, examining the quality of the requests from the Christians on the earth.

"I would say close to one hundred million. What I find interesting is the quality of the prayers. They are very unselfish appeals, which is a far cry from a couple years ago."

Michael paced the golden floor in the Central Prayer Agency.

"Do you believe we have enough to protect Israel?" asked the warrior.

The prayer counter didn't hesitate in his reply.

"Absolutely! Isn't it great that the Lord is in complete charge of this?"

"Yes, it is. Better Him than me! I am perfectly happy to be His messenger," acknowledged the archangel.

Their faces were reddened from a lack of oxygen and an over supply of fear.

"That was close!"

"Yeah, too close!"

The men paused—Ken to thank his Maker, the guard to re-think his position.

"Which door are you talking about?" asked Ken.

There was no response.

"I don't understand why you are helping me in the first place."

The guard stared him square in the eyes.

"My wife was one of the Christians who was taken up to heaven. I never bought the Federation's line that they were judged by God. She was the best thing that ever happened to me. You trust the same God that she did. That's why I am helping you."

He made an attempt to hold back the tears, but to no avail.

"Why didn't you trust Jesus as your Savior when she was with you?"

He could barely speak.

"Because I was, and still am, a hardheaded numskull."

"Ask Him into your heart right now. He'll forgive you. Believe it or not, I was worse than you at one time. I used to be the right-hand man for Immanuel himself," consoled Ken Action.

The guard stared at the dirty floor beneath him. He knew the road to take, but felt as if it was too late.

"Don't worry about me," said the guard. "I'm not good enough to call on God for help. Maybe God will see what I'm doing for you and forgive me for my past," rationalized the depressed man.

Ken silently prayed for him.

"It's not too late for you! God wants desperately to forgive you," persuaded Ken.

The guard shook his head.

"No, it's too late for me."

Ken started to speak, but the guard changed the subject.

"There's a door in the cafeteria that leads to an underground tunnel system. For some reason, they don't have security cameras or bugs in these burrows. They've used these tunnels to ship in supplies for the concentration camp."

Ken began to dream about Tina Marie and himself having a picnic in a peaceful mountain valley.

"Who has the keys?" asked Ken.

"A friend of mine, top brass. He has sympathy for your cause. I think you're guaranteed an out after hearing that you were Immanuel's right-hand man."

Ken was getting nervous.

"When do we put the plan into effect?"

"Tonight! When the moon rises, a jailer will come and order you to clean the cafeteria. The door is located underneath the kitchen stove. I'll arrange the rest. You have two, maybe three minutes. After that, you're on your own. You won't be able to move the stove back over the opening. The jailer will spot it quickly, so move fast!"

"Tina Marie?" begged Ken.

"I don't know."

Ken frowned. He would rather stay in bondage and have Tina Marie free. He knew she would be roadkill for Immanuel if she were on her own in this rugged terrain.

"You're a true friend," thanked Ken. "I'll pray for you."

"Good luck, my friend," uttered the guard. His heart was breaking.

Satan was perched upon his throne. His hands were fingering the Holy Scriptures. He had closely studied the prophet Ezekiel in the past several days, concentrating on chapters thirty-eight and thirty-nine. The acidic drool dripping from his mouth occasionally hit the pages, causing them to catch on fire. Fortunately, he had a collection of Bibles in one of his hidden chambers. They were bounty from one of his many attempts to destroy the Christian church.

"That dictator Jehovah will never succeed in His prophecy!" growled Lucifer. "That fool has given me His battle plans right here in this pitiful Book! I will use these prophesies to show Him who really rules the world!"

Satan took the half-scorched Book, and tossed it into the river of lava flowing around his throne. When the Bible hit bottom, a tongue of flames licked it like it was food for hell.

"Your kingdom will surely collapse!" shouted Satan to a silent heaven. "I will take credit for Your mischief. I will be the people's god! I will show them the beauty of evil. I will make You look like a weak fool. I will stand in Your temple, and I will be worshipped as god!"

Dominic Rosario was gloating. His plan was working without a hitch. The World Church was growing by leaps and bounds. Immanuel believed it was World Federation money that had sparked the religious revival that he secretly scorned. Dominic believed it was his own charismatic style and "God-given" ability to perform miracles.

Dominic was standing by the printing presses of the World Federation Book Company. The look on the False Prophet's face was worth ten thousand words. He picked up one of the newly "expanded" bibles. The revised book was full of his revelations from his god. He began to leaf through the pages, which were still warm from the printers. Dominic looked upon his creation, his eyes wild with excitement. He had reinterpreted every verse in the Bible to fit the worldview of the New Age. He had added thousands of new verses, which were fresh off the lips of Blasphemy. The press was ecstatic over the book, linking its release to the greatest religious event since the birth of Muhammad. The tone of the book was simple. God was a God of love; He approved all behavior as long as it didn't hurt anybody else. It said the World Federation would be used by God to bring peace to the earth. Dominic Rosario appointed himself as the Prophet of the World. Surely, he was the only soul qualified to receive the truths of God. What was strangely absent from the new bible was the book of Revelation. Dominic had dismissed it.

"Do you think it can be done?" asked Daniel.

Timothy's trigger finger was itching for action.

"We have everything in place. My concern is to get them out before they are detected by the camp's computer system. They have motion sensors every six feet, audio equipment that can pick up an ant walking, and video monitors that stretch as far as the eye can see. Somehow, we need to shut down the entire electrical system for at least an hour," said Timothy.

Daniel couldn't see the light.

"But Satan's forces have been heavily guarding the solar processing plant."

Timothy pointed toward his head.

"Remember this, my little angel: they may have the brute, but we have been blessed with the brains!"

Daniel laughed as his eyes scanned the toasted valley floor far beneath them. His feet suddenly slipped on an extra-moist part of the cloud. He mistakenly thought a demon had violated their airspace. He drew his sword and began to swat at the thin air.

"We're being attacked!" screamed Daniel as he made mince-meat of the vanishing vapor.

Timothy grabbed the youngster by the ear as he pulled the weapon from his tense hand.

"Take it easy, little guy. Save those backhands for the enemy."

"Hey, you," growled the guard. "Get off your duff and follow me. The boss has some work that he wants you to do."

Ken grimaced.

"Yes, sir, right away," responded the seemingly dejected inmate.

He slowly pulled his torn body from the floor. He prayed that the captor would not notice the slight bulge in his shirt. It didn't take much to annoy the guard.

"Come on!"

Ken left his cell, took a position in front of the guard, and slowly walked down the cluttered hallway.

Timothy was watching Ken's every move. His human was almost to the cafeteria door when he signaled Daniel to start his diversionary tactics. Daniel zoomed over the camp like a firerocket. He was whooping and hollering at the top of his lungs.

A second lieutenant from Satan's army, recently promoted for poisoning a city's water supply, spotted Daniel.

"Enemy spotted in the northeast sector, condition red!" shouted the demon.

In seconds, hundreds of thorny demons awakened from their slumber.

Timothy spotted them from his lofty perch and instantly signaled Daniel. It took Daniel a few seconds to spot Timothy's message. It was seconds that he couldn't spare. He swung his head around toward the camp to see how close the buzzards were. He panicked as he realized they were less than one hundred feet away. One of Satan's sharpshooters hurled a silver sword toward him. Daniel instinctively ducked. Timothy watched with trepidation as the demon spirit honed in on its target.

Ken went to work near the entrance of the kitchen. He had prayed that the guard would not be specific about where he should start the job. The prayer was graciously answered. The guard was too busy looking out the window to notice Ken. Ken steadily worked his way through the entrance of the kitchen.

The guard was getting annoyed. His mind was on a boxing match that was to air in less than thirty minutes. It was the match of the year, and he was going to miss it, keeping watch on some inmate slowly mopping the floor. His temper raged.

"Hey, buddy, make it quick!"

Ken hesitated, not sure of his next move. As he looked around for the stove, he noticed the filthy floor.

"Excuse me, sir, but it's a real mess in here. I mean, you eat in here, too. It's bad! Gonna take a little time to get it right."

The overweight guard stomped his way toward his inmate. He wanted to see this for himself. As he made his way toward the kitchen, his heavy foot slipped on the slick floor. His plump body hit with such force, Ken thought that he might be dead. He slowly tiptoed toward the body. The guard was completely knocked out. There was no blood, but no sign of life, either. Ken quietly walked into the kitchen, silently placing the mop where no one could see it. He raced over to the eight-burner stove. His eyes scanned around it, looking for a way to move the bulky object. He noticed the wheels on the bottom. He hoped they wouldn't creak as he slowly moved the stove. His ears heard nothing except his own heavy breathing.

There was the door, left open, just as his friend had said. Beneath the entrance, spiraling stairs disappeared into the darkness. He didn't waste a single second. He wiped his shoes off with a dry cloth and began to descend into the pit. He reached into his pants and pulled out a small flashlight. As the light flowed from the flashlight, Ken's eyes were jolted by what they saw.

The hellish fiends were closely tailing Daniel, tossing swords at a rate of one per second. The demons resembled a band of hornets. Timothy quickly sounded his trumpet. He knew it could be several minutes before reinforcements arrived, so he immediately flew toward them with a double-edged dagger in each hand.

"Jehovah God rules!" cried out Timothy with all his might.

A few of the demons broke off their flight path to contest his proclamation, but most continued their pursuit of Daniel.

The demons' lust to make Daniel buzzard bait had caused them to leave their post completely undefended. The first one to put holes in the angel would receive a personal message from Lucifer himself or even an award ceremony.

Daniel maneuvered his spent body around a narrow canyon outside the camp's radar space. He was rapidly losing hope that he could shake the demons. They had dangerously closed in on his position, and were less than ten feet away. The angel's neck began to sense the fiery exhaust from a demon's breath. A few seconds passed, and droplets of molten saliva pelted him from the rear. The demons were seven, then six, feet away. Some were trying to gain ground on their fellow demons by shortcutting the turning radiuses around the granite cliffs. Their folly was fatal. Suddenly there was a boom. Smack! Many collided into bare granite.

Timothy, who was barely outrunning them, quickly nose-dived into a tailspin. The lead ogre on Daniel's tail stretched his blood-stained paws toward the scrambling angel's neck. Timothy positioned his body for an all-out collision.

"My God, what have they done?" uttered Ken as his eyes were assailed by a stack of human skeletons ten feet high. Some of the remains were fresh, leaving a rank odor in the stagnant underground air. It had taken Ken five minutes to reach the bottom of the spiraling stairs, only to be shocked by the sickening truth of Immanuel's killing machine.

Ken's next move would be decided by prayer. He was at a junction of three caves, each disappearing into outer darkness. He noticed one of the roads had tank tracks worn into its moistened surface. Other than an occasional human skeleton perched along the side of the way, there was nothing but black darkness and rats to keep him company. He began to sprint down the dirt track but was forced to slow to a jog. His light couldn't give him the visual distance he needed to proceed safely.

Several minutes passed before he came upon another junction. To his surprise, there were wooden crates stacked to the ceiling with the label "contraband" written in red paint on their sides. He ran to one of the boxes, grabbed a palm-sized Bible, and placed it in his pocket. Suddenly, he sensed movement on the trail ahead. He stopped and bent down close to the earth. He dreaded the thought of a search party.

He stayed hidden for several minutes, desperately trying to discern the noise. His only course of action was to proceed with caution. He needed to escape as quickly as possible. As he inched his way forward, the noise became louder.

"Look out! Dive bomber approaching from the North," yelled the demon in charge of the chase.

Timothy could see the whites of their eyes as he flew straight toward the demons. At twelve hundred miles an hour, his timing had to be impeccable. Daniel had rounded a sharp corner at just that moment. The first four demons were struck with Timothy's sword. The others had the sense to veer away from the incoming missile. Timothy contorted his body as he performed a daring maneuver at the speed of sound. He screamed with all his might. His organs nearly popped out of their places as he made a U-turn and grabbed Daniel from behind. Neither said a word. There was no energy left to talk. It had to be conserved. Both looked over their shoulders to assess the situation. The enemy was not in sight, but they could hear them in the distance.

"I know a hidden cave just a few miles away," whispered Timothy. "If we stay low enough in this gorge, I doubt they will be able to spot us before we make it to safety."

"But they're bound to sniff us out," wheezed Daniel.

"No, they won't. Look!" grinned Timothy.

Dozens of angels from across the desert plain were approaching from all directions.

Ken was silently edging his way closer to the commotion. The sound increased in intensity as he neared, though it remained indiscernible.

"Tina Marie," whispered Ken.

"Ken, is that you?"

"It's me! Where are you?"

"I'm in a corner. There are rats all around me!"

"Don't move," directed Ken. "I'm coming to get you!"

Ken flashed his light toward her voice. All he saw were earthen walls that had been erratically carved by a giant, man-made claw.

"Don't panic, honey! Do you see my light?"

"I can, but barely," answered Tina.

Ken came to another crossroad. He slowly swung his light around to the left. It revealed nothing but empty space, and another disassembled skeleton. It was obvious that a number of people had been tortured in these caves.

"Ken!" shouted Tina Marie.

Ken twisted his body toward her voice, and flashed his light into her eyes.

"Tina Marie! You're safe!"

The two lovers raced toward one another. It had been over six months since they had seen each other, yet the spark had only grown brighter. Neither spoke.

Suddenly, they heard a crude thump on the ceiling directly above them. Both froze in fear.

A dark cloud followed Immanuel to the door. His mind was fogged. Immanuel slowly opened the pair of office doors with both hands.

Dominic Rosario was prepared for Immanuel's storm. The men greeted each other like they were members of the same fraternity.

"Dominic, it's so good to see you! I hope that everything is going well," lied the Antichrist.

"It is well, my friend. The Church is growing by leaps and bounds, thanks to your generosity. I take great joy in helping people," schemed the False Prophet.

The devils shook hands. The door closed behind them. Immanuel sat on the edge of his chair, as if he were uncomfortable with the seating. Dominic observed his restlessness, but wisely refrained from discussing the problem.

"I am pleased with the growing influence that you have with the World Church," parried the world dictator.

"I thank you for the opportunity," responded the False Prophet.

Immanuel's eyes became distant, as if he were in another world.

"Dominic, I am concerned about the Church."

The False Prophet acted surprised.

"Oh? Is there anything I can do?"

"As a matter of fact, there is. The World Church's philosophy is becoming too compatible with that Christian sect's theology. I want some changes made."

Dominic abhorred Immanuel's statement, which sounded more like an order than a suggestion.

"I am doing exactly what God is telling me to do."

"Oh, please," thought the Antichrist.

"Well, then I'm sure that 'God' will tell you we must be sure these Christians are portrayed as what they are. Not some unimportant religious sect. No, they are enemies of the Church!" condescended Immanuel.

Dominic nodded. "They are sick. All of them. Anyone with the slightest bit of enlightenment can see that. I'm doing everything I can to discourage our members from joining that order."

"Dominic, you don't see the big picture. I do. These Christians don't just believe differently. Their beliefs put them in a place of opposition to us—opposition that can only lead to an eventual rebellion. You must obey me in this!"

"I have obeyed you! In fact, I think you will be pleased to hear that I have completely revamped the Bible!"

Immanuel's curiosity was aroused.

"What are you doing with the old Bibles?" inquired the Antichrist.

A smile formed on the False Prophet's face.

"We are burning them. They are outdated. Only the Christians fail to see it."

"A good start, but not enough." A burning intensity appeared in Immanuel's eyes.

"I don't understand. What do you want to do, lock them all up?" said Dominic.

"No," said the Antichrist.

Dominic breathed a sigh of relief, but it was taken quickly away.

"We must put them out of their misery," smiled Immanuel. "All of them!"

The World Federation general was perched on a mountaintop north of the Galilean Sea. The arid mountain range in Israel was peaceful and quiet. The general's troops, numbering in the tens of thousands, were waking from their midday nap.

An aide dashed toward him. His salute was rushed.

"Sir, our five-star general is on the phone."

The general quickly reached into his pocket and pulled out a satellite phone. It was the latest technological breakthrough. It had a miniature dish inside the unit that resembled a solar panel. The top brass in the military, along with a few powerful individuals in the World Federation, had access to this technology. The phone was impossible to tap.

"General Alburn, it's good to hear from you. What can I do for you?" asked the field general.

"We have a big problem on our hands!" explained Immanuel's right-hand man. "The Russians have already taken the majority of the oil fields. They have invited many of their African allies to join them in the plunder! I don't know what is driving them, but I can tell you that we are going to have one hell of a fight on our hands!"

The four-star general was getting nervous.

"Do you want me to move east and engage them?"

"No, I have my orders, and they are for us to sit tight! I'll get back with you when something new comes down the pike. Out."

"But sir, they are—"

The signal had been snapped.

"A politician in charge of a war is like a lunatic in charge of dynamite," cursed the four-star general.

"Reports continue to pour into the Global News Network of bloody battles, tens of thousands of dead and wounded, and the latest fear, which is chemical and biological devastation. Many of the nations joining the Russian land invasion are evading our, and the World Federation's, attempt at communication. The World Federation recently released a statement condemning the unsolicited act of war as a, and I quote, 'cruel, self-serving attempt to plunder the wealth of the Middle East.' The statement goes on to read that 'the World Federation will not stand for this kind of violence, and we assure the world's population that this aggression will not go unpunished! We further believe that the fundamentalist Christian cult movement that has been gaining momentum in the past year has planted the seeds of this violence.' A news conference by Immanuel Bernstate should be starting at any moment to further detail his efforts to squelch this violent betrayal of international law and order," reported the news anchor.

Tina Marie was hanging onto Ken's hand as he frantically led her through the dark channel. The thumping sounds seemed to follow them as they made their way through the mazelike structure.

"Ken, let's go this way," said Tina, as her breathing tried to catch up with her heart rate.

"Why that way?" gasped Ken. "I think we've been that way before."

Tina Marie bent over in anguish.

"You're probably right. But something is telling me this is the way to freedom."

Ken didn't hesitate.

"Let's go with it. Maybe God's trying to tell you something!"

The two raced toward the black hole. Within seconds, the blackness turned to night. They could hear crickets singing in the thin mountain air. They cautiously approached the window to their independence. Ken slowly moved out of the hole, checking for enemy troops. Suddenly, a deafening explosion seized their short-lived peace. Ken jumped back into the cavern and grabbed his fiancée.

"Look, Ken! See it?"

Ken followed her trembling finger. A white mushroom cloud was climbing from the base of the compound. It appeared that the generator station had exploded.

"The electronic eye securing the grounds just blew up!"

"So what?" vented Tina.

"It's our ticket to freedom! They have no way of detecting our escape. They'll be too busy mopping up the mess to notice that we've gone."

Ken latched onto her hand as the two disappeared into the dark of the night.

Daniel and Timothy, who were huddled underneath a bush near the explosion, spotted their humans fleeing to the west.

"That was brilliant," congratulated Daniel.

Timothy took a bow.

"I told you those demons have the brains of donkeys!" gloated the wiser angel.

"The dimwit thought I was turning in my weapon and surrendering. Just as I handed the atom blaster to him, I picked him up and threw him in the generator!"

"Boom!" cried a delighted Daniel.

"Yeah! Boom!" laughed Timothy.

The angels gave each other a "high five" as they watched Tina Marie and Ken embracing on a hillside, far from enemy surveillance.

Dominic was exhausted as he plunged his overworked body into the hotel bed. He wanted to hibernate for at least twenty-four hours, and he decided to turn on the television. As he hit the power switch, the high definition set instantly filled the screen with a visual display that made the old-time television sets seem ancient. The first image was of some fish floating through the waters of the great barrier reef. It was a satellite station that broadcast live, underwater images.

"Next," ordered Dominic.

The machine obeyed by changing the channels. This station, Channel 126, was a different kind of weather channel. It continuously broadcast live and taped segments of intense weather, from hurricanes, typhoons, and tornadoes to arctic blizzards in seventy below zero temperatures. A team of two dozen meteorologists chased these storms, live on the air. Dominic yawned as he continued his search.

"Channel 167," commanded the False Prophet.

The television screen switched stations. There was Immanuel, sitting on a mountaintop, addressing his worldwide audience. He was dressed in a casual white shirt and wrinkle-free khaki pants.

"I come to you today because our world has not yet perfected peace. My dream is your dream, and that is to make every man, woman, and child a prosperous and happy member of the World Federation."

His charisma was contagious; his personality, addictive.

"There are dark forces at work in our world that want to destroy your World Federation! Many of you are wondering why these inhumane people want to see our peace plans wrecked. The answer is simple, but hard to swallow. They worship a god of war, a god who wants war, hunger, suffering, and division. I believe the religious writers from our past called this god Satan, or the master of all lies!"

The Antichrist paused to receive a fresh revelation from Blasphemy, who was joyfully dictating the speech from his seat next to Immanuel.

"A few nations, who believe these lies, have broken away from our Federation and are in the process of destroying much of the Middle East. Don't blame the people of these countries for the cowardly acts of their self-proclaimed leaders. That would be wrong. It is their leaders who want to return to the old order. They want a world that goes to bed at night wondering if they will wake up in the morning. They want to be worshipped, and they use the fears of their people as a whip to keep them down. I want you to know that I will put a stop to this! I have sent a massive contingent of World Federation troops to thwart this uprising. I ask that you put your faith in me!"

Blasphemy stopped dictating, which caused Immanuel to stall. Only the most probing eye noticed the wrinkle in his persona. Immanuel ad-libbed the rest.

"I have ordered your Earth Church leader, Dominic Rosario, to print a new bible for all the citizens of the world."

Dominic hit the wall with his fist.

"You liar," yelped Dominic. "How dare you steal my idea and claim it as your very own!"

"Today, I am sending legislation to the World Congress that will make it against the law to possess any literature that causes people to hate one another. Next week, each citizen will be issued a complimentary bible based on the latest human wisdom and revelations of god. We will ask that each of you find the time to read this enlightened, commonsense approach to god. I want you to find your place in the World Federation."

Immanuel appeared as innocent as a dove.

"From this point forward, we will be getting to know each other on a more intimate basis. Each week, I will be addressing the world on our progress for peace. Until next week, I wish you health, wealth, and peace!"

"You will pay!" shouted Dominic as he clawed at the wall.

Thirteen

Who Is God?

Immanuel sat on the edge of his desk. His right leg rested to one side, and the left barely touched the ground. It was the perfect profile shot for the cameras. The body language was clear: he was relaxed, and in complete control. People could put their hope and confidence in his omnipotence.

"Stand by, sir," requested the camera person.

Immanuel cleared his throat, though no obstruction was there.

"Hello, I wish I had good news to report to you about our success in the Middle East, but I don't. The enemy is now holding 50 percent of the world's oil supply hostage. They are threatening to blow up the underground reserves if we try to attack their positions. Unfortunately, there is nothing that we can do without putting a decade's supply of that precious commodity at risk. The last thing I want is for this to intimately affect your lives. As of now, we do have some shortages of gasoline in a few segments of the globe. But rest assured, I will bring these twisted zealots to justice!"

The Antichrist's eyes didn't blink.

"I want to offer my congratulations to the World Federation police force. They have already rounded up twelve thousand Christian cult members. Soon, all these terrorists will be in jail where they belong. Once we alleviate this plague, peace will return to our earth! Good night, and may the peace that only the World Federation can give be with you!"

"What did you say, sir?" voiced the four-star general with a tinge of panic in his speech.

"The Russian and African contingents are heading directly for Israel," repeated the voice on the other end of the line.

"They have us outnumbered ten to one!" shot back the field general.

The commander's voice was devoid of sympathy.

"You are to maintain your ground. Do not, I repeat, do not engage them in battle. The president of the World Federation has given specific orders to retain a defensive posture only!" ordered Immanuel's faithful servant.

"Why? Is he out of his mind? We'll be skinned alive!"

"You have your orders!" shouted the superior as he slammed the phone down.

The general did everything he could to control his tongue. He picked up a pair of binoculars. The man with forty years of fighting experience peered through the lens, watching the distant mountains. As he panned from north to south, he suddenly spotted something that grabbed his attention. He investigated the sight for several minutes before handing the eyepiece to his aide.

"Get on the phone to all the captains in camp! Tell them to prepare to defend our positions. I don't want one shot fired unless we are attacked first. Got it?" said the general.

The aide appeared confused and a little frightened. He was wise enough not to question orders, no matter how foolish he thought they were.

"Yes, sir," he saluted.

As the lieutenant rushed to the communication center, the general looked up toward the heavens.

"Jesus, I don't know what is going to happen, but I'm prepared to meet You at any moment," he silently prayed.

Two men, dressed in sackcloth, with beards down to their bellies, slowly walked up the stairs of the temple in Jerusalem. Their garments appeared archaic, yet not a blemish was found on either. Each wore sandals on their feet, and appeared to be in their seventies or eighties.

Hundreds of curious onlookers stared at the pair, a few shouted at them. The men appeared out of place, even confused by their surroundings. It was as if they had been in a time capsule for thousands of years and were suddenly catapulted to earth.

The Central Prayer Agency was busier than Wall Street. The archangel Michael paced the golden floor inside his office, waiting for the trumpet to blow. One of the archangel's many workers rushed into his spherical office.

"Four days, maybe less," announced the angelic laborer.

"Thank you, sergeant," responded Michael.

The archangel glared at the earth below. He was thinking about the Battle of Armageddon.

As the men of old stood in the outer temple, neither said a word. They were standing like statues in the wind. A crowd of inquisitive tourists circled around them, asking questions that were completely ignored. Suddenly, the older one raised his hands into the air. His eyes turned to fire as he began to speak.

"Listen, O Israel; repent of your wicked ways, and be saved by our Lord. Turn away from your evil acts. Do not worship the Beast, or you will burn in hell forever!"

As his voice thundered toward the mountains, an enormous storm cloud developed over the city of kings. In a matter of seconds, a clear, peaceful day in Jerusalem had degenerated into a chaotic scene of wind, thunder, and hail.

The gathering crowd, appalled at this old man's message of hate and bigotry, quickly scattered. Lightning plummeted down from the sky as the wind picked up to near-hurricane force. The two men of God stood before the storm with faith that could move mountains. They feared nothing except God Almighty.

Several hours later, news of the supernatural occurrence reached Immanuel. He was at dinner, wining and dining one of his more independent-thinking vice presidents. A waiter handed him a phone.

"Sir, I hate to interrupt your dinner, but I understand that this is urgent," apologized the waiter.

Immanuel nodded his head, trying to appear businesslike in front of the vice president of the Ukraine. The conversation wasn't going the way he wanted anyway. For reasons beyond him, Blasphemy had not given him the capability to do miracles for quite a while. This greatly diminished his influence among his enemies.

"What do you want?" asked Immanuel in a deep bass tone.

The voice on the other end was frantic. Surprisingly, for several minutes, Immanuel listened to the broken English without interrupting. Immanuel's emotions were visible. His dinner companion could hear the person's rushed verbiage from the other end of the transnational line, but the words were indiscernible.

"Who are they?" asked Immanuel with fury in his voice.

The Antichrist dropped his salad fork.

"Are you sick?" he bellowed.

Every conversation in the restaurant stopped.

"I want those two arrested and charged with treason against the World Federation!"

Immanuel was raising eyebrows all across the yacht club. Many of those present were his close friends and advisors. His blood boiled as he digested the next comment from his informer.

"I don't care what kind of powers they may have! They are going up against the greatest governmental power the world has ever seen! Capture and arrest those cultists or I'll—"

Immanuel paused as his eyes scanned the room. The world dictator was providing the entertainment for the night, much to his chagrin. Not a fork or mouth was engaged. He pulled back to regroup. His anger instantly receded from a boil to a simmer. His eyes began to scan individuals in the crowd; each one reacted by quickly looking down at his plate.

"Do your job, or I'll find someone who will!" threatened Immanuel.

He hung up the phone. He looked around the room. No one dared to look at him.

Several days later, a stalemate had developed on the Israeli frontier. The Russian and African troops, under the direct control of the renewed communist government, were showing no signs of advancement. They were camped in a narrow valley due north of Jerusalem. The World Federation's troops were less than ten miles away.

The leader of the Russian contingent was returning the binocular browses of the World Federation's four-star general. Neither wanted a bloodbath, yet neither was willing to back down.

It was noon when the four-star general noticed a puff of smoke rising from the opposing mountain. By the time he realized what it was, one hundred of his men were dead. The blast could be heard for miles. The general screamed into his communicator.

"Attack! Attack!"

Before a weapon could be drawn, the ground began to violently shake. The general was knocked on his back as the upheaval intensified. Fear spread across the camps. The ground began to splinter.

Dread and panic attacked the soldiers as they watched their buddies plunge toward the center of the earth. It was as if the planet were swallowing them whole. Just as the roar of the earthquake subsided, the mountain opposite the World Federation troops exploded. The force of the explosion jolted the valley. Millions of tons of rock and molten lava spewed into the air, causing pandemonium among the troops. A wind of sulfur jetted down the valley, sending tents, and even tanks, flying through the air. The serene mountain was instantly transformed into a volcano of death.

Some of the Russian troops near the edge of the bubbling peak were vaporized by the lava flow. Others tried to escape on foot, only to be swallowed by the three-hundred-degree windstorm. The rest, who thought they were at a safe distance from the boiling mountain, were pelted by burning boulders the size of houses.

The World Federation's army, largely unscathed by the lava and rocks, ran for their lives.

"Base to headquarters!" shouted the terrified general. "We are in retreat! I repeat; we are in retreat!"

The transmission died as the sulfur-rich smoke choked the signal.

The two prophets of God Almighty were standing in the temple that Immanuel had built, preaching the way to heaven. They were given only limited television coverage from a local renegade station in Jerusalem, which was outside the power of the GNN. That publicity was enough to send thousands upon thousands of devout Jews, along with a few tourists, into the temple area to hear their message. Immanuel had managed to keep this news off the global network and was now trying to shut down the local television station.

"Hear, O Israel, what your God has said," preached the fearless man of God.

The temple, and its surrounding area, was jammed with people. Most were there to see miracles; the message was secondary.

Hundreds of World Federation police lined the streets. The patrol was under strict orders to maintain order and to arrest anybody who spoke against the government.

"I am Moses!" exclaimed the bearded giant.

A reverent hush moved across the crowd as the man addressed the onlookers. They didn't know how to react at first.

"Show us a miracle, Moses, so that we can see and believe that it is really you," shouted a woman near the front of the crowd.

Moses ignored the request as he stepped down. The other prophet took his place on the platform. He stared down at the woman begging for a miracle.

"Faith is not a matter of seeing, but of believing," said the other prophet, much to the dismay of the crowd. He slowly raised his head to heaven.

"My God of mercy has graciously allowed me to see the day of His coming! I, too, did not experience death, but was caught up in a whirlwind to the very throne of God!"

A few in the crowd shouted, "Elijah!"

The prophet raised his hands into the darkening sky.

"Yes, I am Elijah. But I am nothing. God Almighty is everything!"

Many of the Jews in the crowd began to taunt the pair of prophets.

"Give us a sign! We want a miracle! Get off the stage, and go home!" clamored the faithless ones.

Elijah and Moses looked at each other with sadness.

"Jehovah God will give you a miracle," condemned Elijah. "For three and one-half years, no rain will fall on His holy city!"

Elijah stepped down and wiped the dust from his feet. An active, menacing cloud quickly rolled in from the Mount of Olives, causing the crowd to disperse like sheep with no shepherd. The rainless cloud brought lightning from horizon to horizon, plunging the crowd into mass hysteria. The men of God did not flinch. They remained in the court of God, their eyes roving through the frenzy, looking for those who had no fear. Several hundred of the onlookers stood in the midst of the storm and remained to hear the prophets.

"Men and women of Israel, you have been called to our ministry. You need to give your whole hearts, minds, and spirits to your Messiah. Forget what you have been taught by those who want to deny His divinity. Jesus is your Messiah! Receive the free gift of eternal life."

The small crowd dropped to their knees. Most were crying to Jehovah God, begging for forgiveness for their past sins and disbelief. What they couldn't see was the Holy Spirit of God descending through the clouds.

"I stand here today as God's spokesman, who swears by God's own holy name, that what we say about salvation is true and necessary for entrance into His glorious rest!" preached Elijah.

"Do you accept Jesus Christ as your Messiah, the chosen Lamb of God?" asked Moses.

They answered, "We do."

Elijah closed his eyes. His hands reached toward heaven. His arms began to tremble as the Holy Spirit connected with his spirit. It was as if he had plugged his body into the city's electrical system, yet this power was more concentrated.

"You will live forever, but now you will live not for your own selfish souls, but for your Messiah, the Lord of the Universe, Jesus Christ!"

Without warning, a sound rang down from heaven. A mighty wind filled the entire arena where they lay prostrate. Suddenly, divided tongues of fire stretched from Elijah's quivering hands to each of the Jewish believers. Each of the Christian Jews jumped to his feet, with many speaking in foreign languages that nobody could understand. It was chaotic, but ordered; robust, yet peaceful; forceful, but gentle.

As Moses and Elijah praised their God, dropping to their knees in reverence, they noticed a few intruders in black uniforms near the edge of the assembly.

Immanuel's cold stare filled the den of his sixty-six room mansion. Things were not going exactly as he had planned. The Antichrist was searching for answers. He rationalized his part in the predicament by blaming others.

The black communicator, the size of a cigarette lighter, began to beep. It was two low tones, followed by a higher pitched sound that aroused his attention. He quickly picked it up.

"This is Immanuel."

"Mr. Bernstate, those characters who call themselves Moses and Elijah have just convinced several hundred Jerusalem citizens to become Christians," said his head security agent for the Middle East.

Immanuel's jaw began to quiver uncontrollably. A barren silence filled the phone line.

"Sir, did you hear what I said? Hundreds of people have deserted to the enemy, in full daylight! They're flaunting their religion in our faces!"

The Antichrist's lips dried up. The news was getting to him, and he knew it.

"Why didn't you arrest them?" calmly asked Immanuel.

The security agent immediately responded.

"Sir, these imposters have the ability to change the weather, and to cause storms to pop up out of nowhere! I even saw lightning come from their fingertips!"

The muscles in Immanuel's body began to shudder as he realized that he wasn't the only one with power.

"I want you to arrest those men. Use deadly force if you must, but I want those felons off the streets of my city before sunset! Do you understand me?"

The security man seemed miffed.

"I will carry out your orders, sir, but I cannot give any guarantee about how many of your officers might be injured or killed. They've never turned their powers against us, at least not yet!"

The decapitated mountain continued to roar as the lava flow engulfed parts of the valley. Nearly 20 percent of the army from Russia and Africa had perished.

Immanuel's troops had retreated to a position twenty miles away, on a ridge of hills high above the smoldering disaster scene. Only a few hundred had lost their lives in the initial blow, with many thousands injured.

The four-star general tried to reestablish communication with his boss. The line was fuzzy but usable. The general prayed for a clear connection. It began to ring, and was quickly picked up by his direct superior.

"What's going on down there?" screamed the voice from the World Federation's primary base in Germany.

"Sir, a volcano suddenly erupted right in their face! We sustained some casualties, but the enemy has been hit extremely hard. Many of them just disintegrated!" recounted the four-star general.

There was a long pause from the other end of the line.

"What is their status right now?" queried the man who was directly responsible to Immanuel.

"One second, sir," said the general as he pulled the binoculars to his ash-stained eyes.

The volcanic plume had dropped the visibility to near zero, but the binoculars had a computer chip allowing the user to see through a cloud or obstruction, similar to the nighttime goggles of the late twentieth century.

As he scanned the lacerated valley, his mouth dropped wide open, causing him to choke on the sulfuric smoke. He dropped the receiver into the ash.

———————

Hundreds of specialized terrorist agents converged on the temple overlooking Jerusalem. They were dressed in black uniforms that were bullet- and laserproof. They had laser machine modules strapped to their chests and were garbed in riot helmets. Some wielded laser-guided missile launchers. A crowd of thousands, who had now gathered to hear the two prophets of God, completely ignored the troops.

"Jehovah God is looking for men who will stand for His never ending law of holiness, righteousness, and love. He has appointed a time in the near future when He will live in Jerusalem. The laws and statutes will flow from His mouth like a never ending stream of pure water, never again to be tainted and twisted by the Evil One, Satan."

With their riot shields raised, the strongly armed contingent pushed and shoved the listeners out of their way. Moses pointed his remarks to the oncoming swarm.

"You people pushing through the crowd. Your hearts are impure, and your motives are weighed against you. You who follow the dictates of the World Federation, headed by the Devil himself, will burn in the unquenchable flames of hell. Repent and come to Jesus, the Savior of the world!"

The leader of the SWAT team raised his laser-guided cannon into the air. He was standing only steps away from the prophets. Nobody could see his face, though his voice could be heard through a loudspeaker that was planted in his canvas coat.

"You cultists are under arrest by the authority of the World Federation!" shouted the colonel.

Neither Moses nor Elijah flinched a muscle. Not one person in the crowd made a sound.

"The authority of God Almighty is far greater than the authority of man!" uttered Elijah in a manner that didn't agree with the commander.

The man in black slowly allowed the butt of his laser machine to drop ever so slightly. It was his sign that he meant business.

"You will leave our presence so that the work of God may continue. You will not be harmed if you promptly obey," spoke Moses.

The leader took his promise as a threat. He quickly dropped his weapon to an offensive position.

"The book of Revelation has spoken! It is written in chapter eleven, and verse three. 'And I will give power to my two witnesses, and they will prophesy one thousand two hundred and sixty days, clothed in sackcloth. These are the two olive trees and the two lampstands standing before the God of the earth. And if anyone wants to harm them, fire proceeds from their mouth and devours their enemies. And if anyone wants to harm them, he must be killed in this manner.'"

The words from Moses infuriated the leader of Immanuel's head-hunting clan. Instead of shooting him at point-blank range, the man lunged at him.

"Ken, where are we now?" asked Tina Marie, who was completely exhausted.

Her mouth was parched from the dry desert wind, and her body was exhausted. Ken watched as she struggled up another mountain.

"I don't think it's too much farther. I know that you want to rest, but if we do, it will increase our chances of being spotted by Immanuel's troops."

"I can't go on any farther."

Ken grabbed her weakened body and carried her in his arms.

"We have to keep going! I'm sure the Dead Sea isn't too far away!"

While she was being cradled, she noticed a gash in his hand.

"Ken, what happened to your hand?"

"Remember when I left you for several minutes to scout out our trail? I didn't want you to know this or worry about it, but I had to slice a hole in my hand to remove that computer tracking chip."

Tina's face was filled with admiration.

"They think I'm somewhere in that river, probably at the bottom of it," said Ken.

"I don't understand, then. Why are we killing ourselves to get away?"

Ken struggled to move the two up the mountain incline.

"Motion sensors. They can track our breathing patterns. We have to keep going!"

As Ken finished his sentence, his eyes lit up. He peered over the top of the mountain. The scenery looked like the bowels of hell, yet Ken was enthused.

The scene was nauseous. The four-star general lowered the binoculars and rubbed his tired eyes. He didn't know if he was dreaming or hallucinating. He slowly raised the eyepiece to his eyes once again. He adjusted the focus, opacity, and gain on the unit, but to no avail. It was real.

"Lieutenant, come over here and take a look at this. Describe to me, in detail, what you see."

His aide dropped the map that he was reading.

"Yes, sir." He took the binoculars from his superior's hands.

The general watched the lieutenant's expression.

The lieutenant pulled the eye enhancers from his flushed face.

"Sir, they are killing each other! I don't think they can see one another through all that haze. They think we are down there, sir!"

At that very moment, the satellite receiver rang. The general grabbed the device.

"This is General Moody!"

"What's going on down there?" asked his commander.

"Sir, I'm sorry that we were cut off. Obviously, we are having some communication problems because of the thick smoke. Sir, the enemy is in the midst of a battle!"

"I told you not to engage the enemy," fumed the general-politician.

"Sir, we didn't! They are literally destroying themselves! The soldiers have turned on one another. My best guess is that the Russians have turned on their African allies."

Moody's boss chuckled.

"When they are finished, go pick up the pieces and report directly to me. Immanuel will be pleased when he hears of our victory."

"But sir, we didn't do anything to claim victory!" asserted General Moody.

Only a dial tone could be heard on the other end of the line.

As the end of the SWAT team leader's rifle neared Moses' head, the prophet of God opened his mouth. Fire, not words, spewed forth, devouring the intruder. His smoldering body lay in ruins as the remaining agents of Immanuel's elite guard dispersed through the stunned crowd.

"People of Jerusalem, we do not delight in death, even in the death of the wicked. But God had prophesied about this time in history, and His Word must come to pass! This is the time to repent of your evil deeds and thoughts. Immanuel Bernstate is the Antichrist of the Bible! He is spoken of in the book of Daniel, chapter eight, verse twenty-three. 'And in the latter time of their kingdom, when the transgressors have reached their fullness, a king shall arise, having fierce features, who understands sinister schemes. His power shall be mighty, but not by his own power; he shall destroy fearfully, and shall prosper and thrive; he shall destroy the mighty, and also the holy people. Through his cunning he shall cause deceit to prosper under his rule; and he shall exalt himself in his heart. He shall destroy many in their prosperity. He shall even rise against the Prince of princes; but he shall be broken without human means.'"

Once again, the Holy Spirit hovered over the temple area, looking for recruits for Jehovah God's army. It took only a minute for 90 percent of the crowd to fall on their knees and repent of their sins.

The emotional scene would be repeated seven days in a row. Exactly one hundred forty-four thousand Jews would come to know their Messiah. Only a few confrontations occurred during this period of intense revival, and each one was met by fiery execution. God's supernatural power caused the war drums inside the World Federation to beat more fiercely than ever.

The makeup artist touched up Immanuel's face as the Antichrist reviewed his speech. He was dressed in a tailored white shirt, dark red tie, and Italian silk suit.

"Thirty seconds before air," announced the camera person.

Immanuel was ready for the kill. The world had seen the images from Jerusalem, with Moses and Elijah preaching to the masses. The GNN camera had recorded the fire gushing from their mouths. It was an obstacle that Immanuel had to clear.

"Stand by, sir," annunciated the camera person.

Immanuel was sitting straight in his chair. His hands were smartly placed together on his desk, and the flag of the World Federation was over his left shoulder.

"Good evening, citizens of the world. I want to thank you for joining me on this very solemn but special occasion. As you probably know, tomorrow is the three and one-half year anniversary of the new world order. I want to celebrate this occasion by delivering the most important message the world has ever known. Join me tomorrow in the historic town of Jerusalem for a revelation that will change your lives forever!"

Immanuel's mood was staid and pressing.

"This evening, I want to tell you why I am choosing Israel. As you know, two men who falsely claim to be Moses and Elijah are stirring up racial and religious hatred in that beautiful city. They have murdered, in cold blood, several World Federation agents. These men and women were trying to protect you when they were ruthlessly killed by some kind of Satanic trick. The Devil is the one who uses fire to destroy his enemies. That is why God has chosen his final punishment to be a lake of fire at the center of the earth. Many have been wondering why we don't arrest these men and charge them with treason and murder. The fact is—"

The Antichrist hesitated. It was as if he didn't want to burden the world with the details of running the planet.

"The truth is, these men are being controlled by the Devil himself. Dominic Rosario has informed me that God has given him a revelation."

The archangel Michael floated over the tragic scene in the Israeli mountains. He was relaying orders to his commanders on the ground who were conducting raids on the enemy troops in the caves. The Devil's demons were frightened.

Several hours earlier, Michael had attacked the demonic hounds directing the invasion. The demons couldn't believe it when thousands of warriors from heaven attacked their cozy masquerade. Most of the demons had foolishly thought they would never deal with a full-scale threat from Jehovah God again. Today was different. Jehovah God had ordered the archangel to destroy the demons and the troops from Russia and Africa. He was to leave the World Federation unscathed.

Suddenly, a black chunk of energy appeared from a cave near the volcano.

"Michael!" barked the approaching phantom.

The archangel turned his head.

"You claim to be righteous and holy, yet you are ordering your angels to kill those innocent humans! How can this be? Is it possible that you and your God are hypocrites? Do not the Scriptures say, 'You shall not murder?'" accused Blasphemy.

The demonic general hovered a few yards from Michael, whose sword was tucked underneath his wings.

The archangel Michael stood like a stone wall. His right hand was only inches from his sword. Blasphemy watched as his trigger finger began to twitch.

"Are you not going to come to your own defense? Is your God not prepared to answer my observation?" tested Blasphemy.

Michael took a deep breath.

"Blasphemy! Report back to your supreme traitor that there are enough Christians to guarantee a fight that he will not forget! We are now strong enough to control any given area of the earth!"

The demon seethed with hatred. His fingernails swiped at his spiritual flesh, sending shots of black ions flying through the sky.

"Big deal! You may have the power to command bits and pieces of the globe! So what! You may control 1 percent of the land mass. It's just like you and your God to think that kind of number is a majority!"

"God is the only One who can make a righteous judgment. Those troops were anything but innocent. As for you and your so-called judgments, one day in the not too distant future, you will have to answer for every stray word that you utter!" exclaimed Michael.

The stinging reprimand ripped Blasphemy apart. He pulled his sword from his holster and lunged toward the archangel. Michael quickly stepped aside, causing Blasphemy to tumble toward the earth.

"You would be a fool to try something so unwise," stated the archangel.

Blasphemy's eyes sizzled with fire. With lightning speed, he catapulted his body into a U-turn.

"You will pay dearly for your words!"

Michael drew his sword. He pointed it toward the oncoming devil.

"It is not your time to die, Blasphemy! Depart from my sight!"

Nobody ordered Blasphemy around, especially not a follower of Jehovah. His sword sliced through the air as if it were a finely tuned meat cutter. Suddenly, a hundred angels rushed to Michael's side. They quickly surrounded Michael with their swords raised. Blasphemy froze.

"Angels, I can take care of this myself. Please finish your inspections!" ordered the mighty angel of God.

Michael's troops slowly withdrew, much to the delight of Blasphemy.

"Finally, I will have the opportunity to destroy you before Satan himself does!"

The demon inched toward his nemesis. The archangel smiled as he put his sword away.

"I believe Satan would not be thrilled to hear that you have tried to destroy the one angel that he despises most. He has specifically ordered all his followers not to lay a paw on me."

Blasphemy stopped dead in his tracks. He slowly backpedaled.

"You're not worth the fight! I could destroy you with one arm tied behind my back!" justified the evil agent.

Michael remained silent. Blasphemy scoured the angel's face.

"I would prefer that you are alive for the day that I rule the world! You will be bowing to me, begging for mercy!" yelled the ogre as he fled to the east.

Immanuel was a master speechwriter. His words were pointed, yet they reeked of doublespeak. The citizens of the world were spellbound by this master of intrigue. He could promise people eternal life, and they would believe him.

"Our religious leader received a fresh vision from our god. It is important for you to understand why we will not prosecute this filth dirtying the streets of Jerusalem."

The camera slowly zoomed closer to the Antichrist. His eyes could hypnotize a greater majority of the audience this way.

"Tomorrow, god will make his appearance on the steps of the Jewish temple. He will leave his place in the heavens and make his home with us!"

Immanuel stared into the camera as if it were the entrance into heaven. A full minute passed before he continued his lies.

"Our bible predicts this, and it will happen tomorrow! Nobody will be required to work during this solemn and joyous occasion. I want every good citizen of the World Federation to be glued to their television system tomorrow at twelve o'clock, Middle Eastern time! Until tomorrow, I bid you a prosperous day!"

The cavern was a respite from the desert heat, an oasis in the midst of a parched land. It was several hundred feet deep and about twenty feet across. The light from the sun faded as Ken and Tina painstakingly edged their way deeper into the darkness. The temperature had dropped from one hundred thirty degrees to less than seventy degrees in a matter of minutes. The cave was littered with rocks, animal bones, and slick spots.

"How much farther must we go, Ken? I can't see the hand in front of my face. I'm happy right here."

"Honey, you're probably right. But I have a hunch that there is something else back here that we need to search for."

Ken stopped at the base of a creek that was silently flowing through the middle of the grotto.

"Tina Marie, you stay here and have a seat on this rock. I'm going to go ahead and find out what that speck of light is."

She squinted to see the light.

"What are you talking about? Stay here with me! What if a wild animal were to come while you're gone?"

He quickly reached his hand toward her face, searching for her cheekbone.

"Honey, it's going to be fine. I'll be back in a couple of minutes!"

He gave her a kiss on the cheek. She was too drained to argue with him.

"Be careful, Ken. I love you!"

Immanuel's private jet was gliding over Europe. The three thorns in Immanuel's side were seated across from him. Each was as stubborn as a rattlesnake and more dangerous than a python. However, they were no match for the great dragon that was breathing down their necks. They could feel the fury of fire coming from his nostrils, yet they remained obstinate.

"Immanuel, I don't understand why you invited me on this little trip of yours to Jerusalem. This talk about God visiting earth is for the movies. Dominic was probably sniffing glue when he received this supposed revelation," quibbled his vice president of France.

"Never mind the religious nonsense. I have a bone to pick with you about my country's share of the World Federation's budget. I'm sick and tired of seeing my people suffer through this recession. I'm completely helpless. I have no power to do anything but suck up to you for a few crumbs!" steamed the vice president of England.

Immanuel's cheek muscles were twitching. It was an omen that neither of the men picked up on.

"I can't agree more with these gentlemen," added the vice president of Germany, Helmut Blitzkrieg. "This is the last straw! When I get back home, I'm going to hold an election in *my* country to see what *my* people want. My guess is, they will choose me over the mess you've given them!"

Immanuel eyed each one of his critics, one by one. It was as if he were measuring them for their caskets. He was operating in slow motion, like he was in some type of time warp.

"Immanuel, are you doing drugs or something?" asked the brave German.

The Antichrist slowly turned his way. He closed his eyes. As he shut the door of the physical realm, he opened his eyes to the spiritual domain. They watched as his eyes began to bubble against his eyelids.

"What is going on here?" yelled the man from Britain.

"The man is psychotic!" raged the Frenchman.

"It's just another reason for us to abandon this maniac before he ruins our countries and the entire world!" castigated the German.

Blasphemy, who had been given temporary control of Immanuel, was getting tired of these nonbelievers.

"You will obey me or suffer in everlasting hell!" thundered the Antichrist.

The monster's eyes began to slowly twitch open. The men were speechless as they stared deeply into Immanuel's eyes.

"Oh, my God!" panicked Helmut.

The dictator's eyes turned bloodred. Instead of being round and small, his pupils were now enlarged and elongated. They were pulsating back and forth between yellow and black.

The diamond chandelier above the Frenchman fell from the ceiling. It landed on his lap, sending throbs of uncontrollable pain through every cell in his body.

The other two men vaulted out of their seats.

"Sit down and shut up!" roared Blasphemy and Immanuel.

The men ignored the Antichrist as they desperately tried to pull the heavy chandelier off their fellow confederate.

Two hungry demons instantly tackled them. The German and the Englishman landed hard on their backs.

"Today, you will know that I am God!" blasphemed the Antichrist.

He stretched his left hand out toward the two men. They cringed in terror as fire spewed from his fingers.

"You will obey!" snarled Immanuel.

Timothy was closely following Ken Action. He was trying to keep him out of harm's way. The senior angel had left Daniel in charge of guarding Tina Marie.

The speck of light that Ken had seen had enlarged. Ken's heart beat wildly as the light brightened. He could now see the footpath. It was obvious that people had recently traveled into this area. Ken didn't know if that was good news or not.

"Daniel, there's something happening ahead of us! Be prepared for anything!" shouted Timothy.

His voice echoed, not once, but three or four times. He hoped that Daniel understood.

The younger angel was trying to calm Tina Marie's nerves when he received the message. He dragged his sword from its holster. His eyes pierced the darkness.

Ken picked up his pace as the rocky path began to smooth out. He became nervous. It appeared as if somebody had recently constructed this road to nowhere. It quickly changed from a narrow footpath of sand to a road of rock three feet wide. Miraculously, it was lined with the most beautiful flowers that he had ever seen. They must have been planted, thought Ken. The light was so bright, Ken had to shield his eyes. He could only see about ten feet in front of him because of the intensity of the glow. His curiosity outweighed his caution.

Timothy was also curious about what was causing this light. His spiritual antenna seemed to indicate that it was friendly, but he couldn't be sure. He weighed his options. He quickly darted toward the light with the sword of righteousness in his right hand.

Immanuel sipped on an espresso laced with vodka. He was comfortably seated in his leather swivel chair. The Antichrist punched a sensor that was molded into the left arm of the unit.

"This is Immanuel. I want you to get rid of those impersonators in Jerusalem. If they get in my way down there, I will personally have your head mounted in my den!"

Immanuel punched the sensor. He wasn't the kind of person to leave any bargaining room.

The sound of his voice awakened the heads of state. Their bodies were sprawled all over the cabin. Immanuel picked up on their moans and groans from beneath him, yet ignored them, as if they were waking dogs. Helmut Blitzkrieg was the first to regain full consciousness.

"Immanuel!" cried out the German.

The Antichrist grinned. He watched intently as the other two became coherent.

"Gentlemen, you are fired. You have shown utter contempt for my policies, and for me personally. As your god, I will uphold my end of the bargain and be merciful to you. That means that I will allow you to live. After this flight, I plan on never seeing your faces again!"

The Frenchman began to complain about his blood-soaked leg.

"I need a doctor! Please help me!"

Satan's disciple ignored him. He pulled up the shade on the airplane window. His private jet was less than a thousand feet off the ground. The city at the center of the earth was smiling at him. Today was the day.

The Devil glared at the prophets of Jehovah God. The enmity possessing his heart could not be controlled. He had to somehow kill those men. Today was his day to shine.

Satan was dressed in a priest's robe. It covered his body from his horns to his paws, but it couldn't cover the noxious smell of his wicked heart.

Timothy zoomed through the tunnel with his heart racing like a hummingbird's wings. He couldn't wait to see what was on the other end. Suddenly, he could see people, hundreds, maybe thousands of them. What were they doing? Why were they there? Who were they? As he reached the end of the road, the cave opened into a stupendous ballroom. It was a miracle. He had never seen anything like it.

Ken Action reached the end seconds later.

"My God! How can this be?" he gasped.

He slowed his pace to a crawl. He wondered if this were heaven. Ken remembered Tina Marie. He had to share this moment with her. He did an about-face, praising God as he dashed back toward the darkness.

"Daniel! Daniel!" shouted Timothy into his transmitter. "We have reached the treasure at the end of the rainbow!"

Fourteen

Let the Games Begin

The following morning, the sun was still on the far end of the earth when Moses and Elijah began to evacuate the Christians from the city to the desert.

It had been two weeks since they first appeared, and in that course of time, one hundred forty-four thousand Jews had pledged their lives to full-time ministry. Tens of thousands more had switched their loyalty from the state to their Creator. These Jews were turning Jerusalem upside down. About a third of the population of this great city had found their Messiah.

The prophets knew from God's Word that today was the day when the Devil would set up shop in Jerusalem. They knew it was time for God's people to flee to the hills. It was there that they would be protected by God for three and one-half years. The prophets knew that any Christian left behind in Jerusalem would face misery beyond comprehension. They warned the Israelites with the words of Zechariah, saying,

"'And it shall come to pass in all the land,' says the LORD, 'that two-thirds in it shall be cut off and die, but one-third shall be left in it: I will bring the one-third through the fire, will refine them as silver is refined, and test them as gold is tested. They will call on My name, and I will answer them. I will say, "This is my people"; and each one will say, "The LORD is my God."'"

Jehovah God had prepared a glorious hideout near the Dead Sea. Elijah and Moses had secretly given directions to this desert location. Since all the roads were monitored by satellites, the exiles were to travel by foot. It was a day's journey from Jerusalem, and the journey was to begin during the night. Nobody would notice that they had disappeared. With Immanuel coming to town, everyone was busy getting prepared for the event of a lifetime.

It was four in the morning. Satan had prepared a meeting for his troops on the earth's sister satellite, the moon. Every follower of the fallen angel was to be there on time or risk one of Satan's infamous temper tantrums. It was the perfect time for God's elect to flee. There wouldn't be a demon in sight to warn the adversaries.

As the earth faded in the distance, it wasn't fading from Satan's thoughts. He wanted the deed to that piece of dirt and would fight to the death for control of it. His warlocks were stationed on the dark side of the moon. As Satan arrived, the crowd began to wildly cheer. They were going to be on the winning side. The demons all wanted their piece of the pie.

Satan's wings were methodically flapping at the zero-gravity atmosphere. He came in for a landing like a great eagle floating toward its nest. His coal-black fur was standing on end. His troops were kneeling on bended knees.

"All hail, Lucifer! King of the heavens! Lord of the air! Master of the earth!" hooted Blasphemy.

The demons were boiling over with anticipation. This was the day that Lucifer had been bragging about for thousands of years. Today was the day that he would break Jehovah God's "spell" on the people of the earth.

Blasphemy slowly bowed as his lifetime nemesis eyed his every move. Fortunately for the general, Lucifer had his mind focused on the great conspiracy.

Lucifer glided over his followers. He circled them, looking for praise. It was his time to be proclaimed God.

"Unholy is the name above all names, Lucifer!" shouted Blasphemy.

His boast was picked up by a solar wind. It traveled at the speed of light across the heavens, reaching the very throne room of Jehovah God.

"It is finished!" announced Jesus Christ.

At that very moment, a trumpet blast shook the heavens.

"Did you hear that?" said Timothy. Daniel stood motionless.

"Let's get up to the throne room of God at once!"

Daniel didn't have time to respond. Timothy started to fly away with Daniel in tow. From the four winds of the earth, every angel advanced toward God's heavenly dwelling. This trumpet detonation had never been heard before.

The rebel of rebels stood on a homemade clump of moon dust. His sullen features were masked by a short-lived joy that can come only from sin. He was king of the hill. In his twisted mind, he was more powerful than anything in the universe, including Jehovah God. Satan turned toward God's throne, which was seven light-years away from the orbiting rock. His pretentious words sent the demons blasting off like a fireworks show.

"Your time is up, Jehovah God! Jesus Christ was given my rightful position as Savior of the world, and I plan to make You pay for it!"

Satan's threat traveled through the glittering cosmic night. It gusted into God's dwelling with the sound of a thousand screams.

Righteous anger welled up inside the Trinity. God had given the traitors of the angelic world over seven thousand years to repent. Their time was up.

Jehovah God motioned for Jesus Christ. Without a word, Jesus approached the emerald throne. The Father's image could have melted a mountain. The two acted as one. They were the same entity but separate beings.

"The time has come to fulfill my Word!" proclaimed the Father. "Give Michael and the angels the power that they need."

Jesus' face was a picture of peace as He left the resplendent presence of His Father. The elders of the church praised Him; the creatures surrounding the throne sang hymns. Suddenly, His angels appeared from the earth. Hundreds of millions of them converged outside the inner throne room to receive their orders. It was as if a star had exploded in their galaxy; light rays pelted them from every direction.

"This must be big!" expressed Daniel as he began to slow down.

Timothy nodded. He was too excited to talk.

The angels of Jehovah God surrounded Jesus Christ.

"Jehovah God wants evil eradicated from the heavens. His Word will be fulfilled today," announced Jesus.

The Savior of the world began to quote Scripture. They were the same words that the apostle John penned on the island of Patmos in the Mediterranean Sea. His perfect words were from the twelfth chapter of the book of Revelation.

"'And war broke out in heaven: Michael and his angels fought with the dragon; and the dragon and his angels fought, but they did not prevail, nor was a place found for them in heaven any longer. So the great dragon was cast out, that serpent of old, called the Devil and Satan, who deceives the whole world; he was cast to the earth, and his angels were cast out with him. Then I heard a loud voice saying in heaven, "Now salvation, and strength, and the kingdom of our God, and the power of His Christ have come, for the accuser of our brethren, who accused them before our God day and night, has been cast down. And they overcame him by the blood of the Lamb and by the word of their testimony, and they did not love their lives to the death. Therefore rejoice, O heavens, and you who dwell in them! Woe to the inhabitants of the earth and the sea! For the devil has come down to you, having great wrath, because he knows that he has a short time.""'

Jesus paused to allow the angels to absorb the fullness of the moment. He raised His hand into the air.

"You have the power to fulfill this prophecy today. Go forth and conquer!"

"Tina Marie, wake up!"

"What, what is it? Oh, Ken, you're okay!"

"Follow me! You will not believe what is at the end of this tunnel!"

"What is it?" yawned Tina.

"I'm not sure, but I can tell you that it is big!"

He searched in the dark and found her hand.

"Let's go!"

Ken was so excited that he almost yanked her hand off as he dragged her into the darkness.

Tina Marie didn't know what to think.

"Ken, slow down. I'm dead tired!" moaned Tina.

"We are just so close. Can you see the light in the distance?" said Ken.

She had trouble focusing.

"I made it to the point where I could see a vast opening! I could have sworn that I saw some kind of crystal building or something!"

"I can't see anything," said Tina.

"Trust me! I promise that I'm not going off the deep end! Don't you see how the light is twinkling with all the colors of the rainbow?"

As the couple approached the opening of the chamber, Ken felt vindicated. Tina Marie dropped to her knees in awe.

It was magnificent. It was the most brilliant thing that she had ever seen. No human mind could imagine it.

"Ken, what is going on here? Have we died and gone to heaven?"

———————

"I will ascend into God's throne room and knock Him into the fires of the sun!" announced Satan as he drew his clenched paw into the air.

The demons hissed their approval. Satan had forced each of his devils to face the ground. After all, it was their duty to bow to their master. He looked toward the earth and howled like a werewolf lusting for blood.

"I am God! I will sit on the mount of the assembly! All the earth will—"

His words abruptly ended. The demons didn't know what to think. Many wanted to look up, but they feared the creature's wrath. Their blind allegiance would seal their fate.

Heaven was invading hell.

"What the—" belched Satan.

Satan's troops didn't flinch. Some demons figured he was testing their loyalty by pretending somebody was attacking him. They didn't see Michael's sword. They didn't see Satan's look of horror. They didn't see their location being surrounded. They were booby-trapped by their submissiveness to the Evil One.

"God has judged you, Satan!" declared the archangel as he swung his sword at the dark one.

His mighty dagger knocked the King of Evil onto the ground. Satan jumped to his feet. The impact dislodged Satan's sword from his holster inside his left wing.

"You have no right to judge me!" growled the dragon.

His demons jumped to their feet but said nothing. They were completely surrounded by the light of God's stalwart army.

"Satan, Jehovah God has judged you, and you have been found guilty!"

The archangel placed his sword on the tip of Lucifer's pointed nose. Nobody from either side dared say a word or even make a move. The strongest angels of all time were nose to nose.

Blasphemy, who was only yards from this cosmic clash, slowly looked around the periphery of the landscape. He realized that they were outnumbered two to one. However, that didn't stop him from making the biggest move of his life.

The city was magnificent. Jehovah God's hand was the sole source of its being. For a distance of seven miles in all directions, one could see pure crystal buildings reaching to the top of the God-made cavern. The streets were made of gold, while jasper, emeralds, sapphire, topaz, and pearls were more abundant than air. A light as bright as the sun emanated from the walls and ceiling of the subterranean shelter.

"Ken, I can't believe what I'm seeing! Who did this?"

Ken Action wrapped his arms around her.

"God did this. But why, I don't know. We'll find out soon."

Ken stared deeply into her eyes.

"You're as beautiful as this or any other thing that God has created."

Tina Marie blushed. She grabbed his hand.

"Let's check this out. Those buildings shaped like towering oak trees have got to be explored."

A set of spiraling golden stairs were attached to the clay exit of the burrow. Tina Marie took the initiative and placed her foot on the first step.

From the air, they looked like an unbroken line of ants, marching to their nest in the hills. Thousands upon thousands of born-again Jews were following Moses and Elijah to their refuge from the storm. Like their ancestors before them who traveled into the desert, they came to follow God's anointed to their promised land. They trusted God with their lives, even to the death.

It was six in the morning. The faithful Jews were miles from Jerusalem. Not one of the enemy had spotted their migration.

Blasphemy thrust his rockets into overdrive. He had one chance to annihilate the enemy, and he wasn't going to pass it up. With the speed of light, he thrust his body toward the archangel as a demonic cannonball. Nobody had time to react. Blasphemy's balled-up body knocked Michael over as if he were a bowling pin.

Michael instantly bounced to his feet. He sliced his sword into the air, sending Blasphemy dodging for cover. Several hundred angels from God's Iron Guard threw themselves at Satan. The war of the heavens had begun.

Immanuel's eyes opened. His face was a ghostly shade of white. He resembled a dead man.

"Blasphemy, where are you? We are less than six hours from our operation. This is not a time to play games with me."

Immanuel's call faded into oblivion. He had no idea that evil was in a fight for its very survival. The Antichrist's mind began to spiral out of control. Blasphemy wasn't answering his distress signal.

"Blasphemy! Answer me! If I burn, you will—"

He quickly snatched the words from the end of his forked tongue. He didn't need to make enemies now, especially not with the one giving him power.

Satan was being tossed to and fro. As soon as he would rid himself of one set of angels, another group would join the brawl. Millions of swords were lashing against the black sky. Most were missing their intended targets. The confrontation had been inevitable. For thousands of years, Jehovah God had allowed Satan and his band of serpents free access to the heavens. He had allowed them to put down the people whom God loved. Jehovah had even given them the freedom to speak falsely about Himself. But now the sand had run through the hourglass.

"Daniel! Watch out behind you!" shouted Timothy as he tried to fend off two demons.

Timothy quickly did an about face, swinging his sword through the air like a trained marshal arts expert. It knocked three demons toward the lit side of the moon.

"Angels, I want every demon routed to the other side of the moon!" trumpeted the archangel Michael as he beat several demons to their knees.

Michael was looking for Satan, who was nowhere to be found. Blasphemy had also disappeared.

The super-angel quickly jetted above the battle to assess the situation. In the distance, he could see Satan's and Blasphemy's spiritual vapor trails polluting space. They had fled like cowards.

His eyes turned back to the dust storm ravishing the dark side of the moon. A clever idea flashed in his mind. He quickly repositioned himself directly above the battleground.

"Your fearless leader Satan and his trusty sidekick Blasphemy have deserted you! It's all over!" shouted Michael.

The force of his voice knocked a few demons on their spiny backs. Every demon, except the feistiest of them, paused to sniff the air. Just the thought of their leader abandoning them was too much to take.

"He's right!" barked the demon Damien. "I saw it with my own eyes!"

The demons watched Damien. The angels watched Michael.

"Satan and Blasphemy are heading to Earth! What do we do?" shouted Damien.

The archangel Michael knew just what to do.

"Angels of God Almighty, hear my plea! You are hereby ordered to destroy every demon that has been left behind. If they escape, allow them to find refuge only on the earth. Every demon remaining in the heavens must be eradicated!"

A supernatural burst of energy filled the angel's swords. Without their master to lead the charge, the devils scattered like a flock of werewolves at the first sign of dawn. Hundreds of millions of them fled to escape their sure defeat. The angels followed closely on their tails.

"Well done, good and faithful servants of Jehovah God!" triumphed the archangel as he kicked one of the fleeing spirits in the tail bone.

Daniel was whooping and hollering. He dropped his sword several times as he waved it in the air.

"Calm down. Save that energy for the next three years. Don't you see where they are going?" observed Timothy.

Daniel slowed down enough to look.

"Where are they going?"

"Earth. They're headed for Earth." For a moment, Timothy and Daniel just watched as the dark cloud of evil approached the troubled planet. "Remember this, Daniel, there has never been a time when every demon has been on the earth. We have a tough road ahead of us."

It was noon, Jerusalem time. Immanuel was dodging the prime minister of Israel's questions.

"I have a right to know what to expect today. I've done everything you've wanted of me without question or hesitation," fumed David Hoffman.

The blood vessels on his forehead were out of control.

"For three long years, I have defended your policies while thousands of my people have died at the hands of Arabs. You've shunned me and slapped me in the face by giving them the ark of the covenant. Now you sit there and tell me to wait? You use my country as your podium, and you think that you have the right to keep me in the dark?"

The Antichrist was unmoved by his emotional appeal. The prime minister stared into the empty eyes of the Beast. It was the worst mistake that he had ever made.

"For your so-called prophet Dominic to say that God is going to visit us today is—"

Suddenly, the Antichrist's hand gripped the prime minister's neck.

"You listen to me! You have no rights. I am the source of all your rights! I thought you got the message a few years ago when my prophet visited you that night!"

Terror filled David's face.

At that very moment, Blasphemy stormed into the hotel room. He was filled with a type of hatred that was foreign even to Immanuel. He didn't waste any time. He plunged his spiritual being inside of Immanuel's body. The Antichrist's body shuddered. Blasphemy reeled with hideous laughter as he took control of the human. He hated Satan, he loathed God, he despised Dominic, he abhorred Immanuel, but he loved himself. He was going to use Immanuel to get back at everybody who had crossed him in one way or another.

"I am God! I created you, and I can destroy you! Bow to me or die!" dictated Blasphemy through Immanuel.

The Antichrist had lost complete control of his body. A bolt of energy resembling lightning nearly missed the prime minister.

"I believe!" cried David as he fainted on the floor.

Blasphemy enjoyed being in the Antichrist's body. He pranced around the suite like a king about to reclaim his kingdom.

Suddenly, Blasphemy's dance was cut short. Something else had entered Immanuel. Blasphemy shook in fear.

Tina Marie was sitting on the edge of a roadside curb made of pure gold. Flowers created from beveled emeralds adorned the surrounding area. The brilliant city radiated heavenly colors. It was more fantastic than she could have possibly imagined. There were colors everywhere. Colors she had never seen before.

"Ken, look at this!" shouted Tina as she began to explore the grass.

He reached down and picked a blade of the perfectly manicured lawn. Another strand of it quickly took its place.

Ken stopped. He heard human voices pouring out of the entrance to the city.

"Who are you to possess my human?" ordered the King of Evil. Immanuel's body began to palpitate.

"Satan," hissed Blasphemy. "You have given him to me to program the way I see fit," lied the five-star general.

The Devil couldn't believe his ears. His sidekick was finally showing his true colors. He didn't need Blasphemy anymore. There were plenty of four-star generals who would give their wings for the opportunity to lead the troops to victory.

"As I expected all along! You are a traitor! You will die!" whispered Lucifer.

Satan's saliva began to boil in his mouth. His blood sizzled.

Blasphemy ripped himself from Immanuel, who was astonished at the spiritual warfare. For the first time in his life, he could actually hear Blasphemy and Satan.

"Blasphemy! Do you have anything to say in your defense before I destroy you!" seethed Satan.

The general shifted into his political mode.

"Sir, I have always had your best interests in mind. Even today, as I stand here a convicted demon, I tell you that I want the best for you and your kingdom of darkness."

"What's going on here?" clamored Immanuel, growing increasingly agitated at the haunting voices surrounding him.

Satan didn't hesitate to give Immanuel an attitude adjustment. The razor sharp claw from the dragon knocked him out.

"Master, I admit to not obeying your orders specifically on a few key points. It's only because you're so busy, and I don't think you have the knowledge of certain significant facts that you might have if you were on the battlefield day and night. I will resign if that is your decision, but trust me when I say that my loss will be your loss! I have prepared Immanuel just the way you like your humans. Give me Dominic Rosario, and I will not let you down."

Blasphemy slowly bowed, hoping that Satan's wrath would be cooled for the moment.

The Devil finished sharpening his sword. He raised it into the air only a few feet from the tip of the general's nose.

"Your life has been a miserable failure from the very start! The only thing that brings more joy to my soul than seeing traitors like you burn is to see my vision of world dominion fulfilled!"

The serpent of old slowly edged his body toward Blasphemy. Satan's sword was as steady as a surgeon's scalpel.

Blasphemy desperately tried to show as little fear as possible. Any sign of fear would be interpreted by Satan as a sign of a guilty conscience. The less guilty he appeared, the better chance that he would be allowed to live.

"Examine my heart, and you will see that what I am saying is true, O cruel master of the most cunning kind," kissed up Blasphemy.

The general's heart began to pound like a bass drum. He couldn't take his eyes off the blade that was dancing closer by the second.

"I will grant your request," uttered Satan. "But I will satisfy my desire to see you suffer, also!"

Without even a hint of warning, the strongest demon ever created plunged his sword into Blasphemy's oval mouth.

The sword slowly did a semicircle around his barbecued heart. The pain was unbearable.

Lucifer carefully watched his reaction as he slowly withdrew the weapon.

"You do fear me!" said the great dragon. "I grant your request! Go and bodily possess Dominic!"

Blasphemy slowly dragged his body off the carpet. He limped toward the door.

"Thank you for sparing my life!" whispered the spirit.

The door to the hotel room closed. Blasphemy hobbled toward the elevator. His vindictive mind was already busy scheming a way to get even.

Moses and Elijah were at the center of the crystal city, welcoming the Israelites to their new home for the next three and one-half years. The look on the weary travelers' faces was one of astonishment.

Ken Action and Tina Marie were hiding. They were baffled by the sheer numbers of people taking asylum in this oasis.

"Who are they, and where in the world did they come from?" whispered Tina as she ducked the glances of a little boy only yards away.

"I haven't a clue. I think we should make our presence known now before they see us hiding and think we're hostile. I think those bearded men over there are the leaders!"

They walked toward Moses and Elijah. It took only a few seconds for the prophets of God to notice them.

"Welcome to our city," responded Moses. "I sense that you love the Lord Jesus Christ!"

Ken stepped forward.

"We do! I'm curious who you are, and what you are doing here. In fact, I'm curious what 'here' is."

"I am Moses, and this is Elijah," began the prophet as Elijah graciously smiled at the two. "We are the two prophets of God Almighty, the God of Israel. This city is a refuge prepared by Jesus Christ to protect and nourish us for a time."

Ken Action dropped to his knees. Tina Marie quickly followed.

"What can we do to help your cause?" begged Ken.

Elijah's smile glistened in God's glory.

"You can start by standing on your feet. Do not worship us, but worship God. We are simply God's servants in this hour of redemption!"

"Are you a Jew?" inquired Moses.

"No," responded Ken.

"God has provided this refuge for the Jewish remnant who are not part of the one hundred forty-four thousand chosen to preach. God is a merciful God. I don't believe that He will mind your staying," assured Moses.

For the moment, Ken and Tina were safe.

———

Hours later, the pomp and circumstance had begun in Jerusalem. The Global News Network had a team of sixty cameras and thirty remote reporters who were live on the scene. It was touted as the greatest event ever to occur in human history. Millions of people from all over the world converged on this mountain city, hoping to touch the garment of God.

Immanuel Bernstate slowly walked toward the microphone located outside the inner sanctuary of the temple. His mind was numbed by Satan's presence. He was not himself. His wicked high priest had possession of him. As Immanuel approached the center of attention, he nodded to the False Prophet, who was seated to his left. On his right was the prime minister of Israel.

As he approached the microphone, he began to chant in an unknown language. The television decoders couldn't decipher it.

Blasphemy, who was seated in Dominic's spirit, wanted to puke. He yearned for the day when he could put that know-it-all tyrant in his rightful place.

Immanuel opened his eyes.

"Welcome to the New Millennia," began Satan through his pawn, Immanuel.

Cheers filled the air. The people of the world wanted to see a god. They wanted to witness miracles. They lusted after the supernatural.

"Today, our spiritual leader has promised us something magnificent. For too long, our world has worshipped an invisible God, a God who seemed uninterested in the affairs of man and woman. Today, god has made a promise to his spokesman, Dominic Rosario. At any moment, he will come to our planet."

As the crowd chanted for their messiah's coming, Immanuel turned and nodded at Dominic. Blasphemy saw the signal. It was time for him to leave the False Prophet and jet toward the eastern horizon.

The streets were littered with people. Nobody could budge a muscle. The mob was pushing forward toward the temple arena, leaving a few trampled in the dust. The atmosphere was filled with anticipation. The eyes of the world were fixated on Immanuel Bernstate, president of the World Federation. He motioned for Dominic to stand and address the throng.

The False Prophet rose from his seat. He shook the Antichrist's outstretched hand and walked to the microphone. He knew that Blasphemy was absent, yet the apostate was poised to begin without him.

"I want to thank you for coming this afternoon to witness history being made. I especially thank our president, Immanuel Bernstate, for organizing this event, and having the confidence in me, and our God!"

The False Prophet bowed toward the man of destruction. The crowd applauded.

"The time is at hand!" announced the False Prophet as he raised his hands toward the overcast sky. "Light is dawning on a miraculous new age."

Several hundred of God's chosen Jewish preachers were in attendance. They were the only ones who knew the significance of what was happening. The world would never be the same again. The sun was setting, not rising.

Immanuel, who was within striking distance of Dominic, looked upward. He was anticipating Blasphemy's arrival at any moment.

Suddenly, a sharp cracking sound rang out from the audience. The crowd was horrified. The False Prophet lunged toward Immanuel.

———————

Ken wanted to stick around and ask the prophets several dozen questions. It was like a dream that had come true.

"Moses, what did you see when you were on the mountain getting the Ten Commandments from God Almighty? What were you thinking? Why did He keep you on that mountain so long? Were you mad when you didn't get to see the Promised Land?" asked the new convert.

Moses smiled.

"Your curiosity is admirable. We will have eternity in heaven for such conversations."

"Please, give us an assignment, and we will carry it out with all our heart and soul," said Ken.

"We'll be leaving this refuge shortly to continue our preaching. You're welcome to join us if you are so led," said Moses.

Ken looked at Tina Marie for her approval.

"It's going to be dangerous," whispered Tina.

Moses overheard her.

"Your life is not of this world!" shared Moses. "Your life is in heaven. Every deed done for the Lord will be credited to you in heaven. Every achievement accomplished for yourself will burn. Do not fear what the world or man can do to you; love God!"

———————

The Antichrist slumped over in excruciating agony. A bullet had pierced his left side, fatally close to his heart. Immanuel was desperately trying to maintain his composure as he dropped to his knees, and then onto his back. Dominic Rosario was by his side, helplessly watching the leader of the world die.

"Get a doctor!" screamed the False Prophet.

The push from the crowd overwhelmed hundreds near the front of the temple square. They were being trampled to death with little remorse from the rest of the crowd. Some men and women were crying. The rest of the crowd were trying to escape to safety.

Several World Federation doctors rushed to his side.

"Is he going to be all right?" asked the False Prophet.

A doctor probed the wound with his fingers. Immanuel cringed in pain.

"We need to get him to our medical truck. It's only a hundred yards to the north of here," said the doctor.

Several medical workers streaked across the temple mound with a stretcher.

The cameras from the Global News Network followed their every move. They carefully moved the president onto the canvas.

By now, the crowd was reacting as if their god had just died. There was complete chaos and confusion. Several hundred police guards surrounding the temple were getting itchy trigger fingers as the pack pushed against their security positions.

"Stay back! The president needs air! We will shoot if we are forced to!" they shouted.

As Immanuel was being carted away from the somber scene, Dominic motioned for peace. Satan wanted calm. Everything was going as planned for now, but he needed his brood to settle down. He jumped out of Immanuel's body and dove headfirst into Dominic's body. The possession jolted Dominic's system. The False Prophet was accustomed to Blasphemy's evil, but the incarnate evil from Satan was beyond comprehension.

Dominic's spine reacted by slowly bending. He walked toward the microphone as Immanuel disappeared into the medical truck.

"People of the world, listen to my words! This vicious and cowardly act was done by forces of evil! You know who they are! They are in your countries, in your cities, even in your neighborhoods! The born-again Christian fanatics are responsible for this violence against not only the World Federation, but also your hopes and dreams!"

Satan used Dominic's eyes to scan the outskirts of town. He saw Blasphemy coming over the horizon.

"Men and women of the world, I am beginning to sense God's presence," spoke the wicked dragon.

"Shouldn't we go down there and stop it?" asked Daniel.

His wings were flapping as fast as his jaw.

"Daniel, don't you understand? God is in control!"

"Doesn't look like it to me!" said the nervous angel.

"Calm down. Let's open up God's Word and see where we are right now. Then you will understand what must come to pass."

Timothy flipped through the Bible before arriving at the book of Revelation.

"'Then I stood on the sand of the sea. And I saw a beast rising up out of the sea, having seven heads and ten horns, and on his horns ten crowns, and on his heads a blasphemous name. Now the beast which I saw was like a leopard, his feet were like the feet of a bear, and his mouth like the mouth of a lion. The dragon gave him his power, his throne, and great authority. And I saw one of his heads as if it had been mortally wounded, and his deadly wound was healed. And all the world marveled and followed the beast. So they worshipped the dragon who gave authority to the beast; and they worshipped the beast, saying, "Who is like the beast? Who is able to make war with him?" And he was given a mouth speaking great things and blasphemies, and he was given authority to continue for forty-two months. Then he opened his mouth in blasphemy against God, to blaspheme His name, His tabernacle, and those who dwell in heaven. It was granted to him to make war with the saints and to overcome them. And authority was given him over every tribe, tongue, and nation. All who dwell on the earth will worship him, whose names have not been written in the Book of Life of the Lamb slain from the foundation of the world. If anyone has an ear, let him hear. He who leads into captivity shall go into captivity; he who kills with the sword must be killed with the sword. Here is the patience and the faith of the saints. Then I saw another beast coming up out of the earth, and he had two horns like a lamb and spoke like a dragon. And he exercises all the authority of the first beast in his presence, and causes the earth and those who dwell in it to worship the first beast, whose deadly wound was healed. He performs great signs, so that he even makes fire come down from heaven on the earth in the sight of men. And he deceives those who dwell on the earth by those signs which he was granted to do in the sight of the beast, telling those who dwell on the earth to make an image to the beast who was wounded by the sword and lived.'"

"Wow! God *is* in control. He knew this all along," said an amazed Daniel.

"Yes, He did. That's why we can trust Him," said Timothy, glancing down at the afflicted planet. "I can feel the prayers of Ken and Tina lifting my wings and energizing my sword. When do we fight?" inquired Daniel.

Timothy patted him on the back.

"Soon, very soon! Unfortunately, it will not be long before you're begging for the war to end!"

The cameras panned across the sky, searching for the first signs of God's presence. The people around the temple looked toward the heavens.

Seeing something in the distance, David Hoffman slowly rose to his feet. His body began to shake uncontrollably.

The people held their breath as it approached. Many fainted. As Blasphemy advanced toward his target, the people's unbelieving hearts were moved. Was it a hallucination? Was it real?

Fifteen

The Great Charade

The spaceship glided across the eastern side of Jerusalem. A hushed reverence possessed the disciples of the World Federation. The reporters for the Global News Network were speechless. As the cameras zoomed in on the foreign object, the viewers at home could see the round ship pulsating with energy.

"It is some type of UFO!" concluded the lead anchor for the worldwide television web. "For nearly one hundred years, people from all over the world have been telling us that they exist. Most of their appeals have fallen on deaf ears. But not today, ladies and gentlemen! The questions are, Who are they? What do they want? Where have they come from? Are they human? How is God involved in all of this? As you can see, Dominic Rosario has dropped to his knees. He had been predicting God's visitation today. Could this be a sign that God is on that ship?"

The crowd's attitude was one of awe and inquiry. No one knew how to act. A few people who had momentarily taken their eyes off the ship had noticed the False Prophet's behavior and mimicked him. People began to drop to their knees and clasp their hands together.

––––––––––

"I want that ship to hover over that medical truck," barked Satan.

"Yes, sir," returned Blasphemy, who really wanted to take the ship and crash it on the dragon's head.

"My God, today we are witnessing the fact that we are not alone," continued the awestruck reporter. "I can only guess how this will change the attitudes of future generations!"

The False Prophet slowly raised his quivering hands into the air. His outstretched palms were reaching toward the ship, as if to say, "I'm not worthy."

"We may very well find out that they are our gods, that they are the ones that humanity has been worshipping since the dawn of the great religions," continued the reporter.

"I couldn't have said it better myself!" laughed Satan from within the False Prophet.

The spaceship continued its trek across the eastern side of the dazed community. It was traveling slowly, allowing the cameras and the world an impeccable view of its intricate design.

It was shaped in an oval on the horizontal dimension, but protruded in the vertical like a spiral pyramid. It was approximately the length of one football field across and three football fields high. An eerie glow streamed from the inner core of the craft. The colored light seemed to surround the ship.

"As you can see, it is now approaching the temple area where millions of people have gathered to celebrate the World Federation. Wait a minute! It seems to be slowing down! The Prophet of the World Church seems to be talking to someone. I'm now getting a message from our lip-reader on the temple grounds. Yes, I see! Are you kidding?"

Moses and Elijah walked up the stairs of the temple in the crystal city. It had four doors that stood for the four winds, twelve sets of golden stairs for the twelve tribes of Israel, and one wooden cross at the top. There were no signs of the old Earth except that one piece of timber that carried Jesus Christ to His victory over mortal death and sin.

As Moses and Elijah reached the top, the crowd gathered at the base of the stairs. Their eyes were forced to squint at God's spokesmen. The light of heaven was deep and lucid.

Jews from all around Israel were rapidly filling the paradisiacal chamber from the outside world. A steady stream of immigrants already had completed the march to their glory land, but many more were lined up for ten miles outside the cave.

The demons, who had returned to Jerusalem from their humiliating defeat on the moon, were outraged. They had just spotted the flood of Jews entering the cave on the north end of the Dead Sea. Not one of the demons had the nerve to pass this crucial information to Satan. Nothing was more meaningful to the Prince of Darkness than claiming his right to be regarded as God.

Moses motioned for the crowd to continue its journey down the golden stairs to paradise.

"Please, Christians, move forward as quickly as possible! Your brothers and sisters are open prey to the wolves of the World Federation!"

"As the redeemed continue to pour in, I would like to update you on what is happening in the outside world," began Elijah.

Nobody said a word. Everyone there had the utmost respect for God's prophets who were bringing the only true message from God's Holy Word.

"Right now, as I speak, the greatest sham against this world is taking place in Jerusalem. I thank God for you, that you were willing to leave your homes and villages, and follow us to a place prepared by Jehovah God. You have displaced yourself and your families, and traveled into a desert not fit for man or beast. You have the faith of the great Jews of the past, who left their homes to obey their merciful Creator."

Tears welled up in the people's eyes. Many closed their eyes and silently thanked God.

"Right now, the Devil is in Jerusalem! If you had not obeyed God, many of you would have been slain by the World Federation! God's angels are busily guarding your Jewish brothers who are fearlessly preaching the Word. The wise among you know that this time was predicted long ago by the apostle John in the book of Revelation. For the next three and one-half years, your home will be here. God has filled this city with everything to sustain your physical needs. His Spirit resides in this place to satisfy your spiritual desires. Soon, Moses and I will go back to preach."

Tina Marie rested her head on Ken's shoulder.

"I'm ready to die for Christ's sake!" said Tina.

Ken hugged her.

"When I think about my past and my hatred for the things of Christ, I can only say that God has performed a miracle in my life! I'm ready to die for Him, too. I see now that there are only two types of people: those for Him, and those against Him."

She embraced him.

"Ken, I've been thinking about it, too. We need to go back to Jerusalem to preach the truth. If one of us is killed, God forbid, it won't be long before we have eternity in heaven to worship our King together!"

The truth of her words struck his heart. He lowered his head. "You're right," he whispered. "You know what this means?"

She smiled. "Yeah."

The announcer's voice had turned broken and shaky. Silence followed as he received the message from his man on the street. The world was on the edge of its seat. After a long, awkward pause, the voice of the Global News Network returned to life.

"People of our fine planet, the message that I have received is incontrovertible. This is not, I repeat, not a speculation or tabloid rumor. Our linguist, who's located less than twenty yards away from our prophet, has informed me that Dominic Rosario is talking to God! God is no longer in heaven! He is in that ship!"

After several minutes of deep meditation and conversation with the occupant of the vessel, Dominic Rosario stood to his feet.

"People of Jerusalem, I have been ordered to ask you to drop to your knees. You are now standing on holy ground! The God of this universe cannot appear to us until we are cleansed of our unbelief. Bow and worship Him. Love Him with all your heart. Adore Him as your Father and Creator!"

As the words spewed from the False Prophet's mouth like poisonous darts, the ship suddenly stopped. The beastly illusion was directly over the medical truck containing Immanuel Bernstate.

Suddenly, the door to the mobile hospital swung open. A despondent doctor lowered his head as he exited the unit.

"People of Jerusalem," he shouted, "Immanuel Bernstate has suffered a lethal injury. Less than three minutes ago, our beloved leader passed away!"

The doctor didn't notice the object floating above him. He was watching the crowd. Many began to wail uncontrollably.

"My God! The president of the World Federation has been assassinated! I repeat, Immanuel Bernstate, long hailed as the one man who can bring peace to the earth, has been killed by a sniper's bullet!"

The lead anchor began to weep. The world was dumbfounded. Why would God, who was in that ship, allow such a tragic event to occur?

Suddenly, a door on the floating fortress began to open. The crowd looked skyward.

"Remember, Blasphemy! Like a king!" demanded Satan. "Your very life depends on it!"

The cameras zoomed in on the opening to the spacecraft. A colored fog streamed from inside the capsule. A snow-white figure emerged wearing a crown of gold. Its eyes blazed like a furnace. Twice the size of an ordinary man, it appeared superhuman. A white robe hid everything except its hands, feet, and head.

The television announcer lowered his voice as he described the astonishing visitor.

"God is here in our midst!" the anchor said in awe. "He is really here! As you can see through the lens of our camera, which is shaking in the hands of our operator, He is surprisingly human in nature. I may be mistaken, but it appears as if you can practically see through Him. It's hard to tell. Our camera lenses are steamed from the vapor coming from His vessel. At this time, I will show reverence for His Majesty by staying silent. I invite you to savor the moment and give Him all your attention."

Satan moved the False Prophet toward the medical truck. His steps were calculated and smooth. The image of their God remained silent as it slowly dropped toward the earth. Blasphemy and Satan had planned to meet near the place that held Immanuel's body.

"Blasphemy!" barked Satan. "Don't think that I won't skin you alive right here in front of the world. Obey me!"

The general acted shocked by his intimidation.

"Lucifer, my master, I will obey your every command!"

Satan was growing weary of his game-playing.

"Blasphemy! You will do just as I order!"

"Yes, master," kissed up Blasphemy.

The mysterious being floated downward. As Blasphemy reached the surface of the earth, Dominic fell on all fours.

At that very moment, Satan lunged out of Dominic's body. Blasphemy departed from his apparition just in time to avoid Satan. The False Prophet's body lay limp at Blasphemy's feet.

"Dominic missed your feeble spirit," belittled Beelzebub. "I only hope that there is enough man left for you to occupy!"

Blasphemy quickly jumped into Dominic's body.

Satan addressed the crowd with eloquence.

"People of the Earth. You are my children. I have come to you today to proclaim peace!"

Grandmothers were on their knees. People were sobbing. The world thought that they were seeing God. It was more than some could take. Thousands all over the temple area were fainting; some were having heart attacks.

Dominic Rosario had been revived. He felt energized. His eyes watered as he listened to the image only a few feet away.

"I love you citizens of the World Federation! From the time that I created the earth, and allowed evolution to take its natural course, I have been watching your race carefully. At times you have pleased me, and at other times, you have troubled me greatly," spoke Satan.

Their god's eyes searched the crowd with the power of a million microscopes.

"My heart is troubled. My servant Immanuel Bernstate has been killed by a Christian's bullet! Today, I will show you the power of God. Immanuel's name means 'God with us.' Today, prophecy is fulfilled, for Immanuel and I shall become one!"

The god-figure slowly traveled through the walls of the medical truck and disappeared from sight.

Dominic leaped to his feet to fill the void. He began to speak.

"Today, the prophet Isaiah's vision of a peaceful future with God at the helm has come to fruition, and I quote, '"The Spirit of the Lord GOD is upon Me, because the LORD has anointed Me to preach good tidings to the poor; He has sent Me to heal the brokenhearted, to proclaim liberty to the captives, and the opening of the prison to those who are bound; to proclaim the acceptable year of the LORD, and the day of vengeance of our God; to comfort all who mourn, to console those who mourn in Zion, to give them beauty for ashes, the oil of joy for mourning, the garment of praise for the spirit of heaviness; that they may be called trees of righteousness, the planting of the LORD, that He may be glorified." And they shall rebuild the old ruins, they shall raise up the former desolations, and they shall repair the ruined cities, the desolations of many generations.'"

The False Prophet happily twisted the meaning of the verses.

"Today, God is here to rebuild the ruins of a world destroyed by the Christian zealots. He has finally come to preach the good news of peace for the earth!"

Dominic's words were cut short by a clamor inside the medical truck.

"Citizens of the World Federation," interrupted the television announcer, "something strange is happening in that truck!"

Without warning, the door blasted open. The crowd jumped back as Immanuel's rigid body floated through the door and over the crowd.

"My God, ladies and gentlemen!" panicked the television host.

Dominic Rosario began to chant to his god. At that very moment, Satan moved through the wall of the truck. He slowly followed the levitating body around the periphery of the temple.

"People of Jerusalem, hear what I have to say!" hypnotized the people's new god. "Immanuel Bernstate died so that I might be glorified! He was killed by a born-again cultist's bullet to prove to you that these destroyers of peace need to be judged for murder. My word says that if a man hates in his heart, then he might as well be a murderer! Many of these self-appointed religious impersonators claim to know me and my ways. They claim to know the truth. The truth cannot be found in them because their father is the Devil! I will judge these lawbreakers with death!"

The crowd cheered feverishly as Satan pulled off the greatest masquerade of all time. Immanuel's dead body continued to circle the field of worshippers as their god slowly followed from behind.

"For thousands of years, I have waited patiently for the human race to evolve into my spiritual light. Many times I have wanted to visit this ailing planet and destroy those who oppress others. However, I waited out of my infinite mercy. I waited until you had evolved enough to make the spiritual jump to the next level and be where I am. Now you see the truth. I am connected to every living thing in the universe. I and the cosmos are one!"

The creature's brasslike hands disappeared behind its flowing garment. Seconds later, they reappeared with a small statue in their grasp.

"This is an idol of my image. Every person on my planet will possess one of these. Pray to it, and I will answer you! My powers are limitless!" thundered Satan with the fury of a thousand cannons.

"I am god, and there is no other! You are to worship me and me alone! I will not stand for any other gods in my place! I have the power to bring down lightning from the cloudless sky! I have the power to judge those who are against me and my people of the World Federation. I even have the power to bring back the dead!"

Suddenly, lightning flashed down from a clear sky. The bolt traveled into the defunct body of Immanuel Bernstate.

"I just can't believe my eyes!" shuddered the anchor. "This is the most amazing display of power that I could have ever imagined!"

Specks of energy began to rotate around Immanuel. The energy began to dive into Immanuel's hardened corpse.

"Immanuel! You are not dead, but are just sleeping," declared the imposter god.

"Angels of the most high, hear my voice!" trumpeted the archangel Michael.

Millions of angelic officers, from colonels to generals, were present to receive their final orders. They were stationed under the waters of the Dead Sea.

Michael gleamed at his comrades. He had known his friends and fellow warriors since the time of the beginning, even before Satan started his war against their God and Creator.

"We have been through much since the great rebellion. I know that our Lord has been extremely pleased with your selfless service during this time of testing."

The officers cheered.

"The plan is simple. We need to protect Moses and Elijah with every weapon we have at our disposal. There are also one hundred forty-four thousand born-again Jews who must have protection for their preaching. The fury of hell will be at our backs, on all sides, and in our faces. Our power will occasionally diminish as Satan tries to destroy the Christians. Many times in the near future, your prayer power could be cut in half, or more. When the Christians are killed, so go their prayers. Do not wander off alone. Stay in groups. And above all, keep your enlisted angels away from the concentrated areas of evil. Are there any questions?"

The archangel scanned the sea of angels. A few hands were raised.

"Alexius, what is on your mind?"

The colonel cleared his throat and glided upward.

"I don't believe we're going to have the angel power to protect every one of the Christian saints on the earth. What are we to do?"

The archangel seemed restless, almost perplexed.

"I have run the numbers also, and it is painfully obvious that many will die at the hands of the Devil. This is God's plan; it is written in His Book, and it is something that we will have to accept. But remember, Alexius, those humans will be with the Lord in heaven when their torture is complete. We need to protect as many of them as possible so that God's purposes will be completed." Michael opened a gold Bible and read, "'And this gospel of the kingdom will be preached in all the world as a witness to all the nations, and then the end will come.'"

Alexius understood. He took his seat among the officers.

"Jesus Christ demands that the entire world hear His saving message. We understand it would not be fair to judge souls to hell when they didn't know how to get to heaven. Therefore, our job is to make sure Christ's saving grace is preached to everyone. When Moses, Elijah, and the hundred thousand and more witnesses complete their jobs, our responsibilities will be done. Hence, we are to concentrate our spiritual warfare around those who are evangelizing for God."

Michael's words were eloquent but pointed.

A general near the back of the flock made a motion to be heard. The archangel graciously gave him the floor.

"Sir, your replies are well-studied. I would like to know what you want of my angels in the Jerusalem sector. As you know, I have been the supreme commander of the region since the birth of Christ. With the Antichrist now stationing his forces within the holy city, I feel that I'll need some major backup support to do my job effectively."

The angel general bowed as he retreated into the angelic mass.

The archangel rubbed his chin. As he considered the question, his wings propelled him to the center of the brackish sea.

"We have the prayer power to control parts of Jerusalem. Jesus assures us that the authority has been granted us to command most of that critical sector. Our Lord will allow much evil to go uncontested for now. Our job will be to protect those who are spreading seed, who are watering His crop, and who are making a difference for heaven."

The cold, expired body of Immanuel Bernstate lay on the stairs of the temple. The spacecraft had completely vanished seconds earlier. Every camera was glued to the body of their fallen leader.

Blasphemy, longing for some spotlight, moved Dominic Rosario toward the carcass.

"Ladies and gentlemen," said the bewildered anchor, "Dominic Rosario is now approaching the great leader's body."

The anchor paused to regroup his thoughts.

The False Prophet was carefully taking one step at a time toward Immanuel.

"I don't know why Dominic Rosario is inching his way to the steps. He is only ten yards or so away from Immanuel Bernstate."

Satan spoke from inside Immanuel's body.

"Get your human to stand over me. You will repeat every word that I tell you to say. Got it? Every word!" raged Satan.

"Yes, my evil king," responded the antagonist.

Seconds later, the False Prophet was standing over the presidential cadaver. The air was still. The people were still. Their hearts waited.

"People of planet Earth," proclaimed Dominic. "With God, anything is possible. Today, the impossible becomes reality!"

Dominic Rosario raised his hands. His shivering fingers were pointed toward the slain president.

"Many across our great planet have doubted the World Federation and the World Church. Many speak of God as an invisible force, a revengeful God destined to throw everybody in hell who disagrees with His ideas. Today, our God is here to refute those malicious claims. As the good book says, 'Eye has not seen, nor ear heard, nor have entered into the heart of woman or man, the things which the World Federation has prepared for those who love it.' Today, I present to you the president of the World Federation, and the God of the universe, Immanuel Bernstate!"

The False Prophet's words had barely sunk in when Immanuel's hand began to twitch.

"My God! Did you see it? He moved!"

The GNN's anchor was losing it.

The False Prophet's hands began to violently shake. Suddenly, miniature bolts of lightning flashed from Dominic's energized fingertips.

The anchor fainted.

Immanuel moved. First, only a finger, then two, then the entire left hand. Hysteria gripped the crowd. Fear mingled with awe spread across the planet like a tidal wave.

"Immanuel, God with us!" cried out the False Prophet. "Let the world know that we serve a risen savior!"

Both hands began to move, then his legs. Pandemonium ruled as Satan unleashed his greatest hoax yet. Then, Immanuel's eyes opened. He instantly stood to his feet, causing Dominic to drop to his knees. The crowd followed suit. Immanuel Bernstate slowly walked up the marble stairs of the temple. When he reached the top, he turned and faced the cameras. His flock was on their knees, sobbing uncontrollably.

"People of my planet," began the great deceiver.

Quiet spread across the masses. The world's conscience was being charred beyond repair.

"I have seen death! I have tasted what glories there are in heaven, and I have been glorified!"

The crowd went berserk. The masses, who had been without God since rejecting Jesus Christ, were overwhelmed with emotion.

"I am the one who created the Earth! I am the one who created you! I have the power of life and death! I have chosen this time to bring good tidings of joy, to bring eternal peace to my planet! I am the god of all religion! I am the one who judges! Hell exists only for one group of people, and they are those who oppose the truth, who oppose my purposes!"

Immanuel's demeanor was different. With Satan at the helm, he moved with unabashed arrogance. He preached about religious pride being evil, yet his own body language condemned him. Satan's logic was flawed, yet the people's minds were numb.

"I have a vision!" shouted Immanuel at the top of his lungs. "I see a world where peace is not a promise, but a reality. I see a world where the young child can play at the den of a cobra's nest. I see a world where there is no rich man and no poor widow. I see a world where religion is outlawed."

Dominic Rosario did a double take. Blasphemy could not believe what he had just heard. No religion translated into no power for the world prophet. It was the worst thing that could ever happen to him.

Every demon was buzzing through the air like locusts swarming over wheat. Their objective was to control the minds of the people. Today was a historical day in their squalid history. Satan owned the government, the Church, the lines of communication, and the hearts of the people. There was nothing to stop Immanuel now. He was evil incarnate and proud of it.

The Antichrist looked toward the sky.

"I see over one hundred thousand Jews who have fled our city this morning. They are running away from me because they know that their deeds are evil. They are fleeing my light because they prefer the darkness of their iniquity."

Satan raised Immanuel's hands into the air. His body began to shake as the tranquil sky fell apart.

"I will not put up with a people bent on twisting who I am. The foolhardy Israelites who have followed the underground Christian revolt against me will be brought to justice!"

Fire rained down from heaven. The balls of lightning appeared as if meteors, and vanished just above the crowd's heads.

"Immanuel! Immanuel! Immanuel! Immanuel!" bellowed the brood of satanic converts.

It was a high beyond reality. Satan was tasting his first sample of deity. There was no looking back. It was full steam ahead.

"Citizens of the World Federation, hear my word and believe. You are to go back to your cities, towns, and neighborhoods. Go to your families and live life as you always have, except this time you will be able to see and hear your god. I want you to obey me. Think for yourself, but consider my word final. You are to work for the common good of your fellow man and woman, as well as the World Federation. Forget what the Christian church put into your minds about God. I am your god, and there is no other!"

Suddenly, one of Immanuel's closest handlers rushed to his side.

"Sir, I have a confirmed report that over ten thousand Jews are near the Dead Sea. We have them where we want them."

Immanuel ignored him.

At that moment, a struggle broke out near the outer edge of the crowd. Somebody was struggling with Immanuel's line of defense. Several guards were on top of an individual. The ruckus captured Immanuel's attention.

"As I speak, there is somebody in this crowd who does not agree with the words of god. This is to be expected. Bring them on the stage to challenge me face-to-face."

The global guardians hustled the individual up the temple stairs. His right eye was swollen and his cheeks were bloodied. As they dragged the man closer to the untamed Beast, a few in America recognized the troublemaker as one of their own.

Immanuel appeared cordial to the intruder.

"Please state your name for the world to hear," beguiled Satan.

The American seemed a bit hesitant. He looked around, then faced his oppressor with a defiant tone.

"My name is Bill Thomas."

Immanuel grinned at him.

"I was a cabinet member for the president of the United States. I defected when I discovered that he was selling out the sovereignty of the United States to a heathen like you, Immanuel Bernstate!"

The Antichrist took a deep breath. It was important that god remain calm. The crowd couldn't believe what they were hearing. How could someone criticize God, to His face?

"I have given you the opportunity to be heard, and all you want to do is malign me and my fine organization."

Immanuel's face thinned as he changed attitudes.

"Are you a born-again bigot, Mr. Thomas?" examined Lucifer.

A peace that the Antichrist could never possess filled Bill's face.

"No, I am not a born-again bigot. I am a born-again Christian who loves God. You are not God! You are a man impersonating God for your own egotistical ends!"

Immanuel cut him off. He didn't need his godhood questioned at this point in his ministry. The Beast placed his hands behind his back as he slowly marched around the American.

"So you don't believe that you are talking to God. You don't believe the miracles that you have seen. Your faith is misplaced and has led you astray."

Immanuel paused, which was a fatal flaw in his strategy. Bill Thomas saw the gaping hole and ran with the ball.

"Listen to me, people of the world. Jesus Christ loves you. He hates sin, but loves people. Read the original Bible and you will see that all of this was—"

Concentrated energy poured from Immanuel's fingers. It hit Bill Thomas with such force that it knocked him sixty feet backward. The crowd gasped. The guards quickly raced to Bill's side and checked for a pulse.

"He's dead, sir," stated the sentry in a matter-of-fact tone.

The Antichrist turned toward the crowd. He appeared saddened by the unfortunate event.

"I do not desire to end anyone's life. I do not want to see my creation in hell. But I am a god who must keep order, or our house will fall into disrepute. This man is a perfect example of an individual who spreads the flames of hatred. This is the type of revolutionary that hell was made for. I warn you not to be like him, or face the consequences of eternity in Gehenna."

Satan closed his eyes. The False Prophet ran to his side, as if he were a dog that had been called by a silent whistle. Dominic stood by his side as Immanuel dropped into a trance. The world watched as the two seemed to bond into one. Both the Antichrist and the False Prophet were in a supernatural stupor. They suddenly opened their eyes, which now appeared glazed and distant.

"As I speak, Bill Thomas has reached the gates of hell," fabricated Satan. "He is being shackled by the innkeeper, and tossed into a horrid world of his own making!"

The Antichrist faced the False Prophet.

"Hear my voice, people of the world. The World Church will be undergoing some important changes in the near future. My representative on Earth, Dominic Rosario, will be my man to implement these changes. By next week, I want every church, temple, and synagogue on the face of the planet to have an image of me in the front of their worship facilities."

The spellbound flock cheered.

"Get lost, Blasphemy!" retorted Satan.

Dominic wisely exited the stage.

"At this very moment, the World Federation troops are ready to overtake the Christian anarchists in the desert near the Dead Sea. They will be judged severely," promised the Evil One.

The Jewish Christians were lined up at the entrance to the cavern, awaiting the opportunity to enter their place of rest. Suddenly, screams of horror encompassed the back of the line. Fear spread like wildfire.

"My God, they're coming after us!" yelled a widow as she lost her footing.

Like a flood of water rushing down a hillside, the ruthless troops from the World Federation marched on their position.

The news reached Moses and Elijah in the nick of time. They were standing outside God's crystal temple, electing elders.

"People of Israel, Satan is attacking our people in the desert. Bow with me as we claim God's promise of protection."

The assemblage fervently prayed for God's miraculous intervention.

As Immanuel's army neared its target, something beyond explanation transpired. The thirty thousand troops were less than a hundred yards away when the ground beneath them collapsed. A sinkhole the size of a small town gobbled up every enemy of Jehovah God.

Sixteen

The Evil Blossom

D aniel was curled up in the corner of a Jerusalem apartment, studying the book of Revelation. Timothy had given him the idea to meditate on God's plan, hoping that it would help him prepare for the upcoming battles.

Ken and Tina were asleep. Months earlier, they had begged the prophets to marry them. There, in the cave, amid God's miraculous handiwork, they committed their lives to each other. Now that memory seemed as far away as the moon. They had returned to Jerusalem to stand for truth.

Daniel would occasionally glance up at the humans that he was protecting. He loved them unconditionally, especially Tina Marie. She was a lot like him. Ken's wife was loving and sweet, yet excitable. His emotional attachment to her went beyond the call of duty.

"Daniel," shouted Timothy as he swooped into the room.

The shock of Timothy's intrusion sent Daniel careening against the wall. Timothy had caught him off in thought, his guard down, once again.

"I was just over at the temple area. Something big is happening there today."

Daniel tried to regain his rattled senses.

"Can't you enter a little more quietly?"

Timothy punched him on the wing in a nonthreatening manner.

"Sure I can. But I don't expect Satan's little friends to be so kind."

"So what's going on out there today?" wondered Daniel.

"I'm not entirely sure, but I did see some members of Satan's elite force hiding behind the temple mount."

"Do you think it's Armageddon?" said Daniel.

"No way, not yet! That's three years away! But I am wondering if they are planning an attack on our witnesses, Moses and Elijah."

Daniel raised his forefinger into the air as if he were Superman.

"They will have to trample my body into the dust of the earth and send my body into the flames before I allow such a dreadful thing to happen," reacted the emotional roller coaster.

Timothy laughed.

The room was familiar; the times were not. The smoky chamber beneath the chic Swiss hotel was full of bankers and egos. Everybody was there except Immanuel Bernstate. He loved to keep people waiting and make a grand entrance to grab as much attention as possible. The conversations were filled with emotion as the bankers discussed a solution to their dilemma. A few didn't think there was a problem. Some believed the government had no business redistributing wealth. Most had no trouble with government policy, as long as it wasn't their assets that were being confiscated. The chaos was shattered as Immanuel strutted out of the elevator.

He was wearing a black suit and sun-yellow tie. It was the first time that the group had ever witnessed their leader in anything but a bloodred tie. Satan would pick Immanuel's ties from now on. Immanuel was carrying a briefcase by his side as he made a straight path for the front of the table.

"Gentlemen, I thank you for coming today. I have less than an hour so I will have to make this quick," announced Immanuel as he took a seat.

Every eye was focused on the man who would ransom his children for the deed to the world.

"We have a problem," began Immanuel with the help of Satan. "The people are expecting much from me, and I want to deliver it to them. When I created the world—"

A few scoffed. Satan picked up on their lack of loyalty. He answered the dissension with a sudden burst of energy toward the elevator. It missed the control panel by an inch. All murmuring died, and Immanuel smiled. He would do anything necessary to demand allegiance, especially from those who had the power to damage his credibility.

"As I said, I created a world where men were given a free will. You gentlemen have free wills to walk the walk with me or follow your own path. In any case, I have found it necessary to borrow 90 percent of your assets, payable to the World Federation, immediately."

One could hear the heavy breath of Lord Birmingham as Immanuel severed their friendship. The deafening silence didn't sit well with the Antichrist. He quickly made eye contact with each of the men. Their cold stares were to be expected.

"Sir, I have the utmost respect for you and your policies," flattered Birmingham, "but this is a travesty. You are violating an unspoken contract with the men who put you into power. You yourself said that we would share in the success of the World Federation."

The bankers at the oval table seemed frightened. Immanuel didn't know if he should read that as a plus or a minus. He was worried that the others would follow Lord Birmingham into mutiny.

Satan caused the Antichrist's rigid body to stand up. He slowly walked around the room. His cocky attitude was the final straw for Lord Birmingham.

"My dear Lord Birmingham," began Satan, "you have been the fearless leader of this little club for some time, and I applaud you for your pursuit of profit. But, sir, profit is not everything!"

The Antichrist's voice resembled a father speaking down to his prodigal son.

"Birmingham, you've been a success, according to the horizontal playing field of life. You have accumulated enough riches to feed a medium-sized country for a decade. Certainly more than you need for yourself."

The men were confused.

"Unfortunately, your life will not be judged horizontally; it will be judged vertically. What have you done for God?"

Immanuel smiled. "What have you done for me?"

Immanuel continued walking around the table, placing his hand on each man's shoulder. "Don't you see? I'm helping you make the right decision. I'm assuring you of a blissful eternity." He paused.

"If I were to use 90 percent of your money to feed the poor and clothe the oppressed, you wouldn't miss it a bit. Your lives here wouldn't really change. Ah, but your eternity, now there's where the change would be!"

The men were shaking their heads in disbelief.

Immanuel was leaning on Lord Birmingham's chair, hoping that the banker would lose his cool. Birmingham stood to meet him face-to-face.

"You, Immanuel Bernstate, are a demagogue of the worst kind. You couldn't care less about the sick and poor of this world. You don't advocate helping the underprivileged and those in need. They don't need your salvation, and neither do we!"

The others remained motionless. They were waiting for a lightning bolt to fry Lord Birmingham. They were cowards. Most of them preferred life with a few concessions to their integrity than to die a martyr's death to uphold their principles.

Immanuel placed his hand over Lord Birmingham's shaking finger. He slowly placed it back at its owner's side. The Antichrist's behavior was astonishingly modest and sober.

"As god, I forgive you for your lack of understanding," said Immanuel.

"I don't forgive you for 'borrowing' my ark of the covenant!" shouted Birmingham.

Immanuel smiled. "*Your* ark? Really? I thought it belonged to God."

Lord Birmingham was taken so off guard by Immanuel's statement that, in disgust, he plopped back down into his seat.

"You have lost your mind, Immanuel! This god thing is going to your head! You may have powers, but I don't believe for a second that you are God!"

No one seconded his remark.

"You don't?" smiled Immanuel.

"No, I don't," said Birmingham. "If you are God, then how is it that you have to rely on evil to accomplish your objectives?"

The verbal jab didn't faze the Antichrist. The bankers were exchanging snide facial expressions.

"My patience is waxing thin with you, dear Birmingham. You are but a child trying to understand his father's job. You are not stupid, but you are ignorant," voiced the Antichrist.

Lord Birmingham's eyes rolled.

"I only use evil because I must meet evil on its own territory." Immanuel stared at him with a look so intense that it silenced any further questions. No one questioned his logic, or lack thereof.

The sunlight strained its way through the vinyl blinds. Tina was the first to respond. The clock was flashing two-thirty in the morning. She poked Ken in the back.

"Ken, wake up, the electricity went off again last night."

Ken rolled his haggard body on its side.

"What time is it, honey?" mumbled Ken.

Tina jumped out of bed.

"I don't know. But the sun is up. We have that meeting at eight. The sun rises at seven something."

"Daniel, did you know about that meeting?" checked Timothy.

"Yeah, I'm the one who helped them with the connections." responded Daniel.

"Then why didn't you do something to wake them up?" questioned Timothy.

Daniel poked his head behind his wings.

"I'm sorry. I was so much into the prophecy stuff that I forgot."

"Get over to the Mount of Olives and stall them. They can't miss this meeting, or our work will be set back for months!"

Immanuel's proclamation of godhood brought sweeping changes to the World Federation. Each citizen of the new world order was required to have an invisible computerized tattoo ingrained in the palm or forehead. The citizens of the World Federation were more than happy to obey Immanuel's order. He promised that this new program would save enough money to bring prosperity to every person on the planet. Every financial transaction would be tabulated and taxed by this new computer setup. The benefits far outweighed any inconveniences. It took less than ten minutes in a World Federation doctor's office to guarantee financial freedom for the rest of one's life.

Criminals could not operate because the cashless system put them out of business. Those who didn't pay their fair share of the tax burden would be exposed. Billions would be saved because there would be no need to pay people to police drug trafficking, counterfeiting, stealing, or a host of other money-related crimes. Everybody who received this mark was required to swear their allegiance to the World Federation and Immanuel Bernstate. It was their symbolic act of obedience to their new god. In a speech several weeks after his proclaimed godhood, Immanuel compared it to baptism.

Immanuel's true motives were masked by his public propaganda. He was frantically trying to smoke out the underground Christian revolt that had continuously dented his plans. He figured that if he could keep them from buying food, they would eventually break under the pressure of an empty stomach. It was wishful thinking because, as he tightened his grip on the world's merchant system, the Christians' resolve swelled. It didn't make sense to the Antichrist. They were hardheaded hoodlums who loved pain, thought the Devil. Every time that he lowered the hammer on the Christian renegades, their numbers increased.

Since proclaiming himself god, he had already tortured over six million Christians. He had tried mind- and conscience- altering drugs. For some odd reason, they had little effect on the zealots. He directed the World Federation police force to publicly torment them into submission. That directive seemed to backfire in his face. While 95 percent of the populace loved to see the Christians burn, the other 5 percent joined them. He hired a team of psychological investigators to find out what made them tick. Satan's mind could not fathom why some people would join a quickly dying group of people destined for torment. A few of those who took the assignment were converted by the Christians. No matter what the hardship, they were at peace. Immanuel was promising a manufactured peace, but the Christians had a real peace that politics and money could not buy.

It was difficult for Immanuel to admit, but war could occur at any moment. Even though he had proclaimed himself god of the world, there were splinter groups all around the world who had unhindered access to weapons of semi-mass destruction. There were even rumors of nuclear warheads being sold to the highest bidder. The World Federation was powerless to control the bartering of individuals in every remote cubbyhole on the planet. His political statisticians estimated that Immanuel had a 90 percent following. This rating would never make the evening news. Even a 10 percent faction among the citizens of the new world order could bring devastating effects. Immanuel's mouthpiece, the GNN, was strictly prohibited from reporting any news that could be detrimental to his long-term goals.

———

Lord Birmingham silently hissed as he watched Immanuel disappear behind the elevator doors. The lord glanced around the room. His friends were watching him carefully.

"Gentlemen, I believe we have created a monster!"

He smacked the perspiration rolling down his cheeks. Nobody dared to speak.

"We must do something to stop this madman! Trust me, gentlemen. This man won't stop until he has every last penny from our pockets. He knows that we have the power to bring him down."

The embittered bankers seemed nervous by the force of his fighting words.

"I want to know something right now!" exclaimed Lord Birmingham as he slammed his fist on the table. "How many of you truly believe that Immanuel is God?"

His eyes darted from man to man. Lord Birmingham wasn't sure if they would be honest with him or even themselves. No one moved a muscle, which relieved the lord.

"All right, then, if this man is not God, and we all seem to agree with that, then we must take him down!"

One of the more quiet members of the group forced his hand into the air.

"Lord Birmingham, I don't believe that he is God, but his powers are real and frightening."

"Unfortunately, I agree," consoled the lord. "I can't fathom these miraculous powers of his. That UFO thing I think I can explain, but the lightning stuff and the moving objects are disturbing. Nevertheless, gentlemen, we can't let this little two-bit Houdini walk off with what we've worked so hard to enjoy."

"But, Lord Birmingham, this man does have the power to kill us," offered the CEO of Germany's largest bank.

Lord Birmingham stood to his feet, placing his hands on the desk in front of him.

"I'm sure he already has our cemetery plots arranged at one of his Christian concentration camps."

Many shook their heads in agreement. Lord Birmingham's heart began to race.

"The way I see it, we must go to war with this maniac! We must take back control before it is too late!"

"Don't you think that it is already too late?" asked the banker from Switzerland.

Lord Birmingham swung his eyes toward the pessimist.

"No, I do not. I have a plan that will put Immanuel back into the pit that he crawled out of," responded the lord.

"I would like to hear that," reacted another banker.

Lord Birmingham took his seat again. He folded his trembling hands and hid them on his lap.

"Here's the plan. We do not pay him the 90 percent ransom. We earmark that money for groups scattered across the globe that are fighting the World Federation. Even though I don't agree with the Christians, I believe that they are the most organized, so they should get a large slice of that pie. They will use our gold for food and shelter. The underground bartering is almost entirely driven by precious metals, so that should get us over the computer, cashless system hurdle. I have connections who have ready access to conventional, chemical, nuclear, and biological weapons. We distribute them to the Muslim fundamentalists. Some of the Islamic militants dream about the day when they can die for their god."

"How about the Christians? If they have the numbers, shouldn't we get those to them?" wondered the man from Germany.

Lord Birmingham gritted his teeth as he thought about the idea.

"I've spoken to a few of them in the past several months, and I don't believe that they would use the weapons even if we gave them to them on a silver platter. They don't believe in force. They will take our gold and silver if it means the difference between starving or living, but that's about it. On the other hand, the Muslims will thank Allah for the opportunity to blow up a city or two if it means destroying Satan's throne. We must go into hiding immediately. My guess is, Immanuel has already dispatched a team to keep an eye on us. He already has the cashless system that tracks our every move, and I'll be willing to bet my life that he is having us tracked by satellite right now."

The Englishman stood to his feet. His admiration for Birmingham's courage was apparent. He was the voice in the group that was seldom heard, but was highly respected.

"Lord Birmingham, I have been sitting here for some time without saying a word. But I must end my silence. I believe that this journey could be deadly to us all!"

The man's lips were broad and aged. He was the oldest and wisest of the group.

"Even so, I support you 100 percent. This man is not God. I don't know if you gentlemen believe any of the Bible, and I'm not talking about their new edition, but my King James Version. Don't get me wrong. I'm not a Christian, but I do find it amazing that most of the predictions in that Book are now coming true! This man is not God; he is a devil, the Devil! He must be stopped at any cost!"

The Englishman sat down.

"Thank you, sir, for your endorsement," said Birmingham.

Lord Birmingham looked around the room.

"Well, at this point, I think it would be prudent if we took a vote. All those in favor, please raise your right hand."

The Englishman's hand was the first to sign on. Seconds later, a couple more slowly crept up over their shoulders. The remaining bankers finally signaled their approval. Lord Birmingham was relieved.

Tina and Ken crept their way across town, hoping that they wouldn't be spotted by one of the World Federation patrol units. It had become too dangerous to drive, since Immanuel had ordered every car to be occupied by a certified world citizen. If a person didn't accept the computerized tattoo identifying him as a patriotic citizen, he was not permitted food, water, or a driver's license. In fact, every car was fitted with a transmitter that was used to track it anywhere on the planet. A supercomputer in Brussels was linked to a series of spy satellites. It was capable of locating every car on the planet, within the range of a foot. Fortunately, for Tina and Ken, gas was in short supply, which meant most people walked from place to place anyway. They just hoped that they wouldn't stand out in the crowd.

It was painfully difficult to walk on eggshells and make it look as if you were on a Sunday afternoon stroll. They had heard horror stories about some of their friends looking guilty, and then ending up in Immanuel's claws. The global police force had been trained to interpret fear as the one quality necessary to indict a person for treason. Some Christians allowed the peace of God Almighty to be overruled by the frightful idea of the consequences awaiting those who didn't believe in Immanuel's godhood.

"Tina, it's going to be fine. You need to trust God. Don't fear Immanuel. The only thing that he can do to us is kill our body, not our souls," reminded Ken.

Tina's breathing returned to normal.

"You're right. I'm just worried about this meeting. What if I say the wrong thing?"

Ken squeezed her hand as they turned the corner. The Jerusalem temple, which was trodden by Satan, loomed in the distance.

"We can trust these men. They are part of the one hundred forty-four thousand."

Tina's eyes were roving from corner to corner, searching for any sign of danger.

"What if they are part of the underground police? Some of Immanuel's own are infiltrating our members."

Timothy, who was stationed on a rooftop near his humans, noticed a black fog of demons approaching.

"Daniel, bombers are advancing on our positions! Cut them off before they recognize our people!"

"Let's get over there immediately. Those raiders may alert one of the secret police about Tina and Ken."

The young angel stormed into the enemy line feet first. His sword pierced their outer defenses before being stopped by an alert sergeant.

"Enemy on the deck!" buzzed the stunned demon.

There were twelve of them and one of him. The numbers didn't look promising for the angel voted most likely to pick a fight with a pack of grizzly bears.

Timothy abandoned his position. With his sword whirling through the air, he rolled his body into the form of an oblong missile and shot toward them.

As Daniel pulled his body away from the demons, Timothy steamrolled into the tyrants. The bold tactic was similar to a kid playing with a bee's nest. Make the hit; then run as fast as you can.

"Get over to the temple immediately. Our leaders are there to protect you," shouted Timothy.

Daniel closed his eyes as he kicked his wings into supersonic thruster mode. Two of the twelve villains were snapping at his feet.

As he neared the temple area, Moses and Elijah were preaching in clear view of the planetary police. Daniel's angelic comrades were standing like a wall of water several hundred feet high. Captains, colonels, and even generals were standing guard on the outskirts of the altar. They were daring any demon to flaunt themselves near their high caliber weaponry. Surprisingly, there had been few disputes.

The demons gnawing at Daniel's feet were blinded by the light of these angels. They covered their dark eyes in agony as they retreated. Daniel looked behind him. He stuck his tongue out at the fleeing ghosts.

Ken and Tina had reached their destination.

The old warehouse had been used in the 1980s for seafood imports. It had been deserted for years. The exterior was in bad shape. Years of dry weather had colored the stone brown. The wood used for the doors and windows was infested with termites.

Ken glanced down one of the side streets. There appeared to be a side entrance, away from the hustle and bustle of the main artery.

"There it is," whispered Ken. "They said to go through that entrance and wait for them near the staircase."

They proceeded with caution toward the back alley. As they edged their way toward the side door, several birds were aroused from their nests. The birds screamed.

"Oh no! What was that?"

Ken yanked his neck upward. He spotted the birds as they loudly announced their departure. He grabbed Tina's hand and jerked her into the downtrodden structure.

"Sorry I had to do that, but if somebody nearby saw us in that passageway, my guess is, the police would be here to break some bones," surmised Ken.

"It smells like dead fish in here," objected Tina as she pinched her nose.

"This used to be a seafood storage warehouse a long time ago. Hey, there are the stairs," pointed Ken.

The inside of the building was in far worse shape than the outside. Parts of the floor were caved in. Light was swallowed up by the dust that had collected over the decades.

It took several minutes for the couple to safely make it to the other side of the structure. At times, it was like traversing a maze. Everywhere they turned, the floor had disappeared. Finally, they reached the stairs, gladdened that another board hadn't given way to time.

"So what do we do now?" asked Tina.

"Well, I guess we sit back and wait." He strained to see his watch. "I hope that they didn't give up on us. It looks like we are about twenty minutes late."

"We didn't give up on you," came a voice from the dark.

The sound made them freeze. Ken wasn't sure how to react.

"Where are you?" responded Ken as he tightened his grip on Tina's hand.

"We are right here," said one of the men as they revealed their position under the stairs. "Sorry to make you a little nervous, but you can never be too careful nowadays."

The two men were both dressed in casual clothes. They were wearing sandals, and loose-fitting long pants to shield them from the sun's heat.

"Are you sure that you are both ready for this?" asked the taller individual, who couldn't have been older than thirty years.

Tina stepped up to shake their hands.

"Well, I would like to introduce ourselves. I understand that we have mutual friends."

Ken took her cue.

"I'm Ken Action."

"I'm Tina Action."

They exchanged handshakes.

"Any suggestions on how to do this without getting caught?" asked Ken with a note of nervousness in his voice.

The elder man cleared his throat.

"The key is prayer. Pray that God would give you the wisdom that you will need and the protection of His angels. I can only imagine the spiritual warfare going on around this city since Immanuel announced his godhood."

Daniel, who had recently flown in after checking out some of Moses' speech, heard the last comment.

"You got that right, man!" shouted Daniel.

He knew that they couldn't hear him, but that didn't stop him from sounding off.

"How many Bibles do you have?" asked Ken.

The younger of the evangelists thought about it for a few seconds.

"I guess we have about ten thousand pocket Bibles left. You can have as many as you need, as long as you promise God that you will use them wisely and cautiously," responded the Israelite, who appeared as if he hadn't slept in days.

"Where are they?" asked Tina.

"I have them hidden in one of those collapsed areas in that corner over there," pointed the elder evangelist.

Suddenly, sirens began to wail outside the building. They seemed to get louder as the four looked at each other with dismay.

"Are they coming after us?" asked Tina as her eyes darted toward the partially open side door.

"I don't have a clue," responded the more composed Bible smuggler, "but we'd better take cover!"

The men motioned for Ken and Tina to follow them behind the stairs. There was a trap door underneath them. The men opened it without saying a word. Beneath the stairs, a ladder carried them into a pitch-black cellar.

"A few of the rungs are missing on this ladder. Be careful," whispered one of the men as Ken and Tina grabbed onto the rotting wood.

Quickly, but carefully, all four made it safely into the musty dungeon just in time. Tina panicked as she heard four, maybe five, voices just above the trap door. Ken put his hand over her mouth.

"It's going to be okay," whispered Ken.

Daniel and Timothy weren't sure what to do. The good news was that the police didn't have any demons attached to them. The bad news was that the global witch hunters knew somebody had been there minutes earlier, and they weren't about to give up their search very easily. There was a hefty bonus for anybody responsible for the arrest and conviction of Bible smugglers. With Satan's brand of justice, an arrest was the same as a conviction.

"We have to do something!" whispered Daniel.

"I'm thinking, I'm thinking!" responded Timothy.

His eyes skimmed the warehouse. Something on the opposite side entangled his eye. There were some wooden cases perched on an overhead compartment.

"I've got it!" announced Timothy. "Follow me."

Timothy jumped on one of the cases.

"Sergeant, there is a trap door behind the stairs." The private banged the butt of his laser gun on the loosely hinged door.

The four prayed as if their lives depended on it. The prayers raced toward their guardian angels, and immediately strengthened them.

"Praise God!" shouted Timothy as he knocked one of the boxes off its lofty mount.

The box smashed through the window.

The protectors of the planet charged toward the side door.

Timothy flew through the window with Daniel on his tail. He picked up one of the pieces of the broken box and tossed it down the alley.

"They're making a run for it!" blared the sergeant as he sprinted toward the boulevard.

"Give it to me straight," spoke Immanuel.

His tie was hanging loosely around his neck. His feet were resting on his desk. Vice President Colt glared at his god.

"I do not want to be the one to give you this information, your majesty, but I have sworn an oath to you, and I intend to carry that out," prepared the sniveling American.

Immanuel rolled his eyes.

"Just get on with it. Remember, I am god. I can do anything!"

Vice President Colt read his prepared statement without looking up.

"Your majesty, Moses and Elijah continue to wreak havoc on your plans. They have organized an underground Bible planting campaign. Its objective is to refute Dominic's bible and call you a liar. Many people are buying this line."

Colt paused, hoping Immanuel would vent some steam. He didn't want to be there during a violent eruption.

"Sir, we have confirmations from all over the globe of intense fighting. Somehow, people are getting weapons. Many are resorting to the older weapons. Our bureaucracy is in place, your majesty, but food is in increasingly short supply. People aren't working like they used to. We will survive, for now, sir, but if these skirmishes continue to accelerate, we may have a difficult time feeding the people."

Immanuel nodded his head, as if he had been expecting the report. He placed his hands into a position of prayer and raised them to his empty face.

"Did we receive the electronic check from Lord Birmingham yet?"

"I am sure that it was some minor oversight," explained Colt. "Maybe it was lost in the computer somehow," stretched the vice president as he tried to skirt the issue.

Immanuel cracked his knuckles.

"Your pandering for those self-appointed big shots irritates me. Give me the facts and do your job, and I will take care of the reasoning."

"Yes, your excellency. The forty trillion ECU check has not reached our hands."

The American glanced at his notes.

"You may find this of some interest. An extraordinary amount of gold and silver has been turning up in the Middle East, and among some in the Christian corner."

Immanuel's eyes stopped blinking. Hell was about to overtake him. He was putting two and two together, and it was equaling twelve disloyal bankers.

"Get out of here!" roared the monster.

Vice President Colt was happy to oblige. As Immanuel leaped out of his seat, the American quickly exited and left his notes lying on the floor.

Satan began to shake Immanuel.

"They have double-crossed me! Nobody backstabs me and lives to tell about it!" smoldered Immanuel.

He tried to calm the volcano inside of him. His eyes shifted to his computer.

"Computer," said Immanuel.

The screen instantly lit up.

"Ring my security chief!"

Seconds later, the chief appeared on his screen.

"Where are they?" sniffed Immanuel.

The man dropped his chin into his chest.

"Your majesty, I have just been informed that we lost them somewhere in the Colorado Rockies," lamented the chief. The man was twitching uncontrollably.

"You are fired! Report to my office immediately! I have a score to settle with you! Computer off!"

The screen died. Immanuel glanced at his security system, which tracked each of his employees.

"Security system on. Follow number 676."

The hot-tempered dragon watched the screen as his security chief exited his office. He followed the computer dot through the hallway. Suddenly, the chief's marker took a U-turn. It raced toward one of the main exits in the building.

Immanuel chuckled.

"Security system, lock all doors!"

The security chief was less than five feet from the steel door when it slammed shut. The chief crashed into the door.

Immanuel bolted out of his seat. It was the first time in months that he didn't take the elevator. As he glided down the stairs in record time, his mind was dreaming of the most nauseating execution of torture that he could fathom. Seconds later, he dashed through the first-floor door, slowing his pace as he neared the fool.

The chief was barely conscious. One of his eyes was swollen shut by the force of the blow. The Devil didn't waste any time in making an example out of the frail human.

"You have let down the people of the World Federation by your incompetence. You have tried to run from my justice," Satan said in a tone reserved for his most hated enemies.

Several dozen employees were watching. Nobody moved or dared to say a word.

"You must die! The earth must purge you from her system!"

Immanuel dropped to his knees by the side of the sniveling chief. Unfortunately, he was now fully conscious. Satan placed his claws on the man's swaying head and began to chant. The man began to scream as the spell attacked his central nervous system. Electrical impulses traveled from Immanuel's fingers into every nerve fiber in the chief's quivering body. He literally set every nerve ending on fire.

"No! No!" squealed the security chief as his heart began to sputter.

Those witnessing the execution were too aghast to respond outwardly.

Satan's claws were latched onto the chief's skull.

"I see the fire! Oh, my God, I can feel the flames!" shrieked the chief as his body spiraled into death's cold grip.

Suddenly, the storm had passed. The chief's battered body lay lifeless near the entrance of the World Federation headquarters. Immanuel wiped the sweat and blood from his hands as he stood. His subjects pretended that they hadn't seen a thing. It was business as usual.

"Insurrection's only just punishment is death!" announced Immanuel as he casually tossed his dirtied handkerchief into the trash.

"Repent, people of the world, and be baptized into the kingdom of the one true God!" preached Moses.

The crowd was unrepentant. Several hundred devoted World Federation citizens were standing outside the gates of the temple square throwing insults the prophets' way.

"The God of Israel will judge the inhabitants of the earth in less than three years. You still have time to give your lives over to the only sinless Man who walked the earth. Jesus Christ is the Savior of the world!" proclaimed Elijah.

The mob taunting the prophets of God Almighty were slinging rocks in their direction. Miraculously, not a single stone came close to the objects of God's affection.

"Get off your high horse, and come down and fight like a man!" shouted a soldier at the front of the angry audience.

"The kingdom of God is not about violence. Its fruit is peace and love," countered Moses.

The soldier continued his verbal assault.

"You are both liars and will go straight to hell! It's the Christians who love war! It's the Christians who refuse to accept peace! It's the Christians who reject Immanuel as the god of gods! Even that worthless Bible of old had to be burned! The final book in that piece of hate speech glorifies billions of people being killed by God!"

The prophets were patient enough to allow the man to finish.

"People of Jerusalem, billions will be killed! Many will be murdered by Immanuel Bernstate. Many more will die when the God of the universe judges humanity because they are a stiff-necked, proud, disobedient race. The Bible says that there can be no peace for the wicked. It says that peace will come only when Jesus Christ establishes His throne on the earth. Immanuel Bernstate is no Jesus Christ. He is a beast; he is Satan, the Devil incarnate!"

Their God-given words ripped at the souls of the onlookers like a butcher's knife slices through meat.

Several thousand demons converged on the angry mob. The enraged humans began foaming at the mouth as the demons took control. They stormed toward the prophets of God. As their feet trampled the dusty earth, a cloud of soot swept toward Moses and Elijah. The prophets instantly responded. Lightning radiated from their fingers toward the approaching mob.

Hours later, Immanuel slammed the stop button on his VCR. It was painfully apparent that he was powerless to stop these prophets of God. He glared at his new security chief. His eyes were black as night.

"I don't want to see this happen again," murmured Immanuel. "Wherever these Moses and Elijah characters go, I want the area cleared of pedestrians."

"Sir, why don't you confront them and judge them the way you did my predecessor?" the new chief boldly asked.

"Don't question my wisdom!" shouted Immanuel as he hurled a chunk of gold from his desk.

The million-dollar rock missed the chief by a hair. Immanuel slowed down his heartbeat as he leisurely rose to his feet.

"My ways are not your ways. I have my reasons. My eyes continuously roam the earth, searching for the wisest way to further peace. You are a peon; I am god!"

The man quickly excused himself.

"I will take care of this immediately, master!"

Several weeks had passed since the prophets had ordered fire from heaven. Immanuel's heart had grown colder toward their power and their God. The Global News Network was working overtime to cover over Immanuel's dirty little secret. Food and water shortages had reached epidemic levels. Millions of the world citizenry had starved, adding fire to the separatist movement. Russia, Asia, and Africa were hit especially hard by shortages. Hostilities between people who had food and those who did not were becoming epidemic. Entire provinces in Africa and Russia were amassing armies for the sole purpose of capturing food from their neighboring districts. The World Federation's corrupt system of food distribution was plagued with inefficiency and bribery. A person would have to work a sixteen-hour day just to feed himself.

The influence of the Christians was fast being liquidated by the forces of darkness. Every week, the secret police would arrest hundreds of thousands of people. However, many of the God-fearing people were blessed. God used Lord Birmingham's gold and silver to feed and clothe them. The underground economy had roots all around the globe. Many in the World Federation's elite police forces turned an eye to the illegal smuggling operations. They would make more in a day through bribery than they normally would in a year. Their loyalty extended as far as their wallets.

Immanuel's scientists, whom he had kidnapped from every sphere of the globe, had devised a machine that rearranged the molecular makeup of any living organism. In short, it provided a death that was slow and extremely painful. Every Christian who was strapped to it was promised deliverance from death if he would disavow his faith in God Almighty and follow Immanuel by receiving the tattoo on his forehead or hand. Fewer than 1 percent took the bait. Miraculously, they felt little pain with God by their side.

Seventeen

Birth Pains

Lord Birmingham and his brotherhood had moved six times during the past year. Their network of money laundering and distribution to Immanuel's enemies was barely traceable. They were now hiding in a mansion deep in Siberia. Centuries ago, a Russian czar had occupied this castle on a mountaintop. It had over one hundred rooms, including a ballroom that could easily house three hundred guests. Fourteen fireplaces worked overtime keeping the mutineers warm. In the land of the midnight sun, the European money men were busily formulating strategies for how to best annihilate the so-called god of the Earth.

Lord Birmingham was comfortably seated in a seventeenth-century armchair, sipping some of Italy's finest wine. The computer screen, secretly tied into the World Federation's mainframe, spewed forth a wealth of spy information.

"The way I see it, gentlemen, Immanuel has lost control of over 50 percent of his empire, directly due to our—how shall I put it—global generosity."

The Englishman was not as cavalier. He paced the floor. "Our present income will run out in about a year. What do we do once the gold and silver are spent?"

The lord was the spitting image of the Russian czar in the painting that was hanging over the mantle. Many of these men were descendants of kings, czars, and tyrants.

Lord Birmingham stared at the computer terminal.

"Relax. It will only be a few months until the war and peasant uprising finish him off. Here. Pour yourself some of this marvelous Italian wine. It's quite good."

The German banker didn't look convinced.

"We should have a contingency plan, just in case your plan fails."

The lord glanced away from the screen. His bloodshot eyes stared out of the medieval window and into the frozen wasteland.

He was growing weary of being in forced hiding. He would give half his fortune to bask under the Riviera sunlight. He would give his entire fortune to stall what he knew was inevitable.

"Unfortunately, Immanuel is not the only one running out of time," sighed the lord. "Our little demagogue will eventually sniff us out. When it happens, I suggest that you have the contingency plan that Helmut's concerned about. A quick and painless exit would be wise." Birmingham poured the remainder of the wine into his glass. "From what I have been reading, his brand of torture redefines the term *cruel and unusual punishment!*"

The affluent billionaires grew pale and fidgeted in their seats. Pain was a foreign entity to most of them. Death was out of the question.

Tina watched Ken as he handed out the contraband Bibles. They were on a busy street corner, only a quarter mile from the gates of Satan's temple. Moses and Elijah were preaching to anyone who would listen. Few seemed interested. Ken and Tina knew that God was protecting the prophets. They wisely decided to hang onto their coattails, hoping this would keep them safe. Their mission was to place a real Bible into the hands of every person who wanted to know the truth. World Federation spies were everywhere. Every time they offered someone a Bible, it could be the last time. Many times in the past, they had watched with sorrow as somebody would request a Bible, and then tear it up into a zillion pieces only a few feet from them.

As the sun began to set, the street started to clear of people. Ken sighed.

"We're running low on Bibles. How are we going to get more? I can't believe our friends are dead! I mean, it's all so crazy. Brutally murdered for giving us some Bibles."

Ken picked up his box of Bibles.

"Why haven't we been arrested yet? What are they waiting for?"

Tina rubbed his shoulder as she peered around the square. The World Federation police seemed to ignore them. "We have to keep our eyes on Jesus, Ken. On Jesus."

As the duo walked toward their apartment, the earth began to shake violently. The Bibles, perched on Ken's shoulders, plummeted to the ground. Ken and Tina shielded their heads with their hands. The streetlights swayed. Electrical lines shredded like soggy spaghetti. The terrifying sound of cracking concrete and shattering glass was everywhere. Just in time, Ken poked his head from beneath his hands. A four-story building on the other side of the street was collapsing in their direction. Ken screamed as he grabbed Tina's hand and pulled her toward safety.

"Good job, Daniel!" shouted Timothy.

Daniel's quick thinking had saved his humans' lives.

With the same amount of warning, the seismic trembling stopped. The sound of destruction was replaced by the sound of wailing. Ken had moved Tina and himself under a park bench. Tina's leg was bleeding, but it looked like a minor wound. Ken was nervous.

"I think we should get you back home to clean up that wound."

Ken picked up his wife. Bricks, mortar, and concrete blocks were everywhere. A few of the buildings had completely collapsed. Ken had to sidestep gaping holes in the road. It looked like a war zone. A brown teddy bear coated with blood was lying on the street. Tears filled Ken's eyes.

"The news continues to pour in from around the globe," reported the anchor for the Global News Network. "A nuclear bomb has been detonated on the United States of Europe. Ground zero was near Paris. At this point, we have no reliable reports from this area. Reports continue to pour in about earthquakes around the globe. Standing by right now, I have the Director of the World Federation's earthquake center at our studio in New York."

The television screen split in two. On the left was the male anchor; on the right, a man in his mid- to late fifties.

"Mr. Blankwell, could you please give us the latest on this worldwide earthquake?"

"Well, at this point, it appears as if the entire world has experienced a once in a lifetime upheaval. The seismographs are ill-equipped to pick up simultaneous earthquakes from every corner of the earth, but my best estimates are, the magnitude varied from five on the Richter scale, all the way up to a full-blown nine!"

"I understand that you believe that the nuclear bomb may have had something to do with this?" asked the anchor.

He pushed his glasses into his face.

"That is correct. It can't be a coincidence that these two trage-dies occurred one after another. Once the bomb was detonated, the earthquakes began. In fact, it appears as if the earthquakes spread from Europe to other spots in the world. You must understand that nothing like this has ever happened before. Mankind has never ex-ploded this large a bomb on this area before. The earth is a very fragile being, and I believe that this violent explosion triggered some kind of subterranean jolt that then caused the major faults on the crust of the earth to fall out of their current positions."

"What can we expect in the future? Are we going to see more violent aftershocks?"

"One can never be sure, but my best approximation is the af-tershocks will continue for the next several days. They will natu-rally decrease in intensity with time. I think the big news will be the radioactive fallout in Eastern Europe. The jet stream winds should carry this deadly vapor throughout Switzerland, Germany, and parts of Russia."

"Well, we thank you for your valuable input, sir."

A piece of paper was handed to the anchor, who read it verba-tim.

"This just in to the Global News Network. Immanuel Bern-state, along with his cabinet members, are safe in an undisclosed location. His spokesman said that the president was doing well and will have a statement shortly concerning this cataclysmic event."

Immanuel's nuclear fallout shelter was tucked away in the Swiss Alps, conveniently attached to the Antichrist's command cen-ter. It had been created several years before for this kind of catas-trophe. His satellite system gave him a four-minute warning before the bomb's impact. It was more than enough time to simply open a hidden door behind his deck of computer monitors and jump on a tram to safety.

The fallout shelter resembled a palace cut out of rock. Nearly two hundred million dollars was spent on it. Of course, the taxpay-ers of the world swallowed the bill. The shelter was the size of a small medieval town. There were hundreds of rooms. Immanuel's personal fortune, heavily guarded day and night, was stored in a vault somewhere in this vast space. The World Federation employ-ees who guarded his bounty were never allowed to leave this rocky retreat. They were relieved of duty only upon their death, natural or otherwise. Immanuel rationalized this policy as being necessary for the stability of his empire.

There were a thousand critical employees taking refuge in Immanuel's carved-out mountain. Each had a computer chip implanted inside his palm. This technological breakthrough contained a miniature satellite antenna. Immanuel could send a message to any of his servants with a stroke of a computer key; a microscopic speaker relayed the message instantaneously.

The Antichrist was alone in his imperial bedroom. Satan had left him for the moment. Satan seldom relinquished Immanuel's body, but when he did, the Antichrist seemed dejected, as if he had lost his best friend. Immanuel stared at his computer screens. The devastation that his people were experiencing didn't affect him. Instead, he was fast-forwarding through psychological surveys of the world citizenry. He needed an excuse, a villain, and a hero for explaining the earthquake and atomic bomb. Of course, he would be the hero; that was the easy part. Who would be the villain, and how would the excuse for this tragedy be fashioned?

Immanuel rubbed his eyes as he focused on the list of potential scapegoats. Should Lord Birmingham and his overstuffed banker cronies take the fall? Should he focus on the Christian revolt? It was a hard choice, since he despised both.

———

Satan dove into the cathedral. Dominic, with his spirit guide, Blasphemy, was in a prayer meeting for the casualties. Thousands of people were weeping. The death toll was in the millions; the emotional toll was immeasurable.

"We pray for the dead, that their souls would find their rest in Immanuel's hands. We pray for the families of the lost ones, that their peace would flow like honey."

In the midst of Dominic's supplication, Satan, with his sword drawn, confronted Blasphemy.

"Where are Lord Birmingham and his bandits located?" hissed the snake.

The five-star general jumped out of Dominic's body. The quick transition caused the False Prophet to begin babbling. Blasphemy bowed.

"My king, I have no idea what you are talking about! For the past year, I have obeyed you to the fullest extent of my ability. Are they the ones who are responsible for this world calamity?" inquired Blasphemy.

Blasphemy didn't dare challenge Satan. The time was not yet right. With his laser eyes, the dragon scrutinized the general.

"You are telling the truth," admitted Satan. "Those bankers are behind this bombing. They have been hiding out since my announcement and are doing everything possible to disrupt my reign. You are hereby ordered to release your possession of Dominic Rosario and hunt down these apostates. I want them brought to me alive!"

Satan slashed his silver sword to within inches of Blasphemy's smirk. The threat erased Blasphemy's insolent attitude.

"Get on the job immediately! I must remain with Immanuel. He needs me now more than ever."

Ken dipped a dishcloth in some cold water. Hot water was a luxury that they didn't have.

"This may hurt a little," cautioned Ken as he dabbed the cotton rag on her wound.

"You don't have to fuss. It's fine. Just a simple cut."

Ken reached for the alcohol. He looked at the label and then at Tina.

"This is going to hurt. Are you ready?"

"I can handle it."

"I'll tell you what. To get your mind off the pain, let's turn on the GNN. I'm sure they're having a field day with this one."

His wife didn't object.

Ken pushed the button and was paralyzed by the painful pictures of the unedited video from Paris, France.

"Ladies and Gentlemen, we apologize for the graphic video that we are running. Our cameraman, who is wearing a space suit to protect him from the nuclear radiation, is sending these pictures back to us live. We do not have the ability to edit them at this time."

"Ken, those poor people!"

Tears began to well up in Tina's eyes.

"Honey, we're in God's care. We knew that things were going to get tough."

Tina began to weep as Ken held her in his arms.

Although they knew that God was in control, their faith was tested by such devastation.

Timothy and Daniel were both watching the transmission. Their hearts wilted at the grizzly scenes. Every building in sight was completely destroyed. The destruction was so complete that not a tree was left standing. Much of the debris was stained with human blood.

"Timothy, why is God allowing this? It's so difficult to fathom."

Timothy was wise enough not to question God, but he knew he had a responsibility to his younger angel and his humans. Without a word, he opened a nearby Bible and started reading from the book of Revelation.

"'When He opened the fourth seal, I heard the voice of the fourth living creature saying, "Come and see." So I looked, and behold, a pale horse. And the name of him who sat on it was Death, and Hades followed with him. And power was given to them over a fourth of the earth, to kill with sword, with hunger, with death, and by the beasts of the earth.'"

Timothy closed the Bible. He spoke softly to his young friend.

"Our God is a God of love, but also of justice, Daniel. I'm sure it pains Him, too. He offered the world His son. Tell me, Daniel. What more could He have done to save them from all this?"

Daniel sighed.

"Come on," said Timothy. "We have more to do."

The two spirits flew through the roof and headed toward the south of town. They settled on a mountaintop close to Cairo, Egypt.

"Do you see that city over there?" asked Timothy.

Daniel was trying to catch his breath.

"I think I can."

The makeshift tent city occupied about sixty-six square miles. An electronic security fence the height of the Berlin wall dared anybody to tinker with its purpose. There was little sign of human life, other than the World Federation guards making their evening rounds. A gruesome smell violated the surrounding desert air.

"Whatever this place is, it gives me the creeps," coughed Daniel.

"Keep it down. There are enemy troops patrolling this area every few minutes."

Both angels lowered their bodies toward the earth.

319

"Nobody has an accurate count except for Jehovah God, but it is estimated that twenty to sixty million Christians have been brutally executed here in the last year."

Daniel was having a difficult time handling the painful truth. Timothy remained strong for his pupil, but his heart ached beyond comprehension.

"Satan is killing the saints of God. Jehovah God isn't doing the killing here. Satan is the murderer."

Daniel finally understood.

"Now I get it. God is allowing the evil to occur. He's not the one who creates it; He only created a person's free will," said Daniel.

"Yes."

Timothy opened his Bible. "I think I can show you where we are on Revelation's timeline. It will settle your heart to see that God is in control:

"'I looked when He opened the sixth seal, and behold, there was a great earthquake; and the sun became black as sackcloth of hair, and the moon became like blood. And the stars of heaven fell to the earth, as a fig tree drops its late figs when it is shaken by a mighty wind. Then the sky receded as a scroll when it is rolled up, and every mountain and island was moved out of its place. And the kings of the earth, the great men, the rich men, the commanders, the mighty men, every slave and every free man, hid themselves in the caves and in the rocks of the mountains, and said to the mountains and rocks, "Fall on us and hide us from the face of Him who sits on the throne and from the wrath of the Lamb! For the great day of His wrath has come, and who is able to stand?"'"

"Do you see, Daniel? The nuclear bomb over Europe literally caused the sky to roll up."

Daniel was stunned to see the book of Revelation come alive like this.

"We have the bomb, and the effects of the bomb, listed here. The sun and the moon will change their appearance because of the nuclear fallout. The worldwide earthquake was triggered by the bomb. And listen to this, Daniel. Right now, Immanuel and all of his rich conspirators are hiding in their homemade mountain near Geneva. And you can bet that everybody is going to have to take cover from the nuclear fallout."

"And then everyone turns to God for help, right?" hoped Daniel.

"No, Daniel," sighed Timothy. "I wish that were true."

Timothy started to read again. "'Fall on us and hide us from the face of Him who sits on the throne and from the wrath of the Lamb!'"

Daniel was dejected at this thought. "They're not sorry for their sins, are they?"

"No, Daniel. I know it's incredible to us, but they're not. They are simply admitting that God exists and that He has power. In the book of James, it says that even the demons believe in God and shudder at His power. They are no better off than the demons."

Blasphemy was cruising high above the Earth. His wings sliced through the frigid, thin air. He thought of himself as an eagle; majestic, strong, and beautiful. Jehovah God saw it differently.

Blasphemy's eyes browsed the Earth. The spreading clouds and radiation from the nuclear attack hindered his vision.

"I'm finally free!" celebrated Blasphemy.

What a difference this year had made. A year ago, he was drooling to possess the False Prophet of the world. However, lust is so quickly bored. He wanted more. He wanted it all. Blasphemy's eyes latched themselves onto a microwave tower in a mountain range near the North Sea. The demon aligned himself with the faint signal as he made a dash for its source. He landed near a newly constructed steel tower. Dozens of communication devices were bolted to the beam. It appeared as if a television station was broadcasting from the middle of the frozen tundra. It didn't add up. Even though he hadn't been intimately involved in the propaganda side of things, he did know that this was out of the ordinary. There would be no reason for the Global News Network to set up shop in this vast wasteland of ice. Somebody was hiding here. Blasphemy wasn't bored anymore.

"What's the latest?" tested Immanuel.

He stared at his prison warden, who had been Immanuel's hit man several years earlier. He lived for death. When he was a child, he had a toy guillotine.

"Your majesty, everything is proceeding without a hitch. We must have five tons of gold stored in the vault at the prison. Somebody was bankrolling those Christians."

"Excellent! You have once again pleased me! Let's arrange a transfer of that bounty tomorrow afternoon."

"Your command will be carried out this afternoon," upped the killer.

Immanuel's respect for the hired hit man-turned-administrator could not have been measured. He was a man after his own, baneful heart.

"Give me your best estimate on numbers," asked the Devil.

"I haven't run all the numbers yet, but I can give you a rough estimate. We have six camps in every sector, and six sectors around the globe. Each camp has judged between two and five million felons. So two times thirty-six is seventy-two million, and five times thirty-six is one hundred eighty million. Average that number out and we have about one hundred twenty-five million put out of their misery!"

The head of the World Federation prison system saw his mission of murder as a divine calling.

"Very good indeed," motioned Immanuel. "What is your most popular method of execution?"

"The atomizer! It is the most effective. I don't know how they endure the pain. Even under the highest setting they just keep whispering 'Jesus, Jesus, Jesus!'"

Satan cringed.

Tina was fading off to sleep. Ken hoped her pain had subsided. He kept the volume low on the television, being careful not to bother his wife.

"In less than half an hour, the great Immanuel Bernstate will address the world about these troubling circumstances," reported the world anchor. "In the meantime, we have some new information on the bomb and ensuing earthquake. The global police force is reporting that the Christian revolutionaries were behind this death and carnage. A plane was apparently stolen from a military facility outside London, less than forty-five minutes before the bomb blast. Radar shows the plane over Paris at the time of the detonation. It attempted to land on a remote landing strip in a western province of Russia. Minutes later, the World Federation police arrested two men, both identified as Christian rebels!"

Ken turned off the sound on the television. "Why am I not surprised," he muttered.

"Ken, what's wrong?" mumbled Tina.

"Sorry I woke you. I'm just getting sick and tired of all the lies. I feel like we are banging our heads against a brick wall."

"How long do you think we have?" wondered Tina as she placed her head on his chest.

"It will be a miracle if we make it six, maybe seven months."

Immanuel's face suddenly appeared on the screen.

"Let's turn up the sound," said Ken. "The Devil is about to speak again."

———————

Blasphemy sneered as he noticed a column of smoke spiraling toward the sky.

"Dinner," mumbled the demon as he shot toward the pollution.

His eyes spotted the historic chateau. It was located on a mountain that overlooked the frozen tundra. He didn't waste any time in penetrating the stone walls.

Blasphemy couldn't believe his beady little eyes. There they were, the twelve thorns. This was the greatest opportunity that he would ever have. He would handle them with care.

He moved over to Lord Birmingham's side. The lord of the Order was sleeping. The demon plunged himself into his dream.

The sky was purple, the grass was gold. Lord Birmingham was seated on a throne of gold. Immanuel was bowing to him.

"You are a worthless piece of trash," Birmingham berated Immanuel, who was on his knees, weeping. "You wanted to rule the world, and you can't even snivel properly! Kiss my feet and beg for my mercy," dreamed the banker.

Blasphemy entered the dream as a talking dove. He glided down toward the throne, singing songs of praise to the new king.

"You will succeed in your conquest of the world. You will devour Immanuel with the power of your mind. You will control him, and every other human on the face of the Earth, if you will only take my advice."

The beauty, charm, and eloquence of the dove seemed inviting to Lord Birmingham.

"What advice do you have, my friend?"

"Immanuel's power lies in the spiritual realm. You need to tap this great bastion of energy before you can claim your treasure. You are not competing on a level playing field until you accept my wisdom and power."

Lord Birmingham's ears were itching for Blasphemy's message.

The dove sailed around his head before landing on his left shoulder.

"Who are you?" Lord Birmingham asked.

"I was the wisest man to ever walk the planet. I never died a natural death. My spirit has been roaming the planet for centuries, searching for a soul worthy to bind with my own. I have finally found it! We will team up and defeat the greatest evil ever to pollute Mother Earth!"

The dove jumped into Lord Birmingham's lap. It spread its wings across his lap. "The ark of the covenant is the key!" whispered the bird. "Whoever possesses it wins the war! I know Immanuel stole it, and I know where it is. Would you like to get it back?"

The dream faded into reality. The crispness of the picture turned dull. Lord Birmingham didn't want to wake up. He tried to force the dream to continue, but only succeeded in disappointing himself. As his eyes slowly opened, he scanned the room for the dove. Disappointed, he realized that it was gone.

Immanuel courted the camera like it was his lover.

"Citizens of my world, I have come before you this day, saddened by the upheavals that have rocked our Earth."

His eyes watered slightly, a recently acquired skill.

"Many of you are tuning in today to find out vital information about loved ones. Our good friends at the Global News Network are working overtime to help you with that critical information."

Immanuel's tone changed.

"But I have a higher purpose for speaking to you tonight. I want you to understand why pain and suffering must occur. The Earth is in the middle of giving birth. That's right. The old order is passing away; and the new order, built on peace, prosperity, and liberty, is approaching. I gave my creatures the ability to choose me or discard me. Those who want to kill me have created a war zone on my creation. Their right to hate me and you has caused everybody pain and suffering. A group of Christian warriors has brutally attacked an innocent city today," lied the Devil. "Millions are dead, and countless thousands of others are gone due to the accompanying earthquakes. This terror must stop."

Immanuel's face turned pale. He folded his hands on his leg.

"Effective immediately, every world citizen is to be on guard for these terrorists! Every person who does not have my mark should be assumed to be armed and dangerous. These people will think nothing about cutting your throat and leaving you to choke on your blood. These terrorists are forcing my hand. I must assert my authority in this matter, or you could suffer the same fate as those in Paris!"

He took a measured pause.

"Today, I am ordering my police force to take drastic measures. Anyone who refuses to be called by my name will be guilty of high treason! In the past, I thought denying them food and buying privileges would make them come to their senses. But my mercy has ended! Anyone who does not have my mark of allegiance will be pronounced guilty. They will be charged with the worst of crimes and will be executed on the spot!"

Immanuel's face resembled a thunderhead—ominous, breathtaking, and frightening.

"Christians, you will pay for your crimes against humanity! I know that you are watching. You have a choice. Accept me and my mark of loyalty, or meet me as your judge in this life, and in your afterlife!"

Lord Birmingham tossed upon his bed. He couldn't sleep. The harder he tried to doze off, the more it eluded him. The only thing that he could think of was that dove. He wisely kept his dreams to himself. He didn't want anyone to think that he had gone off the deep end. His eyes roamed the room. A bottle of sleeping pills had been placed on the counter at the entrance of his bathroom. He didn't remember putting them there. He yanked the covers off his clammy body, walked over to the counter, and picked up the bottle.

"Take one or two before bed," read Lord Birmingham to himself. Blasphemy was crouched in the corner of the shower.

"Two will help you sleep," whispered Blasphemy.

Birmingham embraced the thought as his own, took two of the pills, and fumbled around for a glass of water.

"This is too easy," chuckled Blasphemy.

The front door crashed off its hinges with a thunderous clap. Ken and Tina were in their bedroom. Daniel and Timothy, who

325

were guarding them, were suddenly attacked from behind by a swarm of demons. They had no time to react.

"It's the police!" gasped Ken.

"Help us, God!" screamed Tina.

"I heard a voice in there, Captain!" shouted one of the police-men.

The five intruders were dressed in army fatigues. Each had a laser rifle in his hands, capable of torching an armored truck.

Ken moved toward the window lock. Tina held onto her hus-band as the bedroom doorknob began to shake.

"Hurry, Ken! They're at the door!"

Ken was too shaken to talk. The window latch had rusted over.

"I'll kick it in, sir," responded the largest of the men.

"I can't get it!" gasped Ken as he gave the window one last shove.

The corroded latch cracked. Just as Ken opened the window, their bedroom door caved inward.

Tina screamed. "Follow me!" Ken said as he dove feetfirst out of the second-story window.

"Ken!" Tina leaned out the window.

Their eyes met. Ken's arms were raised in the air.

"Tina, jump! Honey, jump!" she started to jump when her con-torted body was pulled back in by the animals in police uniforms.

Tina tried to cry out to Ken, but a hand swiftly muzzled her mouth.

Ken was staring up at the window in shock. What should he do? Stay and get arrested, too? With Immanuel's edict, they'd both be executed on the spot. His beloved Tina—Ken felt an urging in his spirit to run. He would have to leave Tina to God's love and will.

"Well, look what we have here, sir," laughed one of the younger agents.

"Lord Jesus, help!" prayed Tina.

They let go of her. "It's not too late for any of you. Jesus will still—"

"Shut up! Shut up or we'll cut you up right here!" barked the commanding officer as he waved his laser gun near her throat.

Tina dropped to her knees. She had had hundreds of night-mares about this day, but she never dreamed that she would handle it with such faith. God's promises were coming true because it was as if the Holy Spirit of God was completely taking over. She silently prayed, not for protection, but to know how to respond. If she was going to die, she wanted these men to have one last chance to know about her God.

The youngest agent struck her on the cheek with his left palm.

"You listen to me. Because of your kind, millions are dead in Paris. You pray for my soul and say you love me, and then blow people up!"

"We didn't cause the violence. Jesus wouldn't—"

The commander kicked her in the stomach.

Daniel and Timothy couldn't help her. They had been knocked out cold near the corner of the bed.

"Where's your friend?" he demanded.

Tina gasped for air but gave no answer.

He kicked her harder. No response.

The commander ordered his soldier, "Block off every street within five square miles!" He glanced at Tina. "Get rid of her."

A single shot from a laser rifle echoed in the night air.

Ken wept bitterly as he ran through the streets of Jerusalem. He took the darkest streets available. He felt as if his heart had been ripped out of his chest. Tina was in the hands of the enemy. "I shouldn't have jumped first" the thought played over and over in his mind. His legs were rapidly tiring. He wasn't even sure if he was going in the right direction.

"God, please help Tina! Please don't let them harm her! Please, I beg you!"

"Hey!" shouted a sentry from the dark.

Ken dodged the voice by darting into a dimly lit court.

"Stop, or I'll turn you into ashes!"

Ken's legs were turning to mush. A laser beam obliterated the trash can next to him. Then he noticed a staircase. He raced down the stairs, which were steep and wet. Ken had to slow down or risk breaking his neck. He could hear helicopters and see searchlights behind him as he dropped below the surface of the city. Water was everywhere. Before long, he was up to his neck in an underground spring. It was a water tunnel that had been constructed eons ago. "Please save her, God," wept Ken. "Save her."

———

The archangel Michael wept. They were tears of joy, as he watched the faithful remnant come home to heaven. A radiant Tina was among them. He opened a Bible to the seventh chapter of Revelation and began to read. His hands were quivering when he came to verse nine.

"'After these things I looked, and behold, a great multitude which no one could number, of all nations, tribes, peoples, and tongues, standing before the throne and before the Lamb, clothed with white robes, with palm branches in their hands, and crying out with a loud voice, saying, "Salvation belongs to our God who sits on the throne, and to the Lamb!" All the angels stood around the throne and the elders and the four living creatures, and fell on their faces before the throne and worshiped God, saying: "Amen! Blessing and glory and wisdom, thanksgiving and honor and power and might, be to our God forever and ever. Amen." Then one of the elders answered, saying to me, "Who are these arrayed in white robes, and where did they come from?" And I said to him, "Sir, you know." So he said to me, "These are the ones who come out of the great Tribulation, and washed their robes and made them white in the blood of the Lamb. Therefore they are before the throne of God, and serve Him day and night in His temple. And He who sits on the throne will dwell among them. They shall neither hunger anymore nor thirst anymore; the sun shall not strike them, nor any heat; for the Lamb who is in the midst of the throne will shepherd them and lead them to living fountains of waters. And God will wipe away every tear from their eyes."'"

From the time Michael was created, he had given his full heart, soul, and mind to his God. He had never understood humans, not really. Throughout history, the majority of them had scoffed at the Bible. Even many Christians had written off the last book, Revelation. He couldn't make sense of that. The Father had laid bare the future in black and white so that anyone could see it and repent. "What incomprehensible mercy, yet they turned it away," mused Michael. "A prudent man foresees evil and hides himself; the simple pass on and are punished," he sadly quoted from Proverbs.

Michael turned toward God's children in heaven and saw complete peace in their eyes. A tear dropped from his eye as he looked toward the contaminated planet below.

Eighteen

Shifting Sands

In the past eight months, Immanuel had silenced most Christians on the planet, except Moses and Elijah. In fact, he allowed their predictions of judgment to circulate the airwaves on the worldwide cable system. The more adamant the prophets' words were, the happier he was. He had so thoroughly watered the seeds of hatred toward God's people that anything Christian was considered worthy of death. Most people who watched the two prophets of God despised them.

The toxic fallout from the nuclear holocaust over Europe had made refugees of millions of individuals. The death toll from that blast had reached well over ten million, with nearly one million of that number the result of the earthquake of the millennia.

Immanuel had successfully buried the truth from the naive public. Lord Birmingham was behind the bombing, and Immanuel knew it. His top security advisor knew it, as well as a handful of senior agents who were tracking the bankers. The Antichrist was livid at Birmingham, but at the same time, was thankful to him for helping his cause. The bombing had been the impetus that had led to the liquidation of the Christians. He estimated that less than ten million remained on the Earth. He pondered his next move as his white limousine, with the license plate, "GOD," pulled up beside the temple in Jerusalem.

Immanuel was troubled about maintaining his power base.

Blasphemy had disappeared, which meant Dominic Rosario didn't have a suitable guide. The False Prophet didn't have the same religious desire without his spirit advisor. The Earth Church was worshipping Immanuel as God, yet their allegiance was wavering. The people thought of themselves before they thought of him. "That has to stop immediately," thought Immanuel. As he entered the temple, the enchanting atmosphere appeased his jaded mind. There were thousands on their knees as he slowly made his way toward the stage. Millions more were watching on television. A colossal white curtain, six stories high, veiled Immanuel's secret from the rest of the world. For the past several months, construction barriers had hidden Immanuel's mysterious activity. Nobody knew what was underneath the canopy.

The Antichrist moved to the center of the temple with a counterfeit humility. He was dressed in a white robe, and had Dominic's redesigned bible in his hand. Satan's pawn approached the microphone. The cameras from the Global News Network zoomed into the face of the human god.

"My children, I thank you for being here today."

He paused to smile for the camera.

"Today is the day that I have been looking forward to for all of eternity. Today, my children, I am offering you heaven on Earth!"

Ken snatched up a locust as it bounced along the desert floor. He closed his eyes as he bit into its squirming body. The crunching sound made him want to vomit. He had no choice but to eat what was available. The former anchor had no idea where he was. For the past several months, he had wandered through the vast Middle Eastern desert, searching for the hiding place of God's elect. The heat pounded his body. Dust storms popped up out of nowhere. He prayed that God would take his life, so that he could be in paradise with Jesus and with Tina. Something told him to keep moving and to keep fighting.

Ken knew that Jehovah God was with him. Several times, when his will had been broken from a lack of water, an oasis had popped up out of nowhere.

His vision was blurred by the incessant sun. Suddenly, his eyes spotted something about a quarter of a mile in front of him. Over the past several months, Ken could have sworn that he had seen Tina, Sally, and even Jesus Christ. He began to run toward the object. It quickly disappeared behind the crescent rocks. It was the first time that a mirage had moved.

"Hey! Can you help me?" shouted Ken.

A head appeared from behind a rock.

"Who are you?" a voice suspiciously asked.

"I'm lost."

A cloaked man timidly raised his body in full view of Ken.

The man was in his mid-forties, but had aged a decade in less than a year. His hair resembled a mop that had been soaked with sweat and mud. A graying beard covered his face. His body was little more than skin and bones.

Ken offered his hand in friendship. The wanderer was cautious.

"You're not one of the World Federation bullies are you?" asked the man.

Ken respected the question. In fact, he wondered why he had thrown away all caution himself.

"For one thing, a World Federation officer would be carrying a weapon and would have fried you by now. Second, I don't have Immanuel's mark," said Ken.

The man's defenses crumbled. His mouth smiled, but his eyes filled with tears of relief.

"I'm Jim Smith."

He offered his hand. Ken grasped the sunburned hand with all his might.

"Ken Action."

The prolonged handshake calmed their nerves as they stared at each other. Each man was suspicious yet hopeful. Ken broke the silence.

"What are you doing here?"

Tears began to flow down Jim's face.

"It's such a long story," groaned Jim. "Believe it or not, at one time in my life, I was a cabinet member for the president of the United States."

The crowd was tense with anticipation. The hundred twenty-foot curtain began to sway in the breeze.

"You may remember that, when I first revealed my true nature a couple of years ago, I ordered everybody on the face of my planet to carry a statue of me as a sign of their allegiance."

Immanuel's eyes pierced the crowd.

"That order was a precursor to the great things to come. Today, I present to you my power and strength!"

Trumpets sounded as six World Federation jets flew overhead in tight formation.

"I am God, and there is no other!"

The curtain was rent in two. The world beheld its new god.

The towering statue of Immanuel overshadowed the temple. It was fashioned out of pure gold, most of which had been stolen from the Christian saints. This was no ordinary icon. It was alive. Its eyes and mouth moved in unison with the Antichrist. The body was rigid, but it appeared to have life.

"From this day forward, every knee will bow, and every tongue will confess that I am God! Every citizen will pray to this statue of me—morning, noon, and night. I am everywhere! No one can hide from my eyes! I am worthy to be worshipped!"

The flock openly worshipped the statue bearing the mark of the Beast.

"I have promised mankind heaven on earth. Today, I have delivered on my promise! The Christian revolt has been crushed. I alone will reinstate the Garden of Eden!"

Vice President Colt, who was leaning against a corner of the temple, wanted to vomit. Immanuel had put him in charge of this project a few years earlier. This wasn't spiritual; it was science. Computer technology had undergone a quantum leap. The Antichrist's scientists had created a computer that could think. It had the capability of reasoning and experiencing emotion. The face of the statue was lined with a golden plastic mask that was connected to more than a million machine-driven nerve endings. A satellite in space could accurately scan every muscle twitch on Immanuel Bernstate's face. That signal was transferred into a computer code, which was relayed to the Jerusalem statue. In short, it appeared conscious and breathing. It was the perfect masquerade.

"This man is mad!" mumbled the vice president as he applauded with the crowd.

"From this point forward, I no longer see a need for the Earth Church. I will stand over Jerusalem, guarding her precious past and future. I am with you in spirit, and now I am with you in person! Today, I want every church destroyed in order to use its gold, silver, and precious material to take care of my people."

Dominic Rosario stared at his television. "I'm not going down without a fight," vented the Prophet.

Daniel was flying on autopilot, his eyes weary from the relentless search. He wasn't sure how long he had been hunting for his human, Ken Action. Had it been months or years? The angel's heart still ached. He had failed regarding Ken and Tina. The night of the ambush was still clear in his mind. He had sustained a substantial blow to the head. His body was still sore from being stuffed into that tiny vase. He was glad that Timothy had ordered him to find Ken. It gave him something to do. It was a way to make up for his failure.

The sun was turning in for the day. The only good thing about this desert hunt was the glorious sunsets. His wings throbbed with fatigue as he landed in a high desert plain about five hundred miles south of Jerusalem. His body plopped itself down on a smooth rock. He rested his eyes on the horizon and enjoyed God's handiwork. The white clouds transformed from feathered streaks to fiery red flames.

Suddenly, Daniel heard a noise nearby. He dove feetfirst behind a bush. He had finally learned caution.

"You've been through quite a lot," said Ken.

"No more than you or anyone else," offered Jim.

Ken stopped to survey the barren land.

Daniel poked one eye out of the flowering shrub. He thought that he recognized the voice.

"We're south of Jerusalem," surmised Ken. "If we travel at night, and follow that star, we may find our way back to Israel."

Jim frowned. "No way I'm parading out in the open like that. God allowed me to escape one of those nauseating detention camps. I don't want to test His mercy again!"

Daniel wasn't listening to their conversation. He was dancing with joy. He had found his human. He had found Ken.

———

The ark of the covenant was proudly displayed in a bulletproof box. Muslims from all over the world had traveled to see God's tribute to His holiness. Abdul Mohammed was standing nearby, talking with a delegation of separatists.

"I'm not worshipping Immanuel," insisted the Muslim from Egypt.

Abdul shook his head in despair.

"He wanted me to think he was God. I'm ashamed to admit that I fell for his deceit for a moment," said Abdul. "He promised me years ago that we would have free rein over our religion. It was a lie!"

Abdul sat down, allowing the seriousness of the moment to rest on his shoulders. "He is the Devil, and must be stopped at any cost!"

"How do you propose we stop him?" asked the Muslim from Turkey.

"If we can become China's allies, then we have a chance of defeating him. They are not Muslim, but our common ground is that he broke his agreement with them as well, and they want him to pay for it."

The men were huddled near a corner of their mosque. They were being extra cautious not to look suspicious.

"Is it possible to defeat the World Federation military force?" asked the Egyptian.

The men stared at each other. Even with China's help, staging a military coup against the World Federation seemed unattainable.

"China alone can man a two hundred million militia," estimated Abdul. "Much of the Russian element hates China, but they hate Immanuel even more. To them, it would be the lesser of two evils. Yes, they would unite with our force. I have connections in Africa who assure me that they have the precious metals to finance much of the needed weaponry."

A suspicious-looking European strolled by the men.

"God loves all people, and Immanuel is the wisest leader ever to grace this fine earth," parroted Abdul for the ears of the stranger.

The outsider quickly picked up his pace as he realized that he had been spotted.

Abdul looked serious.

"I believe our time frame can be one year from today. If Immanuel is still standing after what we're about to throw at him, then I'll worship him myself!"

Blasphemy's fangs were tightly wrapped around Lord Birmingham's skull. Boiling, spiritual saliva dripped down Birmingham's bewitched face. The leader of the banking cartel had tested every illegal drug known to mankind, but he had never found them stimulating enough to give his life away to them. However, today his mind had been changed, or rather, reprogrammed. His "spiritual guide" Blasphemy was tantalizing his mind and heart more than any manufactured, synthetic substance could ever do.

Lord Birmingham reclined in his black leather chair.

"Ah, I remember when you were a little boy," chanted Blasphemy. He tightened his clamp on the human's head. "You were twelve years old when you mastered your first real deceit!"

The demon's hypnotic recital was going as planned. He floated around the lord's head in the body of a dove.

Lord Birmingham's face struck a smile.

"Yes, I remember," said Birmingham. "I stole my mother's diamond watch and sold it for a hundred thousand! The insurance company never questioned it. You know, I never spent it. I loved to run my hands through those thousand dollar bills every night."

Blasphemy became restless.

"You must fight fire with fire. Immanuel can only be defeated militarily. You have the resources; I have the connections!" beguiled the smooth-talking serpent.

Lord Birmingham's face turned pale.

"The Chinese want Immanuel's head on a platter," Blasphemy continued. "Take away the ark of the covenant from the Muslims, and hell will break out on earth."

Birmingham appeared confused.

"I don't get it."

"Remember the Dome of the Rock that Immanuel destroyed for the Jewish temple? The ark was the payment for the Muslim's loyalty."

Birmingham's eyes were opened.

"Our so-called god will have a holy war on his hands."

The dove cooed. "Without his promised peace, he loses, and we win!"

Birmingham smiled.

"Your wish is my command!" muttered the banker.

"Good!" said the phantom. "Very good!"

Satan yanked himself from Immanuel's body. It was two in the morning. He had three, maybe four hours before his specimen would awake. He flew away, using Blasphemy's name as a curse. The Devil gained altitude. He wanted Lord Birmingham and Blasphemy more than godhood. Revenge controlled his every thought as his eyes studied the landscape.

"I can't stand those sniveling humans," raged the great dragon. "Every last one of them deserves my kind of death!"

Satan suddenly stopped. His ears made a quick radar sweep of the heavens. Not a sound could be heard. For thousands of years, he had learned to tune out the creatures around the throne room of God, who day and night sang praises to their Creator. He believed that Jehovah God intentionally tried to torment him and his soldiers through these hymns of praise. The Devil sniffed the wind. He didn't smell a thing. It was too good to be true.

"That dictator is up to something," he hissed. Satan lusted to know what it was.

The throne room was less than twenty minutes away. He tried to break free from the Earth's gravitational pull. Seconds later, his body nearly cracked in two as it collided with an invisible shield. The force of the blow crippled him for a moment.

"You have been banned from the universe!" trumpeted the archangel Michael from the other side of the floating force field.

The Devil sneered as he tried to regain his kingly composure.

"It's my universe!" screamed Satan as he lunged toward God's spokesangel.

The transparent shield didn't budge or bend.

"You have been banned from God's heaven! The book of Revelation, chapter twelve, verse seven, states, 'And war broke out in heaven: Michael and his angels—'"

"No, no, shut up! Stop it!" shouted Satan as he covered his ears in disgust.

The Devil was reacting like a vampire forced to stare at a cross.

"'Michael and his angels fought with the dragon; and the dragon and his angels fought, but they did not prevail, nor was a place found for them in heaven any longer. So the great dragon was cast out, that serpent of old, called the Devil and Satan, who deceives the whole world; he was cast to the earth, and his angels were cast out with him.'"

The brilliant, shimmering words of truth sliced away at Satan's soul.

"You're a liar! You will pay!" scoffed the dragon as he stumbled backward.

The archangel latched his wings to the solar wind and rocketed toward the throne. For the first time in history, God had ordered a moment of silence. It was a time of sadness yet joy. Jehovah God wanted his creation to recognize the seriousness of the hour.

Lord Birmingham was standing over the double hearth fireplace. He was using a pair of metal tongs to realign the stubborn logs. The flames had died several minutes earlier, and so had the heat. The European wasn't accustomed to manual labor, but found the fire exhilarating.

His colleagues filtered into the medieval meeting chamber as he resuscitated the blaze. He eyed the climbing flames with uncanny interest.

Lord Birmingham was greeted with stares and whispers. They weren't sure what to make of his fascination with the fire. He hauled his eyes away from the combustion and clasped his hands together.

"We have a very long day ahead of us, gentlemen! I have been in very deep thought for some time now, and I believe that I have the answers to our dilemma!"

The men's faces remained somber. Their very existence could hinge on this meeting. The crackling wood in the fireplace relaxed the mood, but only momentarily. The lord was the final one to find his seat.

"Gentlemen," began Birmingham, "we have been badly mistaken about our strategy to take out Immanuel."

He glanced around the table.

"We have been concentrating our resources in the wrong arena. Don't get me wrong. We have had limited wins in regional battles, but the war will surely be lost within the year!"

Blasphemy was beside him to help him through the more difficult turns. Lord Birmingham's eyes turned cold and dark as they stared out the window.

"We must fight fire with fire! I believe that we can muster the military force to extinguish this...magician from hell!"

The men were shocked. His tone and demeanor had changed, and he was offering a strategy they had agreed was not feasible. Their bewildered stares ate away at Birmingham's confidence. Blasphemy quickly took charge. He jumped from man to man, massaging their wills into submission.

The German threw his hands into the air.

"From my point of view, it sounds like instant suicide. Are you crazy?"

Blasphemy hurdled over the Englishman and carved his claws into the German.

"You will listen with open ears," crooned the demon. "Lord Birmingham's intellect far surpasses your own. Immanuel must be stopped at any cost!"

The lord overlooked the German's ignorance. He needed everybody on his side. It was an all-or-nothing deal.

"My intelligence tells me that China has the capability of manning a two hundred million-troop force. They hate Immanuel as much as we do, and are just waiting for someone to come along and make them an offer that they can't refuse."

The men whispered a few comments among themselves.

"Russia lost more than half their force a couple of years ago in the mountains of Israel, but they still have twenty million men ready for combat. They just need the money to oil their gears. As many of you know, Africa has been mining gold like it's going out of style. I have the connections right now. They are promising us twenty tons if we agree to funnel it in to this effort. Immanuel has unwisely forsaken those areas of the globe. They look at it as favoritism; he looks at it as political expediency."

Blasphemy had done his work well. The men around the table seemed interested.

"How did you find out all of this intelligence information?" asked the Englishman.

Lord Birmingham would not discuss his adventure with the dove from his dreams. He didn't want them to have him committed. Blasphemy recognized the opposition. His wings carried him to Lord Birmingham, where he entered his body and spirit. The lord sensed a jolt.

"I was able to break the code in Immanuel's personal computer system. I didn't tell anybody because I was afraid that, the greater the number of individuals who had access to his notebook, the greater chance we would have of being caught."

Nobody challenged his Blasphemy-given answer. His left hand began to twitch as Blasphemy dug deeper into his spirit.

"The final piece of the puzzle comes from the Middle East. The Muslims want his head. They will be willing to supply us with the oil that we will need to carry off this massive operation. Immanuel doesn't have total control over those wells. The locals have been siphoning off a large reserve of fossil fuel that will be at our disposal. They have about five million men who want to die for their god."

The men listened as Birmingham continued. "I believe that the Muslims, though, need something to, let's say, move them along in their thinking."

"What would that be?" asked the Englishman.

"How about somebody stealing their most prized possession," smiled Lord Birmingham.

Satan plunged into Immanuel's body as he opened his eyes. The Devil's abhorrence for Jehovah God was growing exponentially. His frothing passion for vengeance made Immanuel dizzy. The politician-turned-god tried to stand, but collapsed on his bed. He was imagining a white-bearded man with a crown of gold on his head. Every few seconds, a flame of fire would burn a part of the old man's frail body. Soon, the man's body was unrecognizable. Immanuel was feeling joy from this vision. He didn't know that it was Satan's fantasy that he was enjoying. He stumbled onto his feet and made his way to the computer terminal.

"Computer on," mumbled the Antichrist.

There was a number on the screen in bold red letters. Over the years, it had dropped from hundreds of millions, to less than ten thousand.

"Estimated time to complete victory," voiced the Devil.

The yellow-orange light on the computer terminal began to blink. It was thinking.

"Approximately ten months, depending on any additions imposed on the world by Moses and Elijah," responded the voice-activated machine.

"Subtract Moses and Elijah from your equation."

Abdul's eyes scanned the town square. He pulled out a small piece of paper from his coat pocket. His companion shook his hand to make the exchange.

"This is the number to a man named Lord Birmingham. He will be our coordinator," quietly spoke Abdul.

The Arab general, disguised in parson's apparel, seemed to balk.

"How do we know that we can trust him? That title makes me uneasy."

"We can trust him because we have common enemies. He hates Immanuel, and that's enough for me."

The general wasn't satisfied.

Abdul nervously smiled. He needed the general's support.

"He couldn't care less about our religious dispute. This man is amoral and irreligious. His quarrel with Immanuel is over money. He looks at our movement with little interest, which is good for us. We want nothing but our freedom to worship Allah in the true way. He has no quarrel with that."

The men hit the ground as laser shots perforated the square. Woman were screaming; children were crying.

"What's happening?" whispered Abdul as he covered his head with his trembling hands.

The general tried to get a better view of the disturbance, but was deterred by a beam of lethal light that barely missed his head. The only thing that he could see were black boots, hundreds of them, marching across the square.

"This is the World Federation police!" lied a Chinese colonel over a loudspeaker. "Remain calm, and you will not be hurt!"

"They're heading toward the ark of the covenant!" said Abdul as a tear dropped from his eye.

Several dozen of the male bystanders jumped to their feet. They rushed the armed troops. The Chinese spies, who were masquerading as World Federation Police, shot them at point-blank range. The torment from the laser weapons lasted a full minute.

"Do not be like your foolish brothers! You will be killed if you attempt to harm any of us. Stay on your faces until we tell you otherwise!"

The Arab general watched the marching boots move past them. He tried to reposition his body.

"What are they doing?" whispered Abdul.

The general's eyes widened.

"You don't want to know, Abdul!"

"Yes, I do!"

The general was squinting. The setting sun was obstructing his view. Suddenly, a loud explosion shook the ground. The general quickly ducked his head. A rush of wind stormed the square. Wailing soldiers lay on the ground.

"What happened?" fumbled Abdul.

"I...I'm not sure. I think the ark of the covenant was blown up!" guessed the general.

Abdul could not contain his anguish. He slowly rose to his knees. The wind had passed, but the sounds of misery continued. Several Chinese men were on the pavement, writhing in pain. The remaining soldiers were huddled around the men in shock. The ark was still there! Abdul dropped onto his stomach. He breathed a sigh of relief.

"My ark is just fine! Apparently, God did not take kindly to their messing with His dwelling place!"

"I don't understand what happened," said the general.

Abdul pulled his eyes away from his treasure.

"They tried to touch the ark. It's a deadly mistake!"

"What do they want with it?" asked the general as he shook dirt from his hair.

Abdul hadn't thought about that. He lifted his head above the mob, only to be greeted by a soldier's gun.

"Are you Abdul Mohammed?" interrogated the officer.

The first rays from the sun awakened the slumbering men. The morning dew on the desert floor was a sight to behold.

"Jim, wake up! You've got to see the sunrise. It's beautiful!"

The men were in awe.

Ken picked up a small lizard to have for breakfast.

Jim heard the chewing. "What are you eating? No, never mind, don't tell me."

"It's manna from heaven," laughed Ken.

He offered the uneaten half to Jim. "I'm happy to share."

"No thanks. I'll call room service."

They both laughed.

Daniel was listening to their banter. How he enjoyed the company. Isolation and solitude was cruel and unusual punishment for humans and angels alike.

Without a second's warning, something grabbed him from behind. He sensed its hot breath as the creature gave him a bear hug, rendering his weapons useless. Daniel squirmed.

"Let go of me! There are a thousand warriors guarding my position. You'd better leave now!" said Daniel.

"You shouldn't lie," said Timothy.

Daniel didn't trust his ears. He twisted his neck around. Timothy was smiling.

"Timothy, it's you!" leaped Daniel as he hugged him.

His joy quickly turned to anxiety.

"Where's Tina Marie? You saved her, didn't you?"

Timothy didn't say a word. He placed his hands on Daniel's shoulders.

"She's with Jesus."

Daniel tried to command his emotions.

"You would have been proud of her! Two soldiers were touched by her faith and bravery. They gave their lives to Christ."

"I wish that we could have saved her," lamented Daniel.

"God was with her until the end; now she is with Him forever!"

The angels looked at each other. Their memory of her was bittersweet, but they rejoiced that she was now with the Father.

Abdul stared at the officer like he was the Devil. He didn't know how to respond. The soldier kicked him in the gut.

"Are you Abdul Mohammed?"

The Muslim looked over at his general, who slowly shook his head in the negative.

"I don't know who that is, but it is not me," lied the petrified Muslim.

The soldier pulled out a scanning machine, which identified the tattoo marks of the world citizenry. He scanned it above his forehead. The blaring beep told him to go for the hand. He brushed it across Abdul's wrist. The machine could not identify him.

"You are under arrest for treason!" announced the man impersonating a Federation officer.

"You can't do this! I know Immanuel Bernstate personally, and he will have your head for this!"

Abdul's threat backfired.

"Sir, you do not have the necessary credentials as a world citizen!"

"All right, I am Abdul Mohammed. What do you want?"

The soldier hauled him toward the paddy wagon.

"We will get to the bottom of this on our truth machine."

"You will pay dearly for this when Immanuel hears of this atrocity!"

The soldier smacked him in the face.

"Shut up!"

David Hoffman was standing on the balcony of his estate. He rubbed his hands over his face in despair. A political aide stated the obvious.

"It's going to be a year or more before we can get the proper equipment to desalt the water. Thousands could die before then if the World Federation doesn't get its act together."

The prime minister boiled with anger. His first impression of Immanuel had been right on the mark.

"We are at the mercy of that devilish bureaucracy. Maybe a personal phone call to Immanuel could prove some help," said David.

"Sir, I don't believe you have any choice. I doubt Immanuel even knows about the water shortage."

David Hoffman's eye caught a car pulling up at the gate.

"Is that the prophets?"

"I believe so, sir! I wouldn't trust them, sir!"

David looked away.

"I don't know whom to trust anymore. If they really are Moses and Elijah, we should be treating them like kings!"

The two Israelites watched as the car traveled around the dried-up fountain of the mansion. Moses and Elijah slowly exited the blue car and walked toward the door. The prime minister left the third-story balcony. He rushed down the stairs, almost knocking over a servant along the way, and stood by the door as it was opened.

"I am very happy to finally meet you, gentlemen," smiled the prime minister as he reached for their hands.

The prophets appeared gloomy but still hospitable.

"Thank you, Mr. Hoffman," said Moses as he exchanged handshakes.

"We are looking forward to speaking to you about our mission," said Elijah as he extended courtesies.

David forced another smile as he invited them into his den. As the men entered the retreat, their eyes scanned the half modern, half historic hermitage. They seemed to be attracted to the computer system on David's desk.

"I understand that you men claim to be the real Moses and Elijah, from the Holy Scriptures," began the politician. The statement made David feel foolish.

Moses turned away from the computer system and took a seat.

"I did not visit you several years ago, Mr. Hoffman," revealed Moses.

The prime minister was astonished. "How did you...you...how could you know...know that?" faltered the Israelite.

"My God, Jehovah God, the Jewish God that you have disavowed, knows everything under the sun," pointed out Moses. "He knows everything about you."

Visibly shaken, the prime minister moved the conversation in another direction.

"You gentlemen are well known for having the ability to call down fire from heaven, and you claim to have caused this three-year drought. I am a believer in your supernatural powers, but I beg you to allow rain for our parched city. People are going to die if you do not remove this curse!"

The prophets were unmoved by his heartfelt plea.

"Mr. Prime Minister," began Elijah. "Your perspective is earthly, not heavenly. The Bible says that our lives are but a mist that appears from a wave on the ocean. It disappears very quickly. Life on earth is short, very short. Earth is a testing ground for God Almighty. People never die; they live forever. Your choice is where you want to live your afterlife. Where are you planning to spend eternity?" asked Elijah.

The prime minister was desperate. He wanted to talk about the drought, not theology.

"I beg you to do something about this drought. You men will be responsible for killing thousands if you do not remove this curse! You are already responsible for torturing the entire world with your words. Every television set in the world is now carrying your messages daily."

"We have not cursed anybody," responded Moses. "They have done it to themselves. God is a God of love, but also a God of right and wrong. He punishes wrong and blesses right! This city, and the entire world, has chosen to follow the Devil himself! When they repent, God will relent!"

David Hoffman felt a rush of serenity envelop his body. The archangel Gabriel had just arrived with the Holy Spirit.

"If you would like, we'll pray for you," said Moses.

The prime minister didn't know how to respond. His heart was divided, and his mind was perplexed.

"Well, I guess. I don't see why not. Please include a prayer for our city," begged Mr. Hoffman.

"We will," smiled Elijah.

The prophets dropped to their knees. Their humility was evident. David followed.

"Jehovah God," prayed Moses. "We beseech you to save this city from its sins. We pray that your Son, Jesus Christ, would overtake the evil from within this city. Lord, we pray that you would chip away at the scales covering David's eyes from the truth. Save him from his sins and from the clutches of the Evil One!"

The Holy Spirit encircled the shaking politician. The archangel Gabriel stood guard against the Enemy, which was precariously close at hand.

"Lord, give David a heart molded after Your own image," prayed Elijah. "Oil the door to his soul so that it might open and allow You to indwell him. Give him the desire to be in the family of the one true God of Israel. Amen."

The prophets opened their eyes. David's were closed. His body was shaking out of control. The struggle for his heart was quickly being decided. The trembling settled as he opened his eyes. He looked at Moses and then Elijah. David collapsed in their arms and wept as his Messiah healed his soul.

"Thank you, God. Thank you, Lord," he said over and over.

Moses and Elijah were overjoyed.

"Your decision has made it dangerous for you to stay here," said Elijah. "We can offer you refuge from Immanuel in a hideout not too far from here."

Tears continued to stream down David's face.

"No, I am going to stand up to Immanuel. People must know!"

Dominic Rosario paced Immanuel's secretary's office. He was bitter and broken. His limousine had traveled past several dozen churches that were being torn down. It broke his heart and his pride. Without warning, Immanuel swung open his doors.

"My friend, Dominic Rosario, come in! We have much to catch up on since my last decree!" smirked Satan.

The False Prophet would rather have died than to have given up his church.

"I hope you have a good explanation for all of this!" said a riled up Dominic, as he entered Immanuel's office. The two men sat down.

"It must pain you to see the churches of the world disassembled right before your eyes," jabbed Immanuel.

Dominic didn't respond. He wanted to punch Immanuel.

"Somewhere in that bible of yours, it says that the greatest blessings come to those who are going through the fires of life."

Immanuel tipped back in his chair as he nibbled on a pencil.

"I am promoting you, Dominic!"

The False Prophet looked at him as if he were insane.

"You destroy my church, the very essence of my lifeblood, and you tell me it's a promotion!"

"I want you to join me here in Geneva. You are to be by my side during every public appearance. You will be responsible for making every man, woman, and child worship me as their one and only God. I know that you have lost your supernatural powers, but I plan on giving them back to you. In fact, I will give you the ability to call down fire from heaven, to move objects at will. You are to make them believe that they can be God, too."

The False Prophet was dumbfounded yet suspicious.

"What's the catch?"

Satan's smile curled downward.

"There is no catch, Dominic," explained Immanuel. "The people don't need churches when God is on the earth. Churches represent me. My image in Jerusalem should suffice."

Dominic's eyes locked into Satan's seductiveness.

"I thank you, master, for this opportunity! When I'm finished, everybody on this planet will know of your power and glory!"

Immanuel's expression turned pale and bleak.

"Do you have any opinions about Moses and Elijah? My satellite has just picked up some damning information about their escapades in Jerusalem. It seems that the prime minister of Israel has succumbed to their message."

The False Prophet appeared stunned by the developing news. He thought that he had David Hoffman in his pocket.

"Maybe this is an effort to infiltrate their little fraternity."

Satan hadn't thought of that. If that was true, the prime minister hadn't bothered informing anybody of his underground activities. That alone was worthy of the death penalty.

"I don't have any public appearances until next week. Get down there and find out what is happening. The last thing I need is to see that Jew make his hideous decision public!"

Abdul had been tied to a metal chair.

"So I hear that you have a problem with the truth," said the Chinese scientist in charge of the truth detector.

Abdul hoped that this man had a soul. He had heard horror stories about mad scientists.

"Immanuel and I have some unfinished business. I would hate to see what will happen to the individual who kills or tortures one of his allies!"

Abdul's calculated threat was a risk, but a necessary one. The Asian eyeballed the Muslim for a moment before firing up his invention.

"Some people don't like God," stated the soldier.

He placed a pair of rubberlike suction cups near Abdul's temples. The mind machine was 100 percent effective. The only hazard was, the contraption often annihilated the brain altogether.

The scientist punched the power button. An inverse reactor began humming like a vulture over a carcass. Abdul began to pray to Allah.

He felt as if his brain were being sucked out of his ears.

"Are you Abdul Mohammed?"

"Yes," responded Abdul.

Anguish invaded his face as the pain became unbearable.

"Does Immanuel Bernstate know you personally?" smirked the scientist, who was expecting a negative response.

"Yes, he does!"

The Chinese man smiled as Abdul nodded his head yes.

"I was hoping you would say that," laughed the Chinese scientist as he powered the machine ever higher.

"No!" screamed Abdul as death began to overtake him.

"We need this war more than you need your life!" justified the Asian as the Muslim leader breathed his last gasp of air.

Nineteen

Sound the Trumpets

The Global News Network was in a state of alert. Meteorologists called it unprecedented. Out of nowhere, huge thunderstorms had blossomed over one-third of the globe. There wasn't a spot in the United States of Europe, or in the new Russia, that had been left untouched. Immanuel stared at his television.

"Once again, the earth is being pounded by another catastrophe. This time, it seems that nature herself is displeased!" editorialized the news reporter.

The lady anchor was polished but not attractive. Immanuel had ordered a personnel restructuring of the Global News Network. He wanted the anchors to look average, to be believable and trustworthy.

"At this very moment, a huge cyclone is spreading intense lightning all over the European and Russian territories! Lightning is setting entire forests ablaze! Many observers report that hail the size of grapefruit has destroyed much of their crops. We also have reports that blood is mixing with the hail, creating widespread panic. Standing by right now is the senior meteorologist of the Global News Network, Kelly Stanton, who will hopefully shed some light on this bizarre outbreak of Mother Nature."

The television screen split in two. A normally jovial gentleman in his late thirties was standing behind a weather map. His joy was missing today.

"Mr. Stanton, could you please tell us when you believe this hurricane will be over with?" begged the anchor.

"To be honest with you, there is no scientific reason behind this storm. Every weather map that I have tells me that this should not be happening. By the way, this is not a hurricane, but a gigantic thunderstorm that seems to have popped up out of nowhere!"

The anchor was annoyed with his honesty. She wanted positive answers.

349

"Maybe you could fill us in on this blood mixed with hail?"

The meteorologist pondered her question for a moment.

"Hail of this type is extremely rare. It is possible that the chunks of ice are killing birds in the air, thereby creating bloodied hailstones."

The anchor smiled. It was a stretch, but any explanation was a comfort.

"Thank you very much, Mr. Stanton."

Her face filled the screen again as she scanned some of the latest news releases.

"The reports from the field are numbing. One-third of the globe is on fire! I understand that almost everything in the European and Russian sectors has been torched. Some buildings are being saved by the heroic efforts of global fire fighters, but most of the vegetation seems to have gone up in smoke!"

The television continued to blare the disturbing events. Satan moved Immanuel to his mahogany desk. He sat down. His yellow eyes narrowed in anger. He began to drum his fingernails on the desktop, nails that were now long and sharp, like claws.

"Do you think this is going to stop me?" fumed Satan as he glared toward heaven.

Ken and Jim were huddled in a small cave outside Jerusalem. The hailstones outside the cave were pounding the sand.

The thunder and lightning were like nothing that either one had ever experienced.

Fear tried to enter Jim's heart. He looked over at Ken, whose face showed anxiety.

Jim pulled his Bible from his shirt pocket and began to read.

"'So the seven angels who had the seven trumpets prepared themselves to sound. The first angel sounded: And hail and fire followed, mingled with blood, and they were thrown to the Earth. And a third of the trees were burned up, and all green grass was burned up.'"

Jim closed his Bible.

"This is the first trumpet blast! We don't need to be afraid. It'll be over soon," offered Jim.

"I know," said Ken.

A peace came over them as they continued to watch the storm.

The prime minister stepped up to the pulpit outside the gates of the temple. He feared no one but God Almighty. Immanuel's image towered over him. There were thousands inside the temple square, worshipping Immanuel's idol. A few dozen people had encircled Moses, Elijah, and David Hoffman.

"Are you sure that you want to do this?" asked Moses as he surveyed the crowd.

David smiled. Words weren't needed.

Elijah patted him on the back. He admired his courage. "The Lord will reward you handsomely!"

Hundreds more were gathering around their makeshift podium. Many were whispering to their friends.

David Hoffman cleared his throat as he faced the crowd and the cameras of the Global News Network.

"People of Jerusalem, I have an announcement to make, and I pray that you will give me the opportunity to speak my entire mind."

The gathering company became silent.

"These two men have not been preaching hate, but the truth!"

The throng of Jerusalem citizens, who thought of Immanuel as the Messiah of Israel, picked up some stones.

"That's blasphemy!" shouted one as he gripped his stone tightly.

"I love Israel!" countered David, standing his ground. "Read your own Scriptures. All the major prophets in our history were condemned by the people of the time. This is not new. You have been lied to! Immanuel is the Antichrist! Jesus Christ is your Messiah, and He will come in the clouds soon to deliver you into paradise!"

The crowd's hatred could not be contained. A few of the younger men threw stones the size of baseballs toward the prime minister. One slammed into his knee.

"Your hatred of my words will not change the truth about Jesus Christ!"

Moses and Elijah were about to use God's power to save the prime minister. He motioned for them to back off.

"My life means nothing if I cannot speak the truth on my own. They will get me sooner than later when I leave here."

The prophets backed off as the crowd shouted obscenities at Hoffman. Blood was dripping from his knee as he continued his brave speech.

"You don't understand what you're doing! Jesus Christ changed my life, and He can change yours, too, if you will only open your eyes!"

A large, burly man at the front of the mob pulled out a handgun.

"Liar! Blasphemer!" screamed the globalist as he fired a shot toward the prime minister.

The bullet lodged right between his eyes. The crowd scattered as the prime minister plunged to the ground. He was killed instantly. The man began to shake as he turned his weapon toward Moses and Elijah.

"You are just like your forefathers!" decried Moses as he lifted his finger toward the murderer. "You kill God's prophets in your twisted justice! You must die for your sins!"

The man fired several rounds of ammunition toward the prophets. Miraculously, every one of them missed. Fire burst from Moses' fingers as the man tried to make an escape. It engulfed him with such fury that only ashes were left.

Immanuel straightened his cuffs as he cleared his throat. A makeup artist was powdering his nose when he received another urgent phone call.

"Sir, I think you may want to speak to this person," said an aide as he lifted the phone into the air.

"Two minutes to air, your majesty," announced the camera person.

"Tell him to call back," chided the Antichrist.

The aide wisely took a message. Immanuel looked at himself in the mirror.

"You missed a spot on my forehead!" barked Satan through Immanuel.

The lady rushed over to him and quickly corrected the problem.

"One minute to air!"

Immanuel glanced down at his notes. His assistant placed the message in front of his face. He quickly tried to digest the message as he read it to himself.

"Immanuel, a fast-moving asteroid the size of a small city was picked up by World Federation radar. It apparently made an impact somewhere in the Atlantic Ocean. A tidal wave warning has been issued for the North American and European coasts! Not good!"

The Antichrist looked up calmly. No one could have imagined what he had just read.

"Ten seconds, sir."

Immanuel cracked his knuckles as he readied himself for the world. Every channel on the global cable system automatically switched into the live transmission.

"Good afternoon, citizens of the World Federation. A very tragic storm has swept through Europe and Russia, leaving much of this region of the globe burned and charred. As your god, I will do everything I can to get you back on your feet. Many of you are wondering how such a tragedy can occur with your god shouldering the governments of the world."

Satan stared into the camera.

"Your faith in me is built not only in good times but also in bad times. My bible states unequivocally that tragedy softens the heart. I will provide for my children, but you must have the faith that moves mountains. I did not cause this terrible disaster. But I cannot stop this type of event, either. I set my universe up to function independently of me. Therefore, adverse conditions can arise at any time. I expect neighbors to help one another and bond as if they were one. This is an opportunity to test your faith in me and in all of humanity!"

Immanuel paused as he stared at the piece of paper.

"Leave it alone," kicked Satan.

"Expect more upheavals in nature as the Earth is born into an era of peace and tranquility. We are all connected to Mother Earth. Focus your prayers. You have the power to calm Mother Nature. Until we all think as one, birth pains will continue."

Several thousand miles away, Immanuel's twelve little thorns stared at the television screen in disgust. Lord Birmingham stood up.

"This man is beyond comprehension. He actually had the gall to say that these disasters are because everybody doesn't agree with him!" Lord Birmingham wiped his brow as he sat back down. "Unfortunately, they will buy the lie. Every bit of it."

"When do we send the troops out, Lord Birmingham?" inquired the German banker.

Birmingham placed his pipe back in his mouth as he relaxed in his armchair. All eyes were on him.

"If you want to kill a vampire, you have to drive a stake right through his heart!"

The bankers didn't understand what he was trying to say. Lord Birmingham smiled.

"We need to drive a stake right through the heart of Immanuel's kingdom. The heart is in Jerusalem, where that technological marvel is located, but we can't get into that airspace. The next best thing would be Europe and the Middle East."

Birmingham smirked.

"We can put a dent into his 'holier than thou' image by taking out the water supply and creating a slight disturbance in the Muslim world."

"With what?" responded the German.

Lord Birmingham picked up his glass of water. He smiled as he spit into it.

An hour later, the Global News Network interrupted regular programming.

"As many of you know, a tidal wave warning has been issued for the entire American Eastern seaboard and Western European coastline. Our worst fears have been realized!"

The screen cut to a video camera that was secured on top of a skyscraper in Miami, Florida.

"This video was shot just moments ago. I warn you that these pictures are graphic!"

The man paused as he allowed the pictures to tell the story. The water around Miami Beach had completely disappeared. Suddenly, a bubble of water appeared on the horizon. The bubble of water quickly turned into an enormous wall of water several hundred feet high. People were running for their lives as the water invaded the beach and moved inland. The force of the crash rocked the building so severely that the camera went blank.

"Reports are pouring in from the Canadian coastline to the Brazilian coast, all the way across to parts of Europe and even Africa. This wave of terror has engulfed everything in its path! Nearly one-third of the world's coastlines appear to have been demolished. An asteroid, the size of a mountain, is the cause of this disaster. Astronomers have been quoted as saying, "It popped up out of nowhere! We should have seen it decades ago!" It plunged into the heart of the Atlantic Ocean several hours ago, sending energy equivalent to one thousand nuclear bombs to the shores of our great continents!"

Daniel and Timothy were flying in circles around their humans, watching for enemy invaders. Ken and Jim were within fifty miles of Jerusalem.

"The second trumpet has sounded!" shouted an angel as it traveled at lightning speed across the desert.

"What does that mean?" asked a nervous Daniel.

Timothy opened his Bible and began reading from the eighth chapter of Revelation to his shaking comrade.

Daniel drew closer to Timothy.

"'Then the second angel sounded: and something like a great mountain burning with fire was thrown into the sea, and a third of the sea became blood. And a third of the living creatures in the sea died, and a third of the ships were destroyed.'"

"That's what's been happening," said Daniel.

"Yes, but God is in control."

Suddenly, a large group of demons darted past them. The angels hid under some desert brush. This was no ordinary group of evil spirits, and both angels knew it.

God was desperately trying to send the world a message. Those who had the mark of the Beast and believed that Immanuel was their god were not listening. The people of the world rationalized away the judgments of God. They blamed a fickle Mother Nature, they accused the Christians of polluting the spiritual airwaves, and they incriminated those who didn't pray to Immanuel enough for the healing of the planet.

Roughly one-third of the Earth had been mangled by the natural disasters. In biblical terms, the Earth was vomiting up its inhabitants.

The fire that had ravished one-third of the planet had obliterated much of the food supply. The storm had lasted only seven hours, but the effects would last a lifetime. In addition, with one-third of the ships destroyed, the resources of the Earth could not be distributed equitably. Immanuel snubbed his nose at Russia, the Middle East, and China, leaving billions of people to fend for themselves. His spy satellites had spotted a massive buildup of troops in those refractory regions, so he tried to starve their citizens into submission.

"Clear out of my office immediately!" squalled Immanuel.

They scattered. Immanuel dropped into his seat. He closed his eyes in search of his invisible beacon.

"What do I do?" searched Immanuel as he grabbed a deep breath. "What or who is against us? Every time I think that we have made inroads, something like this happens!"

Satan didn't appreciate the wavering faith of his disciple.

"Your problem is simple, human," whispered Satan. "Your faith is too fragile. You must believe, or die a coward's death!"

The Serpent's reprimand terrorized Immanuel. He feared the power that possessed him. It controlled his every thought as if it owned his body.

"What do I say to the world if this kind of thing continues?" questioned Immanuel.

"You will say nothing! I will use Moses and Elijah."

"What is it?" asked a scientist at the World Federation science research station.

His coworker was shaken. The tightly covered plastic flask that he was holding suddenly slipped through his fingers and bounced off the floor. He scrambled to retrieve it.

"I don't know what this is, sir, but it is so deadly that a few drops of it can kill millions, almost instantly!"

His boss shrugged his shoulders.

"So what? We have identified several dozen of those chemicals in the past twenty years."

"Sir, you don't understand!" voiced the junior scientist.

He attempted to hide his shaking hands in the pockets of his white uniform.

"This water came from the ocean where that asteroid landed!"

His superior suddenly grew pale. He dropped into the hard-wood chair.

"How many specimens do you have?"

"Enough to know that every living thing in the Atlantic will be dead within the next week!"

Timothy searched his memory. He recognized the demon squad but couldn't remember from where.

"Daniel, Satan is planning something big in Jerusalem. I don't know what, but it could completely change our plan. Maybe it's not such a hot idea to lead Jim and Ken over there right now."

"Is there a safe place in the mountains surrounding Jerusalem where we can go? You know, a place where we can watch, but still be out of danger?"

Timothy pondered Daniel's question. His face began to glow.

"I was in Jerusalem when David was king more than three thousand years ago. I remember a concealed cave on the Mount of Olives where he hid. It's possible to get them there, but the cave might not be a secret anymore."

The angels glanced down at their humans.

"I have a feeling that God wants us to do something," said Ken.

Jim had reservations. "With no resources? What could we possibly do?"

"We can pray, Jim," smiled Ken. "We still have that."

———

Lord Birmingham sported a beard, a mustache, and a cane. He was standing in a remote region of Geneva, begging for bread. In his beggar's basket lay a dead bird, an outdated dollar bill worth less than the paper that it was printed on, two live earthworms, and a threatening notice informing him of his illegal activity.

He scanned the muddy roadway. He discreetly pulled up his sleeve to glance at his Rolex. It was 3:00 P.M.

"Lord Birmingham, do not leave!" whispered a voice from behind him.

The European obeyed. He continued panhandling. Several people looked at him in disgust.

"I need food! Please have mercy on me!" he begged.

The people passed.

"A container is buried in a shallow grave exactly thirty feet behind you. It is marked with a dead squirrel. It should do the job nicely."

"What's in it for you?" Birmingham asked. The man laughed.

"Let's just say, divine justice."

"How can I contact you in the future?"

"I was never here," said Vice President Colt.

Birmingham heard footsteps fading quickly into the distance.

The banker counted off thirty feet. A charred squirrel marked the spot. The European dropped to his knees as he dug through the ashy soil. As he saw metal peeking out of the dirt, he sped up his effort. He hesitantly reached down and picked up a round metal container.

Later that evening, Vice President Colt was snuggled up on his favorite bar stool inside a posh Geneva hotel. Ever since Immanuel had proclaimed himself God, Colt had considered himself a lone voice of reason calling out in the wilderness. The only problem was, he couldn't risk telling anyone his true feelings.

As the vice president inhaled another vodka on the rocks, a man dressed in a black woolen overcoat appeared on the stool beside him. The words "News Emergency," flashed on the twenty-foot digital television. A middle-aged male anchor appeared on the screen.

"This just in from the wires of the Global News Network. The meteor that struck the Atlantic Ocean last week, killing tens of thousands from Africa to the Americas to Europe, has not finished with the world just yet."

Vice President Colt was captivated by the headlines. For the first time in nearly seven years, his direct actions would make world news. That's the kind of raw power he remembered and coveted.

"Scientists from the World Federation have announced that a deadly bacteria was carried on that meteor. At this point, every fish within one million square miles of the impact point has died. This foreign chemical has not been identified by our scientists yet.

"The leading experts have assured us that this will affect only the water in the ocean. It will not, I repeat, will not, affect local drinking water."

Colt swished a shot of vodka in his mouth. That wasn't the news that he was waiting for.

The vice president glanced at the person beside him. He could barely see the man's eyes.

"Excuse me, what time do you have?" asked the vice president as he fiddled with his shot glass.

The man glanced at a clock on the wall.

"It's seven o'clock," mumbled the stranger.

Vice President Colt smirked as he turned toward the television screen.

"The global food shortage is reaching epidemic levels. With the latest disaster that struck one-third of our oceans, many are wondering when the seafood will be safe to consume," continued the news anchor.

Lord Birmingham's palms were sweating as he placed the round steel container inside a nuclear-tipped missile.

"How much of the water do you believe it will poison?" asked the Frenchman.

Lord Birmingham slowly backed away from the killing machine.

"A few drops of this stuff in a water system could kill millions!"

"Isn't there any other way that we can accomplish our objectives?" asked the German banker as he rubbed his chapped face.

Birmingham walked toward the men.

"I wish there were an easier answer. This is our only alternative. When this chemical gets into the jet stream, and eventually into the rainwater, it will poison the drinking water in possibly a third of the Earth! It will break Immanuel's back, I promise!"

The men hurried to their fallout shelter. They knew these weapons were old and unpredictable. If the propulsion system failed, they would at least have an underground cave to live in until their food ran out. They were strangely quiet as they filed into the subterranean grotto.

After Lord Birmingham sealed the rock door, he quickly turned toward the discharge gear. His right hand was steady as he placed it on the green button. Placing his left hand on a key, he turned to face his team. Blank stares greeted him. Without blinking an eye, Lord Birmingham turned the key and pushed the button.

"This is phase one, gentlemen. Phase two begins when Immanuel's thievery comes back to bite him!"

Colt glanced up at the clock as he guzzled his eighth drink. It was eight o'clock. The foreigner beside him, who sipped on a Coke, remained quiet. The television screen blurred as the vice president succumbed to the alcohol. Suddenly, another news flash interrupted the programming.

"Ladies and gentlemen, we have just received a distressing report from the province of Spain. Apparently, another nuclear bomb has been launched!"

"This is it," he thought. He had to get back to work immediately. He couldn't wait to see the look on Immanuel's face. "Treason never felt better," thought Colt. As he stumbled out of the door, the stranger quickly followed. The vice president was standing beside the ash-covered curb, motioning for a taxi. The figure slowly moved in behind him.

"Immanuel wants you to know that you are going to hell!" whispered the hit man as he stuck a needle into his back.

The message barely had time to register in his mind before the drug reached his heart. The American president instantly collapsed and died.

The archangel Michael hovered over the Earth. His eyes teared as he read from the eighth chapter of the book of Revelation.

"'Then the third angel sounded: and a great star fell from heaven, burning like a torch, and it fell on a third of the rivers and on the springs of water. The name of the star is Wormwood. A third of the waters became wormwood, and many men died from the water, because it was made bitter.'"

The archangel knew that when the apostle John had seen this nuclear-tipped missile sailing through the sky, he must have thought that it was a falling star. He had seen the engine exhaust and compared it to a torch.

One-third of the Earth's water resources were defiled.

The Evil One's time was running out.

A week later, Immanuel was standing amid the ruins of the old Roman empire, preparing for another television appearance. His eyes stared at the long columns of carved rock that had been tossed like toothpicks along the hilly landscape. He had strategically chosen this popular tourist location in Rome.

"Your majesty, thirty seconds to air," stated a new camera person.

Immanuel ignored him as he adjusted his cuffs. The old camera man had forgotten to give him an important cue several days earlier. He was found at the bottom of a sewer hole.

"Focus on those prophets," instructed Satan.

"Yes," smiled Immanuel.

"You're on!" cued the cameraperson.

"My citizens of the world, I stand before you today at the cradle of modern civilization."

The camera panned the ruins of the Roman empire.

"This is what the prophets Moses and Elijah want to see. They feed on death and destruction. Today, nearly one-third of our world has been destroyed by their predictions. The latest nuclear bomb to strike the world has obliterated Spain and parts of southern France. Even worse, these terrorists, who call themselves 'prophets,' attached a poison to the warhead that has contaminated every lake, river, and stream in Europe, Russia, parts of Asia, and the Middle East. These men are so hideously inspired by hatred and malice that they brag on international television about this catastrophe as 'judgments of their God'!"

The camera moved from Immanuel's somber face to a dark grayish-brown sky.

"It is noontime here in Rome, yet the sun doesn't shine. Scientists call this phenomenon a nuclear winter. One-third of the globe has been affected. My scientists tell me it could be months before many see the sun or the moon again!"

Immanuel paused, letting his audience catch up with him.

"For nearly three and one-half years, I have allowed these so-called prophets to exist. I have shown them mercy above the call of duty. Now, my mercy has been exhausted!"

The camera zoomed in on the False Prophet, who was standing on the temple of Diana. Dominic raised his hands into the air, as if he were commanding a performance. A bolt of lightning appeared, striking the bare soil surrounding the ancient church.

"Worship Immanuel and give him thanks for his great power and wisdom!" shouted the lying Prophet to all of the world.

The picture slowly faded back to the Antichrist.

"In six days, I will ride into Jerusalem and judge Moses and Elijah. They will be killed as they have killed. The world will then know that I am God!"

The Antichrist was on top of the world. A caravan of sixty vehicles accompanied the leader to the hideout. As it reached its destination, dozens of armed soldiers emerged from their vehicles. Immanuel was the last to appear from his truck. The men were lined in rows as Immanuel approached. Their bodies were rigid, their wills made of concrete. The Antichrist eyed them with a bizarre joy gleaming in his eyes.

"Men, you are the finest soldiers in my world! You will capture all of them alive, and bring them to me for their judgment. I will not tolerate my orders being ignored. If you must, I expect you to give your life for me! Do not allow one of them to slip through your fingers!"

Satan turned toward the stone mansion that was nestled between two ice-covered ridges. Revenge would be sweet. The commander of the SWAT team motioned with his laser gun for the troops to follow him.

As Immanuel neared the mansion, he glanced at his timepiece. It was two in the morning. Everything was perfect. He had promoted the engineer who had pinpointed the location from which the nuclear warhead had been launched. How ignorant, thought Satan. Those idiots must have known that a missile could be tracked to its source.

Immanuel, accompanied by his general, watched gleefully from one hundred yards away as his men penetrated the compound. He heard laser blasts. He turned to the military man, who was drenched with sweat.

"You'd better pray that they do not kill any of them!" grimaced the Antichrist.

"They have been given strict orders to keep their guns on stun. If anyone disobeys me, allow me the luxury of executing the man before you execute me!"

Satan smiled. He was beginning to like this man. The Antichrist and the general stayed a safe distance away until the all clear was given. It had taken less than five minutes. He walked through the front entrance, which led to an immense ballroom. Inside the party room stood the twelve bankers who had given him his kingdom. Their feet and hands were bound by iron shackles.

"It surprises me that it would take 'god' nearly three years to find his enemies!" crowed Lord Birmingham as he tugged at his snare.

The Devil laughed as he slowly walked toward Lord Birmingham.

"You are a fool!" shot back the snake. "I have allowed you this time to make me look good. Nearly every Christian on the face of the Earth has been put to death because of your crusade for justice!"

The other bankers remained silent as their leader poked a spear into Immanuel's story.

"You're so far gone, you even believe your own lies. You're no god! I'm sure that when you die, and you will die, the real God will have a special place for you in His hell!"

Lord Birmingham spit in his face. Satan was delighted.

"It's such a pity. You have the qualities that I admire."

Satan began to pace back and forth in front of the banker.

"All of you deserve to die! You have killed nearly a billion of my people. You have committed high treason against my kingdom. You have stolen my ark and my commandments!"

"Immanuel!" shouted the Englishman. "If you really are God, why don't you prove it?"

The Devil quickly walked over to the challenger.

"So you want proof of my godhood?"

Suddenly, the Englishman was levitated off the ground and thrown toward Lord Birmingham. Both men were knocked down.

Satan grinned as he approached the billionaire traitors. His fingers were twitching.

Lord Birmingham tried to stand but failed.

Immanuel's psychotic laughter enveloped the room. He turned to leave. He had more pressing business on the other side of the world.

"I want all of them brought to Geneva and locked up in my personal prison."

———————

Moses and Elijah were preaching the gospel of Jesus Christ and the impending judgments from the book of Revelation. They knew their road was about to end. It had been a long, hard three and one-half years, but they could hold their heads high and say, "We did God's work."

Satan had longed for the arrival of this day. Immanuel grabbed three hours of sleep on his flight from St. Petersburg, Russia, to Jerusalem. As his eyes opened, Satan greeted him.

"You will do exactly what I say!" Satan words bludgeoned Immanuel's heart.

The Devil coiled his carcass around Immanuel's chest. He slowly applied pressure, and Immanuel began to gasp for air. He feared the thought of a heart attack.

"What are you doing?" panted Immanuel as he wrestled with his body. "I have followed your every order! What more do you want from me?"

The dragon seethed with passion as he tightened his clamp on the human.

"I want your soul!"

The Antichrist began to choke as Satan placed his hands around his neck.

For the moment, Satan relented. Immanuel slowly regained his composure as he stood to leave the plane. A servant handed him his jacket as he descended the spiral stairway of the jet. The sun had risen several hours earlier, yet the clouds brushed darkness across the land. His white limousine, coated with a thin layer of ash, was waiting at the bottom of the stairs.

Moses and Elijah weren't surprised to see tens of thousands of people awaiting their arrival. As they walked toward their make-shift stage, several threats were tossed their way.

Thousands of God's angels were protecting them.

"People of Jerusalem, hear and believe the words of the one holy and true God!" exhorted Moses as Elijah looked on. "For three and one-half years, we have preached the truth. Today, Immanuel threatens to end our life on earth. He will tell you that he is God when he attacks us. I tell you, the time has come for more prophecy to be fulfilled."

The people operating the cameras from the Global News Network turned them off. Immanuel had commanded them to be stopped whenever the prophets foretold the future. The last thing he needed were more converts. The crowds sneered as Elijah read the prophecy. Their hearts were harder than stone.

A few minutes later, Satan's limousine advanced toward the prophets. The crowd continued to pour into the court as the vehicle drove slowly through the anxious masses. The cameras turned on as Satan appeared and walked toward the prophets of God.

"Immanuel, Immanuel, Immanuel!" chanted the crowd.

Moses and Elijah held their ground as they watched the enemy of men's souls come toward them.

"Judge them for their wickedness!" shouted an onlooker.

"Make them pay!" yelled another.

Moses and Elijah closed their eyes as they prayed.

"God of the heavens, the Lord of our souls, we pray not for our will, but for Yours. We pray for our enemies, that they might see the truth. Amen."

Nobody could hear their petition except the Antichrist. Immanuel was less than six feet away when he turned to address the world. The chaos subsided.

"I stand before you today as the only true god of the universe! Behind me are impersonators. They are con men who have a spirit of evil. They have no power over me, because if they did, they would kill me right now!"

The Devil immediately twisted his body around to meet his adversaries. The look of peace and contentment on their faces made him want to vomit.

"If you are the representatives of the one and true God, then prove it. Strike me dead!"

Moses and Elijah were silent. They reacted just as Jesus had when His accusers had arraigned Him for blasphemy. They had demanded a sign from Jesus, but He had refused.

The electric atmosphere was charged with hatred and lies. Satan's demons surrounded the stage and began to attack it with all their might. They could have been easily overcome, but the commander of the angels ordered his troops to withdraw. Not a single angel questioned the directive. The demons had won, without a fight. Satan watched with glee as his troops swarmed the area.

"I pronounce you guilty of murder," shouted the Antichrist.

The demons began to possess many in the crowd as the assembly hissed at the prophets.

"I pronounce you guilty of lying, stealing, and impersonating God's spokesmen. I find you guilty of provoking my wrath," yelled Satan as he brought up lightning from hell.

The bolt of electricity belted their bodies. Moses and Elijah dropped to the ground with their hands in the air. They were praising God as they breathed their last breaths.

Satan turned toward his subjects.

"Many have questioned my power and godhood because of these so-called prophets."

He gazed at the camera as if it were a nugget of pure gold.

"All evil has now been removed from the face of my Earth! Soon, the nuclear winter will end. A new and glorious period of peace will follow!"

Satan glanced at the dead bodies.

"This calls for a celebration! Today is a day to give thanks! God has arrived on Earth, and his enemies have scattered! Celebrate your new lives on an earth of tolerance and tranquility! From this point forward, Christmas will be honored on this day. Peace on earth has arrived!"

Twenty

A Stunned World

I t had been three days since Satan had killed Moses and Elijah in full view of the entire world. The Global News Network repeated the tragic event over and over again, until the pictures were singed into the people's consciousness. Night and day, the cameras remained fixated on the prophets' dead bodies. Moses and Elijah remained on the dirty street as a warning to those who opposed Immanuel.

The world was in the midst of the greatest celebration in recorded history. Satan, against the better advice of his economists, granted all world citizens a credit of one thousand ECUs on their World Federation buying cards. It was to be a six-day festival to commemorate the birth of a new world. Satan stressed the importance of adopting a new attitude, a new mind, and a new core set of values where he was God. The truths of the old Bible were seared from the memories of the people.

Satan had another reason to celebrate. He was the proud owner of twelve bankers, who now took up residence in a dungeon several stories belowground under the World Federation's main headquarters. His northern nemesis, Russia, had been captured, and his southern enemies had been destroyed. The Devil had weathered the storm.

It was Sunday evening, and Satan was in a meeting with his top aides. They could not come to an agreement about whether to allow Moses and Elijah a decent Jewish burial to appease the Israelites. One of his cabinet members, a Jew by birth, had personally inspected the bodies hours earlier and confirmed that the bodies were not decaying. Satan demanded that the media not be informed about this. The dragon's aides were shaken by the phenomenon. He brushed it aside as a freak of nature. No one dared to take it any further. They watched the television screen with their intrepid leader.

"I don't believe that we should continue this desecration any longer," voiced his concerned media spokesman. "We need to move on with more positive reforms instead of watching two dead men rot in the street!"

The Prince of Darkness nodded his head.

"Your majesty," began an aide, "I believe that you're using this unique situation beautifully! Every minute that those men's cold bodies are displayed on every cable channel out there, the stronger your appeal becomes! The people universally hate them!"

Satan glanced at the dead bodies.

"Gentlemen, Moses and Elijah are the very reason that I have succeeded in bringing the world together. I used them until their purpose had been exhausted. We will wait until the six-day celebration is complete; then we will cremate them on the temple altar in Jerusalem."

Satan's leading scientist timidly raised his hand.

The Antichrist glanced his way before returning his eyes to the prophets' bodies.

"I know what you are thinking," said the Antichrist. "You want to study the bodies before we burn them."

"Your majesty, if I can just find out what is causing this supernatural event, I could possibly double or even triple our life span!"

The Devil lowered his voice.

"I will not allow any kind of tinkering with their bodies."

His tone sent shivers down his hireling's spines.

"I want all of you out of my office immediately!" ordered Satan as he turned away from the television screen.

The men started to race out of the office when the scientist pointed toward the television screen in horror.

"They are...I...don't...don't believe...it!" he stammered.

The Devil watched his aides as their faces began to fill with horror. Immanuel nearly swallowed his tongue as he turned toward the television.

———————

Blasphemy soared across the Italian mountains, cursing every molecule of air along the way. He was homeless and destitute. Earlier in the week, he had been bragging to himself about his greatness. The five-star deserter had slipped through the claws of Satan without the Devil's even knowing it. Seconds before Immanuel's troops had ransacked his hideout, Blasphemy had escaped through the underground tunnel system.

But now Blasphemy was a fugitive with nowhere to go. He didn't trust his troops. After all, one of the greatest attributes of a fallen angel was backstabbing. He passed over Rome and plunged toward the city of seven hills. He would make a house call on an old friend.

Moses and Elijah slowly stood to their feet. A huge white cloud began to descend on them as the world watched in utter panic. The announcer for the Global News Network quickly cut into the breaking news story.

"Oh, my God!" yelled the reporter. "This must be some kind of supernatural trick! People of the world, Moses and Elijah are alive!"

The president of the Global News Network was in Satan's office watching in horror.

A mysterious smirk appeared on Immanuel who was completely possessed by Satan himself.

"Cut the cameras now!" ordered Satan.

Moses and Elijah were gazing into heaven as the transparent cloud curled around their feet. The heavenly vapor seemed to have a mind of its own as it circled the men's worn bodies.

"Come up here!" thundered a voice from heaven.

Moses and Elijah were lifted by the cloud into the sky and quickly disappeared.

Seconds later, the television screen turned to snow. However, it was too late. The world had seen a true resurrection. People's hearts from every corner of the globe were struck with fear. The Devil's stranglehold had been loosened.

Satan stared into the empty television screen. "I see that you want to play hardball," seethed the Devil.

Timothy and Daniel were in better spirits as they neared the last mountain range before Jerusalem. They considered it a miracle that they hadn't been spotted by the enemy. They and their humans were still safe. Satan had allowed a drunken orgy for the past three and one-half days. The demons were so confident that they had won the ultimate battle that they had completely dropped their defenses.

Suddenly, crude howls of anguish filtered from the north. Timothy recognized the distress signals from Satan's camp.

Daniel nervously looked at him to make sense of the hellish sounds.

"Something has sent the demons into shock!" said Timothy, who stared toward Jerusalem.

Without warning, the earth began to shake violently. Ken and Jim dropped to the ground.

"This earthquake is worse than the first one!" shouted Ken above the sound of the rumbling.

A few loose rocks began to tumble down the hill as the men covered their heads.

"Do you think that this is Armageddon?" yelled Jim.

The agitated earth began to calm as the men prayed for their safety. It had passed as quickly as it had come. Jim and Ken lifted themselves off the sand.

"The next earthquake on the prophecy map is not Armageddon!" shouted Ken. "Apparently, Moses and Elijah have been raised from the dead!"

Ken reached for his Bible and opened it to chapter eleven in the book of Revelation. Jim looked over his shoulder as he began to read from verse seven.

"'When they finish their testimony, the beast that ascends out of the bottomless pit will make war against them, overcome them, and kill them. And their dead bodies will lie in the street of the great city which spiritually is called Sodom and Egypt, where also our Lord was crucified. Then those from the peoples, tribes, tongues, and nations will see their dead bodies three-and-a-half days, and not allow their dead bodies to be put into graves. And those who dwell on the earth will rejoice over them, make merry, and send gifts to one another, because these two prophets tormented those who dwell on the earth. Now after the three-and-a-half days the breath of life from God entered them, and they stood on their feet, and great fear fell on those who saw them. And they heard a loud voice from heaven saying to them, "Come up here." And they ascended to heaven in a cloud, and their enemies saw them. In the same hour there was a great earthquake, and a tenth of the city fell. In the earthquake seven thousand people were killed, and the rest were afraid and gave glory to the God of heaven.'"

Ken and Jim stared at each other. It was impossible for them to communicate their feelings. Their God was keeping every last one of His promises, and the world still hated Him with a passion.

"This is the perfect opportunity for us to make a run for it!" realized Ken as he knocked the sand out of his shoes.

"How do you figure?" asked Jim.

Ken's eyes were glued to the Mount of Olives, which he could barely see in the distance.

"The police in Jerusalem will have their hands full. Most of the buildings will be severely damaged or destroyed. They will barely be able to keep order in the streets. I doubt that they will notice two people walking in from the desert."

Jim wasn't hard to convince.

"Where do we go?"

"I don't know. But I'm sure we have guardian angels protecting us and guiding us. God will use them to place us where He wants us."

Timothy and Daniel felt a rush of joy in their spirits as they realized their humans knew that they were there.

———

The archangel Michael watched with mixed emotions as a mighty angel plummeted toward the Earth like a falling star. The war for the universe had lasted more than seven thousand years, yet now it was just months away from being completed. His mind began to recount God's words from the ninth chapter of Revelation. He muttered them softly to himself as he glided over the Middle East at an altitude of seven hundred miles.

"'Then the fifth angel sounded: and I saw a star fallen from heaven to the earth. To him was given the key to the bottomless pit. And he opened the bottomless pit, and smoke arose out of the pit like the smoke of a great furnace.'"

The powerful angel, who had been given the order from Jehovah God Himself, continued to plunge toward the earth. Michael followed behind him as he reached a remote location in northern Iran, and plunged deep beneath the surface of the earth. The archangel dashed into the cloud cover from the nuclear fallout. It was nearly eight miles thick. The archangel recognized the location as the original spot of the Garden of Eden. My, how it has changed, Michael thought with a sigh.

———

Immanuel was alone in his office, staring into a beveled mirror on the other side of the room. He knew that he had been duped, yet it didn't matter. It had been weeks since he had been able to think clearly. Satan had controlled every part of his being. Suddenly, the image in the mirror was engulfed in flames as the Devil appeared in the reflection.

"Immanuel!" seethed the Serpent.

The Antichrist straightened his body. He needed Satan more now than a newborn needs his mother.

"Yes, your majesty!"

"It's a hoax. It never happened. Somebody stole the bodies." The haunting image in the mirror sprang toward Immanuel, who was helpless.

Dominic was having lunch at an exclusive Roman restaurant. He was dining with friends, discussing the latest in theological thought. Dozens of plants lined the eatery, many of which were being choked by the lack of sunlight.

"My bible, and my revelations, fully support the idea of God existing in human form. Immanuel is the fulfillment of those ancient predictions," argued Dominic.

The religious men accompanying Dominic were once Immanuel's followers, but were now having second thoughts. The terrifying plagues that were gripping the globe were weighing on their minds.

"I don't believe it anymore," said one of the men as he dropped his dinner fork. "Immanuel's a fraud! I know that I can be killed for my opinion, but that's the way I feel!"

Blasphemy, who was loitering in the shadows, was pleased. He had visited each of these men in their dreams during the previous night, hoping to plant seeds of doubt that could bring in a bountiful harvest. If he could only get Dominic on his side, Satan's blueprint for world domination would burn.

"Let's just say that you're right. Let's just say that Immanuel is not God," played Dominic. "He has given me the power to perform miracles that one could only have dreamed of. How do you explain that?"

Dominic's closest friend took the challenge.

"Listen, Dominic," said the man as he leaned toward his longtime friend. "We all know that Satan has powers that we don't understand fully. The old Bible said that there'd be a time when Satan would masquerade as God, in the form of a man. You have much to lose if you agree with us, but you have more to lose if you don't!"

Self-righteous anger boiled inside the False Prophet. He moved his plate toward the center of the table in disgust.

"Is that a threat of some kind? Are you suggesting that I will lose my soul if I don't agree with your theological opinion?"

"You can interpret my words in whatever fashion you desire. Your association with this man will be placed on the scales of God's justice system."

Blasphemy jumped into Dominic's spirit.

"Maybe the problem is, God hasn't found the right person to possess bodily. Maybe He has been disappointed in Immanuel, and wants someone of..." Dominic paused, "of more noble and moral character."

The archangel stood and surveyed the vast wasteland before him. He was remembering the paradise that Jehovah God had created here some seven thousand years earlier. He envisioned the springs of pure water flowing from the earth, fruit trees that glistened in the soft rays of the sun, and Adam and Eve enjoying each other and their paradise. It had been true peace that only Jehovah God can create.

The archangel's pleasant memories dispersed as the ground underneath him began to shake. A mammoth sinkhole was quickly forming. Out of this growing pit came an eerie, smoky substance that billowed upward. The angel that Michael had followed to Earth suddenly appeared from this hellhole. He saluted Michael as he rocketed toward the throne of God. Millions of repulsive, perilous creatures sprouted from this entrance to hell itself. They crawled on their bellies toward the four winds, searching for humans who hadn't placed their trust in the one true God of the universe.

In less than a day, the Devil had set up a mock news conference that resembled a court of law. He had six Jews seated beside him who were willing to say anything for a bribe and to be in the spotlight. The Global News Network had been promoting this event the entire day. Practically every human on the face of the earth was watching.

"Ladies and gentlemen of my good Earth, I once again find myself in a position to condemn those who want to destroy our peace. Yesterday, it appeared as if those two Jewish rebels, whom I personally judged with the death penalty, had come back to life!"

The camera slowly zoomed in for a more intimate profile of their charismatic leader.

"The truth is, it was all a hoax, a cruel hoax. What many of you saw yesterday was state-of-the-art animation masquerading as a resurrection. I have six fine citizens with me today who can testify to you that those rebels never ascended by a cloud into heaven. The bodies were stolen at the exact moment that this travesty occurred. We have recovered the bodies and have cremated them," lied Immanuel.

Satan turned to his well-paid jury of six liars.

"I would like to ask you all if any of you saw a cloud drop down from heaven, and more importantly, if Moses and Elijah actually woke up from their deathbeds?"

They all shook their heads no in unison. The eldest of the group was the only one to speak. He had been memorizing his words all day long.

"I was standing only a few yards from their bodies. At no time did they actually rise from the dead! That idea is absurd! What did happen was that a group of hooded men ran toward the bodies. Using the smoke as cover, they picked them up and carried them away!"

Satan smiled.

"Did you ever see a cloud of any kind coming down out of the sky?" prompted the Devil.

"Absolutely not! We saw a crime. Not a supernatural resurrection!"

The Devil placed his hand over the man's wrist.

"I want to thank you for being brave enough to tell the truth. You have not allowed the fear of these terrorists to cloud your morality."

Satan turned toward the camera, which slowly zoomed in for a close-up of the master manipulator.

"People of the Earth, you have heard an eyewitness account of the truth behind this crime against the state. Once again, these Christian rebels have tried to fool you into believing their phony religion."

Satan relaxed. "My people, you can always trust me to tell you the truth and to protect you from the lies of those who are the enemies of your souls! Rest in my hands. Be at peace."

———

It sounded as if an army were marching toward them. Maybe it was the desert wind rustling against the dried vegetation. Whatever it was, Ken and Jim were scared. They were climbing the desert side of the Mount of Olives, away from the suburbs of Jerusalem. When they were about halfway up the small mountain, the noise became unbearable. The sound was ghostly. They decided to hide in a small cleft in the rocks.

"What do you make of it, Ken?" asked Jim.

"I don't know."

As the daylight grew dim, the horrible sound continued to magnify.

After many nervous hours, Ken and Jim came out of the cave. The entire valley east of Jerusalem was covered with strange-looking insects. They were about the size of the small idols that Immanuel had his people worship.

Ken began to run down the slope toward the valley. Jim thought he had lost his mind.

"What are you doing? You're going to get yourself killed!" pleaded Jim as he tried to catch him.

"No way, man! I'll bet they won't harm us!"

It was only a matter of seconds before they were in the middle of the creatures from hades. The huge, gross insects were like nothing that had ever walked the earth. Suddenly, hundreds of them swarmed around the two saints. The men didn't move or say a word as the bugs surveyed them from head to toe.

"What are they doing?" said Jim as he closed his eyes in disgust.

Ken was far more curious and braver than his counterpart. He put his hand out as if they were man's best friend. The insects ignored his pleasantries.

"They will sting everybody who has sold his soul to Immanuel. They come from hell but are controlled by heaven. We are on their side!"

Suddenly, one of the larger locusts screamed like a demon. It jumped into the air toward the city. The herd of creatures responded to its cry. They began to march toward Jerusalem. Their scorpionlike tails were waving in the air, searching for victims.

The entire earth became covered with these merciless creatures. People were being stung repeatedly. The pain inflicted was beyond description. Most people would go through convulsions, foam at the mouth, and then faint from the agony. Some would hide in their houses, but the locusts would crash through the windows and attack them in their sleep. Others would try to outrun the insects, only to be cornered and stung. There was nowhere to run and nowhere to hide.

Many cursed the God of the heavens. They called on Him to relent. The locusts' bodies were as hard as rocks, so they couldn't be crushed. They were immune to every weapon that man had. Laser guns bounced off them like light off a mirror. Only those who loved the true God were safe.

Immanuel was in his nuclear shelter, recovering from a sting that had ransacked his body. It was as if somebody had placed fire to his every nerve, but denied him the repose of death. His scientists could do nothing to stop them. The insects' tails not only injected a poisonous substance that sent excruciating pain through the body, but also infused a foreign chemical that boosted the immune system. In short, the heinous locusts were designed to torture, but never kill.

It had been nearly twenty-four hours since Immanuel had been attacked. Many of his close associates were amazed at his tolerance for pain. The Antichrist was in his underground office, awaiting the arrival of his leading scientist. He was reviewing some disturbing spy photos that his five-star general had faxed to him only hours before. They showed massive troop buildups in China, Russia, and the Middle East. His general could only estimate the numbers at close to two hundred million. Even his top brass was fidgety about the implications of this distressing news. Satan's thoughts were interrupted by a knock on the door.

"Come in, Peter," said Satan as he tossed the photos to the side.

Peter Kaminsky walked tentatively into the office. He was afraid to make eye contact with his master.

"I take it that all your news is bad," deduced the Devil.

The scientist had just been stung several hours earlier, and he tried unsuccessfully to hide the pain. His hands and neck were in spasms.

"Your excellency, we have never seen anything like this! Unfortunately, the insects' venom is completely impervious to any known substance we've introduced. We can't decipher the chemical structure. We can't—"

The Antichrist didn't want to hear science, excuses, or whining. He wanted answers.

"You are telling me that there is nothing that you can do?"

The scientist was praying to himself that his god would be merciful.

"Every man, woman, and child will go through hell, all because you are dumbfounded over some mysterious chemical!"

Satan quickly looked away from his target, and began to sadistically stare at a golden statue of a lion that was nesting in the corner of his office. It was crafted of pure gold and weighed well over five hundred pounds. The scientist followed his master's eyes. Peter began to shake his head violently back and forth, and raised his hands toward the angry god.

"No, no, please! I will find out the secret if it means not sleeping or eating for the next month!"

Satan stared at his trembling subject. "How are your five children?"

The scientist was confused. "Wh...wh...uh...uh, that's six children, your majesty."

Immanuel got up and walked over to the world map on the wall. He turned his back on the frightened scientist. "Go home and count again!" he said quietly.

———

Timothy and Daniel had successfully guided Jim and Ken into their hideaway on the western side of the Mount of Olives. Their view to the west was of the new temple, the city of Jerusalem, and a gigantic graveyard that Jews had been using for centuries.

Their shelter was a cave where Jews had often hidden from invading armies. It was camouflaged by immense mustard bushes and a few well-placed rocks. Inside the cavern were a busy spring and numerous rodents that Ken and Jim used for dinner.

"What's the plan now?" asked Ken as he reached down for a handful of fresh water.

"I believe our days of evangelism are over at this point," said Jim as he inspected the walls of the cave.

"What are you looking for?"

Jim was looking at the rock like a doctor would examine one of his patients.

"A hidden entrance of some kind. The people who used this cave in the past didn't rely solely on this place for their security. I'm sure that there is another chamber; if only I could—"

Jim's hand suddenly stopped on a humble recess in the wall near the back of the grotto.

"What did you find?" inquired Ken.

"See this little dent in the wall? I bet if I just give it a good push—"

The large rock suddenly creaked as Jim and Ken forced it backward. It left a seven-foot hole in the cave.

The men were speechless as their gazes were returned.

―――――

Dominic, camouflaged as an evening jogger, ducked behind a set of trash cans. He feared that he would be caught, but could no longer endure a life of servitude with Immanuel. This was his one chance to remove Immanuel from his throne and put himself on it. He glanced at his wrist, and then into the sky. A depraved grin appeared on his aging face as he pulled out the satellite receiver. Less than ten thousand individuals in Immanuel's hierarchy possessed this type of phone, and he was one of them.

"Well," Dominic thought, "Immanuel always said, 'Keep your friends close and your enemies closer.'" He chuckled to himself as he dialed.

"Yeah," answered a monotone foreign voice.

"Everything is secure on my end. When are you going to send them?"

The stranger on the other side of the world didn't like questions, especially ones that he couldn't answer.

"You just worry about your end of the bargain."

"And the ark of the covenant?" asked Dominic. "Where is it? It was supposed to be here! Don't cross me, or—"

The man hung up.

"Blasted Chinese! They think that they own the world," grunted the traitor as he hid the phone in a nearby sewage hole.

―――――

Ken and Jim stared at the women and children. Many appeared on the brink of starvation. They resembled human skeletons with a thin coating of life. Jim's flashlight agitated their eyes as he moved it from person to person.

"Who are you?" asked Jim as he slowly approached the group.

A woman dressed in a brown shawl stepped forward.

"Our men were killed by the Antichrist's troops several weeks ago. We fled to this place for security. Nobody knows about it!"

Ken and Jim were dumbfounded. What were they to do with two dozen women and children? Jim glanced at Ken.

"We will do everything we can to help you get some food. Jesus will provide for His own!" stated Jim.

The lady's demeanor was weak physically but strong spiritually. She guided the group into the light with nothing more than a hand gesture.

"We'll go get some food. Stay here and pray that God gives us a safe journey," said Ken.

The middle-aged Jewish lady was horrified.

"Don't go; you'll be killed! You'll be—"

Jim interrupted. "We're not risking very much. Praise God, time is short for all of us."

The woman was touched by their kindness. She hugged both of them as they left.

The angel Timothy peered out from the cave and looked for enemy demons.

"Anything out there?" asked Daniel, with a hint of testiness in his tone.

Timothy slowly pulled his head into the den. His familiar smile had been stolen by the seriousness of the situation.

"I counted at least a hundred of those warlocks soaring around the mountain like vultures. It doesn't look good," he sighed as he rubbed the handle of his shining sword.

The room was filled with rumors of invasion. Nearly one hundred military men from all over the globe were seated in Immanuel's war chamber.

The five-star general, covered with medals, was trying to gently educate Immanuel.

"Your excellency," bowed the general as the others looked on, "two hundred million men could be destroyed easily if we had the resources at hand. Unfortunately, with gas and oil being extinct, all we have are men, horses, and laser guns. We have no strategic advantage over the Chinese and Russian armies without firepower. If they have more men, they will have the upper hand. And consider this, the Muslims are livid over losing the ark."

The trembling general quickly took his seat as Satan stared a hole through him.

The Devil pulled his bitten body from its seat. He never took his eyes off the general. He walked over to the general's chair and paced back and forth behind him as he spoke.

"Outnumbered?" he said, placing his hand on the general's shoulder. "They have the upper hand?" he continued, digging his claws into the general's flesh.

The general's body twitched as he attempted to look chivalrous. The Devil glanced at the portraits of Napoleon, Caesar, and Stalin that covered the wall.

"Your lack of faith in my power is a poison that must not be allowed to spread! You are not worthy to lead our fine world citizens into a battle of righteousness! You are hereby fired from your duties!"

Satan's decree hit the military man like a freight train. He recklessly jumped out of his seat.

"You can't do that! I am the only man who can—"

Lightning burst from Satan's finger. The agonizing pain brought the proud man to his knees. Nobody dared flinch a muscle as they watched Immanuel humiliate their once fearless leader.

"You have been weighed on my scales of justice and have been found lacking," judged Satan.

The Devil slowly walked to the general as the others watched in horror. Satan lunged out of Immanuel's body. He placed his icy claws around the general's neck and squeezed him like an overripe orange. Immanuel stood a few feet away and raised his hands into the stale air.

"You are guilty of treason!"

The general crashed to the floor as he began to choke for air. The struggle quickly ended. He was dead.

"Now, gentlemen, unless there are other opinions, I suggest you get to your assignments!"

The men scurried out of the room. Satan hissed as he glanced at Immanuel's reflection in the mirror.

Weeks passed, yet the plague of locusts continued. The Antichrist blamed the past actions of the Christians as the catalyst for this disaster. He said the nuclear fallout had mutated the genes of the locusts, turning them into creatures from the bowels of hell.

The Devil was unaware of Dominic's betrayal. He had no idea that his most trusted advisor was plotting his overthrow. By day,

Dominic would perform miracles for the television audience, cementing the lie that Immanuel was "God." By night, he was a Judas.

Jim and Ken were weary and dejected. For days they had attempted to infiltrate the city, but had been turned back by impending danger. Timothy and Daniel were close enough to their humans to warn them, in their spirits, that they would not succeed. For nearly a week, the two men had watched helplessly as their new friends suffered from malnutrition.

"I can't stand this anymore," said Ken as he scanned the rocky terrain. "These people need us to do something fast, or they'll die!"

"If we go out there, we won't be doing them any good at all."

The leader of the group overheard the men as she edged their way. Her smile spoke peace to them.

"I'm sorry that you had to overhear our depressing news. There's nothing that we can do," said Jim.

"Why don't we all join hands and pray?" said the woman as she grabbed their hands. "If He answers our prayer, we'll rejoice. If not, we can take comfort in His presence."

They all bowed their heads. One of the children began singing a simple song of love to the Lord. They all joined in as the praises reached toward heaven.

Jim, Ken, and their friends fell asleep worshipping and praying to the Lord.

Early the next morning, they awoke to find their prayers had been answered by Jehovah God. The same manna from heaven that the Israelites had fed on during their years in the desert covered the ground around the cave.

Dominic looked at the gold nugget fashioned in the shape of a lion. It weighed close to fifteen pounds, yet its value could not be measured. It had been found in a remote cave outside Rome several weeks earlier, an idol from her pagan era.

Dominic put the treasure in a plain brown bag and entered the elevator. He pushed the sensor for the bottom floor.

As he stepped into the darkened basement, a man stepped out of the shadows.

"Please take me to the hostages so that I can pray for their souls!" Dominic said.

"You have five minutes," said the warden.

Dominic graciously smiled.

"You will have a mansion in heaven for this divine deed!"

The warden escorted the False Prophet to a steel door. He placed his hand over a round, glowing sensor.

"As you can see, sir, our state-of-the-art security system is the finest in the world," bragged the warden.

"Immanuel will be glad to hear that your system is flawless."

The men approached the inner cell. Once they were beyond the eyes of the cameras, Dominic slid the warden the brown bag containing his priceless reward. The False Prophet slipped into the cell. The warden went into the guards' office and offered his employees an early dinner break.

Dominic approached Lord Birmingham and his colleagues who were tightly chained. They had been underfed and brutalized. Lord Birmingham was sleeping on his feet as the False Prophet neared. Without saying a word, he gently smacked him on the cheek. Lord Birmingham's eyes slowly opened. He thought it was morning. Dominic scratched a message on a pad and shoved it in front of his face.

"Don't say a word. You will recognize me as Dominic Rosario. I am on your side. I can get you out of here if you will tell me who has the ark of the covenant."

Lord Birmingham stared at him as if he were the Devil himself. The bankers were watching with mixed emotions. "Burn in hell!" answered Birmingham, his voice weak.

"Immanuel is planning to have you killed tomorrow. I can help you, if you help me. I need the ark, and I know you know where it is."

Birmingham grunted. "The Arabs have it."

Dominic punched him in the stomach. "Don't lie to me. You had the Chinese steal it from the Arabs to destabilize Immanuel's regime! You have nothing to lose! Join me in destroying the Beast, or die without the satisfaction of knowing that Immanuel could be stopped!"

Lord Birmingham stared at Dominic. He searched his face. "I know where it is," replied Birmingham, his voice lower than a whisper.

Twenty-One

The Battle of Armageddon

The plague of locusts had taken an immense toll on Immanuel's kingdom. Like sand slipping through one's hands, the Antichrist's power base was deteriorating before his eyes. Citizens were being ruthlessly attacked at least once a week by these creatures from hell. Satan could no longer make television appearances. No matter where he hid, the stinging locusts were sure to follow. Every night at midnight, another hellish insect would attack him in his sleep. Satan cursed the God of heaven. He knew that Jehovah God was in control of this pestilence.

Ken, Jim, and the group of believers were enjoying bread from heaven each morning.

"Hey, Ken, help me!" shouted Jim as he collected the cakelike food from the desert vegetation.

Ken ran out of the cave.

"Look at this!" smiled Ken as his eyes feasted on the tiny pieces of bread. "This is our best harvest in months! Each morning I get up, and it's here. It still amazes me."

Timothy and Daniel were stationed several hundred yards away. They were acting as lookouts for their saints. Timothy began to rub his eyes.

"I think this is the longest that I have ever been seated in one place. Even we angels need a vacation from the same old, same old," yawned Timothy.

Daniel stood up to stretch. "There are permanent creases in my wings. If I don't use them soon, they will rot and fall off."

"Hardly," laughed Timothy. "Enjoy the quiet moments when you get them. Soon, you'll need all the strength you have."

The Chinese army was marching westward. For years, Chinese engineers had been working on a road to cross over the high mountains separating them from the Western world. The road had been recently completed, and the only things that had hindered the Chinese army from marching on the West were time, will, and politics. Now, they had all three. The ancient dragon finally raised its head, and it was an awesome sight. Two hundred million Chinese soldiers moved like a dark blanket across the snowy ridges. Marching in one accord and with one purpose, their unified footsteps sounded a beat that would chill any soul.

Blasphemy nestled next to the general of the Chinese army. "Destroy Jerusalem," he whispered.

The general smirked as he glanced toward the ark of the covenant. Twenty soldiers wore harnesses attached to the cart, that was carrying the relic westward.

Satan was in a top secret meeting with his new military leader. The men were hovering over battle plans. The prognosis looked bleak.

"Your majesty, the Chinese army is marching toward the Middle East! I can assure you that they will never make it to Jerusalem. The Russian and Muslim troops are the ones that we will encounter. There are only ten, maybe twenty, million of them. If we station all of the World Federation's one hundred million men in the Middle East, we should easily defeat them."

"What makes you so sure that the Chinese won't be a player?" hissed Satan.

The general grabbed another map from his war chest. He pointed at a long blue streak slithering through the Middle East.

"The Euphrates River, your majesty. There are no bridges that span this great divide. They have all been destroyed. It has been the deciding factor in countless wars in the past. It is really what keeps the East separated from the West."

The Devil sneered.

"It could dry up. Their troops could cross and attack," said Satan, staring at his general.

"The river has never dried up, sir."

"Never?" shot back Satan.

"No, sir. Never. I'd stake my life on it."

"You already did," growled the dragon.

After five months of torture, God finally ended the locusts' scourge. They vanished into thin air. Satan saw this miracle as an opportunity. For the first time since the dreadful pestilence began, the Devil went back on television, proclaiming himself to be God.

"I want that camera shot to be tight, very tight. I want the world to see my eyes."

Nobody challenged the Antichrist.

"Five seconds, four, three, two, one, you're on!" called the floor director.

Immanuel's face filled the television screens around the world. His eyes had a telekinetic effect on his subjects. They said that he was the hope of the world, that he was the answer, that he was the only one worthy of worship.

"It is my joy to report that the plague has been halted! As you know, the nuclear winter that originally created these creatures has been slowly improving. But most importantly, under my supervision, World Federation scientists have created a compound that has killed off all the locusts. It not only extinguished them, but also caused them to disappear."

For the first time in months, Satan's top scientific advisor was enjoying a peaceful evening at home. As he watched Immanuel, he couldn't believe his ears. His boss's lie floored him. How could God lie? He couldn't. He jumped out of his recliner.

"This can't be happening!"

"What?" reacted his spouse.

"God just lied!"

They stared at each other for a moment before glancing back at the television.

"So, what now?" asked his wife.

The advisor glanced at Dominic's revised bible on the coffee table.

"We pray," muttered the man.

She grabbed his hand as they closed their eyes. In the background, the speech continued.

"My dream for you is finally coming to fruition. All of the negative, taunting voices have been disposed of. Next week, I will make a trip to Jerusalem to dedicate our new community of peace on earth."

Immanuel latched his claws to the desk as he screamed out in anguish. He was covered with boils from the top of his head to the bottom of his heels. The blistering boils covered his entire face, making it all but impossible to move his lips. He remained confined to his office. He told his secretary, who was in a similar condition, to tell his closest advisors that he was deep in prayer and could not be disturbed.

The Antichrist was not alone. Anybody who believed that Immanuel was truly God, who shunned the Creator of the universe as a god of hate and stubbornness, was disciplined in like fashion. It was a fulfillment of Revelation, chapter sixteen, verse two: "The first went and poured out his bowl upon the earth, and a foul and loathsome sore came upon the men who had the mark of the beast and those who worshiped his image." The pain from the boils was unspeakable. The truth was that Jehovah God didn't hate any of those afflicted with boils. He wanted repentance. It was tough love. Every individual on the face of the globe had heard the redeeming message of the Son of God. He had given human civilization nearly seven thousand years, yet some still rebuffed the straight and narrow road as judgmental.

The Chinese troops were less than a two days' journey from the Euphrates River. The men were covered with sores. Miraculously, their feet remained clear of the burning wounds. Many believed it was the ark of the covenant that was protecting them.

A robust ghoul in charge of tailing Dominic had just arrived. He saluted Blasphemy in a style reminiscent of the Third Reich.

"Have you found Dominic?" inquired Blasphemy.

"No, master," bowed the demon scout.

"Go find him. Get him here immediately! I need him to tap into the power of the ark!"

Timothy and Daniel were on high alert. Some demons had been loitering on their mountain for the past several nights. It was possible that someone could stumble upon the location of the hideout, so they advised their humans to stay out of sight. Ken and Jim did their best to keep the children entertained. The group remained in the hidden part of the cave with lookouts posting four-hour shifts.

Early the next morning in the throne room of Jehovah God, the Lord motioned for the second angel to make his journey to the battered earth. The third verse of the sixteenth chapter of Revelation was about to be fulfilled: "Then the second angel poured out his bowl on the sea, and it became blood as of a dead man; and every living creature in the sea died."

It was sudden and unexpected. Residents along every coastline of the world noticed an obnoxious stench outside their windows. Further investigation by authorities revealed fish, dolphins, whales, and every form of sea life dead on the ocean's surface.

The Global News Network picked up on the story hours later. Immanuel was just waking from his first good night's sleep in months when his security line buzzed. He tried to ignore it. The ringing continued. It was no use. He rolled over and punched the speaker sensor.

"Yes," said the Devil.

"Your majesty, my apologies for disturbing you," pleaded a disjointed voice from the World Federation's headquarters.

"Speak," said the Beast.

"Your majesty, please turn on the news, sir."

Satan sat up in the bed as he flipped on the television.

"If you are just joining us, let me review the latest on the disaster," reported the anchor.

The television screen showed video from the Atlantic Ocean. You couldn't see water, only dead marine life floating on the sea. When the water occasionally appeared, it seemed to be coated with blood.

"These pictures are from the Atlantic Ocean. From reports received around the world, every ocean and sea resembles a pond of death and debris! At this point, the World Federation has not commented on this disastrous development, but we anticipate some explanation very soon."

The Antichrist jumped out of bed and went over to his computer terminal. Satan couldn't wait to peel away from Immanuel's body, which was covered with oozing sores. He punched a few buttons and began to speak into the voice-activated letter writer.

"To the president of the Global News Network. I will be spending the next week in prayer and fasting in an attempt to ward off the evil supernatural forces attacking my planet."

Nearly a third of the earth's population relied on seafood for their daily staples. Mass starvation would harm his reputation; therefore, he had another plan.

Timothy and Daniel were making plans when they noticed a strange-looking angel soaring across the sky. It appeared as if it were sprinkling some sort of spiritual powder on selected areas around Jerusalem.

"It's the third bowl, isn't it?" asked Daniel as he tugged at Timothy.

Timothy pulled the Book from his wing pocket and handed it to him. Daniel flipped quickly through the pages.

"There it is! I knew it!" said Daniel. "Revelation, chapter sixteen, verses four through seven say, 'Then the third angel poured out his bowl on the rivers and springs of water, and they became blood. And I heard the angel of the waters saying: "You are righteous, O Lord, the One who is and who was and who is to be, because You have judged these things. For they have shed the blood of saints and prophets, and You have given them blood to drink. For it is their just due." And I heard another from the altar saying, "Even so, Lord God Almighty, true and righteous are Your judgments."'"

They watched the angel of judgment like a hawk. In less than a minute, it had disappeared over the northern horizon. Daniel slowly placed the Bible into Timothy's pocket.

"Do you know what this means?" quizzed Timothy as he glanced at their humans.

"How are they going to have water to drink?" answered Daniel.

Timothy sighed.

"Every human on the planet will be dead in a week or less!"

Timothy's eyes gazed at the Valley of Megiddo, also called the Valley of Jehoshaphat. A bittersweet sadness showed in his eyes as he thought about the words of Christ.

———

Satan was deep in thought when the security phone rang.

"Yes?" asked Satan as he poured medicine on his blistering lesions.

"Your majesty, I need to tell you that...uh...well..."

"Get to the point!"

"The plague has...uh...well,...sir, it has affected the rivers and streams! There is no more water to drink, sir! Humans can only survive for three to seven days without water!"

The Devil suddenly forgot about the pain. He flipped the television on. The news anchor was practically in tears.

"Rumor has it that every ounce of water on the planet, from the seas to the smallest of creeks, has been affected by this lethal virus! Water supplies have been contaminated as well! Rioting has broken out all over the globe! The world is clamoring for a miracle from Immanuel! Many are openly challenging him to deliver them from a certain death!"

The screen changed locations from city to city. The scenes were all the same. Tens of thousands of people, covered in burning sores, were shouting for a miracle from their god.

"I have followed your advice. I have done everything that you have told me," said Immanuel.

Hatred boiled over in Satan's hellish heart. War was a certainty in days, and the death of his pawns was a certainty in a week. Jehovah God was doing it again. Satan snarled at the thought of beating Him at His own game. He quickly exited Immanuel's broken body.

"Go to Jerusalem. Meet Dominic there. Fight fire with fire! You need to conquer the Chinese troops. You don't have much time!"

Immanuel collapsed dead on the floor. Satan plunged himself back into the human coat. The heart began to beat again.

The next morning, the hills surrounding Jerusalem were glowing with life as the sun broke through the clouds. The nuclear winter, which had lasted nearly a year, appeared to be breaking up. Hours earlier, Jehovah God had ordered an angel to fly into the sun. Chapter sixteen of the book of Revelation records the prophecy: "Then the fourth angel poured out his bowl on the sun, and power was given to him to scorch men with fire. And men were scorched with great heat, and they blasphemed the name of God who has power over these plagues; and they did not repent and give Him glory."

The angel had turned up the galaxy's burner from simmer to boil. The sun was sending out seven times the energy that it had produced the day before. That increase was rapidly drying up the clouds from the nuclear winter. Sunrise was greeted with hope, but noontime was accosted with curses of the worst kind. The throne of the World Federation was strangely silent. Damaging radiation was burning the people of Earth.

The Chinese troops had met the Russian contingent on the banks of the great Euphrates River. In just the few days since their convergence, the army of two hundred twenty million had dwindled to two hundred million. Without water, the armies were rapidly dying of dehydration.

Blasphemy watched with little concern. He had read the Bible. This was no surprise.

"We will wait. The men need a rest anyway. I see that the sun has finally come out. Maybe that will be good for morale," belched Blasphemy to his Chinese general.

As the sun reached its peak in the brightening sky, Blasphemy noticed something unusual about the troops. They were turning red. They were suffering from an extreme case of sunburn. The intolerable heat was causing many to hallucinate. Blasphemy ignored the misery. If anything, he enjoyed it. He watched the river and waited.

Scientists called it unprecedented. Some called it the end of the world. The unquenchable fury of the sun was beating down on the earth with phenomenal power. The Global News Network quoted one World Federation scientist as saying, "If this keeps up, every living thing will be charred into ashes!" The throne of the Beast alerted the public to the danger, warning everyone to stay in the safety of their houses.

Satan was on his way to Jerusalem to meet Dominic Rosario. He seemed to feed on the sun's increased energy.

He strolled to the waiting limousine. He was the only one not taking cover from the scorching heat. He glanced at a bank thermometer as he stepped into the refuge. It read one hundred nineteen degrees. Once he was safely in his limousine, he picked up his satellite phone. Satan punched in a secret code.

"Yes, your majesty, what may I do for you today?" responded a buoyant voice from a location north of Jerusalem.

"Have you encountered any troops yet?" inquired the enemy of mankind.

The general's voice hesitated.

"No sir, not yet. Do I have new orders?"

Immanuel was waiting for his general to complain about the latest scourge.

"How are the conditions in Israel?" tested the Antichrist. He grunted as his limousine passed a few homeless families burning in the sun.

"Your majesty, the men's spirits are high," lied the general as he turned away from the misery overtaking his troops. "We all are willing to give our lives for you!"

Satan turned his eyes away from the baking city.

"I want victory. If the enemy marches on Jerusalem, you will protect it to the very last man!"

The numbers on Satan's digital clock read 8:56 A.M., yet it was dark outside. The sun wasn't shining. Satan could still see the stars in the sky. He picked up the telephone, which automatically dialed the hotel front desk.

"What time do you have?" demanded Satan as he looked at himself in the reflection from the brass phone.

"Sir, it's nearly nine o'clock. I don't know what's going on. Everyone in the front lobby is having terrible muscle spasms."

Satan slammed down the phone and walked over to the window. The darkness hung over Jerusalem like a black cloak. Satan looked at the sky. "Pull out all your tricks. You'll never be God of this earth! Never!"

"Satan!" shouted a voice from the other side of the door.

The Devil instantly recognized the voice and hissed like a cobra protecting her young.

"Michael! To what do I owe this pleasure?" mocked the dragon.

Michael walked through the door. A shimmering sword occupied his left hand, and he held a glittering Bible in his right.

"Your time of destruction is nearly exhausted. So that you know that my God is a God of His Word, I quote from the book of Revelation, chapter sixteen, verse ten."

"I will never allow you to quote that trash to me!" yelled the Evil One as he lunged toward the angel.

The archangel outmaneuvered the Antichrist as he loudly quoted the prophecy of God.

"'Then the fifth angel poured out his bowl on the throne of the beast, and his kingdom became full of darkness; and they gnawed their tongues because of the pain. They blasphemed the God of heaven because of their pains and their sores, and did not repent of their deeds.'"

Immanuel's broken and welt-ridden body was a testimony to the truth of what Michael read.

"You will pay for your arrogance!" promised Satan.

The archangel Michael frowned at his twisted logic.

"You have mistaken truth for arrogance! Prepare to meet your Maker!"

The serpent hissed as the angel quickly exited through the painted ceiling.

"You will pay!" cried the Beast as he pounded his chest.

———————

Hours later, every television station across the world was no longer functioning. The intense solar activity from the day before had prevented many of the signals from reaching the ground. When dawn never appeared, the stations that had weathered the solar storm were suddenly put out of business by an atmospheric disturbance that could not be identified by World Federation scientists. Many speculated that the sun had literally burnt out, which allowed foreign waves of energy to assault the earth. The entire planet had been plunged into darkness. The scientists that Immanuel owned continued to make up natural reasons for the anarchy in nature. Yesterday, the temperature had climbed to the top of most home thermometers. Today, meteorologists warned of the reverse.

Jehovah God was still in complete control. It had been less than seven hours since the last angel had circled the earth. Events were now unfolding at an exponential rate.

Blasphemy had left the troops to have some solitude under a palm tree in an oasis. His black eyes searched his environment before he opened the Bible. He didn't want any of his demons to see him tinkering with the enemy's Book. He opened it to the book of Revelation, chapter sixteen, verse twelve. Just as he did, he spotted an angel. It appeared as if it were heading directly for the river. Blasphemy's hands melted the cover of the Book as he read it to himself.

"'Then the sixth angel poured out his bowl on the great river Euphrates, and its water was dried up, so that the way of the kings from the east might be prepared.'"

The rebellious demon quickly closed the Bible before it turned to flames. He heard shouts coming from the camp.

"I have the supernatural power of the ark drying up that river!" shouted Blasphemy to a silent heaven.

———————

Hours later, the Chinese troops mounted their horses and crossed the Euphrates River. Starlight led their way. They were heading west with vengeance in their spirits. Blasphemy had left four demons in charge because he had business elsewhere. Blasphemy's defection to his own cause was now a known fact. He had done the unthinkable. He had double-crossed Lucifer. Wanted posters for his whereabouts were seared into the minds of every demon in Satan's swarm. He had to be extra cautious to remain hidden. His spying skills paid huge dividends as he slipped by the World Federation army camp's outer surveillance and into the field headquarters. It took less than a minute to distract the six colonels guarding the World Federation general. Blasphemy crawled into the general's bed. The demon touched the satellite phone, causing it to ring. The groggy general sat up in bed. He grabbed the phone. "Yes, your majesty," said the general.

Blasphemy disguised himself as Immanuel. "Why aren't you marching on Jerusalem? The Chinese will be there by noontime tomorrow. Forget about defending the city. We don't have a chance. They outnumber us almost three to one. Don't give them the satisfaction of razing my city. Destroy it yourself!"

The general almost dropped the phone. He couldn't believe his ears.

"But, sir," he responded, "I thought you wanted us to protect your city!"

"Shut up, you simpleton! Do not question my orders, or I will personally come out there and slash the life out of you!"

The general quickly dressed and mustered the troops. They were less than five hours from the sleeping city.

Ken and Jim were still hiding in the hills when they heard a commotion. The sound alarmed the women and children.

They hurried out of the cave to investigate. Their mountain hideaway gave them a panoramic view of Jerusalem. What they saw shocked them.

World Federation troops were ransacking Jerusalem without mercy. They were killing anything that moved. Thousands of Jews were fleeing for the hills. Many couldn't believe their eyes when they saw their World Federation troops attacking innocent civilians.

The False Prophet Dominic hadn't been seen in weeks. Immanuel figured he was in a similar shape as himself.

Satan remained in the hotel. The wounds covering Immanuel kept him from public view. He waited for his spirit officers to arrive.

A two-star general from Satan's demonic army appeared through the ceiling. He was shaking as he bowed to his master.

"Satan, your troops are ransacking the city!" squealed the spirit.

"Don't you lie to me!" threatened Satan.

The two-star general backed away from Satan.

"Your majesty, I am not lying! I have no reason to. The city is being destroyed by World Federation troops! Your hotel is in the only sector that hasn't been ravished. The ammunition is gone. We're fighting hand to hand. Your general received word from you, sir, that you wanted us to loot the city before the Chinese, Russians, and Muslims did!"

Lava oozed from Satan's nostrils.

"Blasphemy!" hissed the Devil.

Blasphemy and his demonic cronies led the charge as the two hundred million man contingent from the Euphrates advanced on Jerusalem. They were sixty miles to the northeast when they encountered brutal resistance from the World Federation troops. A Chinese general ordered the ark to the rear of the fighting. He was hoping it would provide a miracle for them. Every square foot of Israel from Jerusalem northward was occupied by soldiers. Thousands of men were dying every minute as the battle raged in the Valley of Megiddo. Most of the fighting was hand-to-hand combat. The demons were having a field day. Men were being slaughtered like animals while demons reveled in the glory of their own powers.

Most of the angels of God were gathered outside His throne room. They were preparing for God's greatest victory. The archangel Michael opened his Bible and addressed his brave warriors. His voice cracked as he gently turned the pages of his Creator's promises.

"The time is at hand, angels of the highest God!"

The emotion overwhelming him was fitting for the occasion. He gazed over the vast expanse of brave soldiers.

"Listen as I read from Revelation, chapter nineteen, starting at verse one."

A tear trickled down his brawny cheeks as he cleared his throat.

"'After these things I heard a loud voice of a great multitude in heaven, saying, "Alleluia! Salvation and glory and honor and power belong to the Lord our God'!"

Michael paused as the Christian saints who had been saved from earth began to sing those words. They had run the race faithfully and were at the finish line. Many of the angels wept uncontrollably.

""'For true and righteous are His judgments, because He has judged the great harlot who corrupted the earth with her fornication; and He has avenged on her the blood of His servants shed by her." Again they said, "Alleluia! Her smoke rises up forever and ever!" And the twenty-four elders and the four living creatures fell down and worshiped God who sat on the throne, saying, "Amen! Alleluia!" Then a voice came from the throne, saying, "Praise our God, all you His servants and those who fear Him, both small and great!" And I heard, as it were, the voice of a great multitude, as the sound of many waters and as the sound of mighty thunderings, saying, "Alleluia! For the Lord God Omnipotent reigns!"'"

Ken and Jim were huddled in the cave with their friends. The battle raged outside. Jim stood to his feet and addressed the apprehensive saints. His hand caressed his Bible as his face glowed.

"Today is the day of our salvation!" began Jim as he opened the book of Zechariah. "Today, we will witness the power of the God of the universe!"

The screams of wounded soldiers echoed through the cave. It was hard for the saints not to go out and help them. Jim began to read.

"Chapter fourteen in the book of Zechariah states, 'Behold, the day of the LORD is coming, and your spoil will be divided in your midst. For I will gather all the nations to battle against Jerusalem; the city shall be taken, the houses rifled, and the women ravished. Half of the city shall go into captivity, but the remnant of the people shall not be cut off from the city. Then the LORD will go forth and fight against those nations, as He fights in the day of battle. And in that day His feet will stand on the Mount of Olives, which faces Jerusalem on the east. And the Mount of Olives shall be split in two, from east to west, making a very large valley; half of the mountain shall move toward the north and half of it toward the south. Then you shall flee through My mountain valley, for the mountain valley shall reach to Azal. Yes, you shall flee as you fled from the earthquake in the days of Uzziah king of Judah. Thus the LORD my God will come, and all the saints with You. It shall come to pass in that day that there will be no light; the lights will diminish. It shall be one day which is known to the LORD; neither day nor night. But at evening time it shall happen that it will be light. And in that day it shall be that living waters shall flow from Jerusalem, half of them toward the eastern sea and half of them toward the western sea; in both summer and winter it shall occur. And the LORD shall be King over all the earth.'"

By late afternoon, most of Jerusalem was laid waste. The World Federation and Chinese-Russian forces were fighting one another in a valley northeast of the razed city. All morning Blasphemy had been helping his deluded general to pillage the city. Not one stone was left standing in Immanuel's temple. The casualties were enormous. Blasphemy was concerned about his next move. The five-star demon was reclining on a rock atop the highest peak in Israel, reading the book of Daniel. He had turned to the seventh chapter.

"'I watched till thrones were put in place, and the Ancient of Days was seated; His garment was white as snow, and the hair of His head was like pure wool.'"

Blasphemy cursed the idea of God reigning supreme, yet he needed to know the next move in the enemy's playbook. The only way to successfully double-cross Satan was to take this strategic advantage.

"'His throne was a fiery flame, its wheels a burning fire; a fiery stream issued and came forth from before Him. A thousand thousands ministered to Him; ten thousand times ten thousand stood before Him. The court was seated, and the books were opened. I watched then because of the sound of the pompous words which the horn was speaking; I watched till the beast was slain, and its body destroyed and given to the burning flame.'"

Blasphemy shouted obscenities. Revenge was even sweeter than he thought.

"Satan will be destroyed! I will be king!" belched the demon as he continued to read. "'As for the rest of the beasts, they had their dominion taken away, yet their lives were prolonged for a season and a time. I was watching in the night visions, and behold, One like the Son of Man, coming with the clouds of heaven! He came to the Ancient of Days, and they brought Him near before Him. Then to Him was given dominion and glory and a kingdom.'"

Blasphemy hissed at the thought of Christ being King over him. However, his curiosity took over, and he continued his adventure into the truth.

"'That all peoples, nations, and languages should serve Him. His dominion is an everlasting dominion, which shall not pass away, and His kingdom the one which shall not be destroyed.'"

Blasphemy spit into the dirt as he ripped that part of the Bible out. He balled it up and tossed it into the dust. He flew high into the air, reversed course, then headed feet first toward God's Book. The force of the explosion crushed the Bible into an indiscernible pile of paper.

"Jesus Christ will never rule over me! Trash! Pure trash!" mocked Blasphemy as he headed toward the ark of the covenant.

Satan rushed out of the hotel to his waiting limousine. The streets were littered with corpses. He ignored the death and destruction.

"Driver, to the temple, immediately!" ordered the Devil.

Dominic was on his hotel room floor, writhing in pain. He picked up the new bible from the coffee table. As he leafed through the pages, his hands began to tremble. The False Prophet started to tear the pages from his blasphemous book. "It's not my fault!" he screamed as he clawed at his head.

Ken and Jim were outside the cave and on their knees in prayer. Dead soldiers littered the ground around them as they watched the eastern horizon.

"Lord Jesus, help!" pleaded Jim. Ken stood up.

"Is there anyone alive out there?" yelled Ken, and he gently checked the corpses.

Timothy opened his Bible to the book of the Revelation and began reading from it to Daniel. He cried as he read the nineteenth chapter, starting at verse eleven.

"'I saw heaven opened, and behold, a white horse. And He who sat on him was called Faithful and True, and in righteousness He judges and makes war. His eyes were like a flame of fire, and on His head were many crowns. He had a name written that no one knew except Himself. He was clothed with a robe dipped in blood, and His name is called The Word of God. And the armies in heaven, clothed in fine linen, white and clean, followed Him on white horses. Now out of His mouth goes a sharp sword, that with it He should strike the nations. And He Himself will rule them with a rod of iron. He Himself treads the winepress of the fierceness and wrath of Almighty God. And He has on His robe and on His thigh a name written: KING OF KINGS AND LORD OF LORDS.'"

As Timothy finished the verses, his tears suddenly ceased. A flashing, translucent, unblemished white cloud was descending from the pinnacle of heaven itself.

The angels hugged each other as the light from Christ overtook the hillside.

"It's Jesus!" shouted Ken and Jim as they ran toward the light.

The women and children quickly followed as the saints of God dodged the bloody bodies staining the ground. They could see Christ's face. He was absolutely beautiful. Peace was radiating from Him, yet a righteous anger was welling up inside Him. He looked toward the fighting.

Blasphemy was overwhelmed with hatred at the sight of the One whom he had helped to pierce.

"Charge!" he screamed as he led his demons in revolt.

The armies of the earth began to fire at Him what weapons they had left, but it was a futile effort. Jesus Christ slowly descended from a brilliant cloud. Multitudes accompanied Him as He seemingly ignored the war being waged against Him. Ken and Jim were trembling and weeping as the Lord of the universe made eye contact with them. A surge of exhilaration overwhelmed them as Jesus searched their souls.

"Well done, good and faithful servants, come into your Father's rest!" trumpeted the King.

Instantly, the group of Christians began to rise into the electrified air. Thousands from around Jerusalem joined them in the sky.

Blasphemy cursed at the light as he tried to capture Ken and Jim. He lunged at them with both claws, but as his paw swung toward Ken's face, it literally went right through it. Ken didn't notice the assault. The joy filling his spirit could not be measured by human emotions. Nobody uttered a word. They gazed upon their Master with complete loyalty and admiration.

Jesus continued His descent. The heavenly crowd surrounding Him seemed to be feeding on His energy and on His very being. The remaining people of the earth cursed at Him as He neared the Mount of Olives. As His feet touched the top of the mountain, it began to shake violently. The earthquake startled Satan. It caused the Mount of Olives to split apart. Suddenly, a brilliant, blinding shot of heavenly light radiated from the horizon.

"It's the ark of the covenant!" shouted Ken as his body was translated into its heavenly counterpart.

Satan's limousine driver lost control of the vehicle as it rounded a steep curve on the edge of a tall hill.

"No!" roared Satan as the limousine dropped several hundred feet over the cliff.

Just as it was about to hit the rocky bottom of the hill, Jesus motioned with His lustrous hand. The vehicle quickly responded to His calling, and it began to slowly float toward the Lord.

"You have returned!" barked Satan as he covered his eyes from the light.

Jesus remained mute.

"I thought that I finished you off the first time!" seethed the Devil as he took flight. "It brought me great joy to see you die a coward's death on that cross! But this time, I want to do it with my own two hands, just to see how it will feel!" blasphemed the Devil.

Christ's eyes turned away from Satan and toward the False Prophet, who was curled up on the floor of his hotel room, sniveling like a coward.

"Come," ordered Christ.

Dominic was instantly yanked upward, kicking, screaming, cursing, and crying for his freedom. Satan's eyes followed Dominic's contorted body as it whirled toward its Maker. The Devil saw his window of opportunity. He lunged toward Christ. His claws were only inches from Christ's face when he was blinded by the glory of the Lord.

"Guilty!" judged Jesus.

"You overgrown, judgmental—" shrieked Lucifer.

"Quiet!" ordered Jesus as a flaming sword gushed from His mouth. Satan was surrounded by an unbreakable force field. Christ motioned for Dominic to join Satan. The False Prophet's eyes filled with fear as he suddenly found himself joined at the hip with the Devil himself.

Blasphemy, who had ducked under a rock, couldn't control himself any longer. He rocketed toward the Messiah with reckless passion. Michael darted toward the demon, only to be stopped by a gesture from the King. Jesus pointed His nailscarred hand toward the demon general.

"You have no right to—" spat Blasphemy as he was captured by a tornadolike vacuum of pure light.

"It is finished!" announced Jesus as He turned His heavenly army loose on the demons and people polluting the earth.

Timothy, floating in a cloud a safe distance away, recalled chapter twenty of the book of Revelation:

"Then I saw an angel coming down from heaven, having the key to the bottomless pit and a great chain in his hand. He laid hold of the dragon, that serpent of old, who is the Devil and Satan, and bound him for a thousand years; and he cast him into the bottomless pit, and shut him up, and set a seal on him, so that he should deceive the nations no more till the thousand years were finished. But after these things he must be released for a little while...."